THE TOWN OF BABYLON

THE TOWN OF BABYLON

A NOVEL

ALEJANDRO VARELA

ASTRA HOUSE

NEW YORK

This is a work of fiction. Names, characters, places, and incidents are products of the
author's imagination or are used fictitiously. Any resemblance to actual events, locales,
or persons, living or dead, is entirely coincidental.

Astra House
A Division of Astra Publishing House
astrahouse.com
Printed in the United States of America

Library of Congress Cataloging-in-Publication Data

Names: Varela, Alejandro, 1979- author.
Title: The town of Babylon : a novel / Alejandro Varela.
Description: First edition. | New York : Astra House, [2022] |
Summary: "When his father falls ill, Andrés, a professor of public health, returns to his suburban
hometown to tend to his father's recovery. Reevaluating his rocky marriage in the wake of his
husband's infidelity and with little else to do, he decides to attend his twenty-year high school
reunion, where he runs into the long-lost characters of his youth. Jeremy, his first love, is now
married with two children after having been incarcerated and recovering from addiction. Paul,
who Andrés has long suspected of having killed a man in a homophobic attack, is now an
Evangelical minister and father of five. And Simone, Andrés's best friend, is in a psychiatric
institution following a diagnosis of schizophrenia. During this short stay, Andrés confronts these
relationships, the death of his brother, and the many sacrifices his parents made to offer him a
better life. A novel about the essential nature of community in maintaining one's own health,
The Town of Babylon is an intimate portrait of queer, racial, and class identity, a call to reevaluate
the ties of societal bonds and the systems in which they are forged"—Provided by publisher.
Identifiers: LCCN 2021043855 (print) | LCCN 2021043856 (ebook) |
ISBN 9781662601033 (hardcover) | ISBN 9781662601040 (epub)
Subjects: LCSH: Homecoming—Fiction. | Class reunions—Fiction. |
Communities—Fiction. | LCGFT: Novels.
Classification: LCC PS3622.A7413 T69 2022 (print) | LCC PS3622.A7413 (ebook) | DDC 813/.6—dc23
LC record available at https://lccn.loc.gov/2021043855
LC ebook record available at https://lccn.loc.gov/2021043856

First edition
10 9 8 7 6 5 4 3 2 1

Design by Richard Oriolo
The text is set in Dante Regular.
The titles are set in Chubb Regular.

To my parents—Maria, Ernesto, and Miriam—for the running start

To Matias for the safe landing

To everyone who does more than they should with less than they deserve

To those who have never been welcome

And for all the people who know how to share the damn sidewalk

CONTENTS

THE TOWN OF BABYLON

1
SIDEWALKS

The alumni newsletter was sitting on my bed atop a small pyramid of neatly folded towels. It had a January postmark, but the glossy pamphlet remained crisp, no doubt due to my mother's care. On the back, among a scattershot of exclamatory text, it read, "Mark your calendars, Class of '97! Reunion this July! Check St. Iggy's Facebook for updates!"

After mulling it over for a couple days, I visited St. Ignatius's alumni page this afternoon.

THE DAY HAS ARRIVED!!! 7 P.M. UNTIL ***WHENEVER***
(JOE'S RISTORANTE CLOSES AT 11 P.M., BUT DRINKS AT MCCLAIN'S
PUB & LOUNGE AFTER!!! LOL. YOLO! RSVP ASAP.)

I endeavor in life never to be anything more than defensively prejudiced—certainly not haughty—but this sort of unbridled use of capital letters and acronyms should have been omen enough to keep me home.

. . .

Over the last twenty years, these reunions had fleeted through my mind on occasion, the way I might envision a free fall or planes crashing into buildings, which is to say briefly and, at times, with a shudder. I feared, in those moments, the possibility of reviving the past, of slipping irretrievably into its grasp—lamenting, obsessing. Something akin to speaking aloud a long-held secret on the verge of being forgotten. Better left forgotten. In a matter of minutes, all of this will change. Twenty years of abstention, of keeping the past where it belongs, will come to an end.

To complicate matters, I hadn't packed anything appropriate to wear. Is there a standard attire for this sort of occasion? How does one dress for their past? More specifically, a past inside of a present-day Italian restaurant established in 1975, and since remodeled four times, once by each new owner—Italian, Italian American, Puerto Rican, and most recently an immigrant from Kerala. The communist state of India, Kerala is arguably the healthiest and happiest region in the subcontinent. A state whose successes never seem to appear amid the popular images of Indian poverty, Indian elephants, Indian river-bathing, and Indian yogis. I know very little about India, but if I hadn't just mentioned this about Kerala, I'd have been as remiss as everyone else.

Joe's, the Italian restaurant, is six unformed, halfway-harrowing blocks from my parents' home, the home of my youth. Six city blocks aren't much by way of distance. In the city, every block is a microvillage worthy of recognition. Together, six blocks might constitute an entire neighborhood, possibly two, each with its own abiding culture. Here in the suburbs, however, the block is a nearly inconsequential unit of measurement. Here, all movement is coordinate based: *the corner of Main and East 6th* or *behind the Friendly's* or *you know, the old yellow house with the POW flag?* Distance is also measured in time: *twelve minutes door to door* or *twenty-five minutes without traffic* or *I did it in under an hour cuz there were no cops.* And there is no minimum distance for traveling by car. No one walks anywhere, at any time—especially if the stretch of land in question is a six-lane commercial corridor flanked by incomplete sidewalks and a coarse layer of crushed gravel whose low, Wild-West plumes of gray dust materialize at each step.

. . .

The people in the cars zooming past me, if they have taken notice, assume I'm poor, homeless, high, or here illegally, and likely all of the above. If they've given me a closer look—fitted, dark green slacks; summery white linen long-sleeve button-down shirt open somewhat seductively to mid-sternum; brown skin—they might be confused. They might be telling themselves I'm lost or stranded. In their defense, I am the sole person standing on this narrow ledge of pseudo-sidewalk, which ends in about fifty feet. From here, I move onto a borderless tract of wispy grass that appears to have sprouted from the surrounding dirt or from one of the muddy microlagoons that licks its edges, like hair on a pubescent chin or on a dome of advanced age—the alpha or the omega. These anomalous moments of nature are proof that there was once another landscape tucked beneath this capitalist afterthought.

Everyone is racing. To or from a mall, I presume. To buy or return something. To eat, to drink, to bowl, to dance, to watch a movie, or just linger. Doesn't matter if the mall is a short strip with four or five nearly identical, neon-emblazoned storefronts; a behemoth with multiple entrances, food courts, and endless parking; or a sprawling megaplex, as wide as it is gaudy, moated by acres of parking. Doesn't matter. Everyone is eager to get there, which is of particular consequence to me because to reach Joe's, the Italian restaurant, I'll have to wait on the tip of this islet for a breach in traffic.

At least it's summer. At least the dusky sky is a distracting swirl of pinks, oranges, and purples spreading upward from the horizon, as if there were a fire in the distance. A fire that is more or less under control. At least.

It's almost 8 P.M., and there's a slow drip from my armpits. If I back out now, no one will be the wiser—I didn't RSVP. I require only a modicum of temerity and a plan. The route home is simple: turn around, circumnavigate the archipelago of sidewalk islands, cut through one football field–sized parking lot, then camp out at the Applebee's until my parents have gone to bed. Or I could head straight home now, admit defeat, and sit in front of the television set with my father, who's probably going to die soon—not today, but sooner than later.

"We've excised all of the damaged portions of his large intestine. But his fatty liver and diabetes require care, beginning with a reduction in carbohydrates, salt, beer, and wine," my father's doctor explained in the waiting room, nearly three weeks ago. She had a rock climber's steely frame and the matter-of-fact cadence of a small-town mechanic, which left us believing that everything would be okay for now, but one day, it wouldn't be.

"Por favor, vente a casa. He listens to you," my mother pleaded with me last week. "I tell him something, and he says, 'We're all going to die someday,' but when you say it, he listens."

"I can come home this weekend."

"In the hospital, he promised me he would try, but he's already eating papa y arroz y esa carne guisada que le gusta tanto. He sneaks away to el Dominicano. Their portions aren't for old people. Restaurant food is not healthy. And he's not supposed to be driving."

"Mom—"

"A few nights ago, tomó vino. There wasn't much left, but he's not allowed to have any wine. I can't do it on my own. I have to go back to work, and my back hurts from helping him out of bed, off the toilet, in and out of the car. The doctor says it could be months until he has his strength again."

"Mom, I said yes."

"Oh, mi amor! Gracias! You're so good to us. Will Marco come, too?"

"No. I told you, he has his work trip."

"Oh! I forgot—"

"It's fine. It didn't make sense for me to travel with him. He'll be busy."

After a brief pause and some audible breathing, my mother asked if everything was okay between us.

"Yeah. Of course."

"Well, you know your relationship better than I do," she said, with an omniscient tenor that was more irksome than comforting.

A small fissure in the traffic continuum opens up. I won't have to sprint, but neither can I cross the six lanes at my leisure. There's no median; the friable pavement is pocked with faint, atavistic yellows and whites that suggest it hasn't been painted in years, lanes barely delineated one from the other, enticing everyone to swerve by omission. I scurry across like a tense squirrel, lacking the blitheness of my youth, when I was one of a small gang who'd bisect these lanes on low-end ten-speeds, mindlessly returning with sharp words and empty threats the vitriol of the horns and hostilities speeding past.

I'm here.

The restaurant's parking lot, an open-air grid of ten by ten, is halfway filled with gargantuan metal boxes, all of them recently washed and buffed, catching the twilight in their veneers. In this town, one's face to the world is their vehicle. A sleek ride can effectively belie or, at the very least, undercut perceived inadequacies. It can make a shitty life interstitially magnificent. It's been this way since I can remember. Rims, tinted glass, and speaker systems were the reason my friends had jobs in high school. A few traded respectable Jesuit universities far from here for used sports cars—bribes from their parents, in order to avoid private and out-of-state tuitions. For a high school reunion, a car wash is as essential as a new outfit, a haircut, or weight loss.

The restaurant, nondescript and industrial in appearance, abuts a paintball arcade, which is next door to a pool supply store, which shares a lot with a window-siding manufacturer, which is across a narrow side street from a tile company, all of them empty and slatted in the same eggshell-colored vinyl. At the end of this bland chain of businesses is the red-marqueed Uncle Billy's, the electronics store where we'd buy our TVs, VCRs, CD players, refrigerators, microwaves, and washing machines, and where my brother worked as a stock boy in high school, and then a salesman. It's where he died.

Uncle Billy's is run by Uncle Ikbir, who gives my parents the same underwhelming 5 percent discount he's been giving them for the last twenty-odd years. Ikbir has a long, wooly beard and wears a marshmallow-white turban. When he first arrived in this country, he drove a taxi in the city. One night, a coked-out day trader wrote him a five-hundred-dollar check to drive him to the suburbs. Ikbir took notice of how much bigger and greener everything was out here. After dropping the passenger off in his ritzy village, Ikbir got lost and drove twenty miles in the wrong direction, until he happened upon our insignificant town. By then, the sun was coming up, and he could see that the houses were smaller, had ricketier fences, less grass, and were more densely laid out than those he had just seen in the banker's hamlet, but they remained significantly more spacious and private than the fifty-unit apartment building in the city where Ikbir had been living. Not long after that fateful taxi ride into the suburbs, Ikbir picked up and moved to a nearby town. He brought his wife over from Pakistan some years later. A year after that, Uncle Billy sold him the store. According to my brother, Ikbir recounted this origin story every year as part of his staff pep talk during the holiday season. In the early nineties, Ikbir briefly considered changing the store's name to Uncle Ikbir's, but the US had just invaded Iraq because Iraq had invaded Kuwait, and he worried that no one would know the difference between the Middle East and Punjab, and that his name would be bad for business.

If I dawdle outside of Joe's long enough, someone will walk past and recognize me, and I'll be forced to go inside. I may do just that: wait until I have no choice.

This indecisiveness would have amused my brother. *Don't be such a chickenshit*, he might have said. He switched from *fag* to *chickenshit* after I told him I was gay. This was typical of Henry; when I least expected it, he was a good big brother. In fact, when I told him I was worried about coming out to our parents, he came out to them instead—"to test the waters"—a couple of years before I came out to them. After a week, Henry told them he'd been kidding. "Mom was pissed, but dad thought it was funny," he later explained.

My brother was the kind of person who could never muster the courage to ask for a raise or a promotion, who quit several jobs by simply not showing up, who never raised his hand in class, who refused to give simple explanations that would have otherwise extricated him from complicated situations, and who rarely defended himself when it mattered, but he had no problem attending his high school reunion. He didn't stay in touch with many of the friends he'd had back then, but he longed for those years anyway. At some point after high school, which by all measures he'd detested during the actual living of it, nostalgia became his default emotional state. Until the day he died, he referred to that era, sincerely, as the "good old times." As if his remembrances were palliative. My theory: the misery of his adulthood was an order of magnitude greater than the misery of his youth, and over time, less miserable somehow transformed into "good old times." In fact, it rankled my brother that I didn't recall our youth more fondly. As if my memories risked contaminating, or in some way invalidating, his.

"The problem is you think you're better than everyone," he said, the month before his heart attack. He'd said it to me dozens of times before, but this time, he was matter-of-fact about it, and he punctuated it with, "And you probably are."

Better isn't a fair or apt description of how I view myself. I don't think I'm intrinsically better or more important than anyone else, but I admit that I consider myself . . . something. Correct, maybe. After all, I did the things we were supposed to do. I did my homework. I got good grades. I seldom disobeyed my parents. I applied to college. I got into college. I went to graduate school. I got a job teaching at a university. I put down 25 percent for my small apartment. I don't own a car. I buy my produce at the farmers market. I speak three languages well, and a few others so-so. I support a nationalized health service, alternatives to incarceration, and a tripling of the minimum wage. I use LED bulbs. I don't cheat. I avoid high-fructose corn syrup, and I keep plastics out of the dishwasher and refrigerator. I turn the water off while I lather my hands. I consume media created almost exclusively by anyone other than cisgender, able-bodied white men. I apologize when I'm wrong and I try to do better. I vote for the Green Party in the primary and the Democrat in the general election. I wait for my husband to orgasm before I do.

I don't, however, consider myself unique or better. I'm doing the bare minimum. And the bare minimum should have been enough, collectively speaking. It was meant to add up. Instead, here we are, in a gas-guzzling wasteland bereft of sidewalks but with a surfeit of old sports cars on cinder blocks tucked beneath blue tarps.

I might be wrong. About all of it. I often get worked up about these things and later realize that I haven't left sufficient room for the fullness of humanity or for the consequences of history. It's my way.

But I'm not always wrong.

The sound of tires inching over gravel perforates the silence. Another steel behemoth rolls into the lot and I realize that escaping will be more complicated from this moment onward.

2
SUBURBS

They moved to this town by the thousands. From Ireland and from Italy, primarily. Then came the descendants of enslaved Africans from the South—Georgia, Mississippi, Alabama, Louisiana. It was this way for some time. Later, immigrants from Poland arrived. Not many. From Jamaica. Even fewer. From Puerto Rico. From the Dominican Republic. Much later, from Ecuador. From Peru. From Trinidad and Tobago. From India. From Ghana. From Senegal. All of them, by way of the city.

They settled here, in this town, because it was all that remained. The town wasn't along the water, near to the burgeoning industries of war or its fleets of whaling ships. Small businesses, few and brittle, replaced long-ago-abandoned farms. The houses were simple geometric stacks, a triangle atop a square, a square centered on a rectangle, sometimes a trapezoid. Single-family homes spaced apart enough to engender an illusion of independence. The trees had been largely disappeared. So, too, were most of the Pequot and Lenape.

The Irish lived west of the church and the school. Italians lived to the east. Black people occupied six square blocks in the southeast quadrant of the town. The Germans and the English, who'd come to the region earlier, lived elsewhere, in the towns farther east and along the northern and southern coasts. They were the owners of land and commerce, unfriendly and often cruel employers, just as they had been in the city.

Facing a common enemy forced an uneasy peace between the Irish and the Italians. They shared the pews and the classrooms, but rarely did they cross into each other's faintly demarcated neighborhoods—unofficial subdivisions wherein people greeted one another and knew each other's business: the what, the when, the how, and often the why. They helped raise each other's children, fed one another, didn't lock their doors. They attended baptisms and funerals together. Lived and died together. They died old.

Until the next generation. They were the ones who wanted the shinier things that had eluded their parents. They longed for extravagance. They wanted more powerful cars and bigger homes spaced even farther apart than the ones they'd known all their lives. Or they wanted to live in the more cosmopolitan and less crowded versions of the apartment buildings their parents had left behind. They wanted to travel. They wanted to go back to the city—to any city. They believed that distance and anonymity would give them privacy and control over their destinies. A common desire, before and since, especially of those conditioned to want more.

As the second generation scattered and disappeared, the town's battlements were breached, and so, too, were its internal divisions. Those left behind began latching doors. Eyebrows, suspicions, tempers, the cost of living, and walls went up. As did blood pressure, cholesterol, and glucose levels. The town's hitherto inexplicably pristine health worsened. Empty houses on Irish and Italian blocks were filled by newly arrived Poles, mixed Irish and Italian couples who were unconcerned with tradition or unbowed by expectations, a few Black families who wanted what had been dangled before them for generations—bigger homes on wider streets, nearer to everything—and occasionally, a mixed-race, ethnically ambiguous brood, maybe Puerto Rican or Filipino or deep Sicilian or a quarter Black or one-third Indigenous or all of it at once.

Alvaro and Rosario met in the city. They were on the rooftop of an apartment building that resembled all of the other apartment buildings in the neighborhood—a place where one might mistake one block for another if not for the distinct heads, arms, and legs jutting out of windows and dangling from fire escapes.

On Rosario's first night in her new country, there was a party: an assemblage of Colombians mostly, the dominant ethnic group in the neighborhood, but there were others as well. Except for Paraguay, Nicaragua, and Bolivia, every Spanish-speaking country in the Western Hemisphere was represented on that rooftop, along with a few blond white women who worked as the hosts, servers, and managers at the places where the others worked as cashiers, delivery men, and stock boys. Álvaro was one of the Colombians on the roof. He was small—height, weight, and chin—and he had soft, curious eyes and large hair full of loose curls. Rosario heard Álvaro's laughter before she was able to identify him as the source. The sort of full-throated mirth that disarms and ensnares.

They were briefly friends before they were lovers. Álvaro was twenty-one; Rosario was eighteen. She sought a tour guide and a break from civil unrest. Álvaro had been in the country a few years already and proved himself an attentive and tireless distraction. He took Rosario to the tops of the tallest buildings, to the nearest beaches, to the movies, to concerts in smoky cafés, cavernous arenas, and sprawling parks, to restaurants, bars, discotheques, pizza and ice-cream parlors, to church bingo on Friday nights and to mass on Sunday mornings. They were entranced by one another. Before long, they were inseparable. Rosario, who loved the serious glamour of high-heeled shoes, took to wearing flats as both a concession and a tribute to Álvaro, who, barefoot, was only a half inch taller than her. Four months after the rooftop, they were married.

When Rosario became pregnant a few years later, she and Álvaro began taking trips out of the city, to sleepy historic towns and suburbs that proved alluring for their serenity—a life without blaring car horns, grime, drugs, graffiti, violence, sirens, footsteps above, cigarette smoke below, pollution, cockroaches, mice, rats. For a year of aspirational weekends, they visited places they couldn't afford, which only whetted their appetites and made the city seem more unbearable, unsanitary, unsafe. The towns closest and farthest away were too expensive to consider, so they narrowed it down to the in-between places.

Not long before Enrique was born, one of the cooks at the restaurant where Álvaro worked told him of a place. Perfect for new families. The cook had a brother who was married to a *gringa* whose parents lived there. A town not far away, with a reasonable commute back to the city. Un pueblo inventado, said the cook. Still building. Up and up, he explained. Houses were reasonably priced. Two floors, double garages, front lawns, backyards. Álvaro and Rosario visited the industrial town one Sunday and followed the uncreative, albeit effective, signs, *New Homes for a New Life!* They came upon a gated development where only a third of the houses had been erected. The artificial neighborhood wasn't close to the school, the church, or the rows of houses with more space between them, but neither was it far. With their savings and a few loans from family and coworkers, Álvaro and Rosario were able to afford the down payment on a two-story condo with a patio. For five hundred dollars more, they could have added a garage, but Rosario had stopped working after Enrique was born, and a garage seemed like an unjustifiable indulgence with all of the available street parking.

In the months that followed, they drove out to the town every Sunday. They brought Rosario's cousin along one weekend, Álvaro's sister another, and once, the cook and his wife. They picnicked on the hood of the car: egg salad sandwiches, tuna sandwiches, empanadas, toasted pumpernickels with cream cheese, pickles, potato chips, apple juice. They watched the second story appear, then the roof, the windows, one bathroom, a second, a skylight in the third. A few months later, Rosario was pregnant again. A few months after that, they left the city.

Rosario and Álvaro arrived in this country, like many other immigrants before them, hungry, apologetic, oblivious, and from somewhere in worse condition. They were unaware of and unconcerned with what was happening in their new world. A fruitful, protective ignorance. Rosario and Álvaro had come to make a life, as they saw it, on someone else's land. It was incumbent upon them to proceed humbly, to work tirelessly, and to enjoy themselves quietly.

Naturally, Rosario and Álvaro elided politics in all of its forms—no conversations, no groups, no voting, no petitions, no meetings, no causes, no effects. No good had ever come of it. The oppression they encountered was the requisite price of being allowed to live here. Nothing, as far as they were concerned, was discriminatory. They were medium-complected Catholics from Latin America, who were largely untrained at receiving prejudice based on anything immutable. To them, hardship was class-based, and in this country, class was temporary and situational. When Álvaro was offered dishwasher jobs despite applying for server or host positions, he blamed his accent and the ignorance of the manager—never history or a systemic corrosion. When, on Fridays, Rosario was paid less for childcare or housecleaning than what had been advertised, she faulted, first, human error, then greed.

A lack of context meant also that Álvaro and Rosario felt little empathy for anyone who didn't, as far as they were concerned, try hard enough. "Lazy!" Álvaro said many times of many Americanos. "If I spoke the language, I would be a king here." Neither he nor Rosario had considered the long-term effects of living in this country. How it might deplete one's resolve. How for one person to succeed, many would have to fail. How this was a country that practiced a religion of lofty expectations and unattainable goals. How dreams were just that, dreams.

Rosario and Álvaro wouldn't have this hindsight for decades yet. But it didn't take long for them to intuit that there was indeed a pecking order. They might never be Americans, but neither were they held in the lowest regard. That place was occupied by Black people. A phenomenon that had been, through a combination of apathy, denial, and ignorance, easier to ignore in their countries. Here, however, the specter of an even worse life was an added (and unnecessary) incentive to succeed: they didn't have it as bad as others, and they didn't want to be lumped with those others.

The house that had been erected over the course of a year, reasonably priced in their estimation, was surrounded by surly older folk who wanted nothing to do with the new arrivals. Without realizing it, Álvaro and Rosario had moved into a gated complex originally intended, before a dip in the real estate market, as a retirement community.

For a few years, almost none of their neighbors did much more than greet them begrudgingly, and sometimes only because of inertia, before realizing their error and turning away. The exceptions were John, the raspy-voiced septuagenarian widower who brought Rosario and Álvaro freshly killed venison every Saturday, and Patricia and Jason, an Italian-Mexican couple with one child and another on the way, who had also been lured by the housing prices.

Álvaro and Rosario had found their way into a ghost town of sorts, where everyone was either hobbled or recently widowed and typically both. If the neighbors communicated at all, it was by way of notes. Notes tacked onto Álvaro and Rosario's front door or stuck onto their windshield, sometimes with gum—brief, recriminatory missives about parking and garbage pick-up regulations. Álvaro, who was seldom home, was unaffected by the onslaught of ill manners and reproachful looks, the reports of which arrived by way of Rosario. "Así son los Americanos," he reassured her. But Rosario wouldn't excuse any of it. As far as she was concerned, even an unwanted guest was owed respect.

Despite the disdain she felt for her neighbors, Rosario ceded the territory around her. She responded to the unwavering current of incivility by remaining at home, leaving only when it was absolutely necessary: the urgent care clinic, the supermarket, church. At least in the city, she thought, she might entertain herself by watching the stream of passersby from her window. Here, she counted more birds than humans. Without much else to do, it didn't take long for Rosario to master the little that was expected of her, the womanly responsibilities that she'd fulfilled diligently in other people's homes, but only casually in her own. Now, alone but for a baby who was easily entertained by a tower of wooden blocks, Rosario developed a dexterous touch and a keen eye for all matters of the house. A better-kept home would have been difficult to find in that gated community or anywhere else in the town.

And never had there been a boy as quiet, obedient, and spotless as Enrique, who lived perpetually by his mother's side, wound tightly and neat, like the collection of spools and bobbins kept in the small felt box in the middle shelf of her bedroom closet. The world had expectations, and now, she did too. A small smudge, a playful squeal, an unsanctioned foot out onto the patio, a momentary resistance: any of it could trigger Rosario's New World wrath.

In a few short years, Rosario had been rewired, her limbic system reprogrammed, her viscera by turns inflamed, contorted, and shrunken. Whomever she'd been when she'd landed and unpacked her two green leather suitcases, before traipsing through the city with the camera her father had given her at the airport—Para que yo también pueda ver todo lo que ves—she was no longer that person. And there was little proof—the camera had been stolen from her in a park—that she had ever existed as anything other than the self she had become. By her midtwenties, less than a decade after her arrival in this country, Rosario had a husband, a son, a house, an ulcer, two ovarian cysts, and two miscarriages. But her home was clean, and Enrique quiet.

Rosario and Álvaro had been trying for over a year to get pregnant when Andrés was conceived. He was born six weeks premature and at a low birth weight on the two-year anniversary of the house's completion. "The early ones are smarter," said an old man to Rosario as she peered through the glass partition and into the room full of pods and bright lights. Because she'd been raised to treat the advice of elders and complete strangers as an almost paranormal communiqué, the old man's simple words remained with her.

Two brothers couldn't have been more dissimilar. While Enrique was portly, Andrés was scrawny. Where Enrique was aimless and taciturn, Andrés was an arrow shortly after its release. Enrique was disinterested in both school and socializing; Andrés longed for Monday mornings, so that he might, once again, be out in the world, surrounded by his peers. The brothers' differences extended past temperament. They were undeniably cut from the same cloth, but a cloth that was asymmetrical in its design. Enrique was a rich, vibrant brown; Andrés was a duller beige. Andrés had loose, dark curls; Enrique's hair was tighter, almost kinky, reminiscent of a great-uncle that Rosario recalled only in fragments and of Álvaro's paternal grandfather, both of whom the boys had only ever met in the top drawer of Rosario's bedside table—a place of refuge for all of the uncategorizable things: old rubber bands, baby teeth, insurance policies, Social Security cards, dried-up pens, useless pencils, hospital bracelets, bank statements, and bundles of sepia-toned and black-and-white photographs. At times, it seemed that the only common thread between Enrique and Andrés was the cotton-polyester blend in their school uniforms.

In Rosario's and Álvaro's countries, private school was the shortest path to a life worth living, and around here, just as they had been back home, private schools were Catholic schools. Divine intervention, however, came at a nearly insurmountable cost. Each month, the nuns pinned payment slips stamped OVERDUE to Enrique's and Andrés's blazers. Each month, Álvaro tucked a post-dated check into Andrés's backpack and asked him not to bring it to the school office until the final period of the day, guaranteeing that no intrepid nun would have the time to make a deposit before the banks closed.

No matter how many checks bounced, how often utilities were shut off, how many debtors called, how many coins Rosario pulled from couch cushions and Álvaro picked up from the street, how many cold showers they took in the winter because the boiler had stopped working, how much they sweated in the summer because the thermostat couldn't go below seventy-seven degrees, how many half lunches they ate, how many consecutive rice-and-bean dinners Rosario prepared, how many times they had to give the car a push in order to get it to run, how many weighty hands or worn belts landed on soft cheeks or tensed backsides, Rosario insisted her boys continue at the school.

When Andrés and Enrique were old enough to walk to the bus stop alone, Rosario bought a navy-blue skirt suit, sheer nylons, and beige-colored high heels, and she asked Andrés to help her create a résumé.

One of Álvaro's regular customers at the restaurant, a Venezuelans day trader, worked at a large Spanish-based bank in the city, and he offered to put in a good word with human resources.

Rosario agreed to go to the interview, but she feared what her absence at home might engender. Children left to their own devices would end up lazy or in the hands of the devil. She also felt guilt about her desire to leave, something that she had never uttered aloud. An escape from a domesticated life without trajectory, characterized disproportionately by endless waiting:

waiting for her children to wake up, waiting for the washer to complete its cycle, waiting for the water to boil, waiting for her children to come home, waiting for the oven timer to ding, waiting for her children to fall asleep, waiting for her husband to come home. All of it, alone. Rosario wanted her life to have a slope and a pinnacle—nothing overtly lofty, but certainly an ascent. She wanted a career, a desk, a week's worth of skirt suits, pantsuits, and appropriate but severe heels, a commute, colleagues, and a plaza with a fountain where she might eat her lunch. But at some point, she'd concluded that her life would be lived strictly as a wife and mother. Until suddenly it wasn't. After her fourth miscarriage, two of which were in the second trimester, Rosario's doctor told her that her womb was inhospitable.

Everything, it seemed, was inhospitable.

Álvaro worked six days a week at the restaurant, and often all three shifts. Even so, it was never enough. There was always another expense. Mortgage, maintenance, tuitions, car insurance, life insurance, homeowner's insurance, credit cards, remittances for both families, hospital bills from the births and miscarriages, backdoor penicillin, uniforms and school supplies, milk, eggs, beans, rice, meat, cereal, fruit, vegetables, fuel, telephone, electricity, water, cable. Rosario's salary as a receptionist at the bank proved to be a life-sustaining infusion, until the car broke down or taxes were due or someone had unbearable tooth pain. Whenever they'd scaled the mountain, it seemed that the fog would lift, revealing another summit.

Through it all, Enrique and Andrés got along as brothers do. Love and hate alternating with envy and admiration. The natural conditions of love, but also a love under duress. By virtue of being older and present, Enrique became a father figure to Andrés. And Andrés, by default, became like a mother, and specifically, their mother. Before his parents came home each night, he'd rush to finish his homework, to prepare something for dinner, to clean so that he didn't have to see the dreaded exasperation on Rosario's face. The sort of disappointment that makes children into homemakers and soldiers.

And yet, Álvaro and Rosario's affections were present throughout, just beneath the rancor and exhaustion, like old blankets caped in thin layers of dust and, sometimes, fiberglass dust. They knew they'd cobbled together an unsustainable life. Rosario and Álvaro knew it when they lay in bed at night waiting for their blood pressures to drop, heart rates to slow, and cortisol levels to return to their rightful places. Always they were rethinking and regretting their choices, praying for better lives for Enrique and Andrés, and, at times, holding out hope for creating more life, miserable as it might be, until the ring of an alarm clock signaled the beginning of the next day. Again.

3

ITALIAN
RESTAURANTS

I am unsettled by the past. Not a generalized, conceptual, or theoretical past, but three very real and specific events. All of them, deaths. All murders, of a sort. The first was undeniable, even if it remains unpunished and its perpetrator, Paul, at large, and possibly present at this reunion. The second was the inexplicable and abrupt death of my first love. Although no one died, the end of my relationship with Jeremy occurred with the force and expediency of a well-timed blade. The third murder was of my brother, Henry, who died in the most infuriating way one can die—at the hands of a shapeless, invisible system. One that works slowly and surreptitiously, and leaves the victim blaming himself until the bitter end.

A thick velvet barrier hangs between the party and me. I push the black curtain aside and discover another of these soft walls. After it, there's an anteroom with a shin-high oblong coffee table. Name tags sheathed in soft plastic snake along its wooden surface; on its legs are tied red and white balloons—our school's colors. Overhead hangs a banner: *Welcome St. Iggy's Class of 1997.* The cloistered space is festive but also sinister and perfunctory, like *Twin Peaks.*

This is, in a way, purgatory. Silence behind me; entwined, indecipherable murmurs up ahead, growing louder. An inexorable, consuming din.

"Hi. Alumni or spouse?" A clear voice emerges from behind another curtain altogether.

"Excuse me?"

"Are you an alumni or— Andy?"

I consider asking if she means alumnus. I nod instead.

"Nicole," she says and points to her badge: *Nicole Scifelli. Cheerleader. National Honor Society. Chair, Alumni Planning Committee.* Small font.

Her silvery eyes and pinched nose are familiar. Her hair, however, is something recent, an unnatural color—an indecisive blend of blond, red, and brown.

Nicole was the first kid I ever met with divorced parents. I served detention in third grade for lifting her skirt. In seventh grade, I kissed her, mouth closed, during a game of spin the bottle. In high school, we barely spoke, but a few times during senior year she drove me to school. I recall that she steered almost exclusively with her kneecaps throughout the entire fifteen-minute ride, while peering into the sun visor's mirror and applying makeup. It was as impressive as it was bone-chilling. Nicole and I got along just fine, but she suffered greatly for having small breasts—sunken-treasure jokes, surfboard jokes. I'm sure I contributed.

She's no longer flat anywhere. Currently, her cleavage is threatening the flimsy button of her negligee-like black blouse. I feel an urge to apologize, to explain that we were all vile and clueless and that our parents didn't teach us any better; neither did school or society. *I'm sorry, Nicole. Your family was falling apart, and we were all too busy ridiculing you for not meeting impossible, unhealthy, and boringly binary standards. I've seen enough coming-of-age movies to know that you cried yourself to sleep more nights than the rest of us. It didn't help your case that you were bossy as hell, but even that might be history through a misogyny-frosted lens. Maybe you were just being proactive or a born leader.*

"Nicole? Wow. You look amazing," I say, hoping to repair in shorthand what I helped over many years to break.

"Oh, gawd. No way. I didn't even have time to go to the salon today," she says, and tosses behind her the hard, crimped hair that had been resting on her shoulder.

"You know, Mister, I've been trying to get ahold of you for almost twenty years! You're not an easy person to track down. I didn't print a badge for you."

"No problem," I say.

"Before we leave, I want you to fill out an updated contact form. For now, you'll have to make yourself your own name tag." Nicole hands me a sheet of adhesive rectangles and a purple marker. "Do you remember what clubs and sports you were a part of?"

I ran cross-country and track and field. I was in the student government. And the honor society. I wrote for the paper, *The Deacon's Beacon*. "I'd have to give it some thought," I say.

"You were brainy. Just put National Honor Society. And then hurry up and get in here. It's a good turnout. Sixty people so far, but a hundred RSVP'd. Haven't had this many people since the five-year reunion. The complimentary food is going quick, but you can order whatever you want and pay separate."

Nicole slips between the velvet drapes. The curtains part briefly, and I catch a glimpse.

Nine years ago, I ate at this restaurant for the last time, after my brother's funeral. My mother chose Joe's because it was nearby and because it was one of Henry's favorites—the baked ziti, which he ate at least twice a week for most of his adult life, had the perfect ratio of cheese to tomato sauce, he always said. Mostly family came to the lunch that day—two aunts, two uncles, three cousins, their children, my brother's wife and children, my parents—and our neighbor Patty. The meal was quiet except for some ruckus from the kids—batches of second cousins meeting for the first time. Henry would have never permitted his children to make noise. Somewhere before the appetizers, he'd have raised an eyebrow or a tense finger and, without uttering a word, effectively threatened them into submission. On that day, we all ignored it because they weren't particularly loud or annoying—they never were—but I recall filling up with an urge to discipline them nonetheless, if only out of respect for my brother.

Today, I don't recognize the dining room. The soft lamps, white table-cloths, and red wainscoted walls have been replaced with blue-filtered lighting, black tabletops, and a perimeter of crushed velvet. It looks like the template for a nightclub lounge. The wall behind the bar is a mirror of prodigious height and width. The rows of liquor bottles are bookended by large wooden Buddha statues. The staff are all young, a mix of Indian Americans and whites, probably in their last year of high school or first of college. I can no longer decipher if the white is Italian, Irish, or Polish because almost no one remains one or the other anymore. The workers are all dressed in cummerbunds, black bow ties, tuxedo shirts, but no jackets: my father's lifelong uniform. Scattered strategically around the large room are stands with half-eaten trays of hors d'oeuvres—deviled eggs, small slabs of salmon, flaky miniature quiches. Although this remains an Italian restaurant, there is nothing distinctively Italian about the food. A dozen or so bar-height tables without stools are clustered near the center of the space. Atop the tables are crumpled cocktail napkins and tall glasses filled with limp cubes of ice. The event is well attended, but the wall-to-wall mirror gives the impression of a much more crowded room.

"Excuse me. Class of 1997, I would like your attention." Nicole's disembodied voice crackles through the speakers, interrupting Ini Kamoze's "Here Comes the Hotstepper." She informs the room that I've arrived. Late, but I've arrived. Resurrected, she says. "Let's hear it for Andy!" she concludes after the overwrought introduction.

The room claps softly and begins to search itself. I put my head down to avoid eye contact and walk sixteen paces to the bar. "Two gin martinis, straight up, a touch of dirty, three olives."

"A touch of—?"

"Just a splash of olive juice."

"Gin pref—"

"I truly don't care."

The bartender's eyes expand. "Okey dokey."

"Sorry, I'm Andy"—I gesture vaguely into the air, toward wherever Nicole's voice reverberated—"and I haven't seen any of these people in almost twenty years."

"No explanation necessary," says the handsome boy. "This is the fifth reunion this month. They all go the same: Everyone gets wasted. Things get messy. The bright side is, you're either going to have fun or you're going to forget."

I like this advice. *Murderer. I'm the lyrical gangster.* "You're wise for your age," I say. "Don't waste it by staying in this place. Get out while you can."

"Huh?" The bartender gives the ice and gin a vigorous even if brief shake. "This is just a summer gig. I start med school in the fall."

This boy has a square face, dark hair, thick eyebrows, and brown skin darker than mine. Maybe he's the owner's son or nephew. Maybe not. Before I moved away, I didn't know of a single Indian family; now, there are a couple of Indian restaurants—as well as non-Indian restaurants owned by Indians, Indian shelves in the supermarkets' ethnic aisles, a sari boutique in a nearby strip mall, and, according to my mother, several Catholic Indians at 10 A.M. mass on Sundays.

"Wish me luck," I say, but the future doctor has already moved on to someone else.

I eat one broken olive, slug down the first martini, eat a second, sturdier olive, and plop the third inside of the other, untouched martini. I remind myself that I once cared deeply for many of the people here. *Don't be nervous,* I think. Worst case, I won't remember anything tomorrow.

I scan the crowded room. Everywhere are clusters of two and three memories in human shape. A few groups of five. The room is overwhelmingly white, whiter than high school was. Everyone looks as old as I expected. Older than they should. My brain can't help but apply a public health layer to everything—it's what I do for a living. I don't see people in this room; I see chronic risk factors. They pop up over each person, like thought bubbles in a comic strip: drinking, smoking, sedentary living, stress, low self-efficacy, distrust, shame, resentment, low wages, poor food options, trauma, violence, debt. It occurs to me that instead of submitting to tonight's time-travel charade, I could ask Nicole to give me the mic, so that I might present on the harms of capitalism and income inequality. I could explain how chronic stress speeds up wear and tear of the body, and how it makes self-care untenable— the lecture I give to my graduate students on the first day of Introduction to Population Health 301: What Does the Future Hold? Afterward, I could field questions from the audience. But I'd be lucky to get out of this restaurant alive. Everyone here is either a cop or related to one, they're at least one generation removed from union work (except, ironically, the cops), at least half the room identifies as conservative, another half thinks socialists and Nazis are the same thing, three-quarters would agree with the notion that race is a biological construct, four-fifths care more about lowering the price of gasoline than lifting the minimum wage, and all of them are pro-choice Catholics who don't want to talk about it. The only things we have in common are an affinity for fried appetizers and the nook in our frontal lobes reserved for the Goo Goo Dolls and Biggie Smalls.

My pocket buzzes. "Babe, going to bed. Went out with the team for dinner, drinks. Hope your parents are okay. Love you. M."

Marco and I agreed not to talk this week in order to, as per our couples counselor's advice, "think about our individual needs and how they conflict with each other's needs."

I knew Marco would give in first. He didn't want to take a break at all. In fact, on the way to the airport, he offered to cancel his trip and join me at my parents'.

"Your conference is significantly more important than my dad's shrunken colon," I said.

"But you're more important to me."

"Thank you. Maybe though, a week apart will be good for us," I responded, knowing full well that amor de lejos es amor de pendejos. *Long-distance love is for idiots.*

"It's ten days."

"Better still."

"Don't be like this, baby. We'll be okay. It's only a rough patch."

It *is* only a rough patch, but it's the first one in a long time, and it's left my emotions scrambled. I feel half myself, and the half that remains is only two-thirds invested in us.

"You have your boarding pass?" I asked him, when we got to the airport.

"Yes."

"Passport?"

"Yes."

"Phone charger?"

"Uh-huh."

"Your inhaler?"

"Orejas, chill! I have to write and rehearse a speech for my team and find a way to turn three hundred slides into a twenty-minute presentation. I don't need any more stress."

Ears. That's what he calls me because my ears are somewhat big. At the risk of sounding defensive, I don't think they're exceptionally large, but they do stick out a bit, giving the illusion that they're larger than they are. And the lobes are above-average floppy.

Irrespective of our marital troubles, Marco hates planes and goodbyes, which is why I never accompany him to the airport when he travels without me. I don't want to be an audience for his discomfort—the beads of sweat at his brow, the subtle way he nibbles his lower lip. On this occasion, however, I thought a kind gesture might compensate for the kindness I wasn't feeling.

"Sorry for snapping at you," he said, before setting his carry-on on the ground and grabbing me by the waist.

I placed my hand on his chest and exerted a delicate pressure.

"I don't give a fuck about these people," Marco said playfully, knowing how I am about public displays of affection. "I'll fight every last one of them."

I knew he was joking, but a flex in his shoulders told me there was an intemperance too. More proof of his travel anxiety.

"Come here," he said. "Kiss me, and then go."

And I did.

Marco is six hours ahead and intoxicated enough to forget that we agreed not to message each other. He's had two beers. Or two margaritas. Or one of each. But no more than two drinks. He doesn't drink as much as I do. In fact, he'd be appalled at my having just chugged a martini. And he'd be right. There's no reason for me to be this nervous or to, as my therapist says, "submerge my insecurities in gin."

I don't respond to Marco's text.

The Spin Doctors play.

"Andy?"

A short, round-faced woman with long brown hair and frosted tips approaches. I know her. We met in elementary school, and she was often my ride to high school. A Honda Accord. Her grandfather was senile and Sicilian, and he once forgot to lock the gate to their yard, and their Doberman puppy got out and was struck by a school bus, and I had to help her carry the bleeding carcass back to her house.

What is her name? If I blurt out *Lisa* or *Nicole*, I have a 40 percent chance of getting it right. Where is her name tag? She's wearing an inch of makeup, just as she did back then. She was a massive Billy Joel fan—everyone was. Her mom worked at the local supermarket, could smoke a pack of cigarettes in an hour, and adored Meat Loaf, the singer—everyone did. Her family was kind to me in no particular way except that I always felt welcome. When their house burned down in seventh or eighth grade and they were forced into a trailer on their front lawn, my dad brought them dinner from Friendly's. He did this once a week until their house was rebuilt, which astonished me because my parents had never said anything more than *Hello* and *Peace be with you* to her mom. "When is your father going to bring us that good arroz con pollo?" she used to ask when I'd come by after their house had been rebuilt.

"I guess when Friendly's adds it to the menu," I'd respond, pretending that she wasn't joking—I've always been inept at engaging with that type of middling ethnic humor. Besides, I knew nothing of rice and chicken. As a kid, I assumed it was less typical of Colombian or Salvadorian cuisines because my mother didn't prepare it, which in retrospect was completely in character for my mother, who'd never bother with the dish that united all Latin Americans in the eyes of *Americans*.

Marie! That's it! Of course!

"Marie, how are you?" I say.

"'Marie, how are you?' Give me a break, Andy. It's been almost twenty years! Where the fuck have you been? My mom asked your parents a million times to tell you to give me a call. What the fuck?"

There's a tinge of rancor in Marie's voice and in her fluttering violet eyelids and extended eyelashes, but there's no sincerity to her anger. This is merely recrimination as icebreaker—even if it is true what she says about my not keeping in touch.

"How is your mom?" I ask Marie.

"She died. Last year. Cancer."

Marie's eyes fill instantly with thin tears that, through a combination of surface tension and rapid blinking, remain motionless on her eyes. She taps three fingers onto her chest to let me know what type of cancer it was. Without giving it much thought, I reach for her hand, the one that isn't holding a Corona Light. "Shit. I'm sorry, Marie. Your mom was the best. I'll never forget her *Bat Out of Hell* dance parties."

Marie clears her nose with a few inhalations and wipes it with a wrist. "Thanks. You were, like, her favorite, you know. She was happy you never came back. 'What the fuck for?' she used to say. 'Leave that boy out there in the world.'"

Marie's mom surely knew I was gay. She wore eyeliner like a raccoon and poured schnapps into her coffee. She was a suburban drag queen. Certainly, she had gaydar before I knew what gaydar was.

Marie lives one block from where she grew up, she explains. She moved back from Florida when her mother first got sick a few years ago.

"Remember this?" she says, and rolls her eyes.

"MMMBop" plays. Hanson, the blond boy band comprised of science-fearing Christian brothers. Marie's head moves side to side in rhythm with the song. Her waist, too, shifts complicity. She laughs at herself.

Marie recently remarried the father of her two kids, both of whom attend the public schools that we all avoided. "It is what it is," she surmises. Her face contorts into a rictus of underachievement.

According to my parents and the church's monthly newsletter, the *Tea of Galilee*, most of the people I grew up with still baptize their children, but very few send them to Catholic schools. They go instead to catechism classes on the weekends. A mix of fourth-generation white Catholics and the over-achieving children of over worked immigrants fill the parochial seats.

Marie and I exchange numbers because she gives me no choice. Then she flings her hand in the air toward Janna, who in turn calls over Lizzy, who's standing in a circle with Vanessa, Adam, and Chris. Monique pops over briefly on the way to the bathroom. Because she's Black, I want to make a joke about how endangered we non-whites are in this space, but maybe she doesn't appreciate that sort of camaraderie. She shouts that she'll be right back. I'm buzzed and less reticent about interacting with everyone than I was thirty minutes ago. With each successive encounter, I am freer. After a dozen conversations, I make my way back to the bar. Steven, Stephen, Megan, and Meghan part, making space for me to join. One of them reaches back to the bar and hands me a beer. It takes everyone a wide-eyed, open-mouthed moment to remember me. "Wow!" and "Holy shit!" are repeated. Over and over. As are the condolences about my brother. Some don't react much to seeing me, but their eyes narrow into something suspicious. They all tell me about their jobs and children. Everyone has children. Erin has four, LaTeisha three, Monique three, Irene two, Dominic four, Alex four, Greg three. Nicole D. is a nurse, Nicole T. a loan officer, Nicole S. a third-grade teacher and gymnastics instructor, Dina runs a catering business with her sister, Gina makes jewelry, Gino teaches algebra and coaches high school basketball and lacrosse, Jake's a cop, Reggie's a cop, Nicole C. is a cop, Michael L. is a cop, Michael R. is a cop, Colleen is a physician's assistant, and Margaret stays at home with her kids. Some of them see each other regularly, some at events like this one, some at the supermarket, some at church, most only on Facebook.

Of the more than two hundred students in our class, nearly half are now here. But there is no sign of Simone.

Simone was that rare adolescent with unabashed confidence, humor, kindness, and athletic abilities, who occupied the overlapping space between best friend and partner in crime. She lived on the Irish side of town and went to public school until sixth grade. Her parents were professors. History, I believe. She and I were in the same homeroom in seventh grade. In eighth grade, we'd go to an all-ages night at a club in the industrial part of town, where each room represented a different genre of music. Simone only ever wanted to be in the dim, exposed-brick space where they played grunge rock and ran a fog machine. She'd spend the entire night whipping through the mosh pit like a boomerang on fire. After my first busted lip, I took to watching the spectacle from the sidelines. In high school, Simone wore hemp necklaces and was in love with Eddie Vedder. During our freshman year, I roped her into my short-lived racket of supplying alcohol for all the cool kids.

"We just stand outside of 7-Eleven and wait for someone nice to do it for us. The seniors on the volleyball team do it all the time," Simone explained.

Over the course of a few weekends, we filled up our backpacks with Olde English forties and clanked our way to wherever everyone was gathered. Since kids from two counties attended St. Ignatius, sometimes Simone and I would have to travel by bus or train while lugging around nearly fifty pounds of glass and malt liquor.

Once, one of the bottles broke, and the liquor leaked all over the train's vinyl seats, eventually dripping onto the floor and making its way down the aisle.

"Why are we doing this?" Simone asked, as she rushed to pull the fractured forty out of her backpack, while I used notebook paper to sop up the mess.

"I promised."

"Why?"

I shrugged, and she shook her head, half forgiving and half exasperated. I'm sure she thought I was a fool, but she never said so.

When Simone turned sixteen, her parents bought her a used Civic. After that, we were ungovernable, taking secret trips out east, to towns where we were unwelcome but too ignorant and confident to notice. A few times, we drove into the city, parked somewhere downtown, and walked as far north as we could before taking a train back down. But typically, Simone and I would stay nearby, drive to the beach after school, smoke pot.

Simone was nearly six feet tall at thirteen. Her favorite sport was basketball, but she wouldn't try out for the high school team because she didn't like other people's expectations. "Imagine: a tall Black girl playing basketball. How original." Instead, she became St. Ignatius's greatest lacrosse and volleyball player. No one outscored her. During our junior or senior year, she changed her mind, joined the basketball team, and outscored everyone there too. We didn't hang out as much near the end of high school, but it was always happiness and comfort when we were together. In retrospect, we probably fit so well because we were both queer and closeted. Butterflies trapped under glass. One time, we got real drunk and she told me as much—"We're gays in the making," she said. I didn't know what she meant exactly, but I loved the turn of phrase, even if I hated to hear it. "Shut up," I responded. Then I laughed as if she were joking and changed the subject. A couple of years later, in college, I came out to her over the phone. All she said was, "Duh, Andy." There were a few phone calls after that one, but we never saw each other again.

The restaurant couldn't possibly fit any more people, or their memories. My streak of twenty years of avoidance ends at a clip. I get passed around like a team trophy, and frankly, it feels as alien as it does good. In high school, I was a popular kid, but it was a tireless campaign on my part. Always striving to be in the right place, to make people laugh, to be a good dancer, to throw the best parties, to drink more, to smoke everything being passed around, to drop acid, to befriend the beautiful girls so that I might be mistaken for a ladies' man, to keep my grades up, to say yes to everyone, always. I don't know if I was aware of how hard I was trying, but somewhere in me, I sensed that if I ever stopped performing, even for a moment, the audience would leave; so, in a way, I left first. It never occurred to me that they'd remained in their seats.

4

NUNS

I f it hadn't been for Patricia, the neighbor whose husband traveled so often for work that she was effectively raising her children alone, Enrique would have repeated eighth grade—he'd already been held back once. It was Patricia who left messages for Rosario when Enrique didn't show up at the bus stop. It was Patricia who took to knocking on their door after the bus had left with her children and Andrés. ("I'm going to stay right here until you open up.") It was Patricia who drove Enrique to school if she found him at home. ("You're going to make me late for work, honey.")

Enrique took to the routine and the camaraderie. Patricia, to him, wasn't only a neighbor, she was an adult whose concern was unweighted by expectations or consequences—a friend. With her own children, Patricia was imperious, but with Enrique she was accommodating, attentive, and cheerful. He'd never been treated this way before by someone who had no reason to be kind. Patricia was like a family member but without any of the accompanying stress.

Enrique wasn't disruptive or polemic or vicious. In the eyes of Álvaro and Rosario, his most significant shortcoming was how poorly he fared in school, which everyone (parents, teachers, coaches, Andrés) deduced was the result of laziness. It was quite a surprise, then, when his first report card at St. Ignatius was a column of B-pluses—a marked improvement on every school year that had come before. Even more surprising, he seemed to like high school. He was a quiet boy in class and a pleasure to be around, said the nuns. He even made a few friends. From time to time, Patricia still drove him to school, but only because he'd overslept.

Two children doing well in school made the everyday inhumanity seem almost logical and, possibly, necessary for Álvaro and Rosario—the commutes, the long hours, the condescension, the pay, the knowledge that there was no room for improvement in their lives. Álvaro and Rosario believed that if Enrique and Andrés could keep their grades up, they would have no problems, or at least problems different from their own. There was nowhere for their children to go but up. In this country, there were no bombs or checkpoints or young revolutionaries in blond wigs and prosthetic noses or handfuls of Europeans who owned every parcel of land and all of the industries or kidnappings or drug cartels or CIA-trained militias roaming or impermeable class divisions or feral dogs or drunk survivors on every corner or, most importantly, limits. Álvaro and Rosario were guests, and guests owed their hosts deference, but their children owed nothing and could do as they pleased. Certainly, they couldn't fare worse. In fact, Enrique and Andrés were doubly blessed. They held the vantage of outsiders: a bird's-eye view of this country's virtues and iniquities. This was a place with opportunities and inefficiencies; Enrique and Andrés were trained to seize the former and game the latter. They were doing well, and they would continue to do well, Rosario and Álvaro believed. Even so, the warnings rarely abated: *Never end up like us. Look at us. Never be us.*

Enrique and Andrés walked quickly up the sleepy street with no sidewalks, each with a backpack slung over a shoulder of blue wool. It was 7:30 A.M. A humid early-September morning, and they were already sweating through their T-shirts, their white oxford button-downs, their red rayon ties, and their thin, stiff gray slacks. The bus would reach their stop in a couple of minutes.

"Enri—"

"Don't fucking call me that. Everyone at school calls me Henry."

"Henry?"

"That's my name. Don't wear it out."

"No. Enrique in English is exactly the same in Spanish. Proper nouns are—"

"Fuck your proper nouns, shit stain. My name is Henry. You wanna show up to school with your underwear up your ass?"

"Okay, whatever."

"Not whatever. This is my school. And you didn't have to come here. You could have gone to St. Francis or Holy Family. I don't know why you had to follow me here."

St. Ignatius wasn't the best school—that was St. Francis—but it wasn't the worst either—that was Holy Family. Andrés had chosen St. Ignatius because it was the high school where most of his friends were going. He hadn't given any thought to Enrique when he'd made the decision, and now it was too late to go elsewhere.

Andrés wiped his brow with the back of his tie, surreptitiously swallowing whatever was coating his throat. He and Henry had always had a rocky relationship—worsened by adolescence—but Andrés hadn't imagined that Henry hated him this much.

Henry's words slighted Andrés, but they intrigued him too. In fact, he was impressed. Henry had never before evinced anything that signaled a complicated or layered emotion. Whereas Andrés lived perpetually inside of his own mind, obsessively analyzing the minutiae of life, worrying, doubting, full of anger and fear, Henry had maintained the air of someone less troubled, someone incapable of harboring anything against anyone, of cultivating or incubating complex thoughts. Whenever they'd fight, their hatred for one another was as visceral and exaggerated as it was incidental and evanescent. Theirs were the minor emotional scuffles typical of two animals forced into one cage and left unattended.

Henry meant what he'd said, but he hadn't intended to say it. And yet, for a moment afterward, he felt powerful. Until he slid into his seat near the back of the bus and pressed his head against the window. That's when the guilt took hold. And then that, too, vanished.

The high school was big enough for the brothers' paths to seldom cross. Henry didn't go so far as to ignore Andrés, but he kept his greetings small:

waves, head nods, *heys*. At first, Andrés maintained a distance, so as not to upset Henry, but as time went on, he came to see that there were no benefits to being associated with his brother, who didn't provide any of the cachet that some of the other older siblings seemed to, namely access—entry into the upper echelons of the school's hierarchy. Henry wasn't studious enough to be in a club or honor society; he wasn't committed enough to be on a sports team; he wasn't tall, tough, or quirky enough to be part of a clique.

Similarly, Andrés was of no measurable use to Henry.

"He's a dickwad."

"Honey, don't talk like that. He's your brother. The only one you have." Patricia sank into the worn, gray seat of her royal-blue Mustang GT hatchback, a car she had bought with her share of the inheritance her father had left to her and her four sisters after selling his bakery—Giacamo's, the place where locals went for their cannoli, torrone, cheesecakes, and when they didn't want to prepare their own zeppoli for the feasts of St. Joseph or San Gennaro, Three Kings Day, Christmas, New Year's, or Saturdays. The car had a rear spoiler that, to Henry, made it seem as if it might at any second take flight. It was in this car that he'd learned to drive: after-school lessons from Jason, Patricia's husband, whenever he was in town. Andrés, too, was learning to drive in that car. As were Jason and Patricia's daughter, Monica, a bookish kid who wore thick eyeglasses and fleece leggings to school every day, and their son, Vincent, a chubby video gamer who sucked his thumb when no one was looking.

It was the constancy of Patricia's simple advice that comforted Henry, who was drawn to the attention—any attention that wasn't cast primarily as recrimination or retribution or that he wasn't required to split with Andrés.

Patricia had come from a large family where it had been customary to interfere and be interfered with. She was a friend to Henry, but she was a support for everyone else too: complimenting Rosario's "fancy" work clothes, praising Andrés always for his grades and popularity; showing up whenever Álvaro and Rosario's car stalled; driving the brood to the train station, the supermarket, little league, karate class, urgent care, school, the mechanic; reminding the family about picture days, parent-teacher conferences, registration deadlines.

With time, Patricia also became a confidante for Rosario, who, on the one hand, bristled at her neighbor's familiarity and the subtle requirements of friendship, but who was also grateful for a loyal, innocuous presence after nearly twenty years of steeling her perimeter. Rosario resisted the friendship initially out of guilt, suspicion, and spite. Why did her son need attention from someone else? Why was this stranger always willing to help us? Why is she here at all? Rosario came to begrudgingly accept the help that in a previous life and in another place would have been expected and welcome but now felt like an admission of failure.

"I wouldn't worry about the boys," Patricia said, drunk but sturdy, as they said goodbye outside of Rosario's house. Sharing a bottle of prosecco had become a Friday evening ritual once their kids were in high school. "My sister was always jealous of me, but I think it motivated her. She lives out east. Huge house. A pool." Patricia's gum smacked between her molars; her hand rested on the roof of her car. She folded herself to peer into the sideview mirror. "Do I look drunk?"

"No," responded Rosario, distracted, suddenly aware of all the places where the wood was splintering along the chest-high brown-picket fence. "Why? Is Jason home?"

"Gawd no! Not till next week."

At nineteen, Patricia had married someone she'd met on a beach vacation, a barrel-chested man with big teeth. That Jason was Chicano initially estranged her from her family, which in turn led to depression and tremendous weight gain, but when the children turned out white, her family warmed up—the weight, however, remained. Jason sold encyclopedias, after a brief spell with vacuum cleaners, and was gone more often than not, which neither he nor Patricia minded, even if she missed the warmth and possibilities of another body.

"Enrique's not young anymore," Rosario said. "Next year, he has to apply to colleges. I don't think he has the grades to go anywhere." Rosario truly didn't know. She had little understanding of what it took to get into a university. "For the last two years, Cs and Ds. That can't be good enough for a good college."

Rosario was as inebriated after one drink as she was after three. It was this intolerance, and only this, that emboldened her to speak freely about her children's shortcomings.

"Better still. You'll save a ton," continued Patricia. "He can do a couple of years of community college and transfer when he's ready. My cousin's a good tax lawyer, and he went to community college for two years before going to a state school."

"I hope so. Nothing gets through to him." Rosario raised a hand to her mouth and hiccupped. "He doesn't care at all about his future."

"It'll click eventually, Rosie. We just have to keep encouraging them."

Rosario couldn't think of anyone in her life who had ever called her Rosie. She didn't like the nickname, but hearing it made her feel American, just as she did whenever she said "you guys" or "the fridge" or "bucks" instead of "dollars."

He's on the verge of failing. If you want our advice, there's no point in paying all of this tuition. It's clear he doesn't want to be here."

By the time the nuns called Rosario, at the end of his junior year, Henry had been truant for nearly a quarter of the semester.

"Thank you for letting me know. But please don't concern yourself with what we do with our money," Rosario sniped, like a carnivorous plant. She'd taken the call in an empty conference room at work. Rosario didn't care for Sister so-and-so's advice. Nuns were bitter, intransigent devils who'd been responsible for much of her adolescent unhappiness. To complicate matters, Rosario had been, for years, encountering old white women who told her what not to do and how not to say things and how much things cost. She no longer possessed the goodwill and benefit of the doubt that once made these moments bearable.

After every recriminating call or letter from the school, Rosario and Álvaro unleashed a torrent of frustration that produced no ostensible reaction from Henry. They were genuinely worried about his future, but Rosario was also mortified at the attention, at the thought of a roomful of nuns and priests thinking poorly of her son and her family.

"I think it's time for public school!" Álvaro shouted to no one in particular but loud enough for everyone to be imperiled. He, Rosario, and Henry were in the living room, in a triangulated tribunal formation, the threat of taxpayer-funded education now an errant bullet ricocheting, as if in a steel-plated room.

"Maybe you want to go live with your grandparents in El Salvador?" Rosario shouted. This line of rhetorical inquiry, often reserved for the most dismal of report cards, was even less likely to end in action.

Henry remained stone-faced, like a spy trained never to give his captors a moment of satisfaction, focusing instead on small imperfections on the wall ahead.

"How do you expect to find a job without a degree?"

Henry raised and dropped both shoulders in one fluid motion.

"Do you want to live paycheck to paycheck? Do you want to serve people, or do you want them to serve you?"

"I don't care."

"You don't care? ¡Mierda!" Álvaro whacked the side of his own short leg, as if to call a mischievous dog. "You better care because you won't live here forever."

"I don't care."

"You don't care? You'll live on the street, then?"

"I'll join the army."

"The army?" cried Rosario. "Do you know what happens to people who join the army?"

Henry shifted his gaze toward the living room's lifeless orange carpet and away from the chipped paint where Andrés had once thrown a Thundercats doll at him and missed. Henry was rightfully wary of eye contact with the woman who'd compelled him, countless times, to watch *The Deer Hunter*, *Platoon*, and *Jacob's Ladder*, in the hopes of simulating a fear that she'd developed in her youth by simply living through proxy battles of the Cold War.

"If they come back," Rosario shouted, "they come back without legs and arms! They come back crazy. And this country won't do a damn thing to help you. Do you hear me? Nothing! You'll end up on the street begging. Is that what you want?"

Henry uttered another fearless "I don't care."

Conversations like these typically climaxed with the sound of frustration, failure, and anger: a calloused hand's whack on intransigent youth. On those occasions, Henry, who was an otherwise stoic teenager, would surrender a few tears. One time, he mumbled "I hate you" under his breath, and Álvaro responded by taking off his belt and chasing him up the stairs. Andrés remained, in all of those instances, within earshot but out of sight, angry that Henry couldn't make even the simplest of efforts to comply or to merely keep quiet.

After each of these blowups, Andrés would offer to help Henry with his homework or to prepare for a test. It helped, for a few days, but Henry inevitably gave up. "I just don't like it. I don't want to be there. I don't want to be around all those fake people. I want this part to be over."

5

OPEN BAR

The music stops, momentarily revealing the overlapping conversations, all of them drawn in tightly and indistinguishable from one another, as if cinched by one large belt. Reverb jolts the gathered crowd; disgruntled yelps follow before a brief silence serves as a prelude.

"Hello—this on? Yeah? Oh—Class of 1997, I hope you're enjoying the night! We have a couple of hours left here at Joe's." Nicole strains to make her meager voice heard as the collective murmuring resumes. "But remember! We have tables reserved at McClain's for those of you partiers who want to continue the reunion after this! Class of 1997, we have another classmate here. A regular. He's one of only thirty-two gold-star alumni who've been to every single reunion since graduation. Welcome Jeremy Pugliese! Go Tigers!"

Jeremy.

No sooner does she say his name than I feel the blood recede from my face and hands. The ligaments in my jaw steel, and a ghost-like essence passes over my knees, leaving them wobbly. I turn away from the entrance.

Jeremy.

I don't know why he's here. He doesn't live here anymore. A few years back, curiosity got the better of me, and I searched for him online. I found a record of him living north, at least four hours away. I also learned that he'd been arrested for drug possession a decade earlier. The charges were unspecific, but since white people don't get arrested for minor drugs, I assume it was heroin.

Jeremy. Incredible.

It crosses my mind to hide in the bathroom. Just long enough for him to work his way into the room so that I can then sneak out the front door.

What would Marco do? I often ask myself this when I get anxious. Certainly, he'd tell me to relax. *Chill, babe,* he'd say. In fact, he's always telling me to relax. I attribute his placid demeanor to his bedside manner; he's a doctor—a general surgeon who removes the obsolete parts: appendixes, tonsils, gallbladders. And also to his upbringing; he was raised in a large, proud Dominican family within a larger, proud Dominican community.

Marco thinks I'm damaged from having grown up in the only non-white family in a white neighborhood. "You didn't have enough role models or affirmation," he's said blithely, many times. I hate it when he spits public health research findings back at me; I'm the public health researcher in the family. I know he's right, but I somehow can't assimilate into my own experience what I know to be a universal truth.

I rest an elbow on the bar.

"Another gin martini?" asks the aspiring doctor.

"No. A beer. A pilsner, if you have it."

In these sorts of situations, the transition from social cocktail to binge drinking can be seamless. I already sense tomorrow's headache. There was talk, too, of an after-party at someone's house: counter programming to McClain's, with plenty of opportunities for regrets and humiliation to haunt me for years to come. I should slow down.

Doogie Howser hands me a Stella.

"Andy?" It's the silty voice of a much older person, of aged or damaged vocal cords, but it's unmistakably him. "Andy, it's me, Jeremy."

The sweat of my palms mixes with the beer bottle's condensation; I grip the glass firmly. I feel as if I were catching a basketball with my chest. I can't pretend not to hear him; he's standing too close, almost on me. A faster, remixed version of Keith Sweat's "Twisted" fills the room. I'm tempted to walk away, out of Joe's, across the Formula One racetrack, and back to my parents, but I know he'll follow me. Jeremy twenty years ago certainly would have. I can't vouch for this version, but surely, he remembers where my parents live.

Jeremy steps between the bar and me. He's unmistakably an adult. There are shadows tucked between the lines on his face, and the gray strands of his hair are almost in equal proportion to the dirty blonds, all of it dark and shiny with gel. This Francis Bacon portrait of a skid row survivor will replace the ephebe-like Flandrin sketches that have lived in my mind all these years. Coming here has robbed me of something.

"Hey, man," I say unnaturally, "What's up?"

Jeremy pauses to stare through me. The skin around his eyes is sunken and haloed with a faint purple. His lips pull apart, but a small eternity passes before the words sluice out. "It's good to see you. Wasn't sure if you'd ever come to one of these things."

His voice is choppy, nervous. We're like two adjacent earthquakes out of sync, the combined effect of which is a corrective turbulence that cancels out our anxieties.

"I don't think the reunions have ever been so conveniently located," I say.

"True. They're usually south, near St. Iggy's. One year it was out east. By the water. At a fancy place."

"It was a last-minute decision. My dad's sick, and I—"

"I'm sorry, man." Jeremy's face widens. It's a familiar, chivalrous warmth.

I shrug and bite softly at the inside of my lips, as if to communicate, *That's life* or *Thank you.*

"My mom's laid up. Back surgery. Plus arthritis," he says. "I guess it's that time."

"Sorry to hear that," I respond, but what I'd like to say is that according to the health data, it's too early for our parents to be so sick. Mine are only in their sixties, and it's the twenty-first century. Three of my four grandparents, across two countries, lived into their nineties, one past one hundred. All of them died healthy, but my brother couldn't make it to forty. Each generation in this country exhibits poorer health outcomes than the previous generation—the fallout from decades of growing economic inequality. In fact, life expectancy in Ireland is higher than it is here for Irish Americans. Same goes for Italian Americans.

"Yeah, I guess they're getting older," I say.

Jeremy slides both hands into his dark jeans, and just like that, he's eighteen again. Despite the wrinkles around his eyes, lips, and forehead, he's a teenager, a malnourished one. Or a man in recovery. Whatever the case, he's no longer the most beautiful boy I'd ever known.

We nod at one another. Or maybe we're nodding at the circumstances. We remain quiet.

As I study his face, I feel something akin to disappointment. What he's done to himself in the last twenty years is a stain on his family tree. His parents exuded an easy, self-possessed pulchritude that drew stares. His mother was wide-faced and blue-eyed with strawberry blond hair. His father was burly and perennially Mediterranean-skinned, like a bygone movie star or a European who vacations often. Jeremy has fallen into disrepair by comparison. He's a cautionary tale, a lottery winner who files for bankruptcy.

Jeremy presses his hand onto my back, nudging me away from the bar. We're standing in the way of drink traffic.

"You look good," he says. "Like you're in good shape. Not as scrawny as you used to be."

"Shut up."

Jeremy laughs. "Kidding."

"You look like you did in high school," I say, somewhat illogically.

"No, I don't. I can't."

"I mean, I'd recognize you anywhere."

Jeremy's eyes are dim, no longer an egress for electricity, but they manage still to glimmer. The Italian kid with blond hair and blue eyes was a rare bird back then. Most of the other Italians were dark haired and dark eyed and could, in other contexts, be mistaken for Latinx. But Jeremy was white, golden really. I've wondered if north-south dichotomies that affect the world over also existed in Italy. The country, after all, was a collection of city-states with distinct cultures and histories, which didn't coalesce into the American idea of Italy until after World War I. And yet, the Italians in this town cling uniformly and with the zealotry of the Taliban to chicken parm and Columbus Day.

"I'd recognize you too. Those huge ears," he says.

"Fuck you."

"I'm just playing. Can I buy you a drink?"

"It's an open bar."

"Damn." Jeremy reels his hand in from his back pocket before snapping his fingers. He knew it was an open bar. He breaks into a grin for the first time in twenty years.

"A glass of water," I say. "I've had plenty to drink. Actually, I was getting ready to leave when you got here."

"What were you going to do with that?" Jeremy points to the half-full beer in my hand.

"Yeah, well, I meant after this one."

"Can we sit while you finish it?"

"I don't know."

Jeremy's jaw tightens, squaring his face. Not anger, but confusion.

"There are a ton of people I haven't talked to yet. And it is getting late," I explain, hoping to atone for any perceived hostility.

"Andy, I haven't seen you in twenty years."

"Wow. Has it been that long?"

Both of us are aware of how hollow and petty I sound.

Jeremy casts his arm out into a gentle sweep—the short-sleeve button-down burnishes his strapping forearms. He signals toward a bench. "Sit with me for a minute."

I hesitate, and he adds, "C'mon, man."

I'm a stew of emotions; pity is the broth. He's not worth getting upset over, I tell myself. He's not the same person. His sinewy, spiritless frame stands in stark contrast to the body-obsessed adolescent who never missed an opportunity to do shirtless push-ups, who taught me, with whimsy and pride, how to tune up my ten-speed, who walked around my room in a hand-stand while I attempted to do my homework, who forced me to dance with him in his basement. This wretched man could never have been that boy.

The bench is small and recently painted. The strobe lighting above shimmers on the imperfect, streaky black. I set my beer on the floor between my shoes and rest my head on the wall behind us. I'm drunk, legally and viscerally, but still clear minded. And yet, we can't sustain a conversation because of the ghosts who fleet over, around, and between us: "Andy, is that you? Holy shit! How long has it been?" They greet Jeremy, too, but with less élan. A few of them take jabs at my absence: "Well, look who decided to bless us with his presence." "Too good for us, eh?" All of the encounters end with smiles and laughter and clinking glass. The goodwill in the room is palpable and fills all of the empty spaces.

During a lull, I ask Jeremy what he's been up to.

"Construction from May to October. UPS year-round. Nothing fancy," he explains.

Fancy. I've heard this word several times already tonight and throughout most of my youth. It's a catchall. A compliment and a cutdown. A multipurpose assignation that captures well the tension between aspiration and mistrust, between optimism and pessimism. It permeates everything around here, and possibly everywhere in this country.

"Union jobs?"

"No fucking way. If you have a record, the union won't take you," Jeremy says without explanation, without shame. "But I can do tiles pretty good. I got a reputation. A few contractors keep me in mind when jobs come up." There's a touch of hubris in his manner, a harmless brass. His shoulders swell. "But UPS is a total sham. They make us wear the uniforms, but we're all third-party. They won't hire any more people direct. Crap pay, crap benefits."

I think of my UPS guy, a cute Croatian with a broad chest and scrawny legs. I'd assumed all these years that he had a good job, but maybe he's only dressing the part. Union drag.

"No joke. My back is all fucked up, and my deductible is off the charts. That Obama mess."

"Well, health insurance has to cost something. No one wants their taxes raised, but then they want everything state of the art and subsidized." My voice is raised. I realize I feel more affinity for Obama's woefully inadequate health plan than for any of the people in this room.

"Whoa," he says, "I'm not bashing the guy. I voted for him. I just think he coulda gone farther. That's all I'm saying."

"I wasn't defending Obama. I was—"

"What about you?" Jeremy skillfully pivots away from the incendiary. "I bet you got a good job."

"I teach."

"What grade? High school?"

"Graduate school. Public health."

"Like med school?"

"Not really. Medicine treats individuals, and public health is about populations."

Jeremy squints with purpose, but there's vacuousness too. He nods slowly, like an old computer booting up.

"Fuck, man. A professor. I knew it."

His legs are spread wide; his forearms rest on his knees, hands together, fingers interlaced. He looks at me with a mixture of confusion and happiness. It's pride, I think, but not for anything I might have accomplished, instead for him having been right about something.

"I bet that pays pretty good, huh?"

"Not as much as you'd think."

"Enough to get by in the city."

"I have a second job too."

"Really? A professor?"

Truth is, the university pays enough, but only because I'm full-time and tenured.

"As a side gig, I help grassroots groups make connections between their work and public health outcomes. Most of it is pro bono, but some of the bigger orgs pay well."

Jeremy continues squinting and nodding. I stop rambling and let the quiet take over. I look around. I had forgotten where I was, for a moment. "I can't believe it," I say to myself.

"Believe what?"

"What? Nothing."

Jeremy looks at his hands: long, weathered fingers and bulging knuckles. He's somehow damaged and sexy. I'm watching some sort of working-class porn. Wait. All porn is working class. On his left hand is a thin silver ring.

"Married?" Again, I speak without meaning to. It's the martinis.

He curls his fingers up into a soft fist, and the ring disappears. "Yeah, few years now. We've been together like ten, but we got married after our second was born."

"She here?"

"Here?" Jeremy's face rises. "No. No way. The only people who bring some-body to our reunions are trying to show off. People who used to be real busted and lost weight or who ended up with someone out of their league or famous."

"Famous?"

"Remember Janet McCardle?"

"Maybe."

"Pale, freckles, lots of makeup, brown hair."

He's just described 70 percent of the girls in our class. "Oh, right, right," I say.

"She married that weatherman from Channel Four. The blond one."

I don't know who this is.

"You know him, he's been doing the news forever. Anyway, she brought him to a reunion. A while back. Then I heard they got divorced, and she didn't come back after that. I bet you a million bucks she's not here tonight." Jeremy turns both of his palms outward in an exaggerated white-Jesus pose. "You can only really have fun at these things if you come alone," he continues. "Sucks to spend half the time introducing and explaining."

This matter-of-fact wisdom was quintessential Jeremy—a Yoda in Cavar-iccis, with gelled hair. He couldn't get through a book, but he could always read a room well. I was insecure and preoccupied with what everyone else thought of me, but he was casually observant, a young Tarzan swinging from vine to vine, surveying the jungle. And yet, he was the kind of kid who could blow his top, ostensibly from out of nowhere. I lost track of the number of times he kicked a desk or flung it across the room on his way to detention. This anger, just beneath the skin, was familiar to me. It was typical of my family. But Jeremy's anger didn't come from economic stress. He'd endured another type of violence. Without realizing or understanding what he'd survived, I was drawn to his tempestuousness and fragility—just as I would be with most of the boyfriends who followed.

Right now, however, Jeremy seems incapable of anger. He's mangy, middle aged, and mired in defeat.

"Return of the Mack" plays—without irony, as far as I can tell.

Jeremy won't stop peering up at me. If it was 1997, and we were in his parents' basement, I'd run my hand through his hair and pull his face close to mine. I resist an impulse to do so now, despite the absence of adolescent inhibitions. I don't think anyone here would react aggressively to a public display of affection between two men. Tonight, most everyone who's asked me about my wife or girlfriend apologized when I responded "husband," before effusively listing all of the gay people in their lives—siblings, best friends, coworkers, neighbors. A few people changed the subject but weren't excessively rude about it. In fact, everyone seemed more unmoored by my requests to be called Andrés instead of Andy.

All night it's been like this: traveling back and forth—a future inside of a past, or flashes of the past in this future. But Jeremy and I aren't going to kiss because this is also the present, and only a few days ago, I resisted my husband's kiss in the airport because of my purported aversion to PDAs. Making out with Jeremy wouldn't only be a shitty thing to do, it'd be hypocritical.

"What are you thinking?" he asks.

"Not much."

Jeremy raises an index finger toward my face. "Doesn't look like 'not much.'"

"You're a psychic? I thought you were in the tile business."

"You know, we don't have to stay here. We could go somewhere not so noisy."

"Is that your pickup line?"

For a moment, I wonder if I've crossed a threshold, but Jeremy laughs.

"Class of '97, if I could have your attention for a moment." Nicole's amplified voice appears for at least the tenth time; it neutralizes the gentle tension between Jeremy and me and usurps our attention. "We have another latecomer. Please welcome Paul Kowalczyk! Also, if you're the owner of a black Escalade with license plate *D-O-N-T-M-E-S-S*, you left the headlights on."

Paul.

There was a period in middle school when Paul went by Pauly (pronounced: Pawh-lee). It didn't stick, but in retrospect, the *Goodfellas*-style sobriquet was foreboding. All these years, Paul has been like an urban legend to me. I knew he was real, but he was also an extreme character, a personification of evil who couldn't possibly live up to the sinister aura in which I've enveloped him.

After college, after I'd watched the Harvey Milk documentary, after Matthew Shepard, after the Internet became the internet, I thought of tracking Paul down, of siccing the police on him for what he'd done back then, but I couldn't prove that he'd actually murdered anyone. In truth, I don't know that he did.

"He's a minister now," says Jeremy.

"What?"

"Paul. He's a minister. Or some other shit that isn't a priest. Alls I know is he's not Catholic. He runs that church where Carvels was. You okay?"

"What?"

"You look woozy."

"I'm fine—Carvels?"

"You joking? The ice-cream spot, right next to Chung's. The strip mall a few blocks from here," Jeremy says, pointing south. "Near where your parents used to be."

"They're still there," I respond without thinking.

It feels suddenly as if I've dropped unnecessary crumbs. If Jeremy truly didn't know that my parents live in the same place, I've missed an opportunity to remain unfindable. "So, it's a church?" I say.

"Yeah. Looks like a normal storefront, big window, but you can't see inside because it's all curtains. Carvels, man!"

Of course I remember Carvel, the place where my parents would take us for banana splits lacquered in a marshmallow sauce, the place where we bought ice-cream cakes for our birthdays. I just lost my bearings for a moment, and it's easier to let the current take me than to paddle backward.

"How do you know all of this?" I ask.

"Not sure. People talk, I guess."

"You keep in touch with everyone here?"

"Not really. At these things mostly. Sometimes I go back to a basketball game. People go back for that kinda stuff. Homecoming a few years ago. I take my kids to spring carnival. You know how it is: word gets around. Hey, can you wait here a minute?" Jeremy asks.

"Yeah, why?"

"I just want to make sure you won't leave while I go take a piss," he says. I nod.

As he walks away, one of his eyebrows goes up. I don't know what it signifies. Or if he's just being dorky. Something about the way he said "piss" was sexy. It tempts me to follow him, but I tuck myself into a corner instead. I look over at Paul, who is shaking hands with the ceremony of a politician. Stiff-armed, firm grip. He looks like a wide-smile emoji. He's wearing a boxy, cream-colored suit barely a shade darker than his own skin. His face is bloated, his torso inflated, and his head shaved. A skinhead and a Dick Tracy villain all at once.

I met Paul in sixth grade, when we were both twerpy kids who shared a penchant for making everyone laugh. In high school, he grouped off with the other cut-ups who filtered in from the surrounding elementary schools. Paul's humor, which had previously consisted of Beavis and Butthead references and manufactured fart sounds, became, in high school, elaborate pranks that angered teachers and destabilized classes. One of his more amusing tricks involved him asking the teacher a question but miming every third or fourth word, while another classmate, an accomplice at the other end of the room, filled in the missing sounds, creating an uneasy stereo effect that unnerved teachers and left the rest of us suppressing laughter. But Paul always took it too far, as if he were enjoying the discomfort more than the entertainment. At some point in high school, he started bulking up. Everything but his head got big, which made it look like he was wearing one of those padded muscle suits. He transformed, one day to the next, from a jovial kid with a sweet, inviting face into a scowling, intimidating asshole. When he wasn't being sent to detention for disrupting class, he was being suspended for fighting. Rumor was that he was on steroids. One time, he kicked the shit out of Tim Ramos in gym class because of a Polish elbow-slapper joke. (Poor Tim Ramos, the unheard-of mix of Afro-Puerto Rican and Irish, with light brown skin, tight, reddish curls, and a face colonized by acne, never bold enough to pick on someone all by himself, just to pile on after the fact, he went home with a knotted face that day.)

It wasn't until senior year that I realized how truly terrible Paul was. That was when he recounted, to a group of us sitting around a cafeteria table, a story that haunts me still. He and a friend, a guy from the neighborhood, who didn't go to school with us, had driven to Steer Queer, the long-term parking lot by the interstate, which became a de facto cruising ground after dusk. Paul explained that a couple of nights earlier he and this friend had pretended to be gay and lured a guy to an empty parking lot not far from Steer Queer. Once they got there, they got out of their cars. "And as soon as that faggot got on his knees, we beat the shit out of him. When we were done, he looked like a fucking used tampon."

Paul told that story as if he were delivering a joke or recounting the plot of a movie. At first, I smiled, assuming there was a punchline or an unexpected twist imminent, but as he progressed, so did my horror and disbelief. I can't for the life of me recall who was sitting around that cafeteria table, but I remember our collective silence amid the chaos. I think it was the shock. *Sure, gay is gross, but why the fuck would you do all that?* Paul was either unaware of or unperturbed by our lack of reaction, periodically punctuating his account with "sick faggot" and "motherfucking faggot."

Neither will I forget the epilogue of that story, a detail so vivid and chilling, and, I believed, telling. After Paul and his friend left that man groaning and bloodied on the pavement, they drove off, but when they were halfway home, they had to pull over. "I felt so sick about touching that queer, I had to puke my guts out," Paul said, with flared nostrils and spit bubbling in the corners of his mouth. Then he folded over and pretended to throw up on the shiny, speckled floor of the cafeteria. When he lifted his head again, his face was reddened, and his eyes were ablaze.

I was genuinely frightened. I recognized in Paul a tortured sanguinity, a kaleidoscope of the emotions inside of me: the push and pull of desire, belief, and self-hatred. I wanted to get up and leave the cafeteria, but I worried that anything short of approval might register as discomfort, which would signal to Paul and the others that the man on the pavement and I shared something. But I wouldn't have been running away in solidarity; I was, in that moment, afraid of the world. Paul displayed the sort of unhinged hatred that I'd seen occasionally in movies or on the evening news, but never up close. A small shiver runs through me even now, as I realize that our world has contorted itself to confirm onto Paul even an iota of power. His little church is nothing, but I wish it didn't exist. I wish it weren't mere blocks from my family.

You want another glass of water?" asks Jeremy when he returns from the bathroom.

"No, I'll have whatever you're having."

"I'm getting a water."

"Sounds good."

Jeremy strides with broken elegance to the edge of the bar.

"Been sober for a few years now. I don't touch anything," he says as he hands me one red cup and sets the other on the floor beside him. "Except this." Jeremy pulls a pen from his pocket. "Want a hit?"

I do.

He leads me to the back of the restaurant, then through an emergency exit that's propped open. We're surrounded by dumpsters, an old stove, and cases of beer. The scent of warm garbage suffuses the night air.

"It doesn't smell," he explains of the pot. "I could smoke this inside."

"How does this count as sober?"

"It's medicine."

"Uh-huh."

"It's medical grade, man. It helps with my back pain and with my cravings."

I'm all for decriminalization, but I laugh anyway.

"For real," he says, as if convincing me matters. "It's not like the shit we used to smoke. There's no paranoia, no munchies, no fog. Half the time, I don't even remember I smoked. It's super mild. But it works. I got the oils at home too." He extends his arm to pass me the vape pen; a cloud of smoke leaves his mouth and thins out quickly between and above us. It leaves behind an intimacy. I pull from the flattened end of the thin cylinder, and a familiar combination of cigarettes and cologne appears in my nose and mouth.

"Marlboro Reds and . . ." I cough. "Cool Water?"

"Camels and Drakkar. A birthday gift from my wife," he says.

"Last week."

"Huh?"

"Nothing, I—"

"Good memory." Jeremy's face is now a permanent smile. Whether he's high or happy, I don't know.

"I should get back inside," I say. "It's getting late, and I want to make another round before I leave."

"Leave? It's not even nine-thirty."

"I've had enough to drink, trust me."

"Why are you drinking so much?"

"I'm not *drinking so much*. It's a party. And an open bar. I think I drank a reasonable amount considering the circumstances."

"I was just kidding. No big deal."

Just then, the door opens and someone steps outside. She has a drink and an unlit cigarette in her hands; she has a phone tucked between her ear and her shoulder. Her hair is swept up in a braided bun. Before I can conjure up a name or a memory, she says, "Andrés! I heard you were here!"

It's Rhonda Nelson. We used to sit on the bus together. She got good grades, and she played the French horn. Her father was super strict and Jamaican, and although his thick accent differed from my father's, I drew comfort from the fact that my father had this in common with someone else. Rhonda wasn't allowed to go to parties or sleepovers. She was one of the five Black students in my class in elementary school, and one of the twenty or so in our high school class. She's one of three Black people here tonight. In high school, to everyone's surprise, she dated a white boy from public school. He wore gold chains and track suits. Because Rhonda wasn't allowed to drive, she and I only ever caught up when I couldn't find a ride to school and was forced to take the bus. I remember one time, she had her face pressed up against the window, trying to hide her sobbing. It was poignant because Rhonda was as composed a person as I'd ever known, a somewhat anomalous presence during that hormone-heavy era of our lives. The tears were for her boyfriend, who was going to jail. She didn't elaborate, except to say that he'd be gone for a year.

"Let me take this call, and I'll look for you inside," Rhonda says, the phone pressed against her chest. Then she walks away from us.

"I'm sorry if I was rude," I say to Jeremy. "It's just, I wasn't expecting to be here. And I haven't had a drink in a few days. My parents don't keep any alcohol at home anymore because of my dad's new diet. If it weren't for some super flaky bud I found tucked inside an old textbook in the attic—"

"You need weed?"

"No, I—"

"I can set you up while you're here."

"It's alright, I—"

"I mean it. Give me your number."

I don't say anything, and I don't reach for my phone. I hope Rhonda will end her call soon and interrupt us, but she's pacing around the trash bags and crates of empty beer bottles, telling someone, likely a child, not to give grandma a hard time.

"I could just swing by your parents' after work tomorrow," Jeremy says.

"No no. It's okay. Let's talk first." I give him my number.

"I'm calling you now," he says, "so you can save it."

I smile. Then I pull at the door. He holds it open until I'm inside. "Andy"— the din eats away at his voice, and he overcompensates by yelling—"I'm glad you finally showed up to one of these!" His hand appears on my shoulder and squeezes me gently. It's a harmless gesture made by several others tonight, but his touch is unique in its weight and dexterity.

"Honestly, I'm surprised you're here. I'd never have pegged you for a reunion junkie." As soon as I utter that last word, I regret it.

Jeremy doesn't appear to mind; he's too busy taking unabashed liberties with his stare. He puts his hand out. It's rough and warm; the sensation, familiar and erotic. It lasts only a few seconds, but they're long seconds, minutes in another context. I let go and walk into the party.

I grab a beer from the bar and make my way through the crowd of sleeveless dresses and stiff-collared shirts. I greet everyone with the same enthusiasm and stories, like a well-fed parakeet. Midway through each of the brief conversations, I recall all of the pertinent details—street and sibling names, trips, teachers, parties, pets. I don't interrupt; I listen attentively and give everyone a recap of the last twenty years—college, work, grad school, work, marriage, travel. Through it all, I keep an eye out for Simone. Rhonda, who was one of Simone's closest friends, doesn't know why she isn't here tonight. "Call her mom," she says. "Phyllis will know. Do you have her number?" I tell her I do and that I will, knowing full well that I won't. Rhonda lives in Texas. She's a patent lawyer. She has a six-year-old daughter, and a husband in the navy. She's in town for the week to leave her kid with her parents for the month. Something she does every summer. The boy from high school— Dennis—cycled in and out of jail for years. Not long ago, he sent her several messages through Facebook, but Rhonda ignored them. She likes the heat of Texas, even if her town is incredibly conservative. "This place," she says, referring to our current location, "feels like liberal fantasyland compared to where I live."

As I travel through the room, I make an effort to keep a distance from Paul, whose lips are moving, but whose voice I haven't yet heard. Occasionally, I sneak a look at Jeremy; his eyes are, each time, trained on me. He smiles whenever he catches me staring, which I find subtly infuriating at first, but then funny. Right now, he's talking to Sal, Alex, and Greg, the trifecta of cool boys. Salvatore, a stout, soft-spoken first-string defensive tackle with a thin goatee, was my freshman-year crush. One night sophomore year we got high, and he said he wanted to have a staring contest, during which he inched close enough for our lips to touch. I flinched, and he punched me in the arm. Then he laughed and called me a fag. The pain in my arm did nothing to lull my erection, which I could only conceal through an exaggerated pantomime that involved me lying face down on his bedroom floor. Earlier tonight, Sal and I chatted briefly. He's a manager at the nearby Costco. He's dating one of his coworkers, but he doesn't want to marry her: "She has two kids already. They're great kids, but I'm not sure about an insta-family." Sal is boxy and sturdy, like the cars in the lot, but he's mushier than he used to be, best evinced by his mildly droopy jowls and the tautness of his shirt across his shoulders, biceps, and midriff. He voted for McCain in 2008, Obama in 2012, and Trump in 2016—"Women don't know how to drive. How was she going to run a country?"

Alex was one of those guys who smoked immense amounts of pot but never seemed to get high. He was short, tough, and lean, and one of the handful of Puerto Rican kids in our class—the dominant Latinx group. I don't recall ever going over to his house or meeting his parents. I think his dad was a security guard. Alex lived on the cushier rim of an otherwise gritty town that shared a sliver of border with my town, this town. I was lucky to have befriended him early on—a freshman-year global studies project about the practice of foot-binding in tenth-century China. One time, he shoved an older kid against the lockers because he'd called me a fag. Another time, he threatened to beat up someone who'd joked about lacing my joint with PCP. Alex was, in these ways, more of a guardian than a friend. He and a few of the other guys took me under their wings, like Mafia dons, and as a result, I sensed that a certain degree of reverence was expected. They were friends with whom I would never be too direct or familiar, or at ease. After high school, Alex tried to join the marines, but he was rejected because of a heart condition. Then he tried to be a cop, but according to the instructor, he rated too high on an empathy scale. Alex drives a bus for the county now. "Twice, I've been Driver of the Year," he told me earlier. "Came with a bump in salary and a month of movie passes for the family." He's content with the job's benefits, especially the pension. Alex married Charisse, the stoner cheerleader who didn't go to school for a week when Kurt Cobain died. I recall a two-blunt cypher where I took too many hits; after a few minutes, I was a shell of myself, propped up only by my paranoia. Everyone else eyed each other and suppressed laughter. I had gotten too high to care that I was being ridiculed, but Charisse told them all to grow up, walked me to the kitchen, and made me drink a glass of water while she rubbed my back and reassured me that I'd be back to normal in twenty minutes. Charisse didn't come tonight because they couldn't get a babysitter. Alex doesn't vote because "I always forget until after I get home from work and I don't wanna have to go back out. Who cares, they're all the same, you know?"

Then there's Greg, the kid who had the pencil-thin mustache and a Tupac obsession. He wasn't the only white kid in high school who rode around in a tricked-out Celica that could be heard vibrating blocks away, but I didn't know anyone else who got as high as Greg and meditated as deeply on Tupac's lyrics. He was the sort of boy who would become so entranced with "Hail Mary," for example, that the rest of us could leave his room or house and he wouldn't take notice. Greg's high school evolution took everyone by surprise. Freshman year, he was, like many of us, scrawny and high-pitched, but he was popular from the outset because of his basketball skills, which were disproportionate to his stature. Greg grew stronger and more attractive each year, and by junior year, everyone had a crush on him or wanted to be his best friend. All of that changed when his father died—throat cancer. He wasn't the same afterward. Pot became coke; then, heroin. He cheated on Dina with Erica; then he cheated on Erica with Ashley. I recall everyone worrying that he'd show up to their graduation parties high and end up crying in their backyards into the morning. Today he looks alright; he's thin-faced and potbellied. He's a real estate agent, into his third marriage, one kid from each. In fact, it's Greg who's offered up one of his houses for the alternative afterparty—poor Nicole. According to several people, it's an enormous place, with a pool and a hot tub inside the pool.

Greg's McMansion isn't far away, but it's far enough that I'd need a ride, and I don't want to risk getting into a car with anyone here. No one is sober—here or within a five-mile radius—including all of the taxi drivers with their styrofoam cups. That's the way of this and every nearby town. We may not have invented drunk driving, but surely, we've perfected it. If I had to guess, I'd say that at least a third of the room has spent the night in jail. Myself included.

"Leaving so early?" Nicole says, as I make my way through the velvet curtains. Her recently repainted lips are glossy red and catch the light from above.

"I'm tired, and more than a little buzzed."

"Did you see the espresso station in the back?"

"I have to get up early, but thanks for tonight. I'm sure this was a big project to organize."

Nicole runs a long red nail across an eyebrow before a slow smile walks across her face. "My pleasure."

I continue out quickly, until I remember Simone and double back.

"She came to a reunion once—one of the first ones," Nicole says. "But she hasn't responded to anything since. Did you ask Rhonda? They were close."

"Rhonda says she hasn't heard from her in some time."

Nicole shrugs.

"Goodnight. Thanks, again," I say, while stepping through the final velvet curtain.

There's a part of me that wants to remain here, in this moment, with all of these people. The past was rekindled so effortlessly. This opportunity won't come around again soon. I'll never be this age again. My parents might no longer live here during the next reunion, and I won't return to this town for anyone but them. I should go back inside and finish the night, go to a hot-tub party where no one has bathing suits, get fall-down drunk, embarrass myself, kiss Jeremy for the first time in twenty years. The problem is, I've been propping up this wall between them and me for so long that I'm afraid of what will happen if I put my arms up and step out from behind it. Does it fall squarely on me? On them?

I look over at the matrix of steel, glass, and rubber. The lot is now full. It surprises me that the cars are all parked so neatly. It's an unmarked gravel field, and yet everyone has parked equidistant from one another, with sufficient clearance for car doors to swing open. Maybe we aren't a devolved species. I scan the bumpers and back windows. I count six Blue Lives Matter stickers and twice as many Trump decals. How many tires could I slash before someone else comes out of the restaurant? My eyes briefly scour the ground for something sharp before I abandon my plan.

As I approach the main road, a tepid gust runs through my hair and through the spaces between the buttons on my shirt, inflating it subtly. It makes everything good. Better. Bearable. It also radicalizes the nostalgia. I close my eyes and take it in, pretending the particulate matter from the racetrack is missing my nostrils.

"Andy!"

Reverie neutralized.

Nicole wobbles over the loose ground in her life-threatening stilettos. "Andy, I probably shouldn't be telling you this, but I remember you two were close. I heard a couple of people tonight say that she's not well."

"Who?"

"Simone."

"Oh. Is it bad?"

"She's in the hospital."

"Shit. Which one?"

"Not the regular kind," Nicole whispers, as if we're being recorded. "She's in the loony bin."

Loony bin? Christ. This person's a schoolteacher?

"Do you know which psychiatric hospital?" I ask.

"No, sorry. But Puritan, by the interstate, closed a few years ago, so there's a good chance it's the other one, the one that looks like a haunted castle. It was bought by Be Well—they own everything. Across from the new Cheesecake Factory."

"Thanks. I'll look into it."

I speed up toward the street, but Nicole calls out again. "Andy! Why didn't you park in the lot?"

"I walked," I shout back.

"What?" Nicole's face wrinkles, as if I were setting her up for a joke. I say nothing more, and she continues, "Do you want a ride?"

"It's six blocks. I'm good."

"Really, I don't mind."

"It's okay," I respond, and wave as decisively as I can.

"Don't be a stranger!"

Simone.

The phone call in college, during which I came out to her, was one of the last times we spoke. She called another time to let me know she was thinking of transferring schools. Then once more, to tell me she'd dropped out. After a couple of years of not talking, she called my parents' house one Thanksgiving; I happened to answer the phone. She was either drunk or high and almost unintelligible. She needed to tell me something. "We need to talk to you," she kept saying, without clarifying who we was. I searched for a reason to end the call, as if she were a telemarketer. I told her I'd be in touch about hanging out that weekend. "Promise?" she said. "Yeah," I responded. I was a few months out of college then and thinking only of my future, which I couldn't reconcile with my past. Simone felt like all the other people who I used to know, and I didn't want to know anyone I used to know.

If I were in a psychiatric hospital, Simone would come visit me. When we were sixteen, she would have visited every day. She'd have made mixed tapes and brought Swedish Fish. Heck, Simone would have busted me out of there. She'd have hooked an anchor from her car onto the metal bars of my bedroom window. She'd have revved the engine and peeled out. "Andy, get in the fucking car! Get in the fucking car, now!" And I would have because Simone could be eerily authoritative when she wanted to be and because she is one of the best humans I've ever known.

It's certainly the hodgepodge of martinis, beers, and pot talking, but I feel a strong desire to do the same for her now.

Yes! I'm going to bust her out! But first, I'm going to download the first three Pearl Jam albums; I'll play them as the soundtrack to our escape. When we've gotten far enough away, I'll drive her to a 7-Eleven so she can have one of those terrible canned-cheese nacho platters that we used to love.

After that, the sky's the limit, wherever she wants to go. We'll stage our own queer BIPOC retelling of *Thelma & Louise*.

I feel dizzy and a bit nauseated. And suddenly, I have a desperate urge to pee. I won't make it all the way home. I'll go to the Applebee's.

"Wait for me, Simone!" I shout, as I run across the six lanes, an army of headlights approaching on either side.

6
HIGH SCHOOL

Americanos, Rosario and Álvaro called them. *Them* were white people, and Andrés wanted to be like *them*. He might not have realized it or admitted it if he had, but he wanted his skin and eyes to be lighter, his hair to be straighter, his nose to be narrower. But more than that, he wanted the attention and the value that seemed to correspond to *them*. The beauty, the camaraderie, the self-worth.

The relationship between Andrés and white people was paradoxical, marked in equal measure by reverence and disdain. Americanos weren't only standard-bearers for all things aspirational and dominant, they were also ignorant, uncouth, and informal. They were lazy too. They chewed their hamburgers and pizza with their mouths open. They'd never studied a map of the world. They cursed and had tattoos. They didn't wash their hands. They kept pets. They complained about everything. They lacked self-awareness and humility. Ignorance was a primordial value and flag-waving their Olympic sport. And yet, they were in control. They held the reins and the benefit of the doubt. They were the owners, the hosts, and the guards. They demanded explanations and proof. Americanos were the ones who asked for ID. They were the ones who needed to know where you were from and where you were going.

As far as Andrés and his family were concerned, they were guests. And as guests, it was their duty to navigate the perennial discomfort that accompanied being smarter, savvier, harder working, more interesting, and more curious about the world than their hosts. ¿Qué van a saber estos bobos? was a common refrain in Andrés's home. *What do these fools know?* Looking down on los Americanos undercut their size, their ignorance, and their malice. In this way, humility, charity, and pity weren't only pious attributes, they served as buffers and coping mechanisms.

Andrés was both lost and found in this context. He knew, for example, that he and his family were Colombian and Salvadorian and immigrant and different, primarily their color, which he came to know as tanned, olive-skinned, and, on rare occasions, bronzed: euphemisms for his particularly bloated category of mixed race, a designation that was never parsed—then as now. A curdled bloodline that had culminated in a subtle, white-supremacist-fueled self-loathing, prioritizing the Spanish imperialist ancestors over the Indigenous ones and completely ignoring any trace of the African and African Indigenous mestizajes, pretending instead that an entire continent had been born as if by immaculate conception and not through colonization, holding within its own porous, undefined boundaries internecine struggles that mirrored and perpetuated the racism at their inception. A people and a boy desperate to fit in.

Andrés could hardly imagine the scale of everything. What happened to him, he believed, happened to him alone. He was an embodiment of reflections, of norms, foods, spices, language, music, and dances that he knew only superficially, if at all. He traipsed through a haze of expectations, self-hate, and self-importance, the confluence of which concretized his desire to peel everything away and show *them* that he was no different from *them*. And so was seeded a lifetime of contradiction: *Stay out of the midday sun. Avoid bright colors. Cover up. Lower your voice.* At the same time: *Be yourself. Be proud. Be the best. Be.*

Succeed while hiding in plain sight. Be better in order to be equal.

· · ·

In elementary school, there were a few classmates who were worse off than Andrés. Their houses, smaller and shabby. Their parents, disheveled in attire and teeth. They smelled of depression and neglect. They were white people that even white people made fun of. But they were uncommon. Most of Andrés's classmates lived in bigger homes and owned lawn mowers. Their dads had better jobs than his dad; careers, they called them. Their moms had college degrees but didn't typically work outside of the home; the few who did were nurses, teachers, or cashiers at the local shops.

The landscape and scale of everything expanded in high school. Towns mingled, social spheres overlapped, hierarchies twisted into helixes. For at least a few hours of each day, an affluent kid afflicted with acne was effectively a pauper, and a working-class kid with muscles or a dependable three-pointer was king. There were a few more Black and Latinx students. There were spoiled brats who'd been kicked out of better schools in faraway towns, and poorer kids whose families struggled as much as Andrés's. All of them united under one catechism.

But despite everyone's belief in the Holy Trinity and the resurrection of Christ and Lazarus and that Pontius Pilate washed his hands of it all and that Judas had a pocket full of coins and that wine was truly blood, Andrés began to feel different, different in all the ways a kid can feel different.

Before high school, white kids had made up the majority of his neighborhood and school; now, members of Andrés's original long-lost tribe appeared in the wild. Suddenly, he was one of several brown kids.

Andrés had never before felt the need to affirm anything. He'd spent the nine years of elementary school with the same group of kids; he'd been an altar boy, he'd ridden bikes and played basketball with his friends; he'd become, rather unceremoniously, one of *them*. High school changed everything. There was an inexorable sorting, and there was no hiding now: Andrés wasn't white. There it was, a secret that seemed to be at all times broadcast over the PA system.

Although Andrés couldn't deny who he was, neither could he let go of what he'd briefly been. Who, after all, willingly relinquishes their upper hand? White, in a way, remained right. White was safe. White was clean. White was quiet. White was attractive. White was next door. White was on TV. White was on the cover. White were the teachers. White were the doctors. White was the president—all of them. White was the Lord and Savior. White was on top. White was everything.

Black was different. Black was loud. Black was brash. Black was funny. Black was angry. Black was unsafe. Black was the mugshot on the news and the anti-drug PSA. Black was homeless. Black was Eddie Murphy. Black was Jesse Jackson. Black was Michael Jackson. Black was Janet. Black were the Jeffersons, the Winslows, the Bankses, the Cosbys. Black were Michael Jordan, Mike Tyson, and O. J. Black was terrible or glorious, but nothing in between.

Asian was Oriental. Asian was exclusively East Asian. Asian was karate. Asian were the workers at the Chinese restaurants. Asian was one man: Mr. Miyagi and Arnold. (And Lou Diamond Phillips.) Asians built good cars. Asians were the future. Asians were jokes. Asians were punchlines.

American Indians were a chapter in a history book. American Indians were Native Americans. American Indians were the names of states, cities, towns, roads, and waterways. American Indians were face paint and headdresses. American Indians were scrimshaw and wampum and teepees. American Indians yelped and scalped but never spoke. American Indians were mystical, righteous, and invisible. American Indians were either incredibly fit and mythical or diabetic and drunk, but nothing in between.

Who looked like Andrés? Mom. Dad. Brother. Aunt. Uncle. Cousin. Other cousin. Black-and-white pictures of grandparents. Landscapers. Busboys. Porters. Villains. Speedy Gonzales. Ricky Ricardo, sort of. Anita from *West Side Story*. The casts of *Stand and Deliver* and *La Bamba* (except for Lou Diamond Phillips).

To live in the suburbs required resources and government assistance that only whites had once received freely. Everyone else made their way slowly by working thrice as hard in order to live two-thirds as well. Over time, the town changed. Neighborhoods continued to be racially segregated and majority white, but there were spaces and opportunities for interaction. Primarily in the public schools. But also in the parochial schools, despite the segregationist effect of tuition.

Fleetingly and intermittently, school was a leveler. Even though everyone ran back toward what was familiar and easy at the close of each day, students couldn't be prevented from interacting with one another in class, in the cafeteria, on the bus, on the field. A social evolution that was aided by an era in which it was no longer as common or seemly for parents to forbid their children from interacting with others, in particular those others who didn't look like them.

Those who adhered to their prescribed quadrants might avert unnecessary troubles. But anyone who occupied a middle place, who sought validation as a salve for insecurity, or who needed attention to compensate for isolation, that person walked barefoot along a pebbled beach.

Andrés deduced that if everyone liked him, no one would look down on him or accuse him of selling out, of being a poser—after *fag*, the most dishonorable designation imaginable. Andrés was puny, but smart, funny, and acquainted enough with the powder-keg conditions of home to side-step the hormone-enabled beefs typical of adolescence. He weathered the few moments of bullying by pretending and outfoxing, and by surrounding himself with kids who bolstered his credibility and protected him.

By the second week of high school, and after three different kids had called him "undress," Andrés became Andy. Soon after, he found his speed—full tilt. Andy stood furtively on the perimeters of circles, groups, cliques, waiting, surreptitiously edging his way in, fawning and maneuvering toward a thinned coterie of friendships. Friends became collectible things, useful only for how they inflated Andy's value. He might not be one of *them*, but he'd convince *them* otherwise. Luckily for Andy, the business of subsuming insecurities was addictive. There was no drug more potent than being liked by everyone. The sensation was as life-altering as the pain of being disliked by anyone. To complicate matters, Andy wasn't only trying to hide something that wasn't a secret; there was also the secret buried deep within, which he managed at times, sometimes for long stretches, to forget.

By his third year of high school, Andy felt like minor royalty. His future, too, was taking shape. He scored perfectly on his SATs, and Mr. Shanley, the friendlier of the two beleaguered guidance counselors at St. Ignatius, encouraged him to consider colleges far and wide—*Get out of here while you can* was the unspoken sentiment during their fifteen-minute monthly meetings. "Whaddaya got to lose?" was what he actually said.

· · ·

think you're in my seat," said Andy during second-period English lit, to a boy with dirty blond hair, folded blazer cuffs, and a skewed necktie. He must have been new because it was already the third week of the semester, and Andy didn't recognize him.

"I didn't see your name on it."

"I've been sitting here since the first day."

The boy mimed a search of the desk's metal and wood frame. "Show me where your name is."

"There's a seat over there," Andy said, pointing to the back of the room. When the new kid didn't bother to look up, Andy tapped his shoulder. "Excuse me?"

It was only a small touch, but it lit a short fuse. A fuse that Andy had meant, in a way, to light. He knew, even while knowing he shouldn't, that he was imposing himself, crossing a line.

"What the fuck is wrong with you?" The boy shot out of his seat and, with force, shoved Andy, who, along with the desk behind him, crashed onto the ground.

The humiliation and fear jostling for dominance inside of Andy weren't unique—many times, his parents and his brother had laid their hands on him—but these circumstances were unfamiliar. He got to his feet and instinctively approached the boy, who had taken a wide-armed stance, shoulders raised, chest inflated. He had a faint, almost translucent mustache. His skin was as blond as his hair. Up close, his eyes were the bluest Andy had ever seen. And despite the clenched jaw and flared nostrils, the boy's countenance had an almost delicate quality, something soft yet radiant, all the more incongruous for the vapor it was emitting. In addition to the warm moisture speckling Andy's face, a trail of cologne had found its way inside his nostrils. There was also a vibration in his arms and a fire in his chest. It was too late to back down.

Andy knew nothing about this boy except that he was white. And while Andy might be able to back down from a Black boy or even another brown kid, he couldn't back down from a white kid. Not a new white kid. This was the constructed order of things.

If Andy were to throw the first punch, he thought, it'd have to be done soon and repeatedly because the moment he stopped punching, the other boy would find his footing and overpower him. He'd seen it many times before, but always at a remove. His fights with Henry hadn't prepared him for anything. Theirs were living room brawls that mirrored the wrestling matches on TV, and typically ended with him smothered beneath his brother's weight. This, here, was something else, and it wouldn't end well for Andy unless he hit the new boy first. Even still, it wasn't likely to end well.

Or maybe not. The boy wasn't actually much larger than Andy. He was, however, rabid. A crimson spread across the golden-white face and receded from his knuckles.

Andy doubted his chances.

"Mr. Pugliese!" shouted Ms. Cardinale, the English teacher, as she scurried toward the boys and squeezed herself between them. Her hair was large and blond with dark roots that had crept nearly midway up each strand, styled as if from the era when groups of people stared up at the sun in order to watch astronauts disappear into space.

"This is not a very good first impression," she said to the new boy, before turning to Andy. "What is happening here?"

Silence.

"Well?"

The two boys remained locked in their stances, arms and shoulders tensed, eyes wet.

"Okay, you leave me little choice. Class, meet your new classmate: Jeremy Pugliese. Unfortunately, Mr. Pugliese will be spending the first day in detention."

"You too, Andy," she said, before Andy could flash her a penitent look. "It takes two."

Jeremy grabbed his notebook and made his way toward the door, but not before kicking an empty desk in the front row.

"Two days in detention!" Ms. Cardinale shouted.

"Oh, snap!" someone from the back of the room called out. Paul, Andy thought. Always it was Paul with his running commentary. Paul, the scrawny Polish kid who made everyone laugh and had spent all summer lifting weights and now walked the halls punching one hand into the palm of the other.

Andy grabbed his books from the floor. Simone picked up Andy's pen and handed it to him. Her large dream-catcher earrings were flipped upward and tangled. Simone had walked into the room after Ms. Cardinale had stopped the fight. She might have otherwise stepped between Andy and Jeremy. Apart from loyal, Simone was also impulsive and the tallest one in the room. As Andy walked past, she held out her hand for him to slap. "You okay?" she asked.

Andy nodded.

"I'll swing by at lunch," she whispered. "Chicken fingers today."

7
MOM & DAD

¿Y? How was it?"

My mother keeps her back to me as she swirls a wooden spoon through the yellow, white, and clear pools of slowly solidifying egg. An apron is loosely knotted at her waist, mostly for effect because she is a punctilious cook.

"Did you see all those girls that used to follow you around?"

"Mom. No one followed me around."

"They were in love with you. You could have gone out with any girl you wanted."

"Too bad I couldn't be with all the boys I wanted."

"Oh, Andy!"

"What?"

My mother turns the stove off and moves the pan with scrambled eggs to a cool burner. She turns to face me. "Did you really have dates with boys in school? Did we know them? ¿Quién?"

"Are you kidding me with these questions?"

"You can tell me."

"I didn't have dates, but I had crushes here and there. Can we please change the subject?"

"Why didn't you tell us?"

"Do you really think you would have wanted to hear that back then?"

"We are very supportive. We love you no matter what. And we love Marco."

"Now you do, but who knows how you would have reacted back then."

My mother digs a clean wooden spoon out of a drawer, tips the pan, and pushes the eggs onto a clean plate. "¡Ay! Let's not get stuck in the past. We all had to grow up, and we did. Your family could be worse. Don't worry, they're organic. Todo es orgánico."

"What?"

"In case you're wondering about the eggs. Your mother doesn't give you anything that isn't good for you."

"I know, Mom. Don't worry. I'm happy, and non-organic eggs are also wonderful."

"I understand sarcasm."

"I'm not being sarcastic. I just don't want to talk about this stuff."

"I didn't bring it up."

The eggs are in fact delicious. So is the whole wheat toast with raspberry jam. As well as the coffee. "Perfect breakfast," I say. "Thank you."

"I'm glad you like it," she says as she wipes down the counter.

My mother is mistaken. I couldn't have come out to her in high school. Neither of us was ready. My mother is also mistaken about my high school fan club. Although I had many friends who were girls, none of them were fawning over me. And many of the ones who may have been interested in me wouldn't have been allowed to pursue anything.

I know this because Donna Buccio's parents pulled her out of St. Ignatius when they discovered that she was dating Eric Leconte. Eric's crime was being Black. It was the second time that year that a white girl had been taken out of the school for dating a Black boy. Not long after the Donna-and-Eric affair, a group of us (all white, except for me) were hanging out in Marie's basement—surely drinking from her mom's liquor cabinet—and someone asked how our parents would have reacted to a similar situation. All of the girls, except for Marie, said that their parents would have likely done the same as Nicole's parents. Not only that, one of them said, "I wouldn't even be allowed to date you, Andy." Several of the girls nodded along, matter-of-fact, as if it were obvious and I should have known all along. I'd been in the same class with a few of these girls since first grade. I'd shared first, second, and third kisses with some of them. Their parents adored me, sat next to my family at church, had taken me trick-or-treating, and driven me home from birthday parties. I was the kid that all parents liked and trusted, I thought. I didn't want to date any of those girls to begin with, but I certainly didn't want to be told I couldn't.

I didn't breathe a word about that night to anyone, least of all my mother. She would have refused handshakes and peace-be-with-yous at church. She would have stopped smiling at my friends whenever they came over. It would have hurt her immensely to know that all of those families looked down on her children. And she would be as upset about it today as she would have been back then.

¿Estás bien?" my mother asks, as she leans against the counter.

"A little hungover. That's all."

Like a gentle robot, my mother walks to the cupboard, grabs a glass, fills it with water, and sets it next to my plate. Then she puts her mug of coffee in the microwave. After ten seconds, it beeps three times.

"Thank you for coming here. To take care of us," she says as she perches herself on the edge of the chair, ready for her next move. "Old and useless. That's what your parents have become."

"You're not old or useless. You lead full lives. What's happening now is a perfectly normal way for humans to behave. That's what we do. We take care of each other."

"Tu tía Beti can come this weekend, if you want to go back to the city."

"I'm already here. There's no need for her to travel so far. It's great if she comes, but it's not necessary."

"De pronto . . . you want to spend time with Marco?"

"Por dios, Mom. I've only said it thirty times. Marco is on a business trip."

"¿Seguro?"

"Of what? That he's in Namibia? Yes, I'm pretty sure I took him to the airport!"

"Oh, are we being disrespectful to each other this morning?"

"Fine," I say, and take a bite of the toast.

"Are you sure everything is okay between you two?"

"Yes. Why are you asking me?"

"A mother knows her children."

"Well then my future children will be screwed."

My mother responds by raising her chin and closing her eyes. The morning light that passes through the gossamer kitchen curtains bathes her. She looks genuinely peaceful. After a moment, she sets a hand on the table—a long, dark wood slab, too large for the small kitchen it occupies—and rises. She positions herself at the sink.

"Aren't you going to eat?" I ask, in a conciliatory tone.

"I ate this morning," she says, as if my eating breakfast at 7:15 A.M. makes me an immoral sloth. "Arugula, roasted red peppers, un poco de goat cheese, a few capers, and a squeeze of lemon."

"Wow, Mom. You're a proper chef."

"I would have made you some, but I know you don't like arugula."

"I was like twelve when I said that. I eat arugula all the time now. I like arugula."

"Oh. Then tomorrow you can have that."

When she finishes washing the dishes, she sponges down the sink and clears the trap. She dries her hands on a towel and squeezes into her palm a generous dollop of the moisturizer that lives by the dish rack. She lathers her hands in a slow repeated motion, as if she were shaping dough or conjuring a spell.

"What time is Dad's appointment?"

"Tiene que estar en el gastroenterólogo cuarto para las nueve. You should give yourself plenty of time because rush hour on the expressway is terrible before nine."

"Is it the same doctor from the hospital?"

"Yes, but this is at another hospital. Near the Cheesecake Factory."

"Is that, by any chance, near the psychiatric hospital?"

"Exactly. They're separated by one large parking lot. But it's all the same hospital. They're owned by . . ." She pauses and shakes her head. "El demonio."

The devil is Be Well—the hospital conglomerate that bought the psychiatric hospital. For a decade, Be Well has been buying health care institutions, dissolving the unions, and rehiring many of the same employees at significantly reduced salaries—same American tale, different industry. Be Well purchased the clinic where my mom was working as a bill collector after she'd been let go from the bank. Just before the sale took place, the union offered to find her work at another hospital altogether, but most of those positions were graveyard orderly shifts.

"I cleaned houses cuando vine a este país. Después trabajé en el banco por veintiún años. Do you know what I started as?"

"A recep—"

"¡Una recepcionista! Do you know what my title was when the bank fired me?"

"Vice—"

"Vice President of Communications! Do you think I'm going to clean floors now? No, señor. I don't know why I even bothered to join this union," she lamented at the time.

But it wasn't so clear cut. When the bank laid her off years earlier, it did so without warning. It happened on a Friday, just before lunch. The security guards, with whom she'd always gotten along well, sheepishly searched her bags and walked her to the street. Three months of pay and health insurance were her severance package. After twenty-one years. Six months later, the only job she could find was at the clinic twenty minutes from home. For most of her two years there, the union kept her and her colleagues abreast of the negotiations with Be Well. She'd only been an official member of the union for less than a year, but they still made an effort to find her employment when Be Well terminated the contract. The bank, on the other hand, told her at 11:15 A.M. that her position had been terminated, and by 12:30 she was on the commuter train home. After twenty-one years.

"Remember Simone?" I ask. "She's there."

"¿Dónde?"

"At Be—at the psychiatric hospital."

"Oh, my God. Please don't tell me that. That's my worst nightmare. Remember I used to make you and your brother watch *One Flew Over the Cuckoo's Nest* when you were little? I didn't want you to ever end up in one of those places. Pobrecita."

"Mom, it's not a choice, is it? I don't think Simone was bored and wandered into the loony bin."

"That's not nice. It's a psychiatric hospital. How do you think that makes people feel—"

"I know! I was just making a point. Forget it."

I get up to slide my dish into the sink. Before I can turn on the water, she takes over.

"I can wash it," she says tersely.

When I was a kid I had chores, and I often cooked dinner for the four of us. As an adult, anytime I offer to do anything, it's an affront.

While her back is to me, I wipe the crumbs off the table and into my hand.

"Dad's appointment? Eight-forty-five, you said?"

"Sí. And bring something to read because they're always running late, and the waiting room only has the gossip magazines that you don't like. You'll be there a while," she says without turning around.

"Okay. Thanks."

"I left you lunch in the refrigerator, and I'll warm up dinner and make salad when I get home."

"I can make a salad, Mom. Do I need to swing by the market for anything?"

"No! Don't make anything. You've done enough. And I like to wash my own lettuce."

My mother unties her apron with the swift tug of a loose end. Underneath is a variation of the same thin-strapped flowery nightgown she's been wearing most of her adult life—she buys a new one in El Salvador, every few years, always a size larger. She has gained weight recently, but it suits her. She's cute, like a cartoon bear with complex feelings and a creaky back. My mother is approaching sixty-five, but she could be forty. It's her face. It radiates an extraordinary softness. I suspect it's the diligent application of creams and lotions—morning, noon, and night—all of my life. Genetics, too. I'm curious to know what she'd look like if her life hadn't been what it was.

Nowadays, it's her hair that gives her age away. Decades of plucking and dyeing ended a few years ago. Her fully silver, asymmetrical bob gives her a distinguished look, the sophistication she's always sought.

Before I leave the kitchen, she wraps her arms around me. "I love you."

"I know."

She lets go and puts her hands on my face, one on each cheek, and stares deeply into my eyes. I watch hers move as she scans me. "My baby," she says. "¿Cómo estuvo anoche?"

"It was okay. Lots of people. I was surprised by how many. Lots of memories and stories. Everyone was nice. But most of them are Republicans."

"Oof," she says and sways her head. "Trump people everywhere around here."

"Everyone's old and kinda overweight too."

"What's wrong with old and overweight?" she says, only half joking.

"This isn't thick and lovely we're talking about. This is American living. Besides, you're beautiful, Mom."

"I was, once," she responds. "You wouldn't believe it, but I was ninety-nine pounds when I came to this country."

"I know," I say.

I've seen the pictures of her in her short shorts, high heels, and red lips. Happy like I've never really known her.

"Don't let your father get in and out of the car by himself. He's not supposed to exert himself or twist at his waist until the stitches fall out. I'm going to get him up now so he can get ready."

"Okay."

"And make sure he uses his cane," she says, before grabbing the sponge from the sink and wiping down my spot at the table, the area I had left spotless.

"Okay," I respond.

D on't get out yet," I say. "Wait for me."

"I can do it."

"Dad, please! I didn't come all this way for you to tear open your wound." He continues, through groans and discomfort, to pull himself out of the car. "Just wait! Okay?"

"Okay."

It's early, but the sun is already announcing its intentions; it'll be one hundred degrees today. I run around to the passenger side through a thick, invisible cloud of humidity. I lift one of my dad's legs out of the car, and the sweat commences. I lift the other leg.

"Do you want to try with the cane," I ask, "or do you want to put your arms around my neck?"

"I'm already married. Stop flirting with me."

"Dad, cut it out."

"If we don't laugh about this miserable life . . ." He closes his eyes and shakes his head subtly. His worn, ruddy cheeks become veiny purple with strain. He's laughing and he's in pain.

"It's a miserable moment in an otherwise okay life," I say.

My father carries on with his soft chuckle, and touches his head, chest, and each shoulder briefly.

"We could be going through this in Yemen or Palestine," I continue, "or Flint, Michigan."

"That's my worst fear."

"Which part?"

"Being thirsty but not having clean water. Pobre gente."

"That's your worst fear? I thought it was snakes?"

"Those, too."

"Can you wait here while I park?" I ask, after helping him onto the sidewalk.

After I get back into the car, he taps the window with his cane.

"What is it?" I ask.

"Park it in the shade," he says.

"Dad, it's a massive lot, and there isn't a single tree in sight."

"Just try."

Just try is a mellower variation on my father's lifelong mantra: *You can do it.* Another version was *If you can get ninety-eight points, you can get one hundred.* Pleasing my father has always been a Sisyphean task; he is the boulder. Even a perfect test score could somehow prompt a rebuke that left me scrambling and made success feel like a vulnerability. *Didn't I tell you, you could do it? No more excuses.* He wasn't angry or rude with his hairsplitting encouragements, but it was nonetheless clear that trying wasn't sufficient; neither was *Sorry* or *I'll get it right next time* or *The teacher treats me different than the other students* or *I wasn't feeling well*. To his credit, my father modeled the self-discipline he expected of us. He worked long days at the restaurant—breakfast, lunch, and dinner—and never registered a solitary complaint in our presence, even when he had the flu, two broken ribs, strep throat, diverticulitis, cirrhosis, when his father died, when his son died, when his dog died, Election Day, and every holiday except for New Year's Day and the Fourth of July. During the eighties, he worked part time shining shoes and delivering papers, and a few other vague, questionable gigs to fill in the gaps. As a result, my father was probably patient zero for any number of virus and bacteria outbreaks, but, as he liked to remind us often, he was never late with a mortgage payment. *¡Jamás!* He's prouder of that than of anything I have ever accomplished. He came to this country with a tenth-grade education, leaving behind everything he'd ever known and loved, only to be shat on by anyone with half his intelligence, charisma, and melanin, but he learned English and paid all his bills. *¡Americanos pendejos de mierda!*

This perennial survivor mode has depleted him from the inside out, and to make matters worse, somewhere along the way, my dad went from being a Good Samaritan to a child of Reagan. Reagan: the man responsible for the winter when we bathed without hot water. My father will invariably vote for the Democrat, but he scorns anyone who doesn't work as hard as he does, including his children—*Do you know what your mother and I went through?*

I find a recently planted baby tree. It's on a small island of reddish mulch in the center of the parking lot, equidistant from both hospitals. The anemic sapling, with its thin upturned branches, has enough foliage to shade exactly nothing, but it's the best I can do. I can't help but feel proud of myself. I run back to meet my father, who is already inside, waiting at the check-in counter.

"The doctor is stuck in traffic," says the medical assistant. "We'll let you know when he arrives."

I give my dad a container of cubed honeydew and a banana that my mom packed, and I fill his water bottle from the fountain. "Call me when the doctor gets here," I say.

"It's nice, what you're doing for your friend, but be careful."

"I'm just visiting her, Dad. I'm not going to war."

"Don't be a clown. You don't know what those places are like." My dad takes a small packet of salt from his pocket. "Here," he says. "In case of an emergency."

The first time I saw my father after coming out, he gave me a five-pound wholesale bag of restaurant salt packets. "You can throw this in their eyes and run," he said. "Always run, mi'jo. Always."

8
PARKING LOTS

t's 9 A.M., almost ninety degrees, and there is nowhere to hide in this infinite tarmac of white lines. There must be hundreds of cars here, 75 percent of which are SUVs; 90 percent of those are either black or taupe. I'm reminded of a research study that argued that the proliferation of SUVs in the United States was a reflection of the growing mistrust and fear in society, which was, in turn, attributable to the decades-long trend in income inequality. Larger cars, in other words, made people feel safer, not on the road per se, but from one another. Small battalions each in their own tanks.

The psychiatric hospital is castle-like in its structure, complete with conical spires, battlements, and covered parapets. It's abandoned and draped in scaffolding, but a narrow path wends and winds beside and behind the medieval leviathan into a new world with manicured lawns and a sprawling series of interconnected, modern two-story buildings with no shortage of windows, all draped in dark green curtains. There are groundskeepers afoot, most of whom look like distant relatives of mine. Dark green pickup trucks stenciled with *Be Well* plod along, stopping often to unload boxes at one entrance and pick up packages at another. This quaint *Truman Show*–serenity stands in contrast to the wasteland realness of the parking lot and the drab institutional design of the larger hospital beyond it, where I just left my father. I wonder if this pastoral scenery is a temporary campus or the way forward for all of Be Well's business ventures. Merely standing here is therapeutic, and while still wary of capitalism's vice grip on health care, I feel a modicum of optimism for Simone. And for humanity.

I find the entrance and a small waiting area. There's an intercom affixed to a yellowish wall.

"Hello?"

"Hello," breaks through the crackling static.

"Hi. I'm here to see a patient. I think she's a patient. Simone—"

"Visiting hours don't begin until nine-fifteen. Please come back then." Click.

It's nine-ten.

I text my dad and ask if he needs me. "No," he responds, "Take your time."

Now, it's nine-eleven.

My father is happy to be alone because it's cycling season, and although I have never witnessed him riding a bicycle, he can content himself for hours watching the Tour de France on his phone. His passion mirrors mine for tennis, a sport I have no experience playing competitively. In fact, we're in the midst of Wimbledon, and I'd love nothing more than to be sitting in front of a large television set. The truth is I don't even need the matches; I derive pleasure from keeping track of score lines on my phone. There's little love or appreciation of sport in following numbers on a screen, but I cannot help myself. At this point, I know the players well enough to care about their successes and failures irrespective of their athleticism. My obsession is manifold. Every match leads to a change in their rankings, which I track several times a day. At the four Grand Slam tournaments of the year, of which Wimbledon is third, chronologically speaking, each match is worth more, and my concern grows proportionally.

My phone buzzes as I scan the grid of integers—Fabio Fognini, a ribald Italian veteran known for his emotional outbursts, lost the first set to Andy Murray, the feminist Scot whom the English claim as one of their own. Grass is Fognini's worst surface and Murray's best, and none of this is a surprise.

The buzzing was a prelude to a text message: "It was good to catch up. I'm off work at 4. Come here? Or I could swing by your parents'?"

This is someone from last night, a friend from high school. I think it's Jeremy, but I didn't save any of the dozen or so numbers that I pretended to save.

"Sorry, I'm not sure who this is . . ."

"Mr. Popular," they respond. Then, "It's Jeremy."

Immediately, the internal constrictions begin.

How can a high school love have such a destabilizing effect after so much time? I haven't given Jeremy more than a handful of passing thoughts in nearly twenty years. And most of those thoughts were in the early days, triggered by my email; I used his phone number in several of my passwords during college. A terrible way to get over someone. For the first few years, whenever I logged in to my email or my bursar account, a pang of unrequited love coursed through me.

"Better not to come by my place. My parents aren't up for guests."

Blatant lie. My father is always up for guests, and my mother would be tickled to see someone from my past. It would make them both feel younger. In fact, my parents have never understood why I cut everyone off, in part because I've never bothered to give them an explanation, and in part because there is no explanation that they would consider good enough.

The burden to help me disappear after high school fell primarily to my mother. She fielded the inquiries, and provided the excuses: *He's not coming home for this break* or *He had to go back to school early because he has a job on campus.* The only guidance that I imparted to her was that she shouldn't share my contact information.

"I can come to you, but not sure when. I have to be with my dad until my mom gets home from work. Pretty late," I respond to Jeremy. Another lie. My mother is only working part-time these days, at a small medical practice where she spends her days hounding shameless insurance companies to pay their bills, and where she earns roughly one hundred dollars more per month than the cost of her out-of-pocket medical insurance. The work keeps her active and staves off old age. It also saved my dad's life: my mother works for a gastroenterologist, and a poster about colorectal diseases on the wall beside her desk elucidated my dad's symptoms.

"Cool," Jeremy responds, before sending another text: "Looking forward to it."

Looking forward to it. I can't imagine Jeremy uttering such a business-casual phrase.

A subtle alarm or beeping commences, followed by a disembodied voice: "Visiting hours have begun. Please have your identification ready. All bags are subject to search. All packages must be approved."

I'm the only person in the waiting area.

I walk through a door, the one that doesn't lead back outside. I encounter another set of doors; then, a third, but no sign of life. I stand at one end of a narrow beige hallway with a shiny floor made up of large squares, all of them shades of worn beige. Someone with large, listless eyes is standing behind a short table. A yellow kerchief cinches her shiny black hair. Her name tag reads *Chintam, V.*

"ID, please."

Chintam, V. writes my name into the first line of an empty sheet. "Place all of the contents of your pockets in here. You can keep your wallet and your phone." Her long, delicate fingers push a square basket, white and plastic, toward me. I pretend not to have car keys in my pocket.

"Name of the patient?"

Chintam, V. writes Simone's name in the column next to mine and slides a small piece of paper across the table. "Use this to claim your belongings on the way out," she says.

I find it simpler to nod than to point out that I am not leaving behind any of my belongings.

"Have you been here before?"

I shake my head quickly.

"Okay, walk down this hallway here and through those double doors there." Her hand becomes rigid as she extends it. "Then take a left, until you see the desk. The staff on the other side will be expecting you."

This is an overcomplicated trip to somewhere rather close, like eighteenth-century travel between New York and New Jersey.

I cross the Hudson. On the other side, someone appears as if from nowhere and vanishes just as quickly, but not before pointing me toward an orange chair that's bolted to the floor.

I sit alone for nearly five minutes. The waiting area is windowless, unadorned, and shaped like a trapezoid. The harsh fluorescence coming from above combines with the beige motif to give everything a slick yellow film.

"Andy?"

The voice echoes before I manage to see Simone at the mouth of a hallway I hadn't noticed until her figure revealed its dimensions.

"Andy! Andy!" she resumes, with a shouting that makes me awkwardly scan the perimeter.

She's radiant and vibrating, like something carbonated that's been shaken. She's undoubtedly Simone.

"Oh. My. Fucking. God. Andy!" She places one hand on top of the other over her mouth, shrieking and laughing simultaneously. I walk toward her, nervously. I don't know if she's excited to see me or if this is her way of being. It occurs to me that she might be in here because of her irrepressible energy. Simone's troubles might have begun in a mall crowded with skittish white people.

"What the fuck are you doing here, Andy?" she shouts. "Seriously, what the fuck?"

I realize now that I hadn't thought this through. Is it okay to tell her that Nicole told me? Does she even remember Nicole? Will it upset Simone to know that people are talking about her? Is she so unwell that it doesn't matter? Or will it matter more?

"My dad had a doctor's appointment nearby," I say. She doesn't push for details.

We embrace. She's no longer the beanpole I could throw my arms around. There's a density to her, and she smells of industrial soap. When I step back, I notice that she's wearing a *South Park* T-shirt and baggy cargo shorts.

"Let's go sit and talk. I can't believe it!" she screams to herself, before a muttering takes hold. "I can't believe it. I can't believe it. I can't believe it."

We walk toward a bright white-walled area with white tables and white chairs that are also bolted to the floor. Simone walks ahead of me, but turns around periodically. Her eyes are wide and full of disbelief.

One side of the communal space is a wall of enormous windows, the sort of windows I would like to have in my apartment. Their grandeur is undercut by the vertical bars. There are other patients here, not quite a dozen. Some are seated and watching TV, some are milling about dazed. One man is barely holding up his thin drawstring pajama pants. Another grasps at the air, as if he were picking apples. The space is coed, but a clear majority of the patients are white men. Simone is the only woman. And the only Black woman. Suddenly, her situation feels dire.

As we walk toward a table and empty chairs, I cannot help but compulsively scan my perimeter. Brief glimpses are returned with brazen stares—unflinching, hollow, some menacing, all sedated. Everyone is leering at us with abandon, the sort of audaciousness I've only ever experienced in after-hours sex clubs and the suburbs. As the sole visitor, I have usurped everyone's attention, except for the staff. They feel miles away—dressed in white, seated in the center of the room, on a bulletproof island of modular furniture, disaffectedly staring at computers or phones, like mannequins or performance art.

Simone sits with her back to one of the windows. I settle into the chair across from her. An older man who resembles Gary Busey and Nick Nolte ambles nearby. I feel exposed. Scared, actually. I look back at the nurse's station, hoping for reassurance, but none of the staff appear strong or imposing enough to protect me. I make a concerted effort to focus on the small gold loop in Simone's left nostril. I zero in on her short, wayward locs, not all that different from the style she wore in high school, except for the grays that appear as a thin network of capillaries across her otherwise all-black crown.

"Andy, you came to see me! I can't believe it! You're my best friend. Always been!"

Each sentence is louder and more destabilizing than the one before. I want to say, "You're shouting," but we no longer have a relationship capable of sustaining that sort of candor. Besides, what if I trigger something that rebounds onto me?

"It's really good to see you," I say. But suddenly I feel my face quiver. This is my first time in a psychiatric facility, and I'm struck by how much it evokes *One Flew Over the Cuckoo's Nest*, the Milos Forman movie that my mother made me and my brother watch every time it came on the TV. She did this with *Amadeus* and *Cabaret* as well. I think it was her way of exposing to us high(er)brow culture.

"Tell me about you! Tell me everything!" Simone shouts.

"I, uh. Well, where should I start? I, uh—"

"Andy, don't worry about them." Simone's delivery is now in an authoritative whisper. "Focus on me. Don't let them spook you."

This expression of intention and clarity, like a coach in a decisive moment of play, makes me wonder if Simone is faking all of this.

"So, how's life?" she asks, again loud. Then she nervously giggles to herself.

"Good. You know, life."

"I don't, actually." Now, she's stern.

"I meant, I—"

"I'm kidding, Andy. Lighten up." Again she laughs.

Is Simone doing this all for my benefit? *You came all this way, might as well show you I deserve to be here.* She seems well, relative to everyone else here. But something is off-kilter.

I scan the bright room, the bars on the windows, and all of the trapped inhabitants, whose previously curious gazes have transformed into a ring of baleful stares, as antagonistic as they are hungry. I feel warm and a bit tingly in my hands. I tell myself that whatever everyone shares in this space isn't contagious. I can leave whenever I want to. They can't keep me here if I suddenly spin out.

"Are you in town for long?"

"Just a few days. My dad's recovering from surgery, and I'm helping out."

"Good son."

My face starts to ache from its exaggerated smile.

"How's your mom?" I ask.

"Oh, Phyllis? She's okay. We're not talking really," Simone says, nearly pouting. "I still love her, but I'm upset with her right now because I don't like it here. They won't give me nail clippers. Or shoelaces! Look!" Simone points to her construction boots, which are laceless and open. She pulls out one bare, ashy foot with unkempt nails. "They don't have lotion here." Simone massages her ankles in quick, small circles. "The shampoo is bullshit. I can't use it on my hair. And there's no conditioner—Will you bring me some? Please? Please! You're the only friend I have. I love you so much."

Simone's pleas ricochet off the walls and windows. The only thing that would make this moment worse would be if we were on a stage before an entirely white audience, inside of a small propeller plane. At cruising altitude.

Simone lets out a guttural sound that narrows into laughter and then words: "Andy! I. Can't. Fucking. Believe. It. You're here!"

"I hope you don't mind me dropping by like this," I whisper, hoping she'll mimic my soft register. "I would have called first, but I was so close. I figured you could say no once I got here."

"What the fuck, Andy? No way! Do you know how lonely it is here? Except for my mom, no one ever visits me in these places."

"I'm sorry."

"Why? It's not your fault. Unless you're telling people not to visit. Aaaaandyyyyy . . . ? Do you stand outside and turn people away?"

"No, of course not."

"Ha! I'm joking! Fuck! Andy! Holy fuck! Where's your sense of humor?" Simone grips the rounded metal arms of her chair. She's at the crest of a roller coaster, and I'm waiting somewhere on the ground with a bag of popcorn and an oversized orange soda. "You came to visit me! I just can't believe my eyes! Maybe I shouldn't believe my eyes. Maybe I need to have an eye exam. Maybe they can put new ones in. Are you uncomfortable, Andy?"

My face is again scrunched up. I remind myself that noise is okay. That decorum is a cudgel employed by empires.

"Don't be! It's okay. We're okay. Ignore them. Ignore everyone. No one can hurt us." Simone speaks at an unsustainable pace. Her breathing sounds labored, as if wind were moving through a pile of desiccated leaves.

Suddenly she turns away and looks out, not at anything in particular. She furrows her brow. It's as if she's examining particles that only she can see. I remain quiet, unsure if I should interrupt. I watch her nod in affirmation—small, quick bobs of her head—before she turns back to me.

"Tell me something. Where are you? What do you do? Are you married? Is she a model? How's your brother? He was so cute. Did I ever tell you I thought he was cute? I had such a crush on him."

Her questions are stray arrows, and I don't know whether to dodge them or extend my arms and puff out my chest.

"I'm in the city. I teach public health to grad students. I'm married. His name is Marco, and he's very good-looking. But he's not a model; he's a doctor." I pretend to forget her question about my brother. I don't want to deal with her reaction. The moment passes.

Simone's face spreads out, confused and a bit pained, before turning small. Eyes squeezed, lips puckered. I know that look. It's homophobia. Is it possible that Simone has forgotten I'm gay? Has she forgotten that she's gay?

"God bless you," she says. "I'm happy that you're happy."

Her blessing is genuine, but it prickles. I feel something between anger and incredulity. Is she born-again? Did she swap her queerness for a false sense of sanity? I know people like this. My aunt Gloria in Miami who fell on hard times and became born again, and my aunt Teresa, in El Salvador, who transformed from Maoist rebel into devout Catholic.

"I didn't say I was happy." The surliness tumbles out of me before I can give it any consideration.

Simone draws her chin back.

"I'm kidding," I say, hoping to recover the mood previous to this one.

"Oh, fuck you, Andy! You always made me laugh. You're still making me laugh. I can't believe you're here, Andy. I seriously can't believe it. Can you believe it?"

I turn my head side to side.

Simone trains her stare up into the ceiling and out into the distance. Just like that, she disappears again.

All of this triggers a memory: an indigo sky, the wispy remains of sunset, the repetitive thunder of water crashing onto shore. I'm having a bad acid trip on the beach. "I don't feel good," I tell Simone. I regret eating a full tab. On previous occasions, I cut the tiny square into two pieces, and kept the other in my pocket. "Don't be such a pussy," she says. The trip takes me, and before long, I can't handle the immensity of the sky, the water, or the sand. "I really don't feel well," I say. Simone grabs me by the shoulders, and her eyes expand into large, dark planets. She tells me to lie down on the sand. She proceeds to roll over me, back and forth, like a long, heavy log, her pressure and weight binding me to the earth and reminding me that I am real. Calm eventually suffocates the cloudy dissociations and limbic explosions, and relief gives way to muted joy. We were seventeen.

I wonder now when Simone's mental illness began. I wonder, too, what it is. It doesn't feel right to ask. Besides, there's a vernacular to mental health that I don't know.

I feel my phone vibrate against my thigh.

"Simone, I have to go."

"What? No! Don't! You just got here! I'll never forgive you!" With gusto, she comes off the back of her chair and sits up straight, a perfect ninety degrees. Her face is stony before soft lines appear. "It's all good! Thank you. You have no idea what this means to me. Even if I never see you again, I'll remember today for the rest of my life. And the afterlife! I hope you'll remember me too."

"Of course. I'm here aren't I?"

"You are, Andy. You fucking are! Do you really have to go?"

"I do," I say. Immediately, she slumps in her chair. "But I'll come back. I'm here another week."

"You don't have to," Simone says with a dejected air, before sitting up again. "But if you do, please bring me conditioner and nail clippers. And paper bags! You know, those shopping bags with the paper handles? They make really good shoelaces."

I curl downward to put my arms around her.

"Oh, no, you're getting a real hug," she says. "I'll walk you to the front."

The other patients are entranced by the various television screens. On one is a black-and-white movie with Bette Davis. Another has *The Price Is Right*. The third displays *Sesame Street*, with an unfamiliar pink winged puppet waving a magic wand. All of the television sets are muted and encased in hard plastic boxes. At first, it seems like a subtle type of torture, but maybe the limitations are meant to be soothing.

When we arrive at the double doors, I feel a firm squeeze on my arm. "This is it. Freedom," Simone says. Behind us, a few feet away, stands a brawny man with a shaved head and a taut white T-shirt tucked into white pants. We look over at him simultaneously, and he nods.

"Barry's cool," Simone explains. "One of the few staffers I like. We play ball in the yard. Don't let his size fool you, he can get some air."

"How's the rest of the staff?"

"They don't play basketball."

"No, I mean in general."

"They're motherfuckers. They don't let me cut my nails. They go through my comics too. They say they don't, but whenever I get back to my room, nothing is where I left it. I've told them a million times that someone is stealing my money, but they don't care. They look at me like I'm crazy, but I know I'm the sanest person here. I'm just missing things. That's why I don't have conditioner. Someone took it, and these bastards didn't do a damn thing about it. You know, I heard once that Oprah uses a whole bottle of conditioner every time she showers. Every time! I don't need that much."

Whatever Simone is undergoing, it manifests primarily as a frenetic logorrhea. I'm too curious to wait. I ask her why she's here.

"Schizophrenia," she says casually. "I've had it under control for a while. Just some bad luck recently. I'll be back to my old self soon."

Just then, the doors part, making a truculent sound. I don't know how or why they've opened. I walk through quickly, before turning around.

"Bye, Simone."

She smiles and remains quiet. I make my way down the long hallway. Behind me, the heavy doors close slowly; the gears and latches reverberate in the emptiness. When I turn the corner, Simone shouts, "Andy, I love you for coming here! I will never forget this!" Her words are as clear as if there were no doors between us. I realize then that we didn't hug after all.

My father is standing slightly lopsided by the car, resting on his cane, besotted-like.

"How did you find it in this mess of cars?"

"Don't count your old man out," he says, before pinching the breast of his shirt with two fingers. "It's also the smallest car here," he adds, nodding to his silver Prius—a retirement gift from Marco and me, even though my dad is convinced he'll return to the restaurant when he's fully recovered. "You have to use your brain, mi'jo. College doesn't teach you everything."

"Why didn't you wait for me inside?"

"¡Comemierdas!"

"What happened?"

"They rescheduled."

"But the doctor was on his way when I left you."

My father shakes his old, gray head and raises his rounded shoulders briefly. "Waste of my time. I could have been watching La Vuelta at home, instead of this tiny screen," he says and holds out his phone.

"Isn't there anyone else there who can see you?"

"Medicare."

"Fuck."

"Vamos. Este calor es un infierno."

"Okay, don't get in yet. Let me turn on the AC first."

"No importa. I could eat an entire cow. Vamos a Pedro's."

"Mom doesn't want you to eat there."

"Tu madre no tiene que saber todo," he says, knowing full well that she does need to know everything.

"You're going to get me in trouble."

My father brings his two hands together, as if in prayer. "We can share a dish, okay?"

"Okay."

"I'm surprised Pedro's has survived as long as it has," I say, once we're on the road.

"Are you kidding? That place is busier than McDonald's. Los Americanos love our food more than we do." My father beams as if someone somewhere has etched a win in our column.

We're not Dominican, but it is, in a way, our food too. I don't know enough about the agricultural history of the Americas, the colonial influence of Spain, or the contributions of the African diaspora to explain why we find food from the Dominican Republic as interchangeably good as food from Puerto Rico or Cuba or Colombia. But we do. Well, my family does. And in particular, my father, who doesn't pass up an opportunity to be nearer to *our* people. It's the same reason he has always watched TV in Spanish. The news, the variety shows, the documentaries, the soccer matches, all in his mother tongue. He left Colombia when he was sixteen or seventeen—doesn't remember or doesn't want to remember—but he watches TV as if he were attending a reunion or hanging out with friends. A beer in his lap, a smile on his face.

"¿Cómo va todo con Marco?" he asks, as we get onto the highway.

Marco is Dominican, and whenever my dad brings up Pedro's, he brings up Marco shortly thereafter. Conversely, whenever we talk about Marco, my dad asks if I want to go to Pedro's. But his inquiry has the air of conspiracy. Certainly, my mother has put him up to this.

"We're fine. I already told you. He's at a conference."

The truth is, apart from last night's drunk text, and a few one-word messages when he got to London ("Landed"), Johannesburg ("Landed"), and Windhoek ("Landed"), Marco and I haven't spoken since I left him at the airport security line. This isn't normal. We've never not spoken. It's been nearly ten years of talking every day.

The first time we met was all talk. In fact, we chatted online for a week before meeting in person—sushi dinner.

"Are you as good-looking in real life as you are in your picture?"

"No," I said.

"I appreciate your honesty."

"How about you? Are you this good-looking?"

"Better."

"Wow. Confident, eh?"

"Just playing."

But he wasn't lying. Marco is gorgeous on the internet, from across the street, and up close. Rich, dark brown eyes that are always attentive, pronounced cheekbones and dimples that give his face the illusion of a permanent smile, and a sculpted physique like those typically found in museums. Marco has a terrible sense of direction, he's kind to old people, he repeats himself and has bad taste in films and music, and he's a generous lover. After our first night together, I wanted to see him again. After a few weeks, I began wondering about my parents' reactions. Marco being Black was one thing; being Caribbean was another; neither was ideal. Dominicans and Puerto Ricans were the embarrassing cousins of the Latinx family, I'd gathered over the years. Not necessarily from my parents but from the Latinx world at large. *They butcher the language, they're lazy, they're violent, they live off our taxes.* Of course, all of it was political analysis full of effects without proof or causes, with no mention of imperialism, colonialism, capitalism, slavery, racism, or small sample sizes.

Much ado about nothing, it turned out. My parents liked Marco from the outset. It hadn't crossed my mind that they would mistreat him, but I expected at least a wayward eyebrow and maybe a certain degree of frigidity. It never appeared. Nor did my parents' dreaded pet names for one another:

negro and *negra*. But my mother wasn't completely at ease when I brought Marco home for the first time. It was subtle, but several times she told him how handsome he was, in that way that older white women try to mask their racism by complimenting people of color. *You really are quite beautiful. You have such pretty eyes. You are a very attractive girl, boy, person, human, subhuman, second-class citizen, descendant of an enslaved person, Indigenous person, Oriental.* A phenomenon my parents had undoubtedly experienced many times in this country.

As for Marco, it helped his case that he was a doctor who was generous with his consultations and referrals, that he was a good cook, that he danced well, that he rolled his Rs, that he was easygoing, and that my parents were old and no longer as prejudiced as they'd once been. They had also just lost a son and didn't want to risk losing another.

Then again, a colleague of mine researches the ability of humans to carve out exceptions from entire populations. This is how he explains the anti-Black racists who voted for Obama. Apparently people are capable of turning their racism on and off; they just haven't figured out how to make "off" the default.

In any case, my parents love Marco, and they're right to be concerned about us being apart at the moment. I was supposed to be in Namibia with him, but we got into an argument a couple of weeks ago, and I canceled my tickets. Initially, the bickering was about adopting children—he's ready; I'm not—which then led to a rehashing of a few texts I'd seen on his phone between an ex and him, which then spiraled into him rebuking me for my trust issues and for my lack of respect for his privacy, which culminated with my dredging up his infidelity from last year.

"Maybe I shouldn't go on this trip with you."

"Maybe," he responded.

The next day, we made peace, but I used my father's health as a pretext to stay home.

Your mother and I have never spent more than two nights apart in almost fifty years," says my father. "Amor de lejos, amor de pendejos."

"We'll be okay. A little break never hurt anyone."

"You know your relationship best," my father says before extending his arm and pointing toward his side of the windshield. "¡Aquí! Get over to the right lane! Next exit!"

I don't know why he's telling me this. Or why he's shouting. I know exactly how to get there.

9
BASEMENTS

eremy lives on a block of two-story homes with small lawns, vinyl fences, driveways, and sickly maple trees, not far from St. Pete's—the elementary school. One block over is the street where a van full of teenagers opened fire on us with eggs and Super Soaker guns full of piss one Halloween. Our small group was unprepared for the onslaught of yellow. Mikey C., Paul, and I dove behind a hedgerow and only caught a bit of splatter on our costumes—Mike and I were Ghostbusters; Paul was Duff McKagan, the bassist for Guns N' Roses—but the rest of the pack had to run home to wash off the liquid detritus. I didn't recognize the assailants. Paul said they attended McKinley, the middle school named after the US president who'd been shot by an anarchist. Public school kids were, back then, mythical creatures that I'd hear about in passing and sometimes meet at a block party or parking lot carnival. They were usually the poorer or less devout cousins and neighbors of my Catholic school classmates. Troublemakers who peed into water guns.

Most of the houses in this part of town have clapboard siding, and they're painted off-white with red trim, dull blue with white trim, or beige with brown trim. There are no curbs or sidewalks in sight; lawns end abruptly where the street's pavement begins. Small children bike loops or dribble basketballs on their driveways. Every few houses, flowers droop in their beds beneath bay windows. Occasionally, there's an American flag. Always there's one house that's in disrepair. That's where the kids with the ratty uniforms and slovenly parents tended to live. Nowadays, there are two of those houses per block. I've also noticed another trend: bigger, more ostentatious homes (mini-McMansions) stuffed betwixt the older constructions. Whether this reflects wealth or non-union labor or materials made elsewhere for less, I don't know.

Jeremy's lawn is small, but what it lacks in size, it makes up for in verdancy. Water guns, a pedal-less tricycle, and Wiffle balls and bats are strewn about the recently mowed swath of green. A sprinkler oscillates, one hundred eighty degrees: one side, straight up, then the other side. I park in front of his house, on the street, behind an angled black Nissan Altima. Three of its tires are on the pavement; the fourth rests on the short cobblestone perimeter that encircles the lawn.

I can't see what lies beyond the white fence that encloses the side and back of the two-story house. It comes up above my forehead, and there is no visible space between the pickets. I imagine a small patio and an unkempt yard peppered with dog shit.

My mouth is dry. It feels small and inutile. I shouldn't have taken a hit of the old pot—a dime bag that my sister-in-law, Ellie, slid into my stocking during our first Christmas together after Henry died, nearly nine years ago. I've wedged it between two books (*The Count of Monte Cristo* and *Summer of My German Soldier*) in our old bedroom. The brittle, grayish herb retains some of its potency and most of its secondary effects; I'm hungry in addition to cotton-mouthed.

Before I knock, I prepare myself for the possibility of meeting Jeremy's wife. I wonder if she knows that her husband and I spent the last year of high school having sex in his parents' basement and occasionally in my bedroom. Does she know that we loved each other? If they've been together for ten years, it stands to reason that she's asked him about his adolescence, his first time, his first love. These are things that married people know about one another. I know them about Marco—a college friend who's now a well-known theater actor; they remain friends; I'm uncomfortable with it—and he knows them about me. But maybe Jeremy hasn't told his wife. He isn't a particularly loquacious or forthcoming person, or at least he wasn't. An onion with endless skins is what I remember. And maybe she suspects and doesn't want to risk the tears.

Jeremy was always attracted to women and men. I pretended to be, but he actually was. His bi- or pansexuality made me uneasy, primarily because I wanted both of us to feel the same way about everything. But he had a way of making me feel like the center. It didn't matter if we were with friends or in class or at the prom, I knew that his eyes were trained on me, following me around the room, ready to wink in my direction. He was, at least in that way, the abiding star. In retrospect, it's unbelievable that our carelessness didn't betray us more often. I recall one time. He kissed me in an empty hallway, in the moment after the warning bell rang and our classrooms were sealed shut. As Jeremy ran away, down the long blue corridor, I spotted Ms. Van Estren standing in the frame of her door, her face ruddy, nearly apoplectic. She said nothing to me about it, but then misgraded my physics exam a few days later. She claimed to have miscalculated, but I convinced myself I was being sanctioned.

Frankly, I didn't care. I was infected.

Jeremy's confidence was my first sexually transmitted illness. He made me, in a way, carefree. His affections and attentions transformed me into another person. I was popular, but he was cool. A cool kid with good looks and rough edges, who'd been in fights and played baseball, whose reputation cloaked our sins. If our ships sank, at least they would sink together. In the meantime, I spent senior year with outsized self-belief, feeling more attractive, funnier, taller even. One of the best-looking people I'd ever clapped eyes on cared as much about me as I did about him. For adolescent me, that was enough.

Also unique was that Jeremy seemed assured about his feelings for me.

"I love you," he said, as we were lying on his bed one Friday night in January, senior year. Both of us were in boxers, staring up at a 1986 Mets poster on his ceiling.

He said the words without turning to face me. I remained quiet for at least ten seconds, focusing instead on Mookie Wilson's name, forcing myself to wonder about its origins, buying time, trying desperately to control how quickly and loudly I might respond, but the ball of fire that had traveled up from my stomach was detained only briefly in my throat.

"I love you, too."

"Yeah," he said, as if he were confirming what he'd already known.

The four-thirty northern-hemisphere sun strikes a wide angle in the summer, warming my neck and calves and lighting the modest house. I count three small, beige sparrows with mustard beaks perched along the roof's gutter. I knock once for each bird, instead of ringing the cracked buzzer. It crosses my mind to run back to my car. What, after all, will we talk about? I compiled a list of questions on the way over here, most of them silly. Icebreakers, really. Through the living room window, I see a shapeless figure move between shadows before I hear its footsteps.

Jeremy appears behind the mesh of his screen door. "Hey."

"Hey."

His hair is darker and neater than it was last night. His pale face has a reddish tinge, as if he just showered with hot water. He's wearing jeans pulled high on his waist and an unappealing lilac-colored polo shirt. He looks like a dad and a neighbor. He opens the screen door and steps forward, in the process allowing the sunlight to restore his humanity. "Gimme a sec." Jeremy inspects his mailbox and dislodges from it a few envelopes that have been forced into an opening that's too small.

"Come in."

"Should I take my shoes off?" I ask after crossing the threshold.

"What? Why?"

"I don't know. Germs?"

"It's fine. Whatever you want."

Jeremy bisects a narrow, rectangular living room and enters an equally circumscribed kitchen. "Something to drink? I got water, milk, orange juice, or pink wine," he calls out, with his head inside of the refrigerator.

Pink wine. Who doesn't know rosé? I suspect he's uncomfortable saying the word, as if it'll emasculate him.

"I thought you didn't drink," I say.

"I don't. The wine is Tonya's."

It stands to reason that Tonya is his wife, but I don't ask for confirmation. "Water is fine."

"Ice?"

"Yes, please."

He hands me a glass dripping with condensation and sits on a teal sofa across from the armchair I've already claimed. The blues and purples of his clothing and furniture are disorienting, as if his white arms and white face are floating, disembodied.

"So, where are—"

"Do you want—Sorry," he says. "Go ahead."

"No, nothing. I was just wondering where your family is."

"Oh. Tonya took the kids to the pool. At the high school."

"Garfield?" Another assassinated president.

"Yeah. They have swim classes every day in the summer."

"How old are they?"

"Ford is seven. Lincoln is four."

"Like the presidents or the cars?"

"What? Oh. Tonya named them both," he says with a restrained smile. Maybe I've embarrassed him with my penchant for trivia.

"Will they be home soon?"

Jeremy reaches for his phone and glances at its screen. "The class just started. And she usually takes them to Athena's after."

"They remodeled," I say. "I noticed on the way over here."

"Yeah, but it's still the same old diner. Same menu."

"I remember the french fries."

"Still great."

We both smile until it becomes awkward. I look down at the ring of water on my shorts. I wipe the glass with the end of my shirt.

"It's hotter up here. Let's go down to the basement," he says.

M y childhood home didn't have a basement. "The land here wasn't made for basements," my dad has claimed. "But for a few hundred dollars more, we could have had a garage. I'll regret that for the rest of my life." My mother, however, is grateful for the simplicity. "Who would have cleaned the garage?

They get moldy and fill up with junk. I've never seen a clean garage. I think it's a garbage, but they forgot to add the *B*."

All my friends had basements—carpeted, low-ceilinged, wood-paneled, plush-couched dens. It's where everything happened—drinking, darts, dates. I had sex for the first time in a basement. The second time, too. Dozens of times, actually. Jeremy's basement had been designed at some point as a refuge for his father—small kitchen, well-stocked bar, projector, lazily hidden collection of porn on VHS, pull-out couch, bathroom with a tiny shower— but the space became our own whenever his parents were out, which was often.

I went to Jeremy's house for the first time on a Friday in March. It was cold out, but not so cold that I couldn't ride my bike to his place. Jeremy invited me to sleep over because his parents went out on Fridays, and his grandmother didn't care who came by. That first time, I went because he'd been talking to a girl from the neighborhood, and this girl had a friend who, sight unseen, had agreed to be my date for the night. Jeremy said we'd all watch a movie and he'd make screwdrivers and we'd end up making out with our dates, side by side, on the couch. He'd thought it through, he said. By that point, I was a junior who hadn't had sex and I was desperate to catch up to my friends.

The girls didn't show up that night. The one who was meant to be my date got her period, or so said the one who was supposed to be Jeremy's date. Instead, he and I ordered pizza, watched *Friday*, and smoked pot. We became otherworldly and giddy almost immediately, before I entered the familiar paranoia loop. *This high is going to pass. Don't say anything stupid. Don't forget your track meet tomorrow! This high is going to pass. Don't say anything stupid. Don't forget your track meet tomorrow!*

Jeremy, for his part, turned playfully aggressive. He flicked my earlobe whenever I looked away, which only heightened my paranoia. When he tired of that, or maybe because he could tell I was uncomfortable, he began pinching my nipple over my shirt, all the while howling with glee. My guy friends did these kinds of things to each other and to me, but it never occurred to me to do them.

When I got up to use the bathroom, Jeremy smacked my backside and laughed. When I returned, he tried to trip me as I stepped over his legs. When that didn't work, he pushed me onto the couch. I laughed, half-heartedly and artificially, to mask the mix of confusion, anxiety, and arousal that I was feeling. In retrospect, it was rather obvious that he was flirting or trying desperately and unnecessarily to get attention that I would have given freely. It was easier, however, to believe that he was messing around, that my sublimated queerness left me inadequate to the task of being an adolescent boy fluent in the language of horseplay. Whatever I might reciprocate would result in my being pinned beneath him in a wrestling match that I was certain to lose. Jeremy and I were of similar height and weight, but he was fit, while I was nearly malnourished. Every exit pointed toward embarrassment. And still, I was high. The liminal haze allowed me to entertain all possibilities. Was he waiting for me to make a move? Was he as desperate for my unambiguous touch, embrace, or kiss, as I was for his?

As we started to come down, he asked if I wanted to smoke again.

"Nah, I'm good. I have to be up at five-thirty tomorrow and to school by six-thirty. I should probably get going."

"What? C'mon, dude. I thought you were staying over."

"The girls didn't show up, and honestly, it'll be easier to get to school from my house."

"I'll give you a ride. My parents left me a set of car keys in case of an emergency."

"You don't have a license."

"Yeah I do. I got the temporary last week. The new one is coming in the mail."

When it became clear to him that I was resolute, Jeremy started bouncing around me, like a little kid or a desperate puppy.

"You're just down cuz you didn't get any pussy tonight," he said.

"No, I'm not. I'm legitimately tired, and I have to get up early."

"Legitimately?"

"Shut up."

"Fine. You can go, but hang a bit longer. I got something for you. Chill here."

Jeremy vanished into the spare room in the far corner of the basement. Meanwhile, I lay out on the enormous couch, running my fingers against the grain of the soft fibers, gripping the shaggy carpet with my toes, well into the tactile portion of the high. When Jeremy returned, he was holding two nondescript rectangular black boxes. "Which one?" he asked. "Right or left?"

"What are they?"

"Right or left?"

"I don't know. That one," I said, pointing to the one on the right.

Jeremy opened one of the boxes and stuffed the cassette into the VCR. "It's from my dad's collection," he said. Then he walked back to the couch and stood over me. His baggy gray sweatpants were taut from the wide stance. He wore a black tank top, and as he tapped his fists against each other, his bare biceps throbbed. He kneed my thigh. "Move over."

Jeremy and I had gotten to know one another well over the previous months. Ms. Cardinale, our English teacher, had forced us to study together for state exams. I hadn't wanted to pair up with Jeremy because I sensed that I'd be doing the lion's share of the work. I'd also been wary of him since our near fight at the beginning of the school year. During our first study session, Jeremy was effusively recalcitrant: "Dude, I'm not an asshole," he whispered in the library, "I swear. Really, I'm not."

A few times over the next couple of months, he mentioned his dad's porn collection, as if this moment were inevitable. I'd seen porn magazines and porn video catalogs before, but I'd never watched a proper movie. I was, without a doubt, curious, but I was also embarrassed at the thought of watching other people have sex in front of someone else. To make matters worse, I hadn't bothered to change out of my school uniform before coming over. I was wearing thin charcoal-gray slacks, which couldn't, under normal circumstances, hide an erection. I didn't want Jeremy to see me aroused, but neither did I want this time with him to end.

There was a stockroom full of empty boxes in the back of a store. A mustachioed man with enormous arms and legs wore tight clothes. A buxom blonde with similarly tight-fitting clothing appeared without a plausible explanation. Who was she? What was she doing there? After some terse, stolid dialogue, they were naked. I did my best to stay focused on the gyrating bodies, but I couldn't help side-eyeing Jeremy, who periodically adjusted the crotch of his pants and declared his affinity for the synthetic actress, whose artful moans undercut, for me, any semblance of arousal. "She's so fucking hot, man," Jeremy repeated. My eyes rested upon the equally plastic man, whose strength and intensity gave him an almost reddish tint. Physically there was scant difference between the man on the screen and the brawny men my brother and I watched wrestle on television. But whereas the wrestlers appealed to me in the same way that soap operas did, the naked man with the enormous chest, bare ass, and engorged cock awoke the thing inside of me that I spent most of my waking moments trying to quell, the thing I feared more than anything might one day be discovered, the thing I gave myself permission to feel under my bedsheets or in a locked bathroom. When I realized that I wouldn't be able to hide anything, I, too, began talking back to the screen: "So fucking hot. I'd love to bang her." The inauthenticity in my voice was apparent, I believed, and I felt further shamed because of it.

Jeremy got up and scrambled away from the couch without saying a word. I took the opportunity to find the least conspicuous position for my erection. The man on the screen had his back pressed against a rack of easily rattled shelves, hoisting up his partner, who'd wrapped her legs around his waist and her arms around his neck, bouncing up and down on his enormous penis. When Jeremy didn't return right away, I feared he'd gone off to masturbate in private and that I would be forced to do something similar or pretend that I had so that I could leave with my dignity intact, but soon enough he returned with a box of tissues in one hand and a bottle of lotion in the other. He set the items in the yawning crevasse between the cushions. Almost immediately, he loosened the drawstring on his pants and slid them down a few inches. He rubbed himself over his underwear, a pair of briefs, it seemed, but I couldn't be certain because he hadn't pulled his pants low enough for me to see where the underwear ended. I fixated on the otherwise dull blue fabric that had bloated up from his lower body. After a few glances at Jeremy, I was more enthralled than I'd been through the first fifteen minutes of the movie.

My chest and limbs began to tremble. Whatever was happening or not happening between Jeremy and me was about as intimate as anything I'd experienced before, which, up to that point, consisted entirely of a few heavy, alcohol-induced make-out sessions with girls. One of those encounters, only a few weeks earlier, had escalated into the fingering of Monica O'Hearn

(Ecuadorian Irish) in her parents' basement. A part of me had been deep inside of another human, and specifically, inside of the adolescent cup of Christ, but it had been a soulless, solitary experience, during which Monica's feelings were, at best, of secondary importance to my own discomfort. I'd left her home feeling like a creep. In fact, the very use of the word "finger" as a verb connoted something technical and violent. But I'd gone along with the motions because of the race: the checklist of heterosexual credits along the road to fucking. If I'd had sex with Monica, I'd have been on another plane; the next level of life unlocked. I'd have been able to relate to my friends in ways I hadn't yet. I believed, too, that it would lead to transformation; I would become the man that I was expected to be.

Nowhere on my checklist had this encounter with Jeremy appeared, but the silence between us was exciting and passionate, everything that I had expected sex to be.

A subtle, visceral moan escaped Jeremy, and I felt my own breath shorten. I made every effort to keep my gaze trained on the screen and its heaving couple, but inevitably I found myself taking more jittery glances at Jeremy. There were his hands, squeezing the navy blue phallus through his underwear, as if he were gripping a baseball bat, a rounded weapon with a bead of moisture at its head, a growing darkness. There he was, loosening his grip and in one swift motion lifting himself from the couch with a wide arch of his back, simultaneously pushing his pants and underwear below his knees. "Here," he said, after pumping lotion into one of his hands and handing me the bottle with the other.

Even in the locker room at school, the other guys tended to be modest, quickly switching towels out for boxers—never briefs. I wondered for a moment if this was something all my friends did and that I hadn't been privy to. Jeremy's nonchalance confused me. Surely, this was a big deal. Surely, this was meaningful. But he continued stroking himself, staring straight ahead, his eyelids occasionally sliding shut, blunting all of my instincts to react. I looked down at his cock. It was a thick, pasty shaft with a pinkish head, not quite beautiful, but large, bigger than mine. It had no foreskin and was vaguely scarred beneath its head. I had only ever been in this sort of proximity to two other penises, my father's and my brother's, both of which resembled mine. For a moment, I felt as if I were dealing with another species of human.

My inner tremble morphed into something more percussive and conspicuous. I vainly repositioned myself on the couch.

Not participating in this tremendous event suddenly felt odd. I unzipped my pants and lowered them below my thighs, but I kept my Christmas-patterned boxers on, instead using the front flap as egress. I was already wet with pre-cum, and my foreskin made lotion unnecessary. I grabbed some anyway, which proved a terrible decision. The added moisture and slicker hand motion were an unwanted shortcut to climax; I didn't want to finish before Jeremy. Frantically, I searched my memory banks for something antithetical that might interrupt the flow of hormones and blood, something that would level us. I conjured up a memory of myself throwing up in front of a large industrial fan during a birthday party at Chuck E. Cheese. Chunks of projectile vomit blowing back into my face, landing on the game consoles, in the hair of screaming children. The vile replay helped momentarily, but Jeremy was an overpowering presence. Porn en vivo. His tumescent member, his half-exposed six-pack, his tensed forearms, a small trail of hair traveling up to his belly button, and an almost uninterrupted song of moaning right beside me.

I don't remember with certainty if we made eye contact before he came or just after, but I'm certain it happened. He exploded and our gazes met; I finished a few seconds after. Ours were epic, plentiful eruptions that dwarfed the already vigorous effluence to which I was accustomed. There was a brief spell of relief—not quite seconds, but moments—while my eyes remained closed, before the embarrassment, shame, and regret settled into the room. I felt, too, something akin to happiness. An ephemeral internal heat that matched the warmth on my hand, abdomen, and thighs, before the ejaculate cooled. I also felt a softer, deeper warmth on my foot. Something unfamiliar. It was Jeremy. He was fully reclined, one leg bent at the knee, the other extended, his foot gently caressing mine. I don't know if he was aware of what he was doing or if it was a euphoric sort of mindlessness, but it was, in all cases, memorable.

Jeremy sat up, reached for the tissues, and pulled his underwear over the crime scene. I wiped up carelessly and sought refuge in the bathroom, hoping to escape Jeremy and to contain the wave of nausea that was lapping on my insides, a combination of the heathenism and the screwdrivers. I hadn't done anything wrong, I told my newly altered self as I searched the mirror for my previous self.

There was no proof of anything, I thought. Nothing had happened. Nothing to be ashamed of. Nothing to pray about. Nothing to confess. Nothing to regret. But I did regret. I did feel shame. I would pray. Something had indeed happened.

"Where are you going?" Jeremy asked, as I put on my socks and fastened my running cleats to my backpack.

"I just realized I didn't pack my running uniform for tomorrow." This was a lie.

"I can drive you home to get it."

"S'ok. I have my bike. I can be home in fifteen minutes."

"You coming back?"

"No, it's easier to get a ride from my folks tomorrow."

Jeremy kept talking at me, but I didn't register anything, even as he followed me up the stairs and to his garage, where I'd left my bike. "Are you sure?" he shouted, after I'd biked down his driveway and waved goodbye, with my shirt on inside out.

His basement is carpeted green and brings to mind a recently watered lawn or images of the United Nations General Assembly. There's a fifty-inch flat-screen television set anchored onto the wood-paneled walls; there's also a pool table, a dartboard, two plush brown couches, a few dumbbells strewn on the floor, an old wooden desk with small drawers and loose papers— including a stack of utility bills—scattered about, and a slew of framed photographs. Jeremy pulls a vape pen from his pocket and puts the sleek, futuristic tool to his lips. He pulls with effortless devotion.

"Your back bothering you?" I ask.

"Always, but this," he says, without exhaling what he's taken in, "this is just cuz I wanna get stoned. Want?" Tiny bursts of smoke, like exhaust from a sputtering car in the cold months, leave his mouth. "It packs a punch," he warns. "A long punch."

I accept the pen, press a button, and suck. He makes his way to the dark mahogany desk and unlocks the smallest drawer with the smallest key from his key chain. He pulls another pen from the drawer, as well as a small plastic box. His key chain has a tiny pocketknife, which he uses to unseal the box. He unwedges a cartridge, screws it into the pen, and hands me the newly assembled contraption. "All yours for the low, low price of sixty bucks."

Although I half expected this to be a gift, I'm prepared. I pull three twenties from the scrum of bills in my hand.

"Just kidding," he says. "First one's on me."

"You sure?" I ask, but he doesn't respond.

"You need a wallet," he says, as I stuff the money back into my pocket.

"I hate wallets. They're bad for your back. They make your spinal column uneven, or something."

"That's bull. A chiropractor told me it'd have to be a huge wallet." Jeremy mimes with his hands something like a boulder, and I laugh.

The high hits me real fast. I plop down on one of the couches. Jeremy sits on the other smaller one. Vague hints of the anxiety I felt when I arrived echo softly inside of me, but most of it dissipates quickly. I stare at the uneven wood walls, a series of vertical planks, of varying colors and lines; the prominent motif is tree rings—dark holes, where the trees' years spiral into a burnt center. I wonder if the wood is treated to stave off termites, or if this house is one infestation away from collapse. Who built this house, I wonder. Jack? Did Jack build this house? Is this "The House That Jack Built"? Was this the land that he worked by hand? Was this the dream of an uptight man? Wait. Is it *uptight* or *upright*?

I'm partial to Aretha Franklin's early-eighties output, *Get It Right* and *Jump to It* in particular, but I'm also a fan of the Atlantic years.

"The House That Jack Built" is a good song. Underrated song. Too short.

Also underrated, her duet with George Michael. It was a number one song, but it should have been number one for longer. Longer than some of the songs that are number one for months. One of the biggest travesties of justice in the pop music annals is that "One Sweet Day" by Mariah Carey and Boyz II Men was number one for sixteen weeks. I like Mariah Carey and Boyz II Men as much as, and possibly more than, the average person, but that is not the song that should represent the last fifty years of music. From a purely pop perspective, the Aretha-George duet is stronger, but it doesn't belong in the time capsule either, not as long as "Bust a Move" by Young MC, "What Have I Done to Deserve This" by Pet Shop Boys and Dusty Springfield, and "Little Red Corvette" by Prince exist. These are well-crafted pop songs that have managed to cannibalize genres of music and distill something unique, enjoyable, and timeless.

"Dude, you're traveling aren't you?" Jeremy asks.

"Wha? Maybe. A little."

"What are you thinking?"

"Nothing. Just staring at your walls."

Jeremy nods gently while laughing. He asks if I want him to turn on the TV.

The simple question is somehow ridiculous. It angers me too. "I saw you last night for the first time in twenty years, and you want to know if I want to watch TV? What, like *Everybody Loves Raymond*?"

"Okay. Chill."

"I am chill. I'm just being honest. If you turn on that TV, we're not going to talk. We're not going to catch up. I'm not going to know what's happened since—"

"Alright man. Didn't realize pot made you so intense."

"I'm not intense. Just curious."

"Go ahead then. Ask me a question. I'm open."

I can't think of one good question, so I blurt out every question, all the ones I've been holding onto for years, plus the ones I rehearsed in the car ride over here: "Did you go to college? Did you save up enough for that IROC you wanted? Did you date a lot after I left? Did you ever get your wisdom teeth pulled? Did you see the *Friday* sequels? Have you ever left the country? Where were you on 9/11? Were you upset when Prince died? Are you closeted? Did you vote for Bush either time? How about Trump? Does your wife know about me? Why the fuck didn't you come looking for me ever? Why didn't you meet me at the station like you were supposed to?"

The sudden softening of Jeremy's chin and the narrowing of his eyes suggest that he's about to laugh. The heat inside of me, heat that I'd carried around for the last twenty years, has left me suddenly. I feel cold, and my hands tingle. I wish I could measure my temperature so that I could prove to myself that I am in fact colder.

"Fuck, Andy. This shit's supposed to relax you."

"It did. I feel really good about getting that off my chest. Very very very really really really good."

Jeremy's face loses its peace. It reddens and tightens up, like a kid who's being caught sneaking out or back in. "Can't we just leave all that behind us? Let's start new."

"New? I'm here for a few days. I probably won't see you for another twenty years."

Those few words suck the air and the goodwill out of the room. I look down at my cuticles because I don't want to see his feelings. It occurs to me that I've never had a manicure before. Come to think of it, when I was ten, my father came into my room as I was filing my nails with my mother's emery board. "Am I raising a fruitcake?" he asked. The word he used was *mamplora*, a Central American colloquialism that he likely learned in this country, maybe even from my mother. A few years ago, my father accompanied my mother to a beauty salon and succumbed to his curiosity. Now he gets a mani-pedi every couple of months. I don't feel rancor about it. Just funny is all.

Shit, I'm high. Like really high, and I don't want Jeremy to answer my questions. I want to leave.

"Forget it. I was just—"

"Andy, I'm not gonna lie: I missed you. Apart from what, you know, we had, you were my best friend. And I'm real glad you're sitting here."

I remain silent. It feels like he's about to break up with me, twenty years later. Despite his vulnerability—his hand wringing and his cocked head—this amounts to a bullshit confession. In fact, I'm confused about what exactly he's confessing and a bit cross that he has decided to respond to questions that I didn't ask. A familiar tremble in my chest commences, not the trill that accompanies sex, but the one I get when I want to curse out a room, a cop, or a centrist. I focus intensely on the mechanics of standing up.

"Andy, don't go. Please, man."

I ignore him and walk toward the stairs.

"Two semesters of community college. That's all," he says. "My parents helped me buy a used IROC-Z that only had like fifty thousand miles, and I wrecked it a few months later. Drunk. Really fucking drunk. I was lucky to walk away with bruised ribs and a cut on my head." He points to an almost invisible scar on his forehead, at the base of his hairline. "My dad made me pay him back anyway. I didn't go out with anyone serious till Tonya. I fucked around. I fucked around a lot, but no one, like, steady. Yeah, I thought about you. All the time."

I turn back. He's standing, elbows akimbo, his hands interlaced at the knuckles, playing a thumb war with himself.

"What else? Oh, right. I got the two bottom wisdom teeth pulled. My face was real swollen. Like a cartoon character. My mom has pictures of it." Jeremy holds both hands out a few inches on either side of his face to mime the swelling. "I was living at my parents' still on 9/11. I was high as fuck and don't actually remember much about it. My dad knew a guy who worked in one of the smaller buildings. Everyone knew someone. And yeah, too bad about Prince, but you were the big fan. Actually, I thought about you when I saw the news. What was that song you played on repeat?"

"Don't remember."

"It was '7,' right? You loved that song."

In fact, I do like that song, but the one I played endlessly was "Gold." I nod and stare at him with the sort of abandon that no longer corresponds to our relationship. He stares back, and my eyes dart over to a portrait on the wall: a woman with two small children, one on her lap, one in her arms. Tonya, Ford, and Lincoln, I presume. She's light-skinned Black; the children are white-presenting, with thick curly hair. I wonder if Jeremy is the kind of guy who is only attracted to people who aren't white. Before Marco, I dated a guy like that. He had a fetish for brown men. Always checking them out. Always telling me how "fucking hot" I was. His reverence got old by the third month. Eventually, he moved to North Carolina to teach Spanish at a middling university. I wonder if Jeremy has ever slept with a white person. I'm scared to ask. I don't know how to ask such a thing. Is this preoccupation something I should bring up in therapy?

"What about Bush and Trump and the *Friday* sequels?" I ask.

"I voted for Dubya the first time because I wanted something different. I wasn't really thinking. It was the first time I could vote, okay? I didn't know the guy was going to be an idiot. And this last time, I didn't vote for anyone."

I don't say anything because it won't be anything nice. Youth, after all, is no excuse for abject stupidity. Few politicians don't suck, but why pick the one that sucks the most? George W. Bush? Really?

"Was that all your questions? Oh, *Friday*! The third one was better than the second, but not much. They weren't the same without that guy. The one from *Rush Hour*."

"Chris Tucker," I say.

10

BAGELS

My mother works in a narrow L-shaped office with four women her age, all of whom have stiff joints, grandchildren, sciatica, couch-potato husbands, uneven vertebrae, mild alcoholism, white skin, dyed blond hair, thick, tight-jawed regional accents, smokers' voices, phlegmy coughs, and debt. My mother is tired, but won't accept my offer to supplement her pension so that she can stay home. "I like to feel useful," she says. "I've spent too much of my life sitting in this house, and I don't want my final days to be that way too."

One of the paltry perks of an otherwise miserable job is that my mother doesn't work on Thursdays. It's her day for a bagel breakfast.

"I'm allowed to indulge a bit from time to time," she says, interpreting my early morning bleariness as judgment and internalizing her own craving as sin. "Everything in moderation, including moderation. Everything in moderation, including moderation." My mother repeats this mantra to herself while smoothing her hands along her sides down to her hips, as if to redistribute her weight.

Weight. Overweight. Fat. Obese. Healthy. Skinny. Thin. Diet. Over-weight. Fat. Weight Watchers. Jenny Craig. All my life, I've witnessed my mother's struggles. My brother's, too. Also my dad's. And our neighbor Pat-ty's. On the one hand, society's limited beauty standards are a pox on us all, but on the other hand, cortisol. My mother eats small portions and healthy meals, and she's always been active—Jane Fonda's workouts, Tae Bo, power walking, jogging, yoga, Pilates. None of which has proved useful in the battle against the invisible beasts—loneliness, isolation, condescension, self-doubt, fear, loathing, anxiety—who have the home-court advantage in a society that values competition and trumpets personal responsibility while side-eyeing cooperation and denigrating help.

"Lox for me, capers, onions and tomatoes. On a gluten-free bagel. With low-sodium cream cheese. Your father can have half a pumpernickel with tofu cream cheese."

"Do they sell bagels by the half?"

"Very funny." My mother bobbles her head softly and rolls her eyes. "Take my car; it's cleaner than your father's."

"I'm going to the place that's just a few blocks away, no?"

"Between el Chino and your friend's church."

"Paul's not my friend!"

"I'm sorry. Your ex-friend. Anyway, you're right to walk. Exercise is very important. I would go with you if it weren't for my back." Just then, she winces with all of her face. She sets her palm flat on the kitchen counter and emits a sad, exaggerated groan.

For my mother, the only shame greater than limited mobility is the thought of someone misconstruing her immobility as laziness. Even her poor health needs to announce itself in order to be heard.

"Here." My mother pulls a folded twenty from the purse resting on the kitchen counter.

"No."

"Por favor," she says. "You're already doing enough for us."

I take the twenty, so as not to insult her. Later, I will slip it back into her purse.

My mother isn't only paying for bagels, she's compensating me for my discomfort. She knows that it pains me to leave this house. Rather consistently over the last twenty years, I haven't offered to go to the market, I never went bowling with Henry, I resisted all of my mother's attempts at dining out, I went to the movies only for matinee showings on non-holidays. On some visits, I didn't even step out onto the patio.

I hate this place. I hate the town, the neighboring towns, the towns I used to know well, the towns I've never been to, the highways, the main roads, the side roads, the back roads, the left-turn arrows, the no-right-on-red signs, the speeding, the tailgating, the railroad crossings, the parking lots, the malls, the houses, the lawns, the people—above all, the people. The very notion of suburbs. I hate all of it. As far as I can tell, the suburbs are where people go to preserve their ignorance, in service of a delusion they've mistaken for a dream. They tired of the more interesting human experiment and fled. Cowards, the lot. Working class, middle class, and one-percenters alike.

Or maybe I'm just cranky about how early it is. Maybe there are suburbs that work, and it's all more subtle than I've imagined. Maybe some folks have no choice. Anything is possible, I guess. What I am certain of is that I'm embarrassed by this place. And I wish I didn't ever have to return.

It's seven-thirty in the morning, and the warmth is yet bearable. I make my way through the warren of houses, all with a half-timber design redolent of old German villages. The gables, roofs, and windows are framed in dark wood beams, and small red-brick chimneys jut out of all the housetops. The few neighbors I remember from my youth have died or moved to warmer climates; I don't recognize any of the bald or gray-haired domes popping up above fences or any of the sour, wrinkled faces with disdainful eyebrows ducking into cars. No one deigns to greet. This is exactly as it was when I was a child, except I wasn't as attuned to old-white-people incivility back then. I didn't know enough to be slighted by their lack of eye contact and the absence of a hello.

All of this makes me want to walk around with a bullhorn: *My family has been here longer than you! Go back to where you came from! Ireland and Italy are no longer experiencing famine or authoritarianism. The coast is clear!*

The one friendly face belonged to Patty, who moved south recently. Her kids found her an assisted living community with manicured lawns and amenities that she can't properly take advantage of because of her damaged hip and knees. "They all play golf. All day long," she texted me a few months ago. "Trump country but with delicious Spanish food. Come visit!"

Spanish food. She probably meant Cuban or Puerto Rican food.

After Henry died, Patty took to texting me brief missives once a week. *How are you? So proud of you.* Henry was like an honorary son to Patty, and now I've become one too.

Pavement. Pavement. Pavement. Garage. Lawn. Garage. Lawn. Speed bump. Garage. Lawn. Brief sidewalk. Windowless factory. Gray stucco. Windowless office building. Eggshell stucco. Pavement. Traffic light. Liquor store. Pizza place. Laundromat. Deli. Stationery store. Tae kwon do. Nail salon. Revamped 7-Eleven. Artificial lawn. Another brief sidewalk. Yoga studio. Chung's Kitchen. Bag-o-Bagels. Paul's church.

My childhood friend, the homophobic man of God with the small head and dodgy past, has been flickering, like a faulty bulb, in my mind since the reunion. I never told anyone about the tale Paul recounted to us all those years ago. At the time, I didn't see a point. I didn't want to be linked to his story. Neither the gay part nor the violent assault part. Although it pains me to admit it, I didn't feel any solidarity with the anonymous gay man.

And yet, in those days after Paul recounted his Steer Queer episode, all those years ago, I kept an eye on the news. At the time, it was a habit of mine to pick up the local paper from the old vendor who ran the kiosk across the street from St. Ignatius. I also browsed the regional paper that Sister Anne left on the library's reference desk after she'd finished reading it. I watched the news at night with my parents, and I listened to the radio in bed. There were murders, primarily in the city, but all of the violence seemed to happen between people who knew one another. Nothing came close to matching what Paul had told us.

I deduced that he had been exaggerating. Exaggeration, after all, was our dialect. Two kids couldn't have inflicted lasting damage on a grown man, I told myself.

And then came the reports. A body had been found in the back seat of a car, near the wooded area behind the movie theater, not far from an interstate rest stop—Steer Queer. There had been signs of blunt force head trauma. Apparently, he had been dead for several days when a security guard crossed the parking lot to investigate what he'd thought was an abandoned car.

It occurred to me to go to the police, but I couldn't get my dad's voice out of my head: No te metas en los problemas de los demás. It was like Cosa Nostra in our house: *Mind your business.* Despite society's, the Bible's, and Mr. Rogers's entreaties, I was raised to believe that getting involved in the lives of others was more trouble than it was worth, no matter if it was the right thing to do. Be nice to others, yes, but mind your business.

I didn't breathe a word of what I knew or suspected. Not to my parents, not to Henry, not to any friends, not even to Simone or Jeremy. I knew that once I told another person it would come back to haunt me.

I let it go rather quickly. Maybe it was the nature of my transient, adolescent brain. Or maybe I understood that being a snitch, in addition to brown and possibly a fag, was one descriptor too many. Besides, what if the guy in the car wasn't the guy that Paul and his friend had assaulted? Maybe that guy walked away with a black eye. I couldn't accuse Paul of something he hadn't done. And even if Paul had done it, maybe the victim's family didn't want the whole story. Maybe they didn't want to be associated with someone who frequented Steer Queer.

About the dead man. I recall that he was twenty-six, which at the time seemed ancient, and he was a bartender in the city

█ can't avoid Paul's repugnant little storefront church. Whether I'm walking or driving, it's on my route to every place I'm required to go—market, pharmacy, gas station, dad's medical appointments. It has a large, ostentatious neon sign in its window and dark maroon curtains that don't permit passersby even the remotest glimpse inside. *Jesus Rocks!* reads the electric pink cursive, instead of *This congregation is led by a murderer.* At the bottom of the storefront window is a phone number, and a schedule: Tuesdays, 6 P.M. and Sundays, 10:30 A.M. How, I wonder, can an evangelist operation offer only two services per week? Surely, they're not meeting the attendance or recruitment numbers they've set for themselves at the annual convention or around their cauldron. How do they pay to keep those neon lights on? How do they afford the rent?

The entire premise—Paul leading a religious community—is as baffling as it is bleak, like an independent film about a small-minded town that's bathed in self-hate and brims with delusion. I suspect that Paul is closeted and has sought refuge—cover, actually—in God, the primordial agent of obfuscation, the almighty beard.

"Anything else?" asks the redheaded late-teen with freckles and several necklaces. C-I-N-D-Y, reads the most prominent of the gold-plated chains hanging from her neck.

"No. That's all."

"Name?"

"Excuse me?"

"For the order?"

"Oh. Andrés."

"How do you spell that?"

"A-N-D-R-E-S. An accent over the E."

"What?"

"Nothing. Just kidding."

Cindy gives a half-hearted, fully munificent smile. She hands the slip of paper to an older frumpish woman in a hairnet slouching behind her, who then grabs the bagels from the corresponding bins and slices them swiftly. "Any of these toasted?" asks the faceless figure with a smoker's voice. "Yeah. All of them," responds Cindy.

"I'm going to grab an orange juice," I say.

"Sure. I'll ring you up over here when you're ready." The young worker devours her Rs, transforming "sure" into "shaw" and "over" into "ovah."

A small bell affixed to the front door rings.

"Good morning, Cindy!"

"Hi, Mr. K."

"What have I said about that?"

"Saw-ree. Hi, Paw-lee."

I don't need to turn around to confirm anything. I keep my head down and pretend to read through the labels of the juices, teas, and bottled caffeine drinks. The voice orders a dozen bagels, half plain, half rainbow, and two tubs of cream cheese: regular and tofu. "I have the whole family with me next door," he says. "Today is as good a day as any to praise our savior."

"Cool," Cindy says, as she waits for him to slide his credit card and punch in his PIN.

"When am I going to get you over there?"

Cindy remains silent for a moment, eyeing the card-reader's screen. "Hit *OK*," she says. "Sorry, Mr. K, but my mom says we're Catholics, and we go to church on Sundays."

"God is available to us every day, at any time, Cindy. He's here," he says. I crane my neck and, just as I suspected, he's pointing to the spot where his heart is located, which no doubt has been shriveled into a prune-like organ by his lifetime of lies.

My thighs are getting tight from squatting, but I don't want to get up and risk being identified. I continue reading the labels for the countless varieties of orange juice—pulp, no pulp, partial pulp, vitamin D fortified, from concentrate, not from concentrate, with grapefruit, with passion fruit. All of the bottles are made of plastic, and I can't help but multiply the number of containers in this display case by the number of stores in this neighborhood, then, by the number of neighborhoods in this town, and so on, until I imagine something like 7,534,220,160 bottles. I multiply this by 365 days per year, and suddenly, the destruction of Earth vis-à-vis climate change and ruptured whale bellies makes perfect sense.

"ANN-duhrs! Order's up!"

I remain low to the ground, where the air is cool, pretending not to hear my botched name, but Cindy is persistent. "Sir? Hello?" she says several times. "Your bagels are ready." I reach into my pocket and pull out the vape pen. I bring it surreptitiously to my lips and pull much too forcefully before exhaling into my shirt, which absorbs nothing, allowing a sparse plume to expand over the display case. If Cindy has spotted my indiscretion, she's keeping it to herself. I make a harried peace with the possibility that I won't escape Bag-o-Bagels unscathed. I raise a hand toward Cindy, to both acknowledge that I am aware of my outstanding debts and to let her know that I require more time.

After the first inkling of weightlessness, I make my way toward the counter, all the while keeping my back to Paul. I set down five one-liter bottles of orange juice—my parents and I are not juice drinkers, but these bottles have become lifelines, like branches and roots jutting out from the banks of a rapid river, as I stare out at a waterfall in the near distance. I cannot let them go. I buy everything. Cindy bags the orange juice separately from the bagels. I make no effort to retrieve the small collapsible bag from my pocket. I wave, nod, and bite my lower lip all at once. I turn my gaze downward, pretend to inspect the small receipt, and make my way toward the door.

"Andy?" rings out.

Paul collars me, just as my hand lands on the door. I keep on, pretending. "Andrés!" he shouts. "Soy Pablo!"

I have no choice but to whip around with affected surprise. "Paul?"

"Yeah, man. Pretty good, no? My Spanish?"

Before I can respond, Paul grabs the hand that holds the receipt and pulls me in for a big manly hug, replete with back slapping. "Good to see you, bro. I heard you were at the reunion, but I got there late. I must have just missed you. How you been?"

"I'm alright. Can't complain."

Paul's intense grin and glinty eyes suggest genuine happiness, but I assume it's a ploy to get me to join his church or to have sex with him, so that he can throw up and begin all over again, like a homosexual bulimia. I've seen this movie before. He probably has sex with men all the time, but doesn't kiss on the lips, and after ejaculating, he snaps and kicks them out of his house or car or church, or maybe he kills them and cooks them down into small wafers that he then feeds to his congregants. Maybe he infuses the Jesus crackers with pot, in a new-age-y Christian sort of way—or is the Jesus-as-bread phenomenon strictly Catholic?

"I'm next door," he says. "Wait a second. I'll walk out with you."

Paul takes the enormous brown bag of bagels and stuffs it into a thin plastic bag that Cindy holds open for him. It looks like a sack of potatoes wearing a condom.

Paul follows me outside. "My wife is inside with the kids," he says, while pointing to his storefront. "Let me introduce you. She's Cuban. That's how come my Spanish is so good." He laughs heartily at himself, but I don't know which part of what he just said is the joke.

"I wish I could, but I'm—"

"Ah, here's my little man. Milo Joseph, say hi."

The little kid is somewhere between three and six years old. He has dark curly hair and a complexion somewhere between Paul's pasteurized cow milk and my lightly roasted almond. This is the child he and I would have made if such a thing were possible.

"He can be shy," says Paul. "C'mon, MJ, say hi to daddy's friend."

Paul starts to get a bit flustered, and now I'm worried he's one of these parents that flips out when their kids don't do exactly as they're told.

"It's alright, man. He doesn't know me. And I really have to run," I say, which isn't far from the truth. I can already feel one of the orange juice bottles sweating through the paper bag and condensing onto the plastic.

"And here she is, Miss America!" Paul blurts out, in a singsongy way. "Let me introduce you to my wife." Paul extends his knuckly hand toward the petite, hourglass woman walking in our direction. Her face, too, is an hourglass, pinched below the cheekbones. She is clearly the carrier of the dark-and-curly genes. There's a small girl with her thumb in her mouth and a tiara on her head standing beside her. Another child, much younger and swaddled in white, rests in Miss America's arm.

"Honey," she calls out. "The boys are hungry and they're playing with the organ."

Boys? That's five kids by my count. The sack of bagels makes sense. Paul is a no-contraceptive family guy.

"Honey, this is Andrés. A friend since elementary school. Andy, this is mi mujer, Graciela."

"Pleasure to meet you," she says.

Paul's bilingualism is beginning to annoy me. I don't think he's ever once heard me speak Spanish. Not even in school, where I took French. I wonder if Graciela is also put off by his linguistic flourishes. The passivity of her face suggests she's fine with it, possibly proud. And why shouldn't she be? Landing a pale, polyglot prophet must feel like quite a coup.

"Nice to meet you, too," I respond. For a split second, I imagine outing her husband as both a gay man and a murderer.

"He speaks Spanish, too," Paul says, as if he's trying to set me and his wife up on a date.

"That's great, Pauly." The exasperation fraying Graciela's voice betrays her soft smile. She is a person who doesn't want to be trapped in the morning humidity, in an excessively manicured microplaza.

"Where are you from?" I ask, before immediately remembering that Paul already told me and despite detesting the question itself.

"Cuba," she says.

Cuban. Wonderful. I bet she's one of these right-wing types who want all of us to suffer through their PTSD because their parents or grandparents were wealthy landowners who lost their estancias when Castro took over. On the other hand, Castro took it too far. Then again, trying to practice self-determination in the shadow of empire can test anyone's humanity. None of this, however, amounts to a valid explanation for supporting twenty-first-century Republicans.

"And you?" she asks.

I tell her that my father is from Colombia and my mother from El Salvador—after all, it's true.

"That's nice," she says.

There's nowhere useful to go from this point onward. I look down at the strip of grass separating us from the parked cars. It's an extremely bright green, shorn like a military haircut. A few yards away, cars whiz through the heat, steam curling up from the road. Across an ocean, Venus Williams is playing her match against a surly Latvian player known more for her tantrums than her abilities, despite having both.

"I should get going," I say.

"Come by some time," says Graciela. "Our church welcomes everyone."

"You sure you don't have time to come see the place?" asks Paul.

"Wish I could, but—" And, just like that, I realize that I'm high, high above my feelings. I'm looking down on this scene not only from above but from a future point. Not continuing this conversation suddenly feels shortsighted, unnecessarily cold, and a little cowardly. "You know what? Sure. I'd love to see your space."

The large, low-ceilinged room has vibrant blue carpeting and stacks of folded white chairs resting along the gray walls. Three stained-glass triangles dangle over the short stage on the far side of the room, like a mobile over a crib. Off to one side are a large standing keyboard, various stools, mic stands, and three black-matted metal podiums. In a corner, I spot a large wooden instrument with tiered keyboards and long vertical pipes rising from its back. The organ has the glossy veneer and splintered edges of something old and rescued. Instead of a house of worship, the space resembles a recording studio or a basement music venue that should be littered with beer bottles and whisky glasses. I count four electric candelabras, three on the makeshift altar in the center of the raised stage and one on a collapsible table decorated in pamphlets.

Graciela gives a reverential nod and disappears through a side door, with the bagels and a tail of humorless children, each one shorter than the one in front of them.

Paul reaches beneath one of the tables, past the draping cloth, and pulls out a guitar.

"You play?" I ask.

"A little, mostly our hymns."

"And probably some GNR?"

Paul was an obsessive Guns N' Roses fan with an endless collection of their T-shirts. During a string of Halloweens in elementary school, he dressed up as every member of the band, at least once.

"Wow. I haven't thought about them in a long time," he says. "We limit the type of music we play in front of the children."

"Like *Footloose*."

"What?"

"Nothing. How about some 'Paradise City'?"

"You're testing me," he says and grins. "How about this?" Paul sits on one of the four-legged wooden stools and pulls the guitar's strap over his head and shoulder. He lines up his fingers on its ridged neck with one hand; with the other, he strums a few unrecognizable chords. He tightens an ivory-colored peg and repositions his fingers. "This is easier on a piano, but let's see what I can do." He strums once forcefully before switching into a subtle, more graceful movement, something almost classical sounding. It continues for some time.

Paul's quivery voice commences as a whisper, more talking than singing. His small, perfectly round head remains low as he stares, not at me, but out at the empty space beyond us, an imaginary audience. He's sitting in the penumbra of the domineering fluorescence above, doing his best to recreate "November Rain," the Guns N' Roses song. Despite Paul's pleasant voice and adept plucking, he goes on for longer than he should. I'm reminded of the endlessness of this song.

"That's all I remember," Paul says unconvincingly and leans the guitar against the podium. "You a fan?" he asks.

Something about Axl Rose's frenetic swagger and unkempt appearance kept me from the music. I owned the first album, the one with "Welcome to Jungle," but I never listened to it. "Not really. Kinda fair-weather. But I remember you and Mikey C. were really into them."

"That's true," Paul says. "Mikey C., wow. Blast from the past. Someone told me he moved to the West Coast." Paul's lips widen into a half smile. "Mikey C., man. Good memory."

"You'd be surprised at all the things I remember," I say.

Paul squints at me briefly before smiling. He slides the guitar back under the table.

"My wife's like that. Great memory. Maybe it's a Latin thing."

An N of two isn't much of a sample size, I think.

Paul shimmies the weighty podium into the center of the spotlight and looks around the room, as if he's thinking, *There, now everything is in its place.*

"Or maybe it's just that some things are especially memorable," I continue. "You, always wearing those Guns N' Roses shirts. I remember that. I remember your Simpsons impressions and the pranks in class. I also remember that you changed in high school. You were a super nice and friendly guy, who suddenly bulked up and—"

"Lots of guys started working out in high school. My dad had weights in the basement. It was easy to do."

"Yeah, I guess. But you know what else I remember—"

"Shoot, I didn't even ask you if you wanted something to drink. My bad," he says.

"I have a year's worth of orange juice in this bag," I respond. "I'm good. But what I remember, Paul, is a story you once told. In the cafeteria. About Steer Queer."

"What?" Paul runs his hand through his buzz cut and scratches the back of his neck. "Like I said, it's my wife who remembers everything. I have a terrible memory."

"You don't remember going to Steer Queer with a friend and picking up a guy?"

"What the—"

"A guy who you beat up and left for dead in an empty parking lot?"

"Shit man. That's . . . that's not. I don't remember that." Paul's face is somewhere between crimson and neon red. "I'm sure it was a joke. You know how we were back then, always talking big."

"This one was pretty big. Did you know that not long after you told that story a guy was found dead in his car near Steer Queer?"

Paul begins blinking and stuttering. If I didn't abhor this man, I'd feel sorry for him.

"Li-listen, man. I-I don't know wh-what this is about, but, uh, I don't want any trouble. We all make mistakes, but I've accepted Jesus into my life. I'm not the same person anymore. Do you believe—"

"I believe you beat a person unconscious and left him for dead. And I believe that person had parents and friends and maybe a dog who were all damaged forever because of it."

Paul stands perfectly still with his eyes staring blankly and his mouth flattened into an oval, a Jesus fish without a tail.

"What the fuck are you doing?" he asks. "I mean, did someone send you here? Who?"

"Dude, I was just buying bagels, and you came to me. Then you pushed me to meet your wife. And you insisted I come here. You could have left well enough alone."

It's the pot. I'd never have mustered the courage to be this forward otherwise. Problem is, I need another hit. I can feel myself falling back to Earth. Paul's contorted face wakes me to the pain I've inflicted. Without realizing it, I've clenched my fists inside my pockets. No matter how harsh, inappropriate, or poorly planned this encounter is, it's in a way justified, I tell myself. Frankly, it feels good to see a bully losing control, even if I, too, am now a bully.

Paul drops onto one knee with an anvil's gravity. Then the second knee comes down. His hands meet and his fingers enlace. His wounded face is soft; it transforms quickly into something wide and serene. "Our lord and savior Jesus Christ. I accept your challenge against the devil. I will overcome this as I have the many obstacles you have rightfully placed at my feet. I will be the man you have destined me to be. I beg of you to give me strength—"

The door through which Paul's family disappeared earlier opens. "Pauly, are you going to eat—Pauly? What's going on?" asks Graciela. She looks up at me, and I feel the clouds dissipate. I've woken from a nap I had no business taking. "What have you done?" she asks me.

I don't respond and instead reach down for my bags of bagels and juice. "It was nice to meet you," I say.

I leave the sinner and his beards in place and rush out.

I feel like a newborn: raw and easily stimulated. Even the warm air feels strange on my skin—I will need to buy more of this stuff from Jeremy before I head back to the city. I begin walking, at first slowly, but then with more pace. Paul might seek retribution, I tell myself. I've opened a can of worms, certainly. Or maybe I've given him a necessary jolt. I set the orange juice and bagels on the ground, a stretch of sidewalk that ends in about fifty feet, and pull the pot pen from my pocket. I take a long hit and hold it in my chest until I have no choice but to exhale.

Wait a second! Was Paul referring to me as the devil himself, or just an emissary of the dark lord?

It dawns on me that if I had taken my mother's car, I might never have crossed paths with Paul.

11
HENRY

Henry was diagnosed with diabetes when he was twenty-one, nearly fifty years younger than his grandfather was when he was diagnosed with diabetes in Colombia.

For as long as Henry could remember, his parents hadn't only warned him not to overeat, they'd begged him not to. There was Tía Marta on dialysis, Abuelo Hipólito who'd died, Patty who had to inject herself regularly with insulin, one of Rosario's coworkers who was always dizzy, and a couple of elderly neighbors who'd had their feet or legs amputated. All of them clear warnings, ignored.

There were reminders too. Andy regularly made fun of his weight. Once-a-year relatives commented on how chubby he'd gotten at Thanksgiving or Christmas. So had a few of the kids at school. So had the department store labels. So had the mirror. The language varied—"¡Despacio! No comas tan rápido!" or "Fuck you, you fat slob!" or "¡Ay, mi gordito tan lindo!" or "Do I smell bacon, or are those your thighs rubbing together?" or *Husky & Hefty Boys' Uniforms*—but the message was the same: Henry was a loser, incapable of taking care of the one thing that belonged to him, of which he was the primary expert—his body.

Henry wasn't oblivious to his ballooning size, his limitless diet, or his indulgent behaviors, but they were his wild horses—uncooperative, unexplainable, inoperable. Change was unappealing. A slice of pizza was a momentary joy, but an entire pie all to himself was a unique rush that Henry regretted only in the moments after the food reached his stomach, before it passed through his intestines. And then it was time for the next moment of joy—immediate, quantifiable, reliable, distracting, and above all, of his own doing. Why would he sacrifice this proximate happiness for fear of distant consequences? There'd be time to change, he always believed. The interval between now and later.

As an adult, Henry's gluttony was exacerbated by the drum of life, but its inception had come much earlier. He, Álvaro, Rosario, and Andy had lived under a regime of scarcity—they were a family unaware of climate change but inadvertently doing their part to slow it down. Everything was in short supply. Everything was expensive. Close the doors quickly, the AC is on. Close the window, the heat is on. Turn off the lights. Don't leave a bite of food on your plate. Use less of everything. Keep eating. Slow down. Keep eating. Be good. Keep eating. Behave. Lose weight. Do better. Keep eating. A better future. You're going to get sick. A better life. Keep eating.

But there was no better in sight. If there was a critical juncture, Henry had missed it, he thought. He waited instead for a sign. A moment where he might turn all of this around. *Dear God, give me a chance,* he thought in the quiet. But everything continued unchanged. And soon he realized that the only thing worse than worse was remaining the same. Better was not to think about it. Better was to pack a bowl and super-size his second dinner. In his always-distant future, he saw nothing, and there was absolutely nothing wrong with ignoring nothing.

In his final week of high school, Henry rewrote papers and retook exams so that he might finish in time—a kindness from a few sympathetic teachers, as well as an administrative favor, more to keep up the school's reputation than his. Later that summer, he took a check to the community college, but when classes began, he found himself instead smoking pot with friends and being late or not going at all. After his first failed semester, Henry picked up more hours at Uncle Billy's, the electronics and appliance store where he'd worked during his last year of high school. Ikbir, the owner, was flexible with the schedule and thought him a better worker than the others, middle-aged white men who'd resisted the change in ownership and who refused to do anything but sell. Henry, however, was rarely precious. He stocked merchandise, sold large-screen television sets, walked people to their cars, placed the boxes inside their trunks or tied them to their roofs. He swept and wiped and polished. He affixed stickers onto new boxes and picked stickers off of older ones. He worked like an immigrant, Ikbir thought.

But Ikbir was mistaken. Only one generation could be the immigrants. Ikbir, Rosario, and Álvaro had very little room for the contemplation, wallowing, and failure that befell their children.

"You're the only one who works. These guys have been doing this for so long they forgot what it means to sweat." Ikbir often grew frustrated with the second-, third-, and fourth-generation Italian and Irish salesmen he'd inherited when he bought the store. These men knew what they were worth and they knew how far they had fallen. It had been a long time since anyone had expected anything of them.

Henry was glad to have the discounts on the CD and DVD players, on the new TV for his room, on the fridge and washer-dryer for his parents for Christmas and their anniversary. He was happy, too, to have a paycheck; money to spend on baseball cards, fast food, wrestling magazines, CDs that he never listened to, limited-edition coins advertised on cable, and pot. Each bringing its own joy. Henry was paid on Fridays and broke again by Tuesday. A rut of his own making. And yet, most of his needs were being met, so it never dawned on him to worry, to do something different or drastic. There was yet time to change course.

t's normal to be a little jealous. Everyone gets jealous." Patty spoke quickly and kept her eyes on the road, knowing the words would sting.

"I'm not jealous! He worked hard for this, and he deserves all of it. Over there—I see an open spot next to the station wagon."

Patty had picked Henry up after work and driven him to Athena's, the diner where their families often celebrated birthdays and graduations. Rosario, Álvaro, Andy, and Patty's kids, Vincent and Monica, were already wedged inside of two adjacent booths. All of them there to honor Andy and Vincent, who'd gotten their college acceptance letters.

"Really, I'm not lying. It's not that I'm jealous."

"Then what is it?"

"I just—I feel like a loser. Like I should have done all these things first."

"There's still time, honey. You're so young."

"I know, but—this is going to sound stupid, but I just don't feel like the big brother anymore." Henry's voice trembled, and he went quiet. He unbuckled his seatbelt, buttoned up his work shirt—the same white oxford he'd worn in high school—and unpinned his name tag.

"Doesn't matter. You'll be the big brother in some ways, and he'll be the big brother in other ways. That's normal. You'll see. With time."

After Andy left for college, Henry's avenues of escape narrowed. Every day was suffused with reminders of his failures, failures that lingered and layered over themselves, until they became a great weight capable of tipping him over and pinning him to the ground. Although several of his classmates had also stayed home and commuted to college, those kids didn't seem affected by their parents' expectations, or they were better equipped to manage them. Henry, however, could feel the disappointment and, at times, disgust in the room. He knew what his parents thought of him now. The pity on their faces had replaced the desperate hope.

All of this was made unbearable by the stubbornness of time. It never, not for one moment, slowed. Every day, every week, every month sped past, making a reversal increasingly unlikely. "It's embarrassing to be twenty in a classroom full of eighteen-year-olds," he said to Andy when he'd tried to talk him into going back to school. To be twenty-one in a room full of eighteen-year-olds. To be twenty-three in a room full of eighteen-year-olds. To be twenty-five. Thirty. Thirty-one. Whatever it was that was transporting Henry through this life never slowed down long enough for him to hop off.

Never mind why. *How* did this happen? *When* did it happen? We fed them the same baby food. They watched the same television shows. They wore the same clothes and went to the same schools." Rosario pushed her hand carelessly through the air, as if she were unaware that it was holding a glass full of Cabernet.

"Honey, why don't you give me that?" Patty said, while prying the glass from Rosario.

"You know what? They didn't like the same wrestlers. Henry liked André the Giant, and Andy liked the Beefcake Brute."

"Brutus the Barber, I think." Patty laughed a small laugh into her hand before giggling took hold and gave way to jiggling. Then the snorting. "Maybe it's Beefcake Barber the Brute?"

"Patty, stop. This is serious. Henry is ruining his future, and I can't do anything about it."

Patty composed herself and pressed her elbow onto the arm of the sofa in order to get to her feet. "Oh Lord," she said, while rubbing her kneecaps. "I'm going to need new knees."

"Are they expensive?"

"Jason's insurance covers them, but I'm not going under. Doctor says at my weight I might not wake up again. He wants me to lose forty pounds before he'll operate. Can you believe that? How can I exercise if my knees don't work?"

Rosario's eyes were shiny and reddened. She attempted a look of incredulity but ended up closing one eye involuntarily and leaving the other half-open. Even sober, she wasn't good at dissembling what she was feeling, which in this case amounted to *You have no one to blame but yourself.* Rosario, too, struggled with her weight; she was nowhere near the stick figure she'd been when she first came to this country, but that was her problem alone, she thought. Whatever happened to Rosario, Rosario deserved it. And whatever happened to Patty was Patty's fault.

"Everyone has their strengths." Patty pulled car keys from her large, worn leather purse full of dried and broken cosmetics, breath mints, packets of protein-shake powder. "Henry will figure his out. No point in beating yourself up for what you had no control over."

"Maybe."

Rosario often thought back to the neonatal ward of the hospital in the city where Andrés was born. She'd been afraid to have a baby in a suburban hospital, fearing they were ill-equipped to handle an emergency. She'd visited the one only a few miles from their home, but something about it had been eerie. "Estaba limpio, pero había algo—no sé—too quiet. Not unfriendly, but not nice. Prefiero la ciudad," she'd explained to Álvaro.

Luckily, they were visiting Álvaro's sister in the city when Rosario's abdomen tightened and the pain began. Every day of the subsequent six weeks, Rosario sat waiting outside of the room full of incubators for a chance to hold Andrés. It was there that she met the elderly Boricua who was visiting his granddaughter and his great-granddaughter.

"Todo va a estar bien," said the old man.

Rosario pretended not to hear. Rarely had anything worthwhile come of listening to a perfect stranger. This stranger, however, was old, and with age came wisdom, Rosario believed. She also found it difficult to ignore him because he was saying exactly what she wanted to hear. El viejito shuffled over to her, a wool cap under his arm and large moles across his face. "No se preocupe. Bebés prematuros son muy inteligentes."

Maybe that was the reason, Rosario wondered over the years. Maybe the differences between Enrique and Andrés were far out of her control. Andrés, after all, had been forced to work harder from the beginning. Maybe. But she feared another truth: she'd placed too much pressure on Enrique. Instead of deflecting the world's hatred, it'd pierced her, until she'd withstood all that she could, until it began to come out of her and pierced the very ones she'd sought to protect.

Rosario's distaste for and fear of the world had become a lens through which Enrique viewed everything. He hadn't known how to interact with the other kids because he hadn't been exposed to anyone. He didn't know how to interpret himself because he'd never been permitted to be himself. He hadn't ever been allowed to raise his voice (either in joy or from pain) or fall down or run fast. He believed that the only way to be in the world was to be seen and not heard, and preferably unseen too. Both Enrique the boy and Enrique the young man were lonely, fearful people who lacked agency and a proper sense of control over themselves and the world around them. Rosario wished she couldn't see this truth so clearly. She wondered, too, if her son ever would.

At least the classroom portion of his life was over. The daily, inescapable nightmare full of judgment: dreading the questions he couldn't answer, regretting that he hadn't answered the ones he could have, aware of everyone, of all their clothes, muscles, waistlines, cars, gazes, and their facility with each other. Everyone seemed to socialize so naturally, while for him, the business of interaction was merely another exam for which he hadn't studied.

Henry had always found it difficult to retain what little he'd learned in school. Over time, the droning adult at the front of the room became irrelevant to him; whatever was being taught depended on the lessons that had already been taught. It was too late. Occasionally, a class caught Henry's interest, like the day he learned about the Krebs cycle or when he read "Gift of the Magi" or that day in fifth grade when Sister Susan taught them a mnemonic device for the order of operations (Please Excuse My Dear Aunt Sally = Parentheses, Exponents, Multiplication, Division, Addition, Subtraction). In those moments, when learning made sense or approached fun, Henry's posture became rigid. He'd line up his pen and pencil neatly to one side of his notebook. He'd make an effort to write down everything he heard. He'd clean out his backpack. He'd do his homework. But by the second or third day of being a serious student, he'd be back to slouching and gazing.

Often Henry wondered how the others retained the information that in his mind formed a miasma of words and numbers he couldn't see or store coherently. Henry never told anyone, not even Patty, that the reason he cut so many classes was simply fear. He was afraid of being wrong, of being late, of being stupid, of being criticized.

In his own way, Henry tried. He wasn't, after all, immune to the joys that accompanied attention and camaraderie, even if he found the rituals trying and arbitrary. Some kids were popular and some weren't, and he couldn't say definitively why. Over time, Henry gravitated toward meek people—friends, and eventually girlfriends—who loved his ribald, attention-grabbing humor, who let him have his way, who tolerated his intransigence, and who coddled his insecurities. His way, or no way. Henry was the sort of person who would give a classmate his only pen, cover his coworkers' shifts regardless of the impact on his own life, and let the other drivers go first at all-way stop signs, but he was also possessive and mercurial, quick to berate or disown a friend who didn't bend to his will or who crossed boundaries that he'd never demarcated clearly. A rogue pawn exerting control over the other pawns. Made sense. Henry wasn't only being Henry, he was being human, trying any way that he could to empower himself, to find the moments of control over his life, the same control that all living things require for survival.

In their final years of living together, Andy and Henry spoke only when it was necessary. They rarely fought as they had when they were younger, but the distance between them widened. Andy viewed Henry just as Henry viewed himself, as half the person he could have been. When Henry wasn't working or skipping class, he busied himself playing video games, watching baseball, and occasionally bowling with friends or the crew from Billy's. Andy, for his part, was never home. He'd already begun the escape. When he wasn't at cross-country or track practice, he was bussing tables at a catering hall that specialized in lower-middle-class weddings, or he was out with any number of friends, most recently Jeremy, the kid who drove the Grand Am with the flashy silver rims. If Henry and Andy crossed paths at all, it was in the morning, outside the bathroom.

"Hurry up in there! I'll be late for school!"

"I don't give a shit!"

"Don't use up all the hot water!"

"You can always piss on yourself."

"Fuck off."

Or they might meet in the kitchen on a Wednesday evening, when neither of them was working, before their parents came home.

"Could you wash a dish for once in your life?"

"What if you washed your ass crack once in a while?"

"You're an asshole."

"Is that what you like to eat?"

"Fuck off."

Henry and Andy had never been friends, but they'd been allies. To them, it seemed that they were the only two of their kind in the entire neighborhood. The only two with parents who spoke broken English, who worked long hours, and who were always a mix of tired, angry, and affectionate. But a bit of independence gave them the room and propulsion to speed along different trajectories, like a firework that splits in midair.

Somewhere in the final months of living together, their relationship changed again. Andy had caught Henry cutting class a few times, but on each occasion, Henry had acquitted himself by arguing that college was different. "The professors cancel class all the time," he said. "They let you do what you want. They don't care as long as you get the work done."

Andy was unforgiving. He'd been denied use of the family car his senior year so that Henry could drive to school. Andy had Jeremy or Marie to drive him, or one of the Nicoles, and in the worst case, the bus. But driving in the final year of high school was a rite of passage, and missing out had left Andy bitter.

"This is the only way for your brother to get to school," Rosario explained. "We can't give him an excuse to fail."

Andy detested the pitiful and futile coddling his brother received. Henry, in his eyes, made choices, and he should have faced the consequences. More than once, Andy suggested to his parents that they kick Henry out. "He's not a kid! He can find his own place and take care of himself." But Rosario and Álvaro never, even at the heights of their frustration with Henry, entertained the notion of keeping him anything but close, safe. They'd each been younger than Henry when they'd left their countries and their families, and although they never admitted it to each other or to themselves, and certainly not to their children, they regretted their exoduses. Rosario in particular had spent nearly twenty years longing to have her mother, her sister, and her aunts around to help her, to feed her, to comb her hair, to link arms with her on evening strolls, to keep an eye on her children, so that she might go out dancing with Álvaro or get her hair cut or go to the mall or simply put her feet up on a table or a couch. Álvaro, too, had long ago accepted that there was no *living* in this country, only working, but he didn't allow himself to dwell on a mistake that had brought into his life what little he loved. Henry hadn't lived up to their expectations, but Rosario and Álvaro believed that his life would only get worse if he were out in the world alone.

Andy burst into their room and pulled the plug on the game console while Henry was playing Super Mario 64—a slightly dented console returned to Uncle Billy's, which Ikbir couldn't resell or send back to his supplier. This sort of bold move might have ended, even a year earlier, with Andy in a headlock, but the brothers had matured to a place full of threats and little physical violence.

"What the fu—" Henry shouted, as he shot up to his feet.

"What the fuck did you do with the money? Did you keep it?"

Henry's anger was immediately cleaved in two, reduced to something nearer to annoyance. He sat back down on the carpeted floor. "What are you talking about?"

Andy recognized Henry's retreat as an admission.

"That was your school that just called. The bursar's office. They want to be paid. The tuition? They said you haven't been to class in a month."

"Don't worry about it."

"You stole mom and dad's money? What's wrong with you?"

Henry remained silent, cross-legged, staring at his own reflection in the dark television screen.

"Why are you even doing this? Can't you just be honest? If you don't want to go to school, don't go!"

Henry pulled the flesh inside of his mouth between his teeth, leaving his rounded, mildly acned face narrower, but he didn't look up at his brother; instead he stared straight ahead, reacting as he always had when their parents backed him into a corner.

"This is a new low, even for you," said Andy.

"You don't understand shit."

"You're right. This is insane. Don't you care? Don't you want to get out of here? Don't you want to do better? Better than all this?" Andy extended his arm in a way that left Henry wondering if he'd meant the room, the house, or this life.

Henry remained silent for a moment, fiddling with the game controller in his hands, before saying, "No."

"Of course not. I mean, you really are a loser. You just take up space, but don't contribute anything. And you'll probably get away with it, cuz you always do. Maybe you'll even get a new car out of it."

Andy marched toward the door, but his anger by that point had grown so great that he wasn't capable of leaving without first unloading more. "You know what? You deserve all of the shit that comes your way. You're going to have a crap life, but I hope you know that you brought it onto yourself."

Henry plugged the video console back into the wall, not bothering to watch Andy leave. But something had changed. The disappointment and pity that Henry had grown used to glimpsing in his parents' eyes had appeared just now in Andy's. There was truly no one left in his corner.

What little their parents continued to give Henry by way of emotional or material support they now did so begrudgingly, without the same degree of investment. Pity seemed to overshadow love. Andy had been, until that moment, the holdout, the one who might still believe. From time to time, he'd still offered to help Henry with his schoolwork or to cover for him or to remain quiet when the moment called for it. This would be the end of that, Henry thought.

As he sat, furiously tapping at buttons, Henry began to brainstorm where he might go once his parents kicked him out. His options were few. All of his friends still lived with their parents. Their family in the city wouldn't turn him away, but their homes were smaller than this one, and besides, he'd still have to commute back to Uncle Billy's for work. That night, he waited for his parents to storm into the room and set him straight, but when they arrived, all they did was ask if he'd eaten.

"No. I'm not hungry."

"¿Estás bien?" asked Rosario.

Henry sat at his desk with a baseball magazine opened before him and nodded.

Rosario stroked his cheek before kissing his forehead. "Buenas noches, mi amor."

Andy hadn't said a word. And he wouldn't say a word. Later, he'd climb onto the top bunk silently, and in the morning, he'd wait patiently for his turn in the bathroom. In the evenings, he'd no longer bemoan the mess in the kitchen or in their room. His disgust and disappointment were now silent, Henry noticed. Andy was, in a way, done. Eventually, the bursar's office and the enrollment office would call Rosario at work, and she and Álvaro would erupt. In the aftermath, Henry would begin working full time and contributing toward household expenses, but Andy hadn't been the one to tell on him. Henry didn't know what that meant, but it wasn't nothing.

12

PEARL JAM

He died. Massive heart attack. He was at work and passed out. They were never able to revive him after that. They broke most of his ribs giving him CPR."

Simone's face hardens. Her angular cheekbones appear beneath her skin like snow-dusted rocks suddenly revealed by a gust of wind. Her brown eyes moisten.

We're in the same lounge as last time. It's eastward facing and resplendent with the sun's oblique rays. Even her budding tears shimmer in the morning light.

"Henry had worked there on and off for so many years, they didn't have an emergency contact for him. Uncle Billy had to drive to my parents' to tell them."

Simone shifts in her seat. "Who is Uncle Billy?"

"I meant, Uncle Ikbir. Ikbir, actually."

"Who's that?"

"Henry's boss. At the electronics store. Down the way from Joe's. Across from the Applebee's."

Simone shrugs. "We used to go to the RadioShack closer to our place."

"Ikbir was the Sikh guy who owned the place."

"He was sick too?"

"No. Sikh. The religion."

Simone turns her head from side to side. "How do you spell that?" she asks.

"S-I-K-H."

"Where is that from?"

"Like, where it started? I don't know. But I think most Sikh people come from the Punjab region of India or Pakistan."

"Why do you know that?"

"I have two Sikh friends."

"Correction: You have three *sick* friends," Simone says, and cheekily raises her hand. She laughs, and it's the first genuine, non-anxious laugh I've heard from her in twenty years. It's contagious. I laugh, too, but then I become self-conscious. I can't help but feel as if I'm condoning something prejudicial. I think of my friends Heera and Radhika, my neighbors in the city, a middle-class Indian American couple. She's a writer, and he's a filmmaker, and they water our plants when we're away. They certainly wouldn't appreciate the ridicule. On the other hand, they're pretty rad people who would give this situation a pass, considering the nature, intent, and impact of the humor. It's a lazy play on words, not a calculated attack on a religious minority. And the source, too, merits consideration: a person experiencing an acute mental health crisis; a Black woman experiencing an acute mental health crisis. Surely, she's earned some latitude. How can I call out something like this at a moment like this? Hasn't Simone spent most of her life trying to cross a moving finish line? Isn't the weight of expectation substantially greater for her than for most everyone else? Or am I lowering the bar? Would Simone be insulted to know that I'm withholding my discomfort? Maybe she'd want to know that Heera's brother, who wears a head wrap, has been ridiculed, badgered, spat upon, shoved, and threatened numerous times since 9/11, by Islamophobic assholes who think he's Muslim. Ikbir, too, was forced to decorate his storefront with US flags after the attacks. Or maybe this isn't the hill to die on. Maybe there is nothing insulting at all about acknowledging the homophonic nature of *Sikh* and *sick*. Besides, Ikbir has never hired a Black person to work at the store; maybe I don't need to feel too sorry for him. On the other hand, Radhika and Heera have a Black Lives Matter sign in their kitchen window. Fuck, isn't this what Europe wanted all along, to pit its colonies against one another?

"You okay?" she asks excitedly, as a solitary tear rolls down a face that has completed a seamless transition from lachrymose to merry.

I nod. Simone wipes her nose with the back of her hand. I scan the room. It contains the same people from my last visit. Makes sense. Where else would they be?

"I'm sorry, Andy. Really sorry. I didn't know anything about Henry."

"My mom wanted a private ceremony, mostly family. She didn't even want his coworkers or bowling team to come, but my sister-in-law insisted."

"Henry was funny as hell. Sweet guy. Super sweet," Simone says.

"Yeah. A good guy."

"You know we went to a Rage concert together?"

"Rage Against the Machine?"

Simone nods.

"My brother? Really? When?"

"When you got so cool that you didn't answer my calls anymore. I had an extra ticket, and I happened to run into him when I was home one weekend. We got so fucking high. He didn't know who Rage was, but we had fun."

Simone's face crumples up. She cries for real, and it unexpectedly triggers my tears.

"Buck up, camper," she says as I run my palms across my eyes. Hearing her say those words reminds me that she used to say them often.

Simone is not as inconsistent and jittery as she was last time. I tell her so.

"The meds will do that," she says, without elaborating.

"How do you feel?"

"Tired. Really tired. And hungry all the time. But I feel okay."

"I'm glad you're better. I'm glad you're taking your meds."

Simone turns away from me. There's a hint of exasperation, maybe annoyance. She tucks a loose loc behind her ear and looks up at the television set behind me.

It's not the first time she's been put off by me. Yesterday, I came by to drop off a bag of toiletries, but she wouldn't see me. An attendant appeared after I'd been waiting for a few minutes and announced rather stoically,

"She's not in the mood." When I was almost out the door, another white-smocked employee approached me: "Simone's not having a great day. Maybe you could try back tomorrow. The visits are really good for her."

She's cool," Simone says while looking up at one of the screens. She's talking about a talk show host.

"She's very conservative," I respond.

"I look at the person. I see their soul. Are they real? Are they genuine? That's what matters to me."

"I didn't know the naked eye could see a soul."

"You know what I mean, her heart," Simone explains.

"The heart is an organ that pumps blood. That's it."

"Jeez, Andy. What the fuck?"

"I'm sorry, but they have the most inane conversations and the faultiest logic for everything. The times I've watched this show over the years, I swear my blood pressure has gone up."

"You sound like Phyllis. She says they reflect us back to us. Everyone likes them cuz they're familiar."

"I agree with your mom."

"You don't even like Whoopi?"

"I love Whoopi, the actor."

"She's amazing in *Ghost*," Simone declares.

"She was robbed of an Oscar for *The Color Purple*, but that doesn't change the fact that she's one of these liberals who talks a big game but becomes a personal responsibility advocate whenever she's painted into a corner. We need people who can follow a progressive thought all the way through. These five are all anti-intellectual."

"Wow. You're mean," Simone says, before returning her attention to the TV. The grimace on her face suggests she's just caught a whiff of day-old compost. Actually, I don't think she's even looking at the TV. She's doing again what she did the other day: staring into space, but in a focused manner, as if she were having another conversation in addition to ours.

Simone's not wrong; I am mean. I'm also shocked. Simone wasn't a pinko commie in high school, but she wrote a paper once about Angela

Davis, when no one had ever heard of Angela Davis. Her recitation of that paper at the front of Ms. Kerber's class wasn't radically eye-opening, but it was seed-planting. And now she's defending *The View*.

Our silence lingers long enough to become awkward. I contemplate leaving.

"Listen," I say. "I'm sorry about having been so gruff. I don't know why I let them get to me. I guess it's a preoccupation of mine."

"This TV show?"

"No. I worry about how aging makes humans conservative. I think it has something to do with fear. Fear for one's own safety, fear of damage to one's property, fear of new and unknown things. Adult-onset conservatism is also just exhaustion. A lifetime of being optimistic about life's unsolved problems fosters disappointment and, eventually, pessimism. But no one wants to believe they're pessimistic, so they switch perspectives and move the goalposts. The injustices that could have been remedied with more resources or more empathy transform into intractable dilemmas that we then argue must be addressed with austerity and hard knocks, when the truth is that we never pumped in enough resources or empathy to have truly solved anything. Boom: conservative. Or maybe it isn't a consequence of fears, but a fear in and of itself. The very fear of examining the past and our complicity in that past."

Simone's face remains still, eyes slightly strained. "You been rehearsing that?" she asks.

"No. Maybe. Like I said, it's been on my mind."

Simone returns to silence.

"Whoopi's not so bad," I say, by way of an olive branch. It's true, too. Whoopi isn't only *Ghost* and *The Color Purple*. She's *Sister Act* and *Jumpin' Jack Flash* and *The Lion King* and *Star Trek*. She's also funny and an underrated style icon. And probably a loyal friend. "I just expect more from her than a rabid right-winger. She's on our team."

"What team?"

"The non-white team," I say.

"Hmm," says Simone, but I don't know if she's clearing her throat or disdaining me. "TV is bad, but at least women get a chance to run this one."

"Good point."

"Whoopi's alright," she adds, "but Joy's my favorite."

"Mine, too."

(Marco is a fan of the show; it plays in all of the hospital's waiting rooms. His favorite is Sunny: "Blatina, a lawyer, the only one who can make a coherent point. Hands down, Sunny.")

Simone and I both watch the soundless screen for a while. I do my best to follow the closed captions. The hosts are arguing about Trump's travel ban. Whoopi says something pro-immigrant. Then the conservative one says something less pro-immigrant. Then all of them begin speaking at once, and Whoopi cuts to commercial.

"Simone, can I ask you a personal question?"

"Everything's personal. Shoot."

"How does it get to this point? To be in here?"

"This." Simone places a finger on her temple. "Managing *this* is a full-time job. I feel okay now, but sometimes life gets in the way, and *this* gets neglected."

"Aren't the meds enough? If you just stick to them—"

"Not that simple, Andy. Plus, I don't like them." The sour curling of her lips and the folds in her brow suggest that I've hit a nerve. "They make me feel dead on the inside."

"Isn't that better than the alternative?"

"Better? I don't know. I'm going to gain a shit ton of weight. I'm going to sleep all day. And my jaw is going to be numb. So I don't know if that's better. But at least I'll be able to get out of this place."

"Will you live with your mom?"

"Yeah. Unless she wants me to leave."

It dawns on me that I don't know anything about Simone's life anymore. Her mother was kind to me and devoted to Simone, but the last twenty years might have tested her patience. Maybe her mom won't allow her back in. Maybe it's not a good idea for Simone to live with her mother. Does Simone expect me to offer something? Marco and I have a spare bedroom with an expensive pull-out couch that we bought so that his mother or my parents could spend the night whenever they wanted. But why would I offer her my home? We don't know each other.

"I could always go live with my cousin in New Jersey. She's cool. Or maybe Rhonda. Remember Rhonda Nelson? We keep in touch sometimes.

She visited me at the last place. And she sent me this." Simone pulls blue rosary beads from under her *South Park* T-shirt—a different one from last time. Cartman is holding a bag of Cheesy Poofs. "She's coming to see me this week before she goes back to Texas."

I asked Rhonda about Simone at the reunion, and she said she hadn't heard from Simone in a while. I understand now why Rhonda encouraged me to call Simone's mother. She didn't feel right telling me about Simone's business.

"How did this all happen?" I ask Simone.

"What?"

"Your mental health issues. I mean, when did they start?"

"Oh. This time? Or the first time?"

"The first."

"High school or college."

"When I knew you?"

"You still know me, Andy."

"I mean, when we were kids."

"Yeah. That's when these things supposedly start. Lots of changes. Hormones. Stress. Triggers. It's not so bad."

"What? This place?"

"This place? This is the best hospital I've ever been in. You wouldn't believe some of the other places. Here, they take care of you at least. One place called the cops on me. Said I broke a window. I was so far gone, I don't have a single memory of it. Here, it's different. Last week, I saw one of the patients—a short, skinny girl—punch a nurse. Not on purpose, but when she started swinging and throwing herself on the ground she landed a fist right on the nurse's face. The nurse covered her own face with one arm, like a boxer, and with the other she grabbed the woman harder. When it was all done, the nurse even brushed the girl's hair. No cops. This place could be a lot worse."

I'm lost for words. Even in a psychiatric hospital they resort to calling the police? What could the police possibly do that wouldn't make things worse in this scenario?

"You know, I don't mind this, being sick," Simone says matter-of-factly. "I don't really think about it much. It's just part of me. And then suddenly it, like, reminds me it's there. Or something. I don't know. Hardest part is everyone else."

"The people here?"

"No! The people there." Simone points to the window.

I nod.

"And also, these places could be better. Would it kill them to put some flowers in the windows? Or get a few new basketballs? Or those dental floss picks that look like mini–monkey wrenches?"

Simone abruptly crosses one leg over the other and rests an elbow on her knee, tilting her face up. It looks like an uncomfortable way to sit. She gazes again at the television set hanging from the ceiling. "Remember him?" she asks.

"Who?"

"Look! Babyface!"

"The musician?"

I turn back to look at the screen. Babyface is an apt nickname for this man. If he's aged in the last twenty years, it doesn't show.

Simone doesn't respond. She continues staring at the TV, mouth agape, without any semblance of self-consciousness. I take a moment to assess the space. Everyone is quietly observing something: a screen, their fingernails, a window, the ceiling. I am, again, the only visitor. I assume it's because of the early hour.

In the final scene of *Cuckoo's Nest*, after Jack Nicholson's character has been rendered useless by a punitive dose of electroshock therapy, a fellow patient, played by Will Sampson (Muscogee [Creek] Nation), who had pretended all along to be mute, picks up a sink or washing machine and throws it through a window. That's the scene I most recall. In a college film class, I argued that, because the character was American Indian, his escape from the hospital was meant as a critique of imperialism. I no longer stand behind that hypothesis; after all, he could have just as easily made that case for himself. Why was he mute?

I realize that Simone and I won't be able to break out of here; there's nothing not bolted to the floor.

During a commercial break, Simone looks back at me, rather stoically. She begins to sing, or maybe she's humming. Her lips never come apart long enough for me to understand all the words. "I . . . mmm . . . to recognize . . . mmm . . . face."

"That's pretty good," I say when Simone stumbles. But she resumes immediately, and now the humming is familiar. "Hearts . . . mmm . . . thoughts . . . mmm . . . fade . . . mmm." I know the song. It's about a woman in a small town. One day, an ex-lover returns. He's well dressed and drives a nice car, and he walks into the shop where she works. She waits on him with a mixture of excitement and shame.

I wonder if Simone is trying to communicate something to me, or if this is just a song she likes. "Is that from *Vs.* or *Vitalogy*?" I ask, after it becomes obvious that she's done singing.

"Dude! Don't you care about Pearl Jam anymore?"

"I do! I do!"

Simone and I smirk at one another before we slip into an easy, soft laughter. Everything but the setting is familiar and comfortable.

"This is nice," I say.

Simone shuts her eyes. "I'm going to be in here forever, I think."

"Don't say that! You'll be out of here soon. You said—"

"There'll be another place. If not this one, then the next one. And then another. At least when I'm off my meds, I don't think about that."

I see the moisture beading on her eyelashes. This is a time-machine moment. It's not enough to remedy Simone's current situation. Too much has already been lost. To really have an impact, I'd have to prevent it altogether. I'd have to go back to a moment before all of this and warn Simone. *Listen to me, you have a mental illness unfolding inside of you. You should start going to therapy or taking meds.* Frankly, I don't know enough about schizophrenia to know if it's preventable, but certainly a warning wouldn't hurt.

The problem with this sort of utilitarian time travel is that for it to be effective, one has to retain enough of their current self to achieve their desired goals but not so much that they alter their own trajectory.

Actually, the foundational flaw in time travel is that there is no endpoint; one could always travel further back. Why would I stop at Simone if I could prevent Henry's death? Why prevent Henry's death when I could keep my parents from moving to this place? Or from leaving their countries altogether? And why not even go farther. Thwart unjust elections, warn Malcolm X about the Audubon, out J. Edgar Hoover, tamper with the Enola Gay's engine, pistol-whip Andrew Jackson to death, sink Christopher Columbus's ships.

But would any of it endure?

None of the other patients are close enough to hear me, but it doesn't matter. This isn't the place to be self-conscious. I don't care how terrible a singing voice I have.

I dig deep within to recall the lyrics of the Pearl Jam song Simone was just singing. This is not unlike time travel. I remember it. It's a melancholy and wistul song. I'm embarrassed, but I croon a few words, probably the wrong words. I stop, suddenly aware that speaking the word would have been just as effective as singing them.

Simone claps anyway. I take a seated bow.

"I think they medicate us because they don't know how else to deal with our genius." She says this quickly, with a trace of now-or-never desperation.

A part of me understands, even agrees with the sentiment. We are, after all, a society that mistreats people to the point of damage so that we can then use the damage as a pretext for more mistreatment.

It occurs to me that I have to be more deferential to Whoopi Goldberg.

"Why are you here? I mean, why did you come to see me, Andy?"

"Dunno. I just wanted to. I wanted to make sure you were okay."

"I'm okay. This is shit, but I'm used to it."

"And that's all?"

"Honestly, I think this is the plan. A bigger plan from God. I just have to wait it out. Just don't feel sorry for me, Andy. Okay?"

"I don't."

"Yes. You do."

"Maybe, but only because I'm worried."

"Worried? I haven't seen you in . . . I don't remember the last time I saw you. This is how you worry about your friends?"

"If it makes you feel any better, I'm not a particularly great spouse, either. In fact, if I think about it too long, I'm probably not a good son. And don't get me started on what kind of brother I was."

"Okay, Andy, chill." Simone purses her lips before tilting her head to one side. *"I'm the one in here, why are you the one who sounds so miserable? Be. Honest,"* she says, with the droning affect of the caterpillar from *Alice in Wonderland.*

"Honest. Yes, let's," I say. "Let's always be honest."

Simone flashes me a skeptical stare.

"I mean it. Life expectancy in this country is around eighty, give or take. We're nearly halfway through. There's too little time for lies."

"Geez, Andy. Is this how you always are? So . . . I don't know. Nerdy and annoying?"

"Yes."

"I don't remember you this way."

I stay quiet, unsure if I should take this as an insult. Her delivery was anodyne. In fact, I'm not insulted. I'm fully aware of how annoying I am. I can't help it.

"Here's the deal: until now, humanity has operated under the impression that everything has to happen slow as hell, for fear that we'll end up moving at some catastrophic warp speed. But that's bullshit. We can move faster. We have to move faster. Seriously, Simone, don't you want to see the thing happen before your time is up?"

"Hell yes! But what thing?"

"I don't know. Anything. Justice, I guess. Every second, tons of people die before they get a chance to witness it. Why don't we just do it now? Faster. Let's let everyone see it—whatever it is—before it's too late. I don't understand why we can't."

Simone puts her hands over her face.

"What is it? Are you okay?"

"Yeah, I'm fine. I just had a déjà vu moment. I remembered what it was like to be around you."

"Ha ha."

"I'm just playing, Andy. Thanks for the conditioner, by the way." Simone peeks down at the bag of toiletries by her side. "Next time you see me, I won't look like a leftover meal."

"You look fine."

Simone squints again. "What happened to 'Let's always be honest'?"

"Okay, you've looked better."

We both laugh without the slightest bit of misunderstanding, as if time weren't linear.

"Where you headed after this?"

"To pick up my dad."

"Tell him I said hi."

"Will do. In fact, I should go."

"Really?"

"Yeah. My dad is probably done with his appointment."

Simone nods and we both get up. I walk ahead of her. "Hey," she says, "you doing anything while you're here? You going out?"

"Not really. I've gotten a few texts here and there. You remember Marie? She won't stop messaging me. But I don't want to. Honestly, I prefer to stay home with my parents."

"Andy—" Simone gives my shoulder a tight squeeze. I wince before I stop to face her. "Everything was dinosaurs once. And poof, gone. They were here for a long time. You ever think about that? Wow," she says, as if she's just coming to terms with prehistory.

When we get to the main door, I spot Barry, the attendant who plays one-on-one with Simone. His wide torso and well-rounded abdomen test the fabric of his white T-shirt.

"I'll distract him, and you make a run for it," I say.

"Don't tempt me."

Again, we giggle.

Barry's affable face tightens into a sneer. "No funny business over there," he says as we take a few more steps.

"Will I see you again?" Simone asks.

"I have time for another visit before I head back."

"Okay then. It's a date. But you should call first because I might be out of here soon. I should have been gone already, but I'm waiting for an evaluation. And then the paperwork." Simone shakes her head slowly.

"Alright. But what if you're not here? How do I track you down?"

"Phyllis. She's still at the same place."

I extend a fist, and she responds in kind. We pause for a minor explosion before the double doors open with a loud click, and I step over the threshold.

· · ·

How is she?"

My dad is standing beneath the same small narrow-trunked tree with red leaves. The only tree. His cane rests up against the car, and there's a glistening lather to his face.

"Don't you prefer the AC inside of the hospital?" I ask, exasperated, tired of caring.

"No. Mucho aire es malo para uno. It causes asthma," he says, without a firm understanding of how lungs work. I have asthma, and I've never been told to avoid air-conditioning. Or maybe he's right. Maybe science's field of inquiry is too circumscribed and I should have more trust in the empirical evidence put forth by my elders.

"How is she?"

"Simone?"

"No, la reina de España."

"Fine. Medicated. Both of them."

"Mierda!" he says, with an authentic concern. My father hasn't mentioned Simone in almost two decades, but he seems genuinely afflicted by her situation. "¿Está muy mal?"

"No. Better today than the last time."

"Is she hungry? We can pick her up some food."

"I don't think I can bring her food."

"¿Y porqúe? You brought all those shampoos."

"I didn't think to ask. Huh. Maybe she would have appreciated a burger or something."

"Of course. La comida de los hospitales es terrible."

"Next time," I say.

We get into the car and find our way out of the massive chessboard of a parking lot. It's another ninety-plus day of heat, but with much less humidity, which makes it all tolerable. I look over at my father's phone; the screen displays a frantic image of cyclists being crowded by hordes of spectators set against vast farmland in the distance.

"I read this morning that a Colombian is in the lead," I say.

"Los Colombianos somos listos. Give us a chance and we'll win every-thing. I think he has a real chance," my father says proudly. "How's Venus?"

"She's into the semis. Can you believe it? The last three players she faced were half her age."

"Si yo fuera ella, I'd take all my money and go sit on an island somewhere."

"Just one more Wimbledon before she retires, that's all I want. I know she can do it."

"You never know," he says. "¿Qué tal la otra negrita?"

I don't respond. I've had this conversation with my father too many times. I don't want to argue with him again. Silence is as effective as chastising him.

"¿Qué? I don't mean it in a bad way," he said last time. And the time before.

If Serena were a Russian player, he'd ask how la Rusa was doing. Or la Española or la Colombiana, but because she's Black, she doesn't have a country. Also, Serena is one of the most famous people in the world. Why can't he say her name? It's shorthand, but destructive. I hate it.

We argued quite a bit the last time, and I told him that if Marco and I ever adopted children and one of them was Black and he called them el negrito or la negrita, I wouldn't come here anymore. After that, we didn't talk for the rest of the day. I'm glad I stood my ground, but there's something unnatural about reversing the parent-child order of things. And now I'm annoyed that the lesson didn't even stick.

"Serena isn't playing this tournament," I say, after we've left the hospital parking lot.

"My money would have been on her," he responds.

After another silence, one that lasts until we're nearly home, I ask my father if he wants to go to Pedro's. He doesn't say anything, but his assent is clear in his canny smile, as if we're both committing a harmless crime, but a crime nonetheless.

13

THE
NEIGHBORHOOD

Before any of this, there were people. They lived here longer than anyone ever will. They were the people who watched the ships grow from small, innocuous dots on the horizon into hulks tearing the surface waters in half, and they underestimated the hubris, illness, greed, and villainy contained in their hulls.

In retrospect, a policy of unwelcome would have been better. Never greeting a single interloper, but instead killing each one before they could set foot on this verdant, pristine stretch of earth—fierce arrows through torsos and larynxes; jagged rocks flung expertly through the air, denting and blinding Europa; travel-weary bodies submerged forcefully beneath water; throats slit. It might have worked. The great distances between the Old and New Worlds were not, after all, traversed easily; the intruders wouldn't have been able to fall back and seek assistance. And who would have come looking for them? Several of the early invasions were happenstance and couldn't be retraced. Europe would have been left to believe that imperialism was indeed a risky calling and that their loved ones had been lost to the sea—its creatures, its myths, its powers—or, as was the prevailing wisdom in those times, had dropped off its precipitous edges.

Surely, history cannot (and does not) put the blame on the Indigenous people of this land for their own dispossession and decimation. Who, after all, could have foreseen the firepower? Or the microscopic invaders that traveled on the white invaders? Or the scale of brutality? And unless we fool ourselves, there were indeed coordinated, as well as rogue and haphazard, efforts to repel the travelers. Some successful, for a time. But a comprehensive plan of resistance might have required participation from everyone. From all nations of this land. It might have also required the people who were already here to be as cruel and as distrustful, as heartless and as devastating as their intrepid guests. And even if a representative from every nation on the continent had convened and formulated a plan of defense rooted in zero tolerance for the oddly dressed and colorless strangers, someone would have broken ranks. Someone would have argued that the white men, too, were creatures of this earth. Someone would have said that for all their lethal impertinence, these foul-smelling, syphilitic plunderers had the potential for good. That they should be greeted. And sheltered. Fed. Given guidance. Offered replenishments. Which they were.

Who could have expected what came next?

But this is about the people who came later. Hundreds of years later. The people who populated the towns that were built where there had once been forests and farms and who had corralled the people who'd already been here into small bands, some recognized as sovereign nations, some not, without the requisite agency that self-determination requires. This is about the people who were never as welcoming as the people who'd been here first.

The Italians and the Irish weren't interchangeable, but they occupied a similarly feeble status, far below the English, the Welsh, the Germans, the French, and what remained of the Dutch. For a long time, it was acceptable to look down upon them. And many enjoyed doing so in order to veil who they had once been, sometimes in the generation before. In fact, the Italians and the Irish looked down upon each other too. But when they came to this town, they thrived. They worked as cheap labor, in quarries, mines, and factories. They formed their own clubs—Irish places and Italian places—where they danced, played games, smoked plenty, and drank. They built churches and schools. They ate meals heavy in fat, and despite their place in society, their death rates from heart disease were nearly half that of the neighboring towns and of the country as a whole. In fact, the town's life expectancy was higher than the local and national averages by a handful of years. Without meaning to, the townspeople had exceeded expectations.

The town had been a last resort, the place where no one had wanted to live. But those who chose to live here saw only opportunity. Whatever this stretch of earth signified to others didn't matter in the least—to the least. Hope and gratitude filled the homes, streets, and minds of these God-fearing folk.

In a short period of time, the town developed an aura, a protective sphere. An uncommon feeling of familiarity encircled the inhabitants and all of their interactions. Knowing everyone's families. Knowing from which parts of the city they'd come and from which villages their parents had emigrated. Even those who didn't know one another recognized their neighbors' struggles as a simulacrum of their own.

Rows of nearly indistinguishable homes, on equal-sized plots of land. Each filled with three generations: grandparents who spoke with accents; parents who understood the old language but didn't speak it well; and children who knew only a few exclamatory or culinary words. Every family, it seemed, occupied the same place in their American trajectory—not only a cultural and chronological intersection, but an economic one too.

It was their sameness that protected them. It allowed them to be the social creatures that humans are meant to be. Without differences to navigate, life was made simpler. If one, after all, is equal to their neighbor, what is there to fear? What is left to covet? To doubt? They weren't plagued with the sorts of insecurities that run amok in uneven societies. Absent were the wedges that fracture some communities and prevent others from forming.

Apart from communion, humans, like most other animals, require a degree of control over their lives. They deplete faster without it. The healthiest humans have strong bonds within their societies, as well as agency over their destinies. When the former is weak, the latter compensates for the difference. And vice versa.

The townspeople may have worked for others and had very little say over the order of things, but their struggles were shared. Once they were home, they were strengthened. In one meal, one mass, one neighborly interaction, they replenished all that they'd lost in the day. The elevated levels of cortisol and epinephrine that flooded their bodies returned to stasis. The sense of belonging, the support, the respect, the love, and the laughter served as both salves and buffers.

This isn't speculation. This is science.

But these advantages were only ever going to be short-lived in a place designed explicitly to be a hierarchy, where spaces above were limited and everyone below was desperate to ascend. In fact, many of the subsequent interlopers to the town traveled farther and under greater duress to arrive at the same place. They were darker skinned in most cases, spoke languages previously unheard in the town, listened to different music, ate other foods, were newer to the country, and had spent less time in the city before they transitioned to the town. They'd done everything the townspeople had done to get there, but somehow with less help and hospitality. They didn't pour into the town with assistance or explicit permission, like their predecessors, but instead trickled in, each a drop of water, uncertain if it had landed in a lake or a sea, placid or treacherous, too busy navigating the stream to truly care. The new people filled the abandoned blocks and emptied homes, and they took the jobs that white people didn't want and that had been denied to Black and Indigenous people. They ignored the silences and stares. They kept their heads down. They mowed their lawns and painted their homes. They didn't join the clubs or groups. They weren't invited to the dinners or the barbecues. But their children went to the same schools. And they shook each other's hands when the priest told them to. *Peace be with you,* said the new townspeople. *And also with you,* responded the older townspeople, *but don't think for one second that your son can date my daughter or that we'll tolerate your music or the smells of your food. And speak English. This is America. Amen.*

It didn't have to be this way. The townspeople could have been more welcoming. They could have made eye contact. Knocked on the newcomers' doors. Brought them pies. Showed them around. Offered to help. They could have waited for them on the shores and hoped for the best.

· · ·

Phyllis eyed Wesley in the first week of school. He wore his jeans snug and his hair natural, like hers. He stood, bellbottomed and confident, in the back of the carpeted auditorium during orientation.

The next time Phyllis saw Wesley, he was lying on the grass of the main quad with the two other Black boys from biology class. All of the Black students on campus made it a point to know one another and to make eye contact and to create the spaces internally that were otherwise made unavailable to them. During their second semester, Phyllis and Wesley were lab partners in chemistry class, and although Phyllis thought Wesley attractive, she was wary of his confidence. He wasn't always right, but he was never afraid to raise his hand or volunteer himself. She admired his fearlessness, even if the attention he received made her bite the inside of her lip. She had been the same way in high school, always prepared, always with her arm in the air. But her way had a finesse that allowed her to slip in and out of spaces without discomfiting anyone. Wesley, on the other hand, was a system of high-speed winds, unconcerned with its own effects. Someone who seemed to enjoy life as it was happening. The kinship and admiration that Phyllis felt for him was tinged with envy and caution. And yet, she couldn't keep her distance.

During their second year, Phyllis focused on conservation biology, and Wesley switched his major to history. After college, they moved farther north and then south, where she surveyed wetlands and the use of natural grasses to restore coastlines and he studied the role of labor as a catalyst for the New Deal. When Phyllis was three months pregnant, they moved back up north where they'd both found junior teaching positions. They decided to buy a house in the suburbs, away from the city life that unsettled Phyllis. Wesley could withstand the density and grit of a metropolis, in fact thriving in its anonymity and perpetual stimulation, but his desire to please Phyllis dovetailed with his contrarian nature. The idea of moving somewhere quieter and more remote where he might be unwelcomed in excruciatingly polite fashion intrigued him. It was the getting there that proved the most difficult.

Real estate agents refused to show them houses in the better school districts, so Phyllis and Wesley drove through those neighborhoods on the weekends, and found the open houses on their own. They spent more than a year making offers that were rejected or ignored altogether. They bid less, they bid the asking price, they bid more. Their money was no good.

It was Rodney, the security guard at the university where Wesley worked, who told him about the town. "It's not far from here. There's a commuter train. The houses are real nice. Two stories. Front and back yard. Some have garages. My wife grows tomatoes and green beans. Six square blocks reserved just for Black folk. Friendly enough. Good people."

"What do we have to lose?" asked Phyllis, while Simone, their ten-month-old, squeezed sweet potato through her fingers.

"You mean apart from self-respect?"

"Oh, Wes, it's not all that. We live there for a while. Then we find something bigger in a nicer part of town, or in a nicer town."

"No disrespect to Rod, but we both have PhDs, and our money still isn't good enough?"

"It is what it is."

It is what it is was Phyllis's response to everything, always in a raspy, laconic voice, which Wesley found reassuring during the uncertain moments, even if he might have also appreciated her getting riled up sometimes. Something to show that she, too, cared about whatever the thing was that had caused him to get worked up. But that disappointment was only ever fleeting. Wesley was grateful for how grounding Phyllis could be. Grateful when she massaged his shoulders and his neck, grateful for the pressure of her fingertips on his scalp. Grateful that she kept things simple. They were right; it was the world that was wrong.

"Remember, honey, there were dinosaurs here before us. And there will be something else after we're gone," Phyllis said, as she tucked a wad of orange flesh into her daughter's mouth. Then she wiped Simone clean and pulled her out of the high chair. She stood the unsteady baby on her knees, lifting her gently and setting her back down in a fluid, repeated motion, until a soft burp found its own way out. "And what do you think, baby girl?" asked Phyllis. "You think those dinosaurs had more sense than we do?"

The house was only a half mile from the schools, markets, gas stations, and restaurants, but that distance served as a daily reminder of the true distance it measured. The neighborhood, to its credit, had more trees than the rest of the town, which kept it a few degrees cooler in the summer and warmer in the winter. Their home was a one-story ranch-style structure with two bedrooms and a moderate-sized backyard where Phyllis and Wesley put up hammocks and planted tomatoes, peppers, garlic, squash, and strawberries. The neighborhood was as Rodney, the security guard, had said, exclusively Black, and of those Black people, there was an even split between the African Americans whose ancestors had been forced into this country hundreds of years before and those who'd had a more recent arrival, primarily Jamaicans, Haitians, and Trinidadians, along with two Garifuna families from Honduras, and one Senegalese couple. All of whom had lived in the city and eventually made their way to the town. At least twenty of the neighbors could be traced back to George, a bus driver in the city, who had told as many Black people as he could about the neighborhood within the town.

Many of Wesley and Phyllis's neighbors were working-class people whose schooling had ended at seventeen or eighteen. There were also factory workers, salesmen, security guards, police officers, plumbers, and electricians with college degrees. And there was a banker, a pediatrician, a professor of economics, a pilot, and an engineer who worked on HVAC systems for mid-level businesses, all of whom could have afforded to live in much bigger houses and in nicer neighborhoods, but who had, just as Wesley and Phyllis, contented themselves with having yards and living in a suburb with a simple commute to the city.

After six years, and after growing tired of the confined space—"A house with two academics should have a study," Wesley insisted—they sold their home to a young, childless couple (air-traffic controller, nurse) and moved to the west side, an area whose divisions between Irish and Italian had long since wavered, but which remained resolutely white, apart from the few families who, through pride, optimism, or obliviousness, had breached the boundaries.

Phyllis and Wesley had, again, endeavored to find a home in another town, but they'd faced the same manmade problems as before. Realtors only showed them houses in the few scattered Black neighborhoods between their current home and the city, areas that had fallen into deep disrepair over the previous decades. Abandoned homes on ruined streets where, if one looked closely, they could see the lost potential.

"I'm not raising a child in a place where corners are a leap of faith. Frankly, I don't want to live in a place like that either."

"You know what your problem is?" Wesley poked. "You're more comfortable with white nuisance than Black nuisance."

"What is that supposed to mean?"

"Whites are on street corners too. They've got their own ways of menacing. But you're okay with them?"

"I'm not okay with anything. It's all a calculus."

"I see. Well, there's always farther east."

Out east, too far east, was a hamlet established by free Black families at the end of the previous century. Phyllis and Wesley had gone to visit, knowing well they couldn't afford to live there. And that it would add an hour to each leg of their commutes. As it was, they had to time everything right to pick Simone up from her after-school program.

"Maybe one day," responded Phyllis. "A place to retire to," she said, hoping to be conciliatory while simultaneously annoyed that Wesley would suggest it after she'd previously and unambiguously stated her opposition. "The natural landscape can't abide the unbridled construction. Mark my words, that coastline is going to shrink until there's no more beach. It's not logical or ethical to buy out there," she'd said to Wesley after they'd visited the seaside village a few months earlier. It was just like Wesley to forget these moments that for Phyllis were indelible.

The new house was only thirteen blocks from their previous place, but it was nearer to the elementary school, the drug store, the bakery, the car wash, the fish market, the funeral home, two supermarkets, three banks, four gas stations, RadioShack, Mandee, Caldor, and McDonald's. It had two stories, a basement, an attic, a driveway, and a backyard large enough for a garden and a pool. An elderly woman had died after falling down a flight of stairs. Wesley saw the *For Sale* sign in the window and called the number.

Within a week of moving in, someone had left them a spray-painted message on their driveway.

"What's nih-jurs mean?" asked Simone.

"It means, whitey's afraid of losing power," Wesley responded.

"Who's whitey?"

"It's not a word for little children like you," Phyllis said.

Wesley was perched on a wooden stool in the kitchen. He held a small glass bottle of soda in one hand, while the other was pressed onto the granite counter. He eyed his wife with a mix of amusement and exasperation. How would she explain this?

"Can I say it when I'm seven?"

"It's for grown-ups!" Phyllis's voice was raised, as she glared back at Wesley.

"Nih-jurs means grown-ups?"

"No, darling. It's a cuss word. A silly, nasty word that some people don't take seriously enough."

Phyllis never used the word because her father would have slapped it out of her mouth, as he'd done to Phyllis's younger sister once. Wesley wasn't as parsimonious. He quite liked the word, and he resented having to rein himself in, which he did on account of Phyllis, who, if ever she was inclined, was partial to the word Negro. "Negro, please," she might say if a disagreement escalated past the point of lighthearted, like when Wesley had argued that Carter wouldn't be much better than Ford, or when she'd disagreed that cheesecake made with cream cheese was better than cheesecake made with ricotta.

"How can you compare a cake made with fresh, artisanal ingredients to one made with a block of processed pseudo-cheese. Negro, please."

But that was the only N-word Phyllis used.

"Someone cussed at us?" asked Simone, who was sitting cross-legged on the carpeted side of the border between the living room and kitchen. She wore a white Rainbow Brite T-shirt and yellow corduroy pants, her hair was tied in two thick braided pigtails, and her stuffed sheep was tucked beneath her arm in a careless headlock.

"No. It was a joke, honey," said Phyllis. "Sometimes, people make bad jokes. That's all."

It wouldn't be long before Simone heard the word again. Many times more. Usually in passing. Sometimes on TV or the radio. Sometimes up close. Sometimes directed at her. Sometimes coupled with other words. One of the several children named Michael who lived on the block liked to pair it with "giant." This Michael lived in the house with the red door, but all the Michaels said it at least once. Simone had inherited her parents' height, and was in fact much taller than most of the kids her age, and she didn't know which word hurt more. She'd gathered that one was mean and one was dangerous. The first few times, Simone told her mother what the Michaels were calling her, but Phyllis knocked on so many doors that Simone stopped telling her. Instead, Simone became skilled at making eye contact and at momentarily interrupting the rhythm of an interaction: "Don't. Call. Me. That." And then she'd continue playing with the Michaels, the Josephs, the Stevens, the Marys, and the Nicoles.

Phyllis never learned to be as forgiving when it came to their daughter. "Can you believe the nerve of that woman? 'Children will be children' my ass!" Phyllis had gone to meet with Simone's sixth-grade teacher after a few of her classmates had taken to running their fingers through Simone's hair. "I won't send her back into that Wild West middle school. I'd rather she studied in a place with menacing nuns who walk around with long rulers."

"First of all, they don't beat the kids anymore. Second, we don't believe in anything."

"That's not true."

"Oh really, Fraulein Maria. You been going to church without me?"

Phyllis's blue-shaded eyelids fluttered and her chin turned upward, revealing a long, elegant neck and a delicate jawline. She pivoted away from Wesley and started up the electric mixer that she'd paused in order to have the conversation that she'd been avoiding all summer. She whipped cocoa powder and hot water into a thick paste. Into a large bowl, she added the contents of several smaller bowls: flour, eggs, butter, milk, baking powder, sugar. She mixed those too.

"Think of everything she'll have to undo if we set her down this path now," shouted Wesley over the burring.

"We'll talk to her, like we always do. Better to deal with God than to mess with the devils around here." Phyllis set the machine down and poured the batter into two round tins.

"We went to public schools, and look at us, we're fine," Wesley offered, by way of empirical evidence.

"This is the worst-performing district in the entire county. In two counties! We've tried it for six years. It's not working."

Wesley shook his head before wiping crumbs from the counter into his bare hand and depositing them into the sink.

"They really do get you with these property taxes. We are somehow paying more for the same low-quality school," Phyllis said snidely.

Wesley had anticipated the recrimination; Phyllis had been making it since they'd moved into the new house years before, never mind that she, too, had wanted a bigger home. The previous neighborhood may not have been as pretty or as close to anything, but at least they'd had neighbors, real neighbors, Phyllis argued, people who wished them well. People who stopped to talk. People who waved. People who looked you in the eye. People whom she still visited with on the weekends. Here, they'd only moved closer to the lion's mouth, somewhere near its incisors. And for what? Were they in this mess because of a bigger house or because of Wesley's pride?

To make matters worse, Wesley had been passed over again for tenure, and Phyllis hadn't been able to get a job at the same private university as Wesley, but instead worked as an associate professor at a municipal college.

"I just don't want her to be the only Black child," Wesley said, defeated.

"She won't be. The Nelsons send Rhonda there. And they said there are five Black children in the class."

"Out of how many? And does that include Rhonda?"

Phyllis turned on the mixer inside of the now-empty bowl in order to spin the excess batter off the blades. Wesley waited for her to finish before asking again, "How many students in her year?"

"Forty-something."

"Forty closer to fifty?"

"I can't remember." Phyllis choked an involuntary smile by squeezing her lips tightly.

Wesley's jaw squared and his eyes vanished briefly. He wasn't convinced, but he set his arms at his sides.

That autumn, Simone began at St. Peter, the Catholic elementary school across from the Italian bakery and the funeral home. She hated the plaid skirt, but loved the maroon vest. There were three Michaels in her class alone, none of whom were the Michaels from her block.

14
LATE-STAGE CAPITALISM

Pawel, as Paul's father called him, was small for his age, and still he proved more than his mother could bear during childbirth, leaving Jerzy to raise the three children on his own. Jerzy was a spartan man who wore blue jeans, a denim long-sleeve, a bushy mustache, unkempt hair, black boots, and a perpetual look of disappointment. It made Pawel wonder if his father blamed him for his mother's death, an accusation Jerzy had made many times when frustrated or inebriated, both of which he was wont to be. The truth was, Jerzy hadn't cared much for his wife; marrying her had been, at the time, the least complicated way forward. Her death doubled as relief. Jerzy disliked everyone and most things: his life, his children, his unclean three-story house, his own face—although it should be said that Jerzy was an attractive man beneath his contempt, the sort of rugged handsomeness that elicited animalistic urges from others, the kind that triggered smiles and frozen stares.

Jerzy also hated his job; he was a building contractor in the city. He didn't particularly like his crew of employees, his customers, most of whom were wealthy, or their children and pets, all of whom he believed were spoiled, and whose bedrooms often required nooks, pockets, hidden spaces, perfect arches, and other architectural indulgences that were, according to the customer or the self-important architect, never round or square enough or sufficiently big or small, and needed, therefore, to be redone—something that shouldn't have bothered Jerzy, since these exigencies required more labor and ultimately benefited him, but which he nonetheless detested on account of how they protracted interactions that he wished, more than anything, to be over.

In brief, Jerzy was an asshole.

He was also a terrible father and, previously, a horrid husband. It was true that he blamed Pawel for the death of Agnes (née Agnieszka). It was furthermore true that his primary concern for Agnes had been as a mother, a housekeeper, and an obedient lay, all of which she'd performed serviceably. These attributes were of particular relevance to Jerzy; two of the few things he enjoyed in life were sex, so long as it was brief and vertical, and a clean home. As for the children, he hadn't wanted to be a father; he'd needed to be a father. An innate box-checking. He needed to and so he did. To the detriment of everyone involved, Jerzy wanted, even more than to father children, to be left alone.

Agnes had been a perfectly fine parent—patient and tender, concerned that her daughters' teeth were brushed, their bellies full, noses wiped, ears clean, stories told. Agnes tolerated Jerzy because she'd been raised to believe that what little he gave her was near to what she deserved. Agnes spent much and many of her days alone—Jerzy often stayed in the city, sleeping in the empty homes in which he was working, sometimes for a week. Agnes longed for company, which she found periodically in the arms of the only two other Poles she knew in the town: Vera, the cashier at the supermarket who could, to Agnes's disbelief and delight, please her in ways that no one ever had before; and Peter (né Piotr), the mail carrier who replaced the usual carrier during his vacations and sick days, and who, Agnes feared, might have been the father of at least one of her children.

The roots of Jerzy's malcontent had been seeded in the old world and blossomed in the new. He had come from Poland with his parents when he was four years old. His family hadn't wanted to leave, but communism. In particular, it seemed that Stalinism had ruined everything. This was the extent of the explanation that Jerzy's parents gave him whenever he'd asked why they'd left his grandparents and his favorite ice cream and the park with the red flowers and the swing with the padded seat and his trains. His family's perceived losses remained with Jerzy, and the bitterness lingered for all of his life. Jerzy was neither a communist nor a capitalist, but he was, from an early age, viciously stubborn.

Whether Jerzy was aware of his own rancor is unclear. To the world, he was primarily moody and, by turns, stoic. To his children, he was unfeeling and cruel, teasing and berating them, withholding affection, a vengeful style inculcated during his own childhood, which had been a traumatic shuffle between tenements in the city, between schools that would attend to his America-induced muteness, among children who ridiculed him for not speaking and, generally, for being Polish. Jerzy learned quickly that Polish was synonymous with dimwitted. For years, in fact, he believed that the first Poles in this country had been sent here because they'd done so poorly on their exams back home. How else could one explain the blatant and unremitting attacks? It didn't help matters that neither of his parents spoke English. Although they had come from an above-average milieu in Poland, these were not, even prior to the installation of communism, pro-West people. They were, however, both proficient in Italian, which served Jerzy's parents from time to time in the Italian sections of the city, even if nowhere else. Not only couldn't Jerzy communicate with the other children, he couldn't understand the people inside of the television set, which, on its own, could be sufficient explanation for his almost sardonic muteness—*If you won't make yourself clear, neither will I.*

Jerzy had a miserable time here for nearly thirty years, which included but was not limited to the death of his father (a car accident); his below-average intelligence resulting from the aforementioned and consistent school-based ridicule, even after he grew to be a hulking young man with ample shoulders, bulging forearms, and long, thick fingers; his incomplete college career; his and Agnes's exodus to this suburban town bereft of the kind of self-indulgent life that Jerzy had stolen for himself in the city's wee hours, when he could temporarily cease going through the motions of being a man with a paycheck and a wife and a baby, and instead slip out of the apartment and make his way to any number of bars, where he'd drink—no, not vodka, but beer and whisky and sometimes a soda with his whisky, and sometimes a soda with his beer—and occasionally throw darts and always meet a woman or even a man who was drawn to him like a small magnet to a much bigger magnet or to a large steel surface. Jerzy, somehow aware that he held this power over people, would take full advantage in the bathroom stall of the bar or pool hall, or in the alley outside. There was no better place, after all, for the quick, upright sex that he was after, the kind that involved little preparation and minimal cleanup.

All evidence to the contrary, Jerzy was a human with needs, desires even, who didn't find fault in his attractions. He was as fond of sex with men as he was with women, which is to say, he got off either way. In fact, the nature of his work meant that whatever quick and meaningless sex he had during the day was usually with the men who'd constructed the city itself, most of whom were undocumented men from Eastern Europe (including many of his countrymen), Mexico, and Central America. If he had worked with more women, which is to say, if more women had been encouraged to build things, he would have had sex with them too.

This was the man who raised Pawel, mostly through silence and taunts, sometimes with slaps and kicks, twice with a closed fist to his head, once with an airborne bottle of beer. Pawel, who began going by Paul in the second grade, intuited that he was never going to squeeze affection out of his father, so he focused instead on eliciting laughter. Soft-spoken and not unafraid, Paul was a damaged boy. Careful observation might reveal, beneath his placid surface, a stirring, something more turgid threatening to burst through.

Paul's eldest sister, Maggie (née Magda), moved out when she was sixteen to live with her boyfriend's family. She was pregnant a year later. Paul visited her once a week, whenever he cut class. Roxy (née Roksana), the middle branch of this diseased tree, moved to the city as soon as she finished high school. She hated their father and the long stares he gave her friends. She and Magda both had memories of the way their father violently ignored their mother whenever he wasn't berating her. Roxy wanted, from an early age, to be a dancer, a ballerina. She had long limbs and poise, but her movement was mediocre, and yet, she had come to believe that all she lacked were opportunities. In her first month of living in the city, she botched all of her auditions; soon after, she met a man who paid her for sex, supplied her with all manner of drugs, and lent her out to his friends. Within a year, she was HIV-positive and ricocheting from one homeless shelter to another.

Jerzy had made clear to both daughters that once they left, they could never return. Roxy stayed in the city and eventually got sober, found a job bartending, fell off the wagon, pulled herself together once more, and disappeared. Paul and Maggie worried at first and sent her what little money they could both save; they encouraged her to move back home, but ultimately gave up. Her late-night calls—high, rambling, crying, sniffling—transitioned from alarming to irritating to, ultimately, insufferable.

By the time he was sixteen, Paul was on his own. Still at home with Jerzy, but effectively alone. He prepared all of his own meals and cleaned his room, one bathroom, and the kitchen: the areas where his friends were most likely to be when they visited.

Do you have condoms?"

"No."

The heat of embarrassment temporarily supplanted the other heat that had filled the room as well as Paul's loins. With future girlfriends, Paul would insist that they didn't need protection, but in this instance, Vanessa was the experienced one. She'd already had two boyfriends. A few months before, rumor of an abortion she'd had freshman year circled the school. Actually, the abortion had occurred during the Christmas break of sophomore year. Vanessa, in the eyes of most of the other kids, was already an expert at life. She had the confident gait, the measured pauses, and the glare of an adult, which had created a distance filled with awe and insecurity between her and everyone else. She and Paul had been in a few of the remedial classes together, but they met in detention—she for smoking, he for disrupting class. Afterward, they were inseparable.

"It's okay. I have some." Vanessa held the bedsheet at her chest like a movie star and folded over to grab her purse from the floor.

Vanessa lived a few towns over, along the coast, and her family's car-insurance wealth was reflected in her Audi Cabriolet and her authentic Gucci handbag. She'd failed out of the rich-kid Catholic school and had transferred to St. Ignatius after the abortion. It wouldn't be long before she was expelled from there too. Vanessa hated nuns, priests, and not being able to step outside and smoke whenever the mood struck her. She was short and had long, tightly curled blond hair, usually stiff with hairspray and gel. She'd been left behind twice before high school and was nearly two years older than Paul.

After a bit of trouble, Paul fastened the condom and crawled carefully but imprecisely onto Vanessa. His movement was at first slow, before accelerating into a truncated rhythm. A half moan escaped Vanessa's mouth, but her eyes remained locked on his.

"You're not in."

Paul's face was either anguished or elated. "I'm not?"

Vanessa guided him onto his back and mounted his thick, hairless thighs—Paul was committed to hockey, on the ice when possible, but otherwise in rollerblades on his street. No sooner had Vanessa forced him inside of her than he'd finished. He wriggled and heaved for a few seconds before apologizing.

"It's okay, but can you stay in for a little longer?"

"Yes," Paul mumbled, before wincing from the sensitivity.

Back and forth, Vanessa slid, looking like any number of the women Paul had watched on his dad's bedroom cable box with the porn channels. His erection wilted, and his moans were more of pain than pleasure, but watching Vanessa writhe atop him eventually brought a jolt of energy, of blood. He wondered if it was okay for him to fill up the same condom twice, but he didn't ask for fear that he would ruin everything.

It was the combination of his doubts, his pleasure, and Vanessa's rhythm that distracted him from the ambient sounds: a distant dog barking, a car pulling into the driveway, the front door opening and closing, footsteps on the stairs. By the time they heard, or maybe felt, a presence at the door—"Is someone knocking?" Vanessa asked—it was too late. They both turned to find him standing there, silent.

"Holy shit! Dad!"

"Fuck," said Vanessa, before collapsing beside Paul and hiding her face beneath the dark-green pillow.

"Don't stop because of me."

Paul wondered how long Jerzy had been standing in the doorway. Knowing his dad, it might have been a while.

"Dad, get out!"

"Watch your tone, Pawel."

Jerzy didn't have to raise his voice. His whispers were sufficiently threatening. Paul was humiliated, not only by his father's presence, but by his own inability to intercede.

"Young lady, can I have a private word with my son?"

Jerzy knew well that it would be difficult for Vanessa to leave the bed without exposing herself to him, and he made no effort to give her privacy.

Paul turned his head subtly toward the shrouded body beside him. "Sorry," he whispered.

"Could you give me a minute?" Vanessa called out, before sliding up into a seated position.

"Don't worry about me. My eyes are closed," Jerzy responded.

"Gross." Vanessa pulled the sheet forcefully from the bed, leaving Paul fully naked. She wrapped herself, and bent down stiffly to pick up her clothes. The nearer she was to the door, the more pungent the smell of booze. Jerzy's eyes were bloodshot and glassy, his nose red. This was how he came home most days, but typically much later.

Jerzy extended his hand to Vanessa as she approached, knowing that something would be sacrificed if she were to shake it. "My friends call me Jerry," he said. Her face reddened, no longer just in stifled anger and humiliation, but now in fear, too. Vanessa raised her arm over her brow as if to avert a blinding light. Jerzy made no effort to give her the room she needed to leave, making certain to trace a line along her back with his elbow as she squeezed past him.

"What do you want?" Paul asked, still horizontal, a pillow over his midsection.

"A father can't check in on his son?"

"Are you fucking serious?"

"Kid, you will never be old enough for me not to beat your ass."

Paul's chest and arms tensed with a vicious anger and fear. He'd been lifting weights, drinking protein shakes, and taking pills that a friend suggested. He would always be a short kid—according to Jerzy, an embarrassment— but now he was a force. Not to be ignored or trifled with.

"I need you to pay the cable bill this month."

"Why can't you?"

"Business is no good now. Winter slowdown."

"Maybe if you spent less at the bar—"

"Mind your fucking business," Jerzy said, before slapping the pillow shielding his son with the back of his hand.

It wasn't a particularly hard impact, but it made Paul shoot up out of the bed, his shoulders wide, his fists extended and raised. The pillow had dropped to the floor, revealing all of Paul. Jerzy looked at him for a moment before reaching out and taking his son's penis in his hand and giving it a subtle squeeze, as if it were a cow's udder, and he, the farmer.

Paul swatted his father's hand away.

"You should thank me for that." Jerzy stumbled backward but maintained a grin on his face. "Don't know why you turned out so short, but you definitely owe me for your manhood."

Jerzy turned away from Paul, wandered over to the dresser, and ran his hands over the sundry items. Beneath a poster of a large cross decorated in skulls, which read "Appetite for Destruction," was a small box, in the shape and style of a pirate's treasure chest. In it were a few bills, twenties and fives mostly, and a heap of coins—Paul's bounty from mowing lawns and weekend shifts at the bakery. Jerzy stuffed the bills into his pocket and tipped the chest into one hand. He made no effort to pick up the few coins that fell soundlessly onto the carpeted floor. "Thanksson," he said, his words slurred into one.

Vanessa stood in the doorway, dressed in a white long-sleeve shirt and a pleated gray skirt that she typically rolled at the waist several times, but which now reached past her knees. Jerzy walked by her, too busy trying to keep the coins in his hands to pay her any mind. When it seemed he'd disappeared, he called out, "I'm not taking care of any fucking babies. If you need rubbers, I got a bunch." His forced laughter reverberated for a moment before it vanished, along with him.

"Your dad is a fucking creep."

"I know. I'm sorry."

"No. I'm sorry," she said and caressed Paul's face.

He had by this point scrambled to get his clothes on, fearing that his father could return at any moment unannounced.

"You hungry?" he asked.

"Very."

"Taco Bell?" he suggested.

"Sure." Vanessa bit her lower lip, now puffy and dry. She wasn't worried, but neither was she at ease.

Jerzy was crude and scary when sober, but the booze made him sloppy and mercurial. Paul couldn't recall a time when his father wasn't drinking, and it seemed that in the last year, his insobriety occurred with more frequency and more intensity. On a few occasions, late at night, Paul heard a commotion coming from his father's room, two distinct voices making distinct sounds, guttural and occasionally synced. Each time, a green LeSabre was parked across the street, the same man waiting alone and smoking. Paul peered out his window from the darkness of his room, and each time, a full-figured woman in a tight skirt and leather jacket walked from the front of their house to the car. It was the sort of subtle spectacle that Paul had seen in movies and television shows: high heels, choppy gait, and the way she pulled a crumpled pack of cigarettes from her tiny purse.

Paul was embarrassed to have Jerzy as a father. He would have preferred to never bring home any of his friends, least of all Vanessa, but Vanessa wasn't allowed to bring home any boyfriends after her expulsion from St. Francis.

The young pair took to having sex in her car or on the patch of forest between St. Ignatius and the coast, occasionally ducking when the cross-country team ran past. When winter made the car an untenable accommodation, they cut out of school early and went back to Paul's. By this point, they'd grown comfortable with each other's bodies. They'd established a rhythm that worked for Paul and wasn't altogether terrible for Vanessa, who never once came but who extracted tiny pleasures from the encounters, namely, watching Paul squirm under her weight and his convulsions after he'd erupted, scenes of domination that later played out in her mind to useful effect in the comfort of her own bed.

It was during one of their afternoon dalliances that they crossed paths with Jerzy for a second time. Paul had dozed off while Vanessa was cleaning up in the bathroom. It was her screaming and her racing footsteps that roused him. "Fuck your fucking sick dad. I'm not coming back to this fucking dump again." Vanessa slid her clothes over her wet hair and onto her damp skin. Paul begged her to calm down and explain, despite knowing well what and who had caused her outrage. "Don't come near me!" she sniped at him.

After she'd run out of the house, Jerzy came into Paul's room. "Testy bitch, no?"

"What the fuck did you do?"

"Who? Me? I just walked into my bathroom and, surprise, surprise, there was this woman in there that I didn't recognize. I thought someone had broken in."

"You're sick."

"Oh, c'mon. I startled her, that's all."

Jerzy brought the tips of his index and middle fingers to his nose. "Hmm. That's a ripe one," he said after inhaling deeply.

Paul, wearing only boxer shorts, charged the five feet between his father and him, dropping his shoulder just in time to make contact with Jerzy's gut. Jerzy toppled, like an outdated statue, onto the red carpet. Paul, tears streaming over his cheeks, windmilled mistimed punches to his father's shoulders, arms, and chest. "You're a sick fuck!" he shouted repeatedly.

Jerzy hadn't yet caught his breath when his son's fist landed on his nose, reviving him. He grabbed one of Paul's wrists and kneed the boy in the groin. Paul fell to his side, clutching his testicles, while the tributaries of snot, drool, and tears converged at his lips.

"I barely touched her," Jerzy said as he got up. "Just a fucking joke, you little shit. Fucking brat."

"I hate you," Paul said, face down, sobbing into the carpet. "I hate you."

Paul and Vanessa didn't break up; instead, they never spoke another word to one another. Vanessa, for her part, ignored him, and Paul, too embarrassed to approach her, carried on as if nothing had ever happened. The rumor around school was that Vanessa had cheated on Paul and that he'd dumped her.

15

PAUL'S DAD

I have memories of Paul's dad.

I saw him at Steer Queer once. It was in the days before I left for college, after things had ended abruptly with Jeremy and I'd taken to getting drunk every night. I recall the profile of Paul's father, and his elbow resting on the frame of his car window. It was August hot and everyone who drove past was glistening. Paul's dad was one of the dozens of older men who filled the lot that night, windows rolled down, trails of cigarette smoke winding their way out and up. There was both a humming of engines and of humans. One lap around the lot was customary before settling into a parking space and waiting for someone to pull up beside you, to select your cut from the meat market. If you were cruised first, then it was your turn to circle and pull up beside your admirer.

It was in the midst of this sacred, soul-shaking liturgy that I saw him. I wasn't certain it was him because I was, at the time, inebriated, as I was whenever I visited Steer Queer. By the time I completed a second loop, he'd already left the parking lot.

After seeing Paul's dad, I wondered if both father and son made it their business to lure gay men into traps. I wondered, too, how many other people I knew in that lot, how many others might be acting on impulses that, like me, they'd been suppressing all day, all their lives. What if Steer Queer was a rite of passage, ancient Greek–like, each of us young gays waiting to be paired with an older counterpart?

It also occurred to me that someone might be spying on me from a distance, just as I had done to Paul's dad. Immediately, I rolled up my window and pulled out of the lot, only to return the next night, again drunk.

I have other memories of Paul's dad. In eighth grade, we'd go over to Paul's after playing basketball on the courts up the street from his house. A few times, his dad offered us beers. We assumed he was joking and said nothing, instead allowing our laughter to serve as our demurral. Once— and this might have been in ninth grade—Mikey C. said yes and confidently chugged the whole thing before immediately throwing it up, which Paul's dad made him clean up.

I recall, too, that Paul's dad liked to poke fun a lot, in particular at our changing bodies. Our creaky voices were an especially fertile ground for his humor. "You sound like you have some hair on your balls, boy," he'd say to whoever happened to be standing nearby. It was the sort of humor that I detested, but I laughed along with everyone else. "Well, do you?" he'd insist, until someone acquiesced, which only left the rest of us targets for more scrutiny. Paul's dad was, in those moments, like Joe Pesci's character in *Goodfellas*; he unleashed a humor that was coterminous with fear. One time, Kevin, the cool kid with biceps and a speech impediment, called his bluff and pulled down his shorts and underwear for all of us to see. First, he windmilled his dick, before choking his own testicles in a way that expanded the skin and looked terribly painful. I glanced at the spectacle for a moment, but I must have been too candid with my stare because Kevin drew everyone's attention to me immediately: "Are you a fag? Everybody, Andrés wants to touch my balls!" The ridicule lasted only a few minutes, but it felt like an eternity. It lingered, too. Kevin would randomly bring it up in the weeks to come, without context, in front of completely different groups of kids. The irony of that was that I hadn't looked at Kevin because I was attracted to him; it was merely curiosity, like staring at a car accident on the highway.

I wonder now if those sorts of incidents are the reason I still avert my eyes in locker rooms, dressing rooms, and public bathrooms.

As a twelve-year-old, I thought Paul's dad's humor was within the bounds of what was acceptably crass and acceptably male, but after I spotted him in Steer Queer all those years later, I wondered what Paul's dad was after. At some point, I stopped accepting Paul's invitations back to his place after basketball. And then, I stopped playing basketball altogether.

I have one other memory of Paul's dad. In the summer after sixth grade, a few of us were over at Paul's house having a water-gun fight in the backyard. We soaked Paul's dad while he was watering the lawn, and he ran after us with the hose. Paul, his sister, and the kid with the broken teeth who lived next door managed to outrun him, but I couldn't. When Paul's dad caught me, he scooped me up, pulled the cheap drug-store plastic gun from my hand, shoved it down the backside of my pants, and pulled the trigger. I laughed while he did it, but during my struggle to break free, the tip of the gun barrel managed to get inside of me. It didn't penetrate me fully, but it certainly went farther than anything ever had before. I was embarrassed afterward, for no discernible reason. I assumed, then, that it was an accident, which I blamed on my futile attempts to wriggle free, but the sensation remained with me for a long time; the memory, too, is clear. To complicate matters, Paul's dad ended up in a few of my masturbatory fantasies not long afterward. He was, in fact, very attractive.

16

COUPLES COUNSELING

"Should I go?"

"No. Tonya won't be home for at least an hour."

"We're going to hell."

"For this?" Jeremy asks.

"Among other things."

"I'm not going to stress about it."

"What would you do if your wife walked through that door right now?"

"I don't know."

"What will you do if she finds one of my pubes in the bed and asks you straight up if you're cheating on her?"

"I don't know. But I guess I should shake out the sheets after you leave."

"Jeremy, how are you so nonchalant about this?"

"Nonchalant?"

"Untroubled."

"Who says I'm not troubled?"

"But you're not scared that your wife or kids will find out?"

"Not, like, afraid, no. And no disrespect, but I don't want to bring my kids into this."

"I'm sorry."

Jeremy caresses my thigh over the beige sheet. Before long, the gentle massage turns into something more elaborate. He pulls the sheet off of me and runs his hand down the length of my leg, squeezing it at various points along the way, like a doctor or a butcher. "You still run?"

"Three times a week."

"That's good. I need to get to the gym more."

The room is messy. Clothes bloom from partially open drawers. More clothes line the thickly carpeted floor. Atop one of the four wooden dressers, one at each wall, are a few smears of thin gold and silver jewelry, mostly earrings, but necklaces and bracelets too. In the corner, there's an en-suite bathroom. It's been cleaned recently, but there are permanent water stains on the walls, globs of dried toothpaste inside the sink, and dark green and black spots of mold along the ceiling's edges. The grout in the shower has an orange hue.

"How long have you lived here?" I ask. "This place feels familiar."

"Yeah. My uncle Benny used to live here. You met him."

Uncle Benny? Yes, I recall that moniker. "Parrots?" I ask.

"Yeah, he had all those parakeets."

Is there a difference between parrots and parakeets? I wonder.

"Right. Right," I say. "Wow. Didn't we have to feed them once, when he was on vacation?"

"In jail. Uncle Benny had issues." Jeremy takes the thumb of his fisted hand and brings it to his lips. "I guess it runs in the family."

"None of that rings a bell."

"Possible I didn't tell you. Anyway, Benny died a few years back and left me the house. He didn't have kids, so he left me all sorts of shit: gun collection, old coins, antique mallards—"

"Ducks?"

"Yeah, for hunting. Decoys. Each one was worth at least fifty bucks. A few were, like, a thousand. And he had more than two hundred of them. That's how I got my car and took the kids to Disney World. One of the guns was from like the eighteen hundreds. Paid for our place upstate."

"You have another house?"

"Yeah, it's a fixer-upper. I'm still working on it. We're gonna rent it out mostly. But we're headed up there for a week in August."

Fucking white people. Barely eke out a high school degree, spend time locked up, and earn next to nothing, but they're still making bank off of slavery-era memorabilia. Meanwhile, someone mentions reparations, and immediately everyone wants an itemized list of how exactly Black people are going to spend every last dime of their money.

"Cool," I say, suddenly feeling like I'm sleeping with a political norm dressed up as an anomaly. His hand is again traveling the length of my leg. I feel my jaw tense. I grab his wrist. "Jeremy—"

"Here's the deal," he says, while looking at me directly, without a trace of artifice. "I'm not afraid of fucking up anymore. Whatever happens happens. I have to take life as it comes."

He sounds like one of those magic eight-ball toys.

"But it's not just you," I say. "You have—"

"Don't worry about my wife. Let me deal with my family. Listen, man, I don't want to be a dick, but why do you care?"

Jeremy is firm but not visibly upset.

"I don't know. Guilt, I guess. And I'd feel better if I knew she didn't care. If you two had an open relationship."

"Open what? Like cheating?"

"No, not really. Like pre-approved."

Jeremy grabs a cigarette pack from the bedside table.

I pull the bedsheet up and fold it over my lap, as if I were sitting down to a meal. "Forget it," I say.

Jeremy takes a long drag. The smoke he exhales is immediately subsumed, disappearing up his nose or back into his mouth. I don't know. He's like a movie. A movie I've seen many times. A movie I was in once. I reach for his lips. "May I?"

Another mouthful of smoke escapes him, but this one travels upward, toward the stained ceiling. He hands me the perfect cylinder and I squeeze it between two fingers, at the border where the orange and white bits meet. I put it to my lips and pull. I haven't smoked a cigarette in thirteen years. The sensations return quickly, primary of which is fog. Not smoke, but a fog of the mind, followed by a concentric throbbing in my head. I grab Jeremy's forearm, at first gently and then, without meaning to, with more urgency. Somehow this cigarette packs more punch than the pot I've been smoking all week.

"You okay?"

"A little light-headed. It's been a minute since I've had one of these."

Jeremy takes another drag and mumbles to himself.

"What?" I ask.

"I guess I'm a bad influence," he responds. "Like always."

"Says who? I'm a big boy. I'm not doing anything I don't want to be doing."

"Sure, but since Sunday, you smoked pot, cheated on your husband, and now, cigarettes." He holds up three long, knuckly fingers, at least two of which were, moments ago, inside of me. "If we hadn't connected at the reunion, none of this would have happened."

I smile and take another drag; it truly is like riding a bicycle. "I thought you didn't worry about fucking up anymore."

"I'm not worried about me," he says, and hops out of the bed. "Hold up. I gotta piss."

The moment that Jeremy disappears, I remember Marco. Today was his presentation (The Predictive Value of Antiretroviral Therapy and CD4 Count on Cholecyctectomies in HIV-Infected Patients) at the conference— The Global State of AIDS: 35 Years of Health Care Lessons. He had been particularly nervous about condensing three hundred slides into twenty minutes. I should have wished him luck last night. I grab my phone from my pants: "I hope the presentation went well," I send, along with a few heart emojis. Not having sent this earlier feels like an escalation.

This is the fourth day of this, of taking advantage of Jeremy's kids' swim lessons to meet up, get high, and fuck. I told Marco already, but I didn't tell Jeremy that I told Marco. I called Marco as soon as I got home after the first time. He'd just gone to bed.

"Okay," he said, before going quiet.

"Are you upset?"

"Upset? No. I'm not happy about it, but I'd rather talk about this when I get back home."

"Okay, but just so you know, it was only physical. There were no feelings on my part. Plus, I was really high. Honest."

"I believe you," he said.

I've been thinking about this recently. About how it still surprises me when Marco believes me. Early on in our relationship, I would tack on *I swear* or *I'm not lying* to everything—stories, reasons, excuses, explanations. *Sorry I'm late. I missed the bus—I swear.* Or *I didn't read your email. You left the window open on my laptop—I'm not lying.*

I've always been like that. My brother was too. We behaved as if our honesty couldn't be taken for granted. I don't know if it's society's fault or something my parents inculcated or if I picked it up at the record store.

In middle school, my friends and I would bike to Sam Goody on Tuesdays after school; that's when the new music arrived. Every week, I'd stand in the store, committing the singles and album charts to memory, while my friends snaked through the aisles. We did that for two years' worth of Tuesdays, and at some point, it became obvious that the clerks were preoccupied with me. If I remained still, they kept their positions behind the counter. If I moved about the store, they did too. It had never, not for one moment, occurred to me to steal anything, but the clerks made me self-conscious. I began monitoring my movements. Eventually, unzipping my jacket or reaching into my pockets became a test of courage. In an effort to prove that I was a good customer (and maybe even a good person), I spent a lot of money at that store, well more than my friends, who almost never bought anything. All these years later, I still find myself second-guessing my behavior in these settings, often feeling as if I'm performing the role of Human in Department Store instead of being a human in a department store. It's probably why I don't go to department stores.

In any case, I've cheated on Marco, and as long as I continue cheating with Jeremy during this visit, I've decided that it'll all count as one time, and I don't need to tell him anything. Fuzzy math.

But I'm not a complete swine. I apologized to Marco. Even if, frankly, I don't think he deserved the apology, since he cheated first.

It happened after his monthly happy hour with a group of coworkers, last year. Based on Marco's summary of the night, I've gathered that the guy, a friend of his coworker's, whose name I cannot remember (or choose not to, our therapist believes) but whose job title I will never (ever) forget—fashion-trend forecaster for Latin American markets—gave Marco a lot of attention and was just the right degree of outgoing and confident.

"He kept putting his hand on my knee. Laughing at my jokes," Marco explained.

"You don't make jokes."

"You know what I mean."

"So you laughed a lot and suddenly you were having sex?"

"No, babe. He invited me up to his place. We picked up a six-pack. And I know you won't believe me, but—I swear to God—I didn't think anything was going to happen. I knew it was possible, but I really thought that if the moment presented itself, I'd just get up and leave. Really, babe, I mean it, that was it. But the alcohol. They were triple beers," he said earnestly, as if he were teaching me basic math.

"And then what?"

"Babe, c'mon."

"Tell me."

"I don't know. I went to the bathroom at one point, and when I came back out, he wasn't in the living room. And I knew then I should bounce. I even called out something like, 'I should get going,' but then he said, 'I'm in here!' And I just followed the sound of his voice, and when I found him in his room, he was on the edge of his bed. On his knees. Naked. With his back to me."

Marco shrugged with his mouth and shoulders, as if to say, *What could I do?* His reaction served as a reminder that men are, in effect, dogs, only less loyal.

Our therapist believes that I sought out Marco for his dependability, something I've done in all of my relationships as a way to compensate for the uncertainty of my adolescence, which is why his infidelity has hurt me so much. And yet, I've often wondered what it would be like to have a partner who is more spontaneous. Someone who pushes me. To be politically radical. Or sexually adventurous. Not someone who rarely removes his socks. Not someone who watches cable news. In other words, the cheating was the most spontaneous thing Marco had ever done, and there might be something optimistic to draw from it. In the long run.

In the short run, however, I've felt a certain degree of vindication. I'd always believed that I would be disappointed. That's what humans do. Betwixt the love, we hurt one another. In fact, I was as surprised that the infidelity hadn't happened sooner as I was that it happened at all.

Our therapist suggests that we imagine ourselves in the future, as ninety-year-olds who've persevered. "The long view might shrink this one trauma to an almost insignificant degree," she said. It's an effective strategy, but it hasn't erased the moments of doubt. It hasn't kept me from envisioning a road paved with corrosive, lingering distrust, and resentment. To make matters worse, I still don't understand why Marco cheated. "And you might never. Sex is simply fun," explained the therapist.

Jeremy lights another cigarette. The room is silent except for our exhalations. Many times since I quit smoking, I've dreamed of doing it again. Vivid dreams of inhaling and exhaling. After each one, I've awoken relieved. Happy to have not broken my streak, proud of myself even. And yet, here I am undoing everything.

With two fingers, Jeremy crushes the cigarette butt into a small ceramic saucer. "I think we have time to go again."

"How do you have the energy?"

"Ever since I got clean, I'm always horny."

Jeremy turns onto his stomach and runs his warm, skillful tongue in a circle over my nipple, before taking it between his teeth.

"Stop," I say, but he keeps going, moving to the other nipple, and then my neck. He smells like a potion of ashtray, body odor, and spent cologne. I find the combination enrapturing. "Stop, I mean it."

"Oh yeah?" He squeezes my erection through the bedsheet. The bunched-up fabric makes me look more endowed than I am. "Doesn't look like you want me to stop."

"I don't, but I'm sore and I have to go. I don't want to run into your wife or kids."

"I told you, they aren't—"

"I know what you said, but I'd rather play it safe. Besides, what are we doing? I can't pretend the last twenty years didn't happen. Where is this all headed? Are we going to get back together and run away?"

Jeremy looks up, positions himself in the center of the bed, and stares at me attentively. "You serious?" he asks. His face widens, masking the gauntness near his cheekbones. I recognize the emotion. It's optimism. Have I just led him on with a few careless rhetorical questions?

"No. Serious about what?"

"You think this—us—could go somewhere?"

"Jeremy, we're both married. You've got kids. We don't live in the same place."

It doesn't take long for his face and chest to take on a pinkish hue. He's embarrassed. I'd forgotten this look too.

"I'm sorry, but it can't lead to anything. You must see that, no?"

Jeremy doesn't respond. He merely fixes his gaze on the far wall. There's a sad painting of a bowl of fruit, in a style that's indistinguishable from the still lives hanging in every art museum in the world. Seeing it here, in this Home Depot bedroom, in this unkempt house, on this miserable block, in this nothing town, makes me question the role of art.

"Okay," Jeremy says, and again his hand appears on my cock.

I acquiesce. "Fine. But first, tell me, what was the reason? Twenty years ago, we agreed to meet at the train station, on the platform. Why didn't you show up?"

Jeremy exhales aggressively and throws his head back onto the headboard. "Fuck, Andy. You want it every way. You want this to be light and easy, but then you want to bring up the past all the time. What's it gonna be?"

Instead of responding, I take a deep breath. *This isn't me*, I tell myself. *Be thoughtful, Andy. Be mature. Don't get sucked into drama.* "I'm sorry if I upset you. But ten seconds ago, you wanted to talk about running away together. Well, we already tried that, and it didn't turn out well. I have no reason to trust you. No one has ever let me down the way you did."

"Forget it," he says, and climbs off the bed, like a sore loser. He puts on his baggy white briefs. He grabs the condom from the floor and disappears toward the bathroom. It occurs to me to warn him not to leave it in the trash, or risk being discovered, but I choose silence.

The shower runs. I hear the pattern of water change. First it pelts the tub's enamel; then, it softens as the stream hits his body. It becomes loud again; he must have stepped out of the stream to lather up. I rush to get dressed, but I can't find one of my socks. It's one of those small ones that don't come above the ankle and give the impression that one is not wearing socks. They look like homemade ballet shoes. This missing one is maroon. It's not on the floor. Or the bed. Or beneath any of the dressers. Or the piles of their clothes. I consider leaving without it, but what if that one sock dissolves Jeremy and Tonya's marriage? What if that one sock leaves Jeremy pining for me, stalking me? What if I live to regret this one moment? No! I don't care. I'm leaving without the fucking sock. Jeremy's problems are not my problems. Tonya's problems are not my problems. She chose this guy, and if she doesn't have her shit in order, I can't be blamed for it. Maybe they, too, need couples counseling. Maybe their counselor can help them see how they have both contributed to their problems and how they can both contribute to the solutions.

The water stops running. The metal curtain hooks grate against the shower rod. I slip on my shoes, with and without a sock. Jeremy comes out of the bathroom wearing the same underwear. He's swirling a cotton swab in his ear. The blond and gray in his hair are now dark brown and wet. He takes the miniature pugil stick out of his ear. He picks something up off the floor with his toes and passes it to his hand. "This yours?" He holds out the sock. I walk over and try to take it, but he won't let go.

Our gazes overlap briefly before they lock into place. Laser beams. Our hands hold the sock. There's a serenity to his demeanor and his expression, but there's emotion in his eyes desperate to get out.

"What if—I think I still love you," he says.

17

FRIDAY NIGHTS

Fridays were for loosening up.

Rosario and Patricia shared a bottle of iced prosecco or lightly chilled Cabernet and sat by the living room stereo listening to the Beatles or the Pointer Sisters, the Doors or Donna Summer, and occasionally Fleetwood Mac. They recounted their weeks to one another and reminisced aloud with no expectation that the other was paying close attention. Patricia's children were at home playing video games or out at a baseball game with their father when he was in town. Álvaro worked the dinner shift and would be home on the 11:37 P.M. train. Henry was out with friends, upstairs in his room, or working the closing shift at Billy's; he could take the car so long as he promised to pick his father up from the station. Andy was spending the night at Jeremy's.

Rosario saw the men in her life so infrequently—late nights, early mornings, and weekends whenever they rolled out of bed. She should be with them whenever something essential wasn't keeping them apart, she thought. She'd grown accustomed to Álvaro's all-hours schedule, but she was still acclimating to the disappearance of her children. The idea of them sleeping in other people's homes unsettled her. This was, in her eyes, an abdication of her role as a mother. She was implicitly asking complete strangers—Rosario never, if she could help it, interacted with the other parents—to take responsibility for her children, to feed them and provide shelter, maybe even comfort and guidance. It signaled weakness and constituted a sort of debt, she thought.

And yet.

Rosario was glad their aggressive, mercurial energies weren't, at least for one night, colliding with her live-wire exhaustion. She was glad not to have to think too hard about how to navigate their humanity; glad not to feel obliged to care for them; glad, too, not to have to get up from the couch. Whatever guilt, regrets, or doubts clung to her on those evenings of relative peace were drowned in the wine.

Andy and Jeremy spent their Friday nights watching TV or a movie, smoking pot or drinking Jeremy's parents' liquor, making out, having sex once early in the evening, having a second dinner, playing video games, doing a bit of homework, and having sex a second time before going to sleep. Jeremy's parents were seldom home before midnight on Fridays. Apart from Jeremy's grandmother, who kept her distance and was in her room by nine-thirty, Jeremy and Andy were tethered only to one another. They left the basement to collect their meals, to answer the phone, to help grandma move something heavy, and eventually to sleep in Jeremy's bedroom.

Jeremy was an untouchable prince in his house, a kid free to live as he wanted. *Don't give your grandma a hard time* was the only request Andy ever heard Jeremy's parents make. Jeremy walked around the house shirtless and barefoot, he ate whatever he wanted at any hour, he didn't wash dishes, he didn't seem to have chores (although he regularly took out the trash, which Andy deduced was more about showing off his physique to the neighbors as he flexed his way to the street, than about contributing), he cursed freely but rarely with anger, he delivered pizzas on the weekends, which was for Jeremy a video-game-like joyride with periodic interruptions, and he never did homework unless Andy encouraged him to. Jeremy was equal parts carefree and careless.

More reason, Andy thought, for him to be cautious enough for the both of them.

"Dude, sleep on the bed with me." Jeremy interrupted his ritual of lining the floor with a spare comforter and pillows. "Even if my parents came in here, they wouldn't care."

"No, I'm not taking any chances."

But Andy usually relented, and after Jeremy dozed off, he'd move to the floor. In the mornings, Jeremy would drive Andy to St. Ignatius where he'd catch the bus to his cross-country or track meet. This arrangement became a routine, and it carried on for nearly a year before they were caught.

Andy hadn't qualified for the meet that weekend in April, essentially ending his season and his high school running career. Still, he attended practices and was expected to be at all the meets in support of his team. That Friday night, he and Jeremy went to a house party that was broken up early by the police, unleashing, in the process, dozens of inebriated teenage drivers. Jeremy and Andy went back to Jeremy's place, where he mixed orange juice and his father's vodka. They drank until they were sloppy. They had sex and passed out immediately, naked and uncovered on Jeremy's bed. When Jeremy's parents got home, his mother opened the door, with the intention of switching off the light.

She didn't tell her husband what she saw. Jeremy's father would beat them senseless, she thought. He'd throw Andy out onto the street, and possibly Jeremy too. Instead, she waited nervously for the morning's light— first purple, then orange—to slip through the spaces between the blinds and window before she slipped out of bed. She pulled forcefully at Jeremy's shoulder and whispered for him to follow her to the kitchen. "Now," she hissed and threw a pair of boxers at her son. "Put these on!"

Jeremy, barely awake and still a bit drunk, arrived at cognizance quickly. This was serious, like the time his father's appendix burst or when his grandfather died. Jeremy reached for a bedpost and scanned the room. There was Andy, face down, snoring lightly, one leg and half of his ass exposed, the other half of him tangled in the white sheets. It crossed Jeremy's mind in that moment to jump through his second-floor window rather than face what was next, but he put on his underwear, rubbed his eyes, and walked to the kitchen, toward his mother, instead.

"I don't want to know anything," she said as she fitted a filter into the coffee machine. Jeremy blinked repeatedly, trying to adjust to the kitchen's track lighting. "We gave you too much freedom. This is our fault. But it ends today. I don't want to see that boy in this house ever again."

"Ma—"

"Ma nothing. I'm taking him home now. Tell him to get up, get dressed, and to meet me in the driveway."

"I can drive him."

"Jeremy Anthony Pugliese, do you want me to wake your father? Get that disgusting kid out of my house now!"

Jeremy woke Andy by slapping his leg, just hard enough to rouse him. "Dude, get up. My mom knows."

"What?" Andy's mouth, eyes, and throat were parched. He put his hand across his face, unable to give the moment order or urgency.

Jeremy dropped Andy's clothes beside him on the bed. "Hurry. My mom's waiting to take you home."

"Fuck. Really? Did she call my parents? Fuck. For real?" he whispered.

Jeremy nodded. "She didn't tell my pops."

Andy dressed quickly, while Jeremy searched the room for all of Andy's belongings—his backpack and running shoes on the floor, his physics textbook, a notebook, and a few pens and pencils scattered on Jeremy's desk.

As Andy stepped to the door, Jeremy blocked it with his foot. "I can go with you," he said.

"Where? To my parents'? No—wait, your mom isn't taking me to the police or something, is she?"

"No. Geez."

Jeremy's arms were crossed against his bare chest, his hands tucked into his armpits. He was inadvertently flexing, and Andy scanned his bulging biceps, the taut cleavage at his sternum, and the striations of muscle on his forearms and along his midsection. There wasn't an ounce of fat on him. Andy caressed his shoulder.

"What are we going to do?" Jeremy asked.

"I don't know. We'll figure it out. Later."

"I love you," Jeremy whispered.

The room was dark, but Andy caught the glimmer in Jeremy's eyes. They weren't only projecting fear; there was anger too. Anger at his parents and at himself for not being braver.

Andy's socks soaked up the dewy lawn as he crossed it with his shoes in his hands. A plume of exhaust extended from the back of the fogged-up black Lexus in the driveway. Jeremy had once given him a blow job in its back seat, on a night when he'd taken his parents' car without permission.

Andy pulled at the door handle, but the car was locked. Jeremy's mom motioned for him to let go, but Andy tried again too soon, and again it jammed. It took a few more tries for their timing to line up.

"Sorry," Andy said, as he climbed into the back seat. Jeremy's mother said nothing. After a few blocks, she spoke, but only to confirm where she should take a left and, later, where she should take a right. Andy tied his sneakers and sat quietly on his hands for the rest of the ride, suddenly afraid of someone with whom he'd always gotten along well. "They think you're a good kid," Jeremy had said of his parents several times. In fact, they thought Andy was a positive influence who'd kept their son from failing math and English, who had manners at the dinner table, who never caused trouble. "He's a good Mexican," Jeremy's father said once to his wife, knowing well that Andy wasn't Mexican; in fact, he'd said it in defense of Andy, who Jeremy's mother felt had been spending too much time with their son. The demographics of the town and the surrounding towns had been shifting in recent years, and they'd both been secretly disappointed that their son had started a new school and had somehow aligned himself with one of the few non-white kids. "Could be worse," he said to his wife. The parameters of worse were clear even when unspoken.

When they pulled up to Andy's house, the sky was no longer on the verge of anything: it was unmistakably morning. Andy feared that Jeremy's mother would want to speak to his parents, but she remained still as he collected his things and reached for the door.

"If you ever call our house again, I'll tell your parents everything," she said without turning to face him, communicating instead through the rearview mirror.

Andy had spent the brief ride imagining what he might say in this final moment, but all he could muster was a nod before he opened the car door.

"You're sick. But my boy isn't sick. Do you understand me? Don't bring this to my home."

Andy hadn't ever seen her this way. The rectangular reflection of a face petrified in anger, eyes small and piercing, lips retreated—a look that would forever supplant the cautious kindness he'd come to know. He nodded for a second time before climbing out of the car and making his way to the back door of his house, never once looking back, only grateful to hear her roll away.

Andy had made it past one mother, but there was yet another. Even this early, Andy wouldn't be able to avoid Rosario. He'd have to explain himself. Why was he home? Wasn't Jeremy going to drive him to school? Didn't the bus for the track meet leave soon?

There she was, sitting alone at the kitchen table. He scrambled to think of something convincing, other than the truth. It made Andy uneasy not to be able to confide in his mother. He didn't need her as a confidante, but there was an openness to their relationship that was being abrogated more with each day. As unsupportive as she might have been in this matter, Rosario would have defended Andy against Jeremy's mother. *How dare you treat my son this way? I don't need you driving him anywhere. Don't do us any favors. Worry about your idiot, delinquent son, and leave ours alone.*

There was proof of this inner dragon. A few years earlier, Andy had been approaching home after being out with his friends. It was a night in late summer, already dark, but warm enough for shorts and a T-shirt. Álvaro was snoring in front of the television set downstairs. Rosario was upstairs methodically wiping away the layer of Pond's cream she'd caked on in order to clean off the day's makeup. Her face was half-white when she heard Henry call out for her.

Henry had been playing Mike Tyson's Punch-Out when the tin of his brother's voice, indecipherable and dire, but unmistakable, echoed into the room. From the window, he saw two men surrounding Andy on the curb. One man gripped Andy's arm, and the other held his bike upright. Rosario caught only a glimpse before she pushed past Henry and bounded down the stairs in her nightgown, cream still caked on her neck and eyebrows. Even as Álvaro shouted for her to explain what had happened, she continued running. She ran right up to the two men and pulled her son from one of them and the bike from the other, making certain to shove both during the disentanglement. She shouted up a storm of insults, accused the men of being animals, ignorant, uneducated, criminal, child abusers, and rude, before threatening to call the police. The men—one, a retired cop who'd lived across the street for nearly ten years, the other, a fellow retiree—had taken it upon themselves to patrol the neighborhood because of recent reports of theft. Later, the retired cop would claim not to have recognized Andy because of the darkness, but on that night he apologized, lowered his head, and walked away. Rosario had to pour herself a whisky in order to relax. And for years afterward, she resisted going to sleep until her children were home.

Andy feared that Jeremy's mother would have faced a similar wrath. Better, he thought, to leave things as they were: secret, safe, and distant.

"Jeremy and his family were going upstate to visit cousins or something. They dropped me off on the way," Andy explained, while doing his best to move through the kitchen without raising suspicion—quickly, small steps, few pauses, shallow breaths to conceal the odors of Jeremy, of vodka, of bad breath, one brief peck on his mother's crown, in keeping with custom. "I'm gonna go shower. I have to be at school soon. Can you give me a ride?" he called out after he'd disappeared.

"Hmmm," Rosario said to herself.

No longer allowed in Jeremy's house, and with Andy's home not viable because of Henry's unpredictable schedule, the young couple drove to the beach, to the movies, to a state park with ample untouched forest, anywhere they might sneak a kiss, a hand job, a blow job, a clumsy melding, discomfort softened by the newness still of their attraction, everything a pleasure and an education.

A few times they went to Jeremy's place in the afternoon when his grandmother was volunteering at the Knights of Columbus, where she spent every winter and spring helping old Italian men file their taxes. Even if she had been home, Jeremy was certain she wouldn't have said anything—whether she knew what had happened or just didn't care was unclear. The only trouble they faced on those days was Andy's resistance to cutting class; he'd never before missed a day for anything less than severe strep throat.

For a week straight, Jeremy left the same note in Andy's locker: "How about today?"

"No," Andy wrote on the slip of paper he'd then slide into Jeremy's locker.

"C'mon. If not now, when? This is it. You already applied to college. Missing a day isn't gonna fuck with your chances," Jeremy pleaded before dropping Andy off at home one night.

"The school's gonna call my mom."

"Wednesdays, dude. Your last three periods are gym, free, and library. That's the day."

"But I need that library time for a paper that's due in two weeks. If I get my work done in school, we can hang out after. No stress."

"C'mon. It's called homework for a reason. Do that shit at home."

"I don't know."

"All you have to do is sign in for gym. Then we can leave. No one is going to say anything about you missing library or free period. And I'll drive you back for track practice."

"I have to sign in for library or Sister Anne will mark me as absent."

"Sister Anne is senile. Ask anyone—ask Simone!—to sign your name for you."

Jeremy grabbed Andy's hand and kissed each finger. "Please," he said, after each one. When he'd said it five times, Andy's shoulders surrendered.

Asking Simone for help would be tricky. Her father had died at the start of senior year. Ever since, she'd been more withdrawn. Busy, too. In the winter, she'd joined the basketball team, and now she had lacrosse. She was still around, but her interactions with Andy were different, less like synchronized explosions and more like chess. Her calls were infrequent, as were Andy's, whose time away from class now belonged almost exclusively to Jeremy. Asking her for a favor felt odd. She'd certainly do it, but apart from a bimonthly typing class, library hour was the only period he had with her all week. They spent most of it passing notes to one another, Simone drawing caricatures of everyone in the room, and Andy writing descriptions, dialogue, or catchphrases on each—sacrilegious prose and imagery that would have gotten them both suspended.

"I'll ask Simone in typing tomorrow."

. . .

U need 2c him every day? We haven't hung in 4eva," Simone wrote above her drawing of Sister Anne, a frail, hunchbacked interpretation with pointy dragon ears.

"Sorry," Andy wrote back. "Tutoring him in math iii & eng. He's trying to get grades up. Wants to apply late admission to state schools."

"Thought he was going to c.c."

"Guess he's trying to keep options open."

"Okay, how about this Fri?"

"Track meet."

"After? Carnival?"

"Deal," Andy wrote, without clarifying that he'd already made plans to meet Jeremy there.

Simone did as she was asked and signed Andy in. Sister Anne was none the wiser, preoccupied instead with her Philip Roth collection, books she kept on hand but never recommended to the students.

The balmy, chaotic night of carnival arrived. Enormous steel beasts rising up from the school's parking lot, their clunky parts spinning and whirling through the air. Roving adolescence. Screams in motion, nearby, far away, nearby again. The inescapable mix of cloying and savory aromas. Pavement littered with popcorn and peanut shells. An ephemeral world suffused with life.

It started off copasetic, Andy and Simone together, boisterous in their sounds and movements. Until Jeremy arrived. Then Andy was lost. Distracted. Where was Jeremy? What was he doing? Who was he talking to? If Simone stopped for even a moment to talk to anyone, Andy used it as an excuse to scamper off in search of Jeremy, often losing his place in line for a ride.

Barely an hour into the night, Simone left without saying goodbye. She was less annoyed by Andy's flakiness, which she'd come to expect, than deflated by Mary's cruelty.

Mary Ortiz and Simone had shared a hotel room during the volleyball semifinals at the end of the season. Mary—good student, light-skinned, long, shiny black hair, never took off her gold hoops, even on the court—had initiated. She swore she'd seen a ghost in the window of their room. "I'm sleeping with you," she shouted. And without waiting for Simone's reply, she'd slid into the bed, assuming the position of little spoon. For fifteen minutes, Mary alternated between exaggerated yawning and subtle inching, farther and farther back, until there was nowhere to go but in. On. Over. Under. Between. Then the ghost was gone, and Mary moved back to her bed. Her smell lingered—a flowery perfume layered over coconut lotion. It filled Simone's nostrils and remained on her lips and fingers for days. But at practice the following week, the scent curdled. Mary's smiles were awkwardly constructed. Her eyes, her neck, and her waist were aloof. She grew fidgety if they were alone and someone approached. There were a few more sleep-overs, usually on Friday nights, during which Simone's excitement remained only vaguely at bay. She chose a furtive patience, waiting for Mary to make first and second moves. Mary with such soft lips and warm skin and hair that tickled Simone's face, breasts, and stomach. Mary whose fingers felt both tender and exhilarating inside of Simone, and whose insides seemed, to Simone, distinct from her very own, somehow softer and less resistant. Mary so giggly and nimble and perfect to the point of apparition. Mary who was dating Jerrod, the football player who'd graduated the year before. Mary beneath the carnival lights, looking back at Simone but not smiling. Mary who left without saying hello or goodbye. Mary who'd soon announce that she was pregnant with twins, Jerrod Junior and Jerry, due in September when everyone was starting college. Mary who'd be pregnant again the follow-ing year.

Simone's relationship with Mary had fleeted past so quickly. It left Simone wondering how real it had been. Had Mary felt anything at all? Had Simone overreacted to something casual?

Simone kept all of this to herself. Who would she have told anyway? It was her father who had been prone to qualitative research. He'd been the one who kept the inquiries broad. Never assumed anything. Just *Anyone special?* It would have been easier to confide in him. And certainly Simone would have scored points with him by virtue of Mary being Black. "Please, oh please, don't let her bring home a white boy," she'd heard her father say. He'd said it with a humorous tone, but he'd said it more than once.

Simone's mother might have taken it well. Overall, Phyllis was fine, an easy person actually, but she kept a distance about certain things. In fact, she was never around. It seemed there was always a conference or meeting or field trip to attend. Distance was, as far as Simone was concerned, better than the puckered lips, wrinkled nose, and accordion brow that accompanied disapproval.

Simone could have confided in Eleanor. Voted *most unique* in the yearbook, jewelry made from candy, pixie cut, thigh-high striped socks, self-proclaimed bisexual. Eleanor was friendly and had glommed on to Simone during a ski trip at the end of sophomore year. Certainly she sensed something. Simone liked Eleanor well enough, but there was something about Eleanor that was too committed to the truth. Too confident. Too fearless. Or too good at concealing fear. Simone wasn't ready for the sort of honesty that was Eleanor's currency.

And then there was Andy. Familiar and funny. Kind and smart. But also self-centered and melodramatic. He'd been a good friend for years, but was now unreliable to the point of absence. He wasn't someone to confide in, not about this.

Andy knew he'd done Simone wrong, but instead of following her home from the carnival or simply calling, he'd allowed Jeremy to soak up all of his attention, plenty of which was required that night. Jeremy had seen Andy step off the Ferris wheel with another guy, a charmless boy from a competing Catholic school who happened to be standing behind him in line. Jeremy was upset nonetheless. All the way home, he alternated between irrationally angry and irrationally silent.

"Wanna go to the movies?" Andy suggested during one of the silences.

"Or you could just go hang out with your Ferris wheel faggot."

Andy, too, kept quiet after that, lamenting that he hadn't stayed with Simone instead.

It wasn't only Andy's friendships that declined in those months. The previous semester, he'd gotten his first B—physics. If the relationship with Jeremy had bloomed even six months earlier, it's possible Andy wouldn't have gotten into college. Now, it seemed, Jeremy's volatility was being triggered by the acceptances.

Andy's celebrations had been muted around everyone except for his mother, who, for each letter, surprised him with a small gift: a box of eclairs from the expensive bakery near her office, skirt steak on Saturdays, *Working*

Girl on DVD, the *Soul Food* soundtrack, family dinner at Athena's. Henry, for his part, said nothing, which was no particular surprise. By that point, it seemed that he was more of a lodger than a family member. Álvaro's responses were the same after each letter: *I knew you could do it*. The one rejection brought about a variation: "You could have done it."

'll go with you," Jeremy said. They were lying in Jeremy's bed, naked apart from the beads of sweat and a thin sheet. This was the second Wednesday in a row of cutting class. None of the nuns, it seemed, had been the wiser.

"I'll be in a dorm. We can't live together."

"My cousin goes to college, and my mom says he lives in his own place. We could do that. Find an apartment together near whatever college you pick."

"Maybe. But the budgets all include dorms for housing. I don't know if they'll cover any other type of housing. And it's probably more expensive."

"I have some savings. I'll get a job, too. They have pizza places everywhere. Or I can do whatever."

"What about school?"

"They don't have community colleges there?"

"Probably. I don't know. I can call the schools and ask."

Jeremy rolled over from his back onto Andy, both of them still sloppy and moist. "One more?" Before Andy could respond, Jeremy had pinned the underside of Andy's leg to his chest.

"Condom."

"Every time?"

"Sister Mackey says the vagina can have micro-tears that make sexually transmitted infections more likely for the receptive partner. It's gotta be even worse for the anus."

"Dude, you pay way too much attention in class."

"C'mon."

"But you're the only person I'm having sex with. If I wear a condom it's like you're saying you don't trust me."

"I trust you here," Andy said, resting his palm on his chest, "but I have trouble trusting up here." Andy tapped a finger to his temple. "I'd be super nervous after. I promise it has nothing to do with you. My parents would kill me if I got AIDS."

"Couldn't you have gotten AIDS from going inside of me without a condom last week?"

"I guess," Andy responded and smiled. "That was just once."

"That's wack, dude." Jeremy closed his eyes and shook his head slightly, annoyed but also amused. "Fine, but this is my last one; you're going to have to buy the next batch."

"Okay. No problem."

"No problem." Jeremy affected a squeaky voice, before ripping the packet open and reaching for the bottle of hand lotion.

As the time to choose a school neared, Jeremy grew testier, more jealous, unkind. Although they rarely had cause to interact during school, they'd always acknowledged each other—head nods, soft pats on the back, lingering looks and handshakes, once, a stairwell kiss; another time, Jeremy followed Andy into the locker room and playfully massaged him through his boxers until a dime-sized area grew darker and eventually became quarter-sized, causing Andy to panic and pull away. Now it was Jeremy who seemed unsure. He wasn't there in the morning. He wasn't there at lunch. He didn't wait for Andy after school. On Wednesday, there was no sign of him when it was time to cut out early.

Before Jeremy, Andy had been an expert at retreating. Always making an effort to hide how he felt and who he was, measuring himself against the other kids in the room. How did the boys move? Speak? How did the girls? How did the white kids? How did the Black kids? The few other kids who were neither? To what extent could he borrow from one without being admonished or ridiculed by another? Jeremy changed all of that. Andy had never before felt the power and weight of a mutual, romantic love. Being with Jeremy peeled back a layer of artifice, leaving him feeling new and alive, but also vulnerable. *How many layers were there?* he wondered. And how long would he need to be this happy and free before he could actually be a happy and free person? The person he would have been if the world were as it should be. What would become of him now if Jeremy disappeared?

W hat the fuck, man? You scared the shit out of me. How did you get in here? How long have you been in here?"

Andy had cut his last two classes. He'd been sitting in the passenger seat of Jeremy's car for at least an hour. "You left it unlocked."

"Fuck, Andy."

"You've been ignoring me all week. You know I can't call you, and you didn't call me. In the hallways, you look the other way. This morning, in the cafeteria, you got up and left the table when you saw me coming. You haven't given me a ride home since Friday. On Monday, I didn't get on the late bus because I thought you were going to take me home. I had to go back and ask my coach for a ride. That was embarrassing."

Jeremy leaned forward, setting his forehead on the steering wheel. "I'm sorry."

"Why are you being this way? What did I do?"

"You didn't do anything. This is all me."

"*Me?* Aren't I at least part of you now?"

Jeremy lifted his head and turned to face Andy.

"I'm feeling a little crazy," Andy said, in a low voice. "I think about you when we're not together. I hate not being able to call or see you whenever I want. The other night, I was awake in bed just thinking of going to your place and climbing in through your window. I almost did. I got dressed and went downstairs but couldn't find my dad's car keys. I tried to sneak into their room to see if they were in my dad's pants pocket, but he was still awake."

Andy had been rehearsing this monologue for days. He'd managed to say it all, but at a cost. His voice had broken and tears were beading. He wrapped his arm across his face.

"I'm sorry," Jeremy said.

Andy spoke into the crook of his elbow: "But why?"

"I don't know. I'm a fuckup."

Jeremy's voice, too, was now plaited with emotion. Andy, aware that their classmates were scattering about the parking lot, thought twice before taking Jeremy's hand. But it occurred to him that a friend would do this, not only a boyfriend, so he grabbed it.

"You're not." Andy rubbed the sleeve of his shirt across his eyes and his nose.

"I am. I thought if I ignored you, you would leave me alone."

Andy let go of Jeremy's hand. "Why?"

"What am I going to do without you? Without this?" Jeremy shouted. "This is the only thing that makes me feel good. When I'm with you, I feel like something good is happening. Like something good is going to happen."

Jeremy dug the palms of his hands into his eyes, while the tips of his fingers scratched at the top of his head, mussing up his hair.

"Please don't be upset," Andy begged. "What can I do? I don't want to leave you either. We can figure something out. I've narrowed it down to two schools. Both are driving distance away. Five, six hours. You can visit whenever you want, or—I called the school, there's a community college nearby, and we—"

"Let's get married."

Jeremy's red eyes, tousled hair, loosened tie, and unbuttoned shirt made the proposal seem dire and unintended, but also honest. Andy felt little control over his lips, which extended upward into a glorious smile.

"I mean it. I only need you," Jeremy continued. "With you, I'll be happy. I know it. I want to wake up with you and go to sleep with you. I want everything and everyone in our way to just, I don't know, disappear. Everyone tells us our lives are beginning and everything's gonna speed by and we're supposed to make the most of it. If that's true, then I want it to begin now. With you."

Jeremy was shouting. Andy scanned the immediate area around the car. The tailgating portion of the afterschool procession was over, and now everyone was caravanning away, cigarettes lit, hands hanging out of their windows. Andy was torn between happiness and caution, but also envy and admiration. Only a secure person could be as vulnerable as Jeremy had just been; only someone who didn't care what others thought could be so honest.

Jeremy leaned across the gearshift, digging his elbow inadvertently into Andy's thigh, and flicked open the glove compartment. A few papers threatened to spill out as he rifled through the contents. He pulled out a packet of gum, unwrapped two pieces, popped one in his mouth, and was about to take the other before stopping himself. "Want?"

"No, thanks."

Jeremy then took the two thin sheets of foil that had encased the gum and rolled each one up. He tied one around the ring finger of his left hand

and pressed the ends tightly until they held steadily. "Give me your hand," he said.

"What?"

Jeremy took Andy's left hand in his right. "Will you?"

"What?" Andy said, with an artful smirk that transitioned quickly into the widest, most anxious smile he'd ever felt across his face.

"Marry me, Andrés."

"I will."

Andy accepted an offer. It was from a prestigious university that no one from St. Ignatius had ever attended. It was also the one that awarded him the most financial aid. He'd gone with his parents to visit the verdant, hilly campus in May. When he returned, Jeremy was again behaving erratically, changing plans at a moment's notice, sitting taciturn beside him, looking for any reason to disagree with Andy—about food, about a movie, about the color of a passing car. The proposal a couple of weeks earlier had remained a theoretical prospect; they hadn't talked at all about what they would actually do. For some reason or another, Jeremy hadn't been able to contact the community college nearest to Andy's school. Andy wondered if he had changed his mind, but then Jeremy suggested they drive up to the school ("Let's scope it out together"). In the days before the trip, Jeremy's car broke down, and his parents wouldn't loan him one of theirs.

By mid-July, their future remained in limbo. Jeremy was working at Tony's, shaping dough and sweeping. Without a car, he couldn't deliver pizzas and, consequently, collect tips, the source of most of his money. All of this led to more irritability, arguments, and long spells of silence, interrupted only by moments of passion, a pattern similar to the one Andy had known all his life, the downward spiral of fear and affection that he'd grown adept at managing and, occasionally, breaking. It was all made worse by the subterfuge—lying, hiding, borrowing cars—required to see one another.

"What if we ran away?" Andy asked Jeremy.

They were parked in the nearly emptied lot at the beach. Up above, the sky was a severe, almost catastrophic indigo, framed below by dune tops, each sprouting blades of grass, like the new, desperate beginning of a life or its final days. The windows were down, allowing for the intermittent sound of rolling waves slapping against the coast. Everything was at once comforting and ominous. Andy hadn't been here since the end of spring, when he and Simone had dropped acid and hung out on the beach, a reunion and a reconciliation. It'd been a bad trip for Andy; the stress of everything swirling in his life had sucked the light from the hallucinogenic effect and trapped him inside of his own mind. The experience had been both an allegory and a consequence.

"Like run away? Right now?" Jeremy seemed suddenly awake after a few somnambulant weeks.

"No, at the end of the summer. When it's time to go to school, we can go somewhere else instead."

"Hawaii!"

"Hawaii?"

"Yeah. We went a few years ago. A family vacation," Jeremy explained. "It's amazing. The beaches are killer. Beautiful. And it's never cold there."

"No snow?"

"I don't think so."

"But it's really far away. Can we try something closer, like the city? That way we can still be nearby and visit our families. Also, we don't have to go so far for the beach. The beaches in El Salvador are pretty amazing."

"What about El Salvador, then?"

"What? No. I don't want to live there. And you don't speak Spanish."

"I'll be with you. Besides, you can teach me."

Andy looked straight ahead and didn't respond.

"Okay, how about Italy?" Jeremy said. "I have third cousins there."

"Getting there is going to be really expensive. And we don't speak Italian. And—"

"I can say a few words. My nana taught me. Dove il bagno?"

"That it?"

"Acqua per favore?"

Andy snorted.

"Don't make fun."

"I'm not! You just surprised me, that's all. I never heard you speak Italian before. I've never heard your grandmother speak Italian either."

Jeremy's face reddened all over, making Andy nervous. The closest he had come to seeing him this way was during the second or third time they'd had sex. Jeremy had forced himself inside of Andy too quickly, causing Andy to grimace and pull away. Jeremy, immediately contrite, apologized more profusely than he needed to, Andy thought at the time. Afterward, Jeremy grew nervous and reticent.

"It's okay. We can try again," Andy said, when the pain had subsided.

"I don't want to hurt you. I really didn't mean to. I promise."

"I know."

Jeremy's face collapsed, and he began to cry softly.

"Really, it's not that serious. It only hurt for a moment. Don't be upset."

"I know. It's not that."

Jeremy pulled away, as if he were annoyed, possibly angry. He hopped off the bed, put on a T-shirt and boxers, and left the room. Andy waited a moment before following. Jeremy was in the basement, pouring himself a drink. Straight vodka. First one, then another. Andy remained silent beside him, as afraid to stay as he was to leave.

Before long, Jeremy was too drunk to sit up. He began to apologize again. "I'm fucking broken, man. I'm sorry," he said. "I'll always be broken. I'm sorry."

"What are you talking about? Don't say that. It's not true. You're amazing."

"You could do better than me. I'm damaged goods, Andy. It's not my fault. It's him."

"Who? Whose fault about what?"

Between the sobs, Jeremy said, "My cousin." He didn't say anything more after that.

The quiet crying soon transitioned into sleep. Andy watched, nervously alternating between caressing Jeremy's hand and his hair. He wasn't sure at first what Jeremy had meant. He'd talked often about his cousins. There were many. None of whom lived nearby, but they visited. There was one, Tommy or Timmy, who'd stayed with them during his college breaks. A picture of him in swimming trunks and sunglasses sat on a small table in the hallway. A tall, dark-haired beauty on Jeremy's father's side of the family—the well-off relatives. But that's all he'd known of Jeremy's cousin, until now.

Andy wasn't able to get Jeremy back up to his room that night, so he laid him out on the couch and turned him onto his stomach. Then he brought the waste bin from the bathroom and set it on the floor.

In the newspaper that Andy's father brought home from the city most nights, they found ads for apartments. They called several and took the train into the city to visit a few. Through a combination of graduation gifts and savings, they calculated that they could afford first and last month's rent and a security deposit, and still have enough to live for a couple of months.

The few schools Andy might still apply to in the city were no longer accepting applications for the coming year. The few that were wouldn't consider him for financial aid so late in the season. Andy regretted not taking Rosario's advice the year before, when he was making a list of colleges. "Apply to something nearby. Just in case."

"What's the point of leaving if I'm going to be so close?"

"It's important to be near to your family. If you need us, we can be there quickly. And we can meet for lunch or on the weekends. Five hours away is too far."

Andy wasn't listening. The words, yes; the sentiment, however, didn't mean anything to him. He'd been as nearsighted and detached from his family as his age allowed.

In early August, just two weeks before Andy was set to drive north with his parents, he and Jeremy would begin moving into their new place. That was the plan. But without a car, they'd need to spread the move out over several days. They'd meet at the commuter rail station, taking a bag or two each time, until they were fully installed.

"I can bring my TV set, but we'll need to borrow a car."

"I could ask Simone. What about a bed?"

"We can find something cheap. Last few times we were in the city, I saw mattresses on the street. We can try to find one that looks in good shape."

"Is that clean?" Andy asked.

"We'd put our sheets on the bed."

Our sheets, Andy thought. Then he scanned the list in his notebook. "What else? Oh! Pillows, a shower curtain, pots, pans, utensils. A lot of this

I'm already getting for school. And my mom has a spare set of utensils that we never use. I can probably grab a few from there. And there's at least one pot and one pan that—what?" Andy noticed that Jeremy was staring at him, his face tight, suppressing something.

"Nothing," he said.

"What is it?"

Jeremy was sitting in the window seat of Andy's bedroom, barefoot and shirtless. He pulled a small glass pipe from behind his back. "Maybe I took too many hits while you were in the bathroom. I'm high as fuck."

"Dude! You're not supposed to smoke in my room. My mom has a crazy olfactory sense."

"An awful factory? What?"

"Olfactory! A sense of smell."

"Fancy. Anyway, Mr. Awful Factory, chill out. You didn't even smell it. I was careful. I blew the smoke out the window. Want a hit?"

"No. We have too much to do before Tuesday. I have to get a cashier's check for the landlord. I have to finish this list. I have to call the university and let them know I'm not going. I have to find a job—"

"No. You promised. You definitely said you were going to one of the city colleges."

"I looked, but it's complicated, and I'm too late. I'm just going to apply for next year. Maybe even by January. Besides, we need to work. You want cable TV, right?"

"Yeah. But don't worry, man. We'll be good."

Just then, Henry walked into the room.

"What the fuck are you two ass clowns doing? Why isn't this one wearing clothes?" he said, pointing to Jeremy.

"It's hot as balls in here. Your parents don't believe in air-conditioning?"

"No, dick-for, Spanish people like it hot. You didn't know that? Wait up! Are you smoking weed?"

Andy clenched his jaw and fastened his eyes onto Jeremy, before turning to his brother. "He only took one hit. I told—"

"I don't give a fuck. Hand it over. Sharing is caring."

"Henry, the man!" Jeremy said, before passing him the pipe.

．　．　．

Andy and Jeremy grew careless in their affections. In the days preceding their first official trip into the city, there were several moments when anyone paying attention to them could have glimpsed truth: how they sat close to one another on the couch, how Andy fed Jeremy a spoonful of ice cream at the kitchen table, how they kissed unabashedly in the car whenever they greeted or said goodbye, how Andy said "love you" somewhat loudly before he hung up the phone, how Jeremy massaged Andy's shoulders while he wrote up to-do lists at his desk, how they moved in sync and occupied each other's spaces with familiarity just beyond friendship, how they emitted tensions when they disagreed about the mundane things, like what to watch on TV, where to go at night, what to eat.

Rosario noticed. She'd intuited something about Andy years before. Something that made him different. Something that was best to ignore. But over time, she felt the unfolding of that something. She could see that he wasn't a boy as she'd known boys to be. He was gentler in his movements, his timbre, his thoughts, his interests. His girl friends were, in fact, only friends, desperate as she was to see otherwise. Andy seemed to be more concerned with the impression he made on the boys; an energy and a longing to please. And yes, she noticed Jeremy and how Andy behaved around him. How he cared about his appearance and hygiene whenever they were going to meet. How his name was mentioned only in passing at first but then often. How it was always Jeremy calling. How Andy seemed to stop seeing his other friends. What happened to Simone and Marie and Greg and Sal and Alex and Marie and Rhonda and Mike D. or was it Mike C. and Monique and all of the Nicoles. Where had they all gone? Or maybe she was wrong about adolescent boys. Maybe they were all this way. Surely, they all cared about their appearances. All of them had one best friend with whom they spent all of their time. And boys of this age were inappropriate, always joking and crossing lines. Henry wasn't much of a reference point. He hadn't been much for socializing. But he was the exception, and Andy's trajectory was the normal one, she told herself. And maybe this was how boys were in the United States. She couldn't remember truly how they'd behaved back home. Maybe they'd been this way there too. Yes, they joked. Yes, they traveled in pairs when they didn't travel in groups or alone. Everything could be explained.

And ignored. Andy would be leaving soon anyway. Rosario hadn't wanted her boy to leave, but now that her uneasiness grew, she hoped college would set him on the right path, take him from this.

Rosario would have been content enough to continue down this low-visibility road of intentions and hope, if not for the phone call. When Álvaro, Henry, or Andy were home, she didn't typically answer. It was likely to be a friend of the boys' or a bill collector or a telemarketer; she preferred to receive Final Notices in the mail and to avoid telemarketers entirely—oh, the pity for those people trying desperately to sell something, and her inability to say no easily, without first needing to work up her courage or a defensive ire. But on that Friday night, she was alone. Patty had just left. It was too late for a utility company or a vendor, Rosario thought. For the briefest of moments, she entertained the possibility that one of the three men in her life was hurt and that this call might be the terrible news. In the split second before she lifted the receiver from the wall, she wished for the caller to be someone collecting old debts or proposing new ones.

"Good evening," she said.

"Hello," responded a woman.

"Yes?"

"Hi. Is this Andy's mother?"

"Yes. Is everything okay?"

"Yes. Yes. My name is Eva. I'm Jeremy's mom."

18

SUNDAY MASS

So, see you in twenty years?"

"Sounds about right," I say, as I look at my wrist and mime reading a watch that doesn't exist. Jeremy smiles generously and exhales. I wonder if he gets out of my humor what I'm putting in.

It's Sunday, late morning. The men's final is on, but I don't care. Venus lost yesterday. It was a quick affair, but a triumphant tournament nonetheless. At this stage of her career, few could have predicted a run to the final. My father thought it was yet one more piece of evidence that Venus should retire. "She'll regret this in her back and in her knees," he said.

My parents are at church now; Jeremy's wife and children are there too. I wonder, as he and I lie in my room, if our families might be seated near one another, in adjoining pews, or in the same pew, having no knowledge of how they are linked—in this town, it's possible to know only the people who you know, and no one else. Maybe my father has spent the mass covering and uncovering his eyes to make Jeremy's children laugh; my father is like this with all children. Meanwhile, we, the devils, are at home, sinning, as we have been all week. It wasn't sinful twenty years ago, but it is now. Now, our actions have consequences.

Jeremy and I settled back into our cadence rather quickly. The only difference now is how articulated our roles are, no longer defined by the curiosity and discovery that marked our adolescence, when we wanted to know how the entirety of each other functioned. We weren't reckless back then, but we were rapacious hunters and foragers of the body, testing and tasting with abandon, quick to devour and be devoured in equal measure. In the last week, however, there was nothing mutable about how Jeremy and I fucked. We fit like two worn jigsaw pieces. He asserted himself in our first act of reconciliation, and I allowed it. Our bodies settled together quite naturally. Attached, initially, at our mouths, we made our way blindly toward his couch, where we tipped over and our clothes disappeared quick enough to tear seams. Jeremy's mouth settled on my cock before finding its way nimbly and with expedience to my asshole. With each flick and swirl, I moaned louder, which he took, rightfully, as an invitation to continue devouring me, after my asshole, my inner thighs, my balls, my cock again, then back to my asshole, which he spit into before getting onto his knees and slowly pushing the tip of himself inside of me. I didn't stop him because I knew that my physiology would stop him for me; I wouldn't be able to receive the entirety of him without a synthetic lubricant. To my surprise, Jeremy was able to enter me of his own accord, or maybe it was muscle memory. Maybe my body unlocked for him. The ecstasy of the moment didn't erase my fear of disease, but the battle between hypochondria and libidinal joy was won handily by the latter. After we finished, I began to worry. Instantly, I registered the faint tracks on the inside of Jeremy's forearms. I worried that if he was cheating on his wife with me, he'd probably cheated on her before. Then the realization hit me that I, too, had just cheated. I wrapped my arm across my face. It took Jeremy a moment to realize what was happening.

"Are you laughing?" he asked.

When I didn't respond, he put his arms around me awkwardly. "Are you okay? Did I hurt you?"

I shook my head but kept my face covered. He kissed the top of my head and worked his way down to my shoulder and my sides. It tickled, and I involuntarily shifted out of my defensive position.

"Don't worry, I'm safe," he said. "I haven't had sex with anyone but Tonya in years." He confided in me that he'd had hepatitis C years before, but he'd been treated and hadn't had it since.

I nodded, pretending I didn't care and that his assurances were sufficient, but my mood darkened. I felt uncomfortable, angry that there was a person in this world who continued to know me so well and uniquely, after all this time. He was a living embodiment of an invasion of my privacy, and I hated him for it, for having unauthorized access. I also loved him for it.

Each time we had sex in the days that followed, including this morning, we followed a similar pattern, but without tears and with condoms.

Yesterday, as we were lying on his bed, I told him about Paul and the gay bashing and about the bagel shop and the church. Jeremy's advice: mind your business.

"A, you don't even know for sure it was the same guy. B, what's the point? C, Paul's messed up. His dad was a beast. You know he was a predator? Like, legally. He ended up on a sex offender list. Shot himself a few years ago. I'm not surprised Paul's so fucked up. If I were you, I'd pretend it didn't happen. It's in the past."

For Jeremy, it seems that everything is better left in the past. But if the past festers still, isn't that the present? And my past with Jeremy is indeed unsettled. There are still too many unanswered questions.

Why did he back out of a plan that was primarily of his making? Why did his mother tell me, each time I called, that he didn't want to talk to me anymore? Why, on the few occasions when he answered the phone, did he hang up without saying a word? Why didn't he come to his window when I finally worked up the courage to stand outside of it? And why, when his father, who was oblivious to all of it, answered my call and passed him the phone, did Jeremy carry on with a one-sided conversation and hang up abruptly? The obvious answer to all of these questions is that he changed his mind about running away, about us, and about me. But why?

I used to wonder what I had done that was so terrible. What had made him fall out of love with me? And even if he had fallen out of love, certainly he'd gotten used to me—wasn't that reason enough to call, to explain, to respond? Inertia alone should have guided him back to me, just to check in, to say hello. Or goodbye. It didn't have to end with silence. And now he has the gall to gaze at me as if I were a warm, familiar meal?

"I'm sorry," he says. "I was wrong."

This was the same superficial apology I was able to pull from him yesterday. And the day before.

I get up quickly, with care not to spill from my stomach what remains of me and him. My T-shirt is on the floor; I use it to wipe up. I pick up my underwear and sit on the edge of the bed, my back to him. "Tell me more. Help me understand how something with so much momentum and hope can vanish like that. Doesn't have to be exact, but give me something."

He reverts quickly to the recalcitrant boy who was routinely upbraided by short, hoary-headed nuns. He clenches his teeth—there goes his jaw. He glowers at the floor. I don't know any longer if this is anger, frustration, or obfuscation. A long-ago echo of fear reverberates through me. In another setting, with another person, I would walk away. I should walk away.

"I called you like ten times from the train station," I say. "Remember, those were pay-phone days. I couldn't even leave you a message on your parents' machine. Do you have any idea how frustrating that was? At some point, I gave up and got on the train. I convinced myself that I'd messed up the meeting time and that you'd already gone without me. I went to the city, I met the landlord, like an hour late, so he was really upset. He was even more upset when I pulled out of the agreement. Then I had to lug all my shit back home."

Jeremy's chin touches his chest. He refuses to look up.

"What happened? How does someone stop feeling all of a sudden? And please, enough with the 'it's in the past' bullshit."

Jeremy holds his palms up over his eyes, like some sort of prayer ritual.

"You're not going to tell me?"

"Give me a fucking minute," he says loudly, but also stifled, as if something were wedged in his throat. "It's not that it's super hard for me to talk about us back then, but there's so much other shit that happened before and after. I don't want to talk about that, not with you. And I have to think about all of it when I think about us."

The silence that follows endures long enough for me to wonder if I'm going to drive this man to ruin. Do I have a right to demand answers? With his hands still shielding his eyes, he speaks. "I didn't stop loving you just because I didn't show up. It killed me not to meet you. It fucking wrecked me, you have no clue. After you left for school, I fought with my parents a lot. I spiraled. I got, like, three DUIs. I lost my license for six months and then a year. I couldn't get a job. I started fucking around with the wrong people. A little weed became a little coke, some E, some meth, crack, heroin. You name it, I swallowed it, smoked it, snorted it, shot it up. It wasn't your fault—I'm not saying that. I just didn't have a life after you. And plus, I knew what I did to you was fucked up. And the more time went by, the harder it got for me to take it back. Sometimes, life took over, I got jobs, my parents helped me out, I did a few semesters of college, but every time I thought about you and what I did, I felt sick. Plus . . . other shit. Other fucked-up shit I was trying to deal with. And nothing helped, except drugs." Jeremy's voice trails off until it disappears.

"A million times, I started to call you," he continues. "I got your number at school from Marie or Nicole L., but I'd hang up as soon as it started ringing. I remember a week when I called you every night at the same time—I was hoping you would figure it out. I told myself, if you called back, I'd talk to you. But you never picked up. Then I would think about you with someone else, and—I know, I know, what fucking right did I have, right? But it made me sick. Smoking a little herb or drinking another beer helped with that too. Andy, I swear to God, at some point, I woke up and I was twenty-one, and I couldn't believe it. Like, I'd let three years go by, and that also fucked me up. Then it was five years. Then, ten. I wasn't thinking about you every day, only once in a while . . . whenever I ate a bag of Doritos—I don't know why. Whenever Tracy Chapman came on the radio—you remember how many times you played that album? Whenever something important happened, you were the first person I thought about. And that just made me feel worse. I felt like I missed my chance, like . . . if we'd stayed together, I would have grown up and done something with my life."

Jeremy is naked in every way that a person can be naked. He's said it all, exactly as I've always wanted, but I don't take any pleasure from it. I might not have been the cause, but I compounded Jeremy's pain, and I'd known it all along. I knew that I was in a better place than he was. I had a new life to distract me, and he was stuck here. Stuck is what happens here, and I knew it. Even during the times when I was most angry with him, I knew it.

In a way, all of this reminds me of Henry. When he was alive, it pained me to think about him because I knew he wasn't happy. I knew the weight of failure was, for him, as ineffable as it was inescapable. He'd grown up with me, under the same *Just try* and *You can do it* regime. He'd watched me surpass our parents' expectations, and he was haunted by the reminders of what he could have accomplished.

"I'm sorry that your life has been so difficult," I say to Jeremy, as he steps into his briefs.

He drags the back of his hand across his nose. "It's not your fault."

"I'm sorry anyway. I appreciate you telling me all of this."

Jeremy nods and sniffles.

"But you haven't answered my question. The thing I've been asking all along. Why didn't you show up? Was it your family?"

Jeremy pulls a thin, gray T-shirt over his head. "Actually," he says, "it was your family."

"What?"

"I figured Henry never told you."

"Tell me what?"

"About coming to talk to me."

"About what?"

"About you. About us. It wasn't specific. He was clear though." Jeremy wipes his face with the waist of his shirt before I can hand him the box of tissues by my side. "A few days before we were supposed to leave, Henry came by Tony's. He used to come by all the time on his lunch break. Sometimes, we'd have a smoke together."

"Really?"

"Yeah, Henry was a cool guy. And I didn't blame him for anything. He did what was right."

"What did he do?"

"Nothing really. We had a conversation. He told me that my mom called your mom."

"What? When?"

"A few days before we were supposed to leave. My mom told her we were up to something. And that she thought we were planning to run away."

"How could your mom know?"

"I don't know. Lots of ways. I emptied my savings account. I had a bag packed in the closet. I was out late all the time, and I'm sure she knew it was with you. And maybe she heard us on the phone. Might have also been my nana. I think she knew. I'm not sure. What I know is your brother told me that your mom freaked out. She was afraid you were going to miss out on school. The scholarship. And she sent your brother to talk to me."

"I can't believe it," I say. "It's not possible."

Jeremy nods three times slowly.

"I mean, what the fuck. I came out to my parents years after that. And they pretended not to know."

"Your brother never brought that up. I don't know how much my mom told your mom about what she knew. All Henry said was to think about what this would do to you and to your family. That you weren't going to get a chance like that again."

My face is buzzing with anxiety. My hands feel a bit numb. My underwear is bunched up in my hand. I put my head down, almost between my knees.

"You okay?" Jeremy asks.

"Yeah, just wow," I say, without looking at him. I take a few long breaths. "How did he look?"

"Henry?"

"Yeah."

"Regular. Same as usual. I don't remember what he was wearing."

"No. What did he sound like? How did he say all this?"

Jeremy's face shrinks a bit and his gaze goes upward, obliquely, as if he knows exactly where the file cabinet for this memory is located. "I don't know. He wasn't angry, I remember that. But he wasn't happy either. You know how he was, kinda chill. It was a little awkward, but he was sure. Like he was doing what was right. 'Andy's going to have a decent life. My parents worked really hard for it, you know?' That's all he said."

"What did you say?"

"I didn't say anything. I thought maybe he was trying to trick me, and if I said anything he might beat the shit out of me. I just listened."

"Huh."

"Think about that."

"Think about what?"

"No. That was the last thing Henry said that day. 'Think about that.' Think about your parents and stuff like that."

"Why didn't you tell me?"

"Don't know. I guess I thought it was bad news, and I didn't want to give you bad news. I didn't want you to fight with your family."

"But *you* were my family too! We talked about everything."

"Honestly, I was going to ignore it all, but I got to thinking. It sort of made sense, what your brother said. Plus, honest . . . ? I was kind of scared about the whole plan—I was still going to meet you, but I was scared. And then my mom got in my face; she said because you were still seventeen and I was eighteen someone could call the cops on us."

"You believed her?"

"No. Maybe. I don't remember. But she also told me I was being selfish. That I was ruining your life. That you had a chance to do something with yourself. You were going to a great school."

"You should have told me. I could have handled it," I say, compelled to defend my younger self.

"I gave you all that shit about leaving for college, and you changed your life for me. I was selfish. If you'd given that up for me, it would've been hard to go back. You know how it goes. No one gets back on track once they've fallen off. Look at me. You would have got a job in the city and kept telling yourself that you'd go back to school next year. Always next year. But it's never next year. And if we didn't work out, you would have messed up your future for nothing."

"Not for nothing. You weren't nothing. We weren't nothing."

"You know what I mean."

"But maybe I wouldn't have messed up. Maybe I'd be the person I am today, and you would have been with me."

"Gimme a break."

"Why not?" I say, but I don't believe it. He's right. Everyone was right.

I am no longer in love with Jeremy. I am in love with the lust and the time travel, but in this moment I feel the rejection, deeply, because I know that nothing ever could have kept me from meeting him that day twenty years earlier. Nothing and no one.

I slide my underwear on and look up at Jeremy, who's standing, with one knee digging into the mattress, his folded sinewy leg a reminder of how naturally muscular he is. I make my way to him, crawling over the bed. Before he can say or do anything, I wrap my arms around his waist. I dig my face into his chest and squeeze so tight I feel his pelvic bone against my ribs. "Thank you," I say.

19
COMMUNITY COLLEGE

Everything was still wet: the roads, the passing cars, the edges of the windshield. Beads of water trapped the remaining daylight, giving the sunlit evening a glittery veneer. But that didn't keep Henry from speeding a forgivable seven miles over the limit. He knew it was seven because he'd made sure to glance at the dashboard when he heard the siren's whoop. It was the first day of the new semester, and class began in fifteen minutes.

It must have been the right rear taillight that had gotten the officer's attention. It had gone out the day before—at least that's when Henry first noticed it. He'd planned to deal with it over the weekend. Home and work, home and work, school and home: the risk of being stopped before then was low.

As the officer approached, Henry ran his hand along the tangle of dream catchers hanging, like handcrafted spiderwebs, from his rearview mirror. Then he quickly touched his index finger to his cardinal points—forehead, chest, left shoulder, right shoulder.

"Why didn't you stop when you heard the siren?" The man, not much older than Henry, wore sunglasses and kept one hand on his holster.

"I'm sorry, officer. I stopped right away."

"License and registration," he said, his voice severe, like a vault door slamming shut. He was angrier than he had any reason to be. "Wait here."

A cowboy, Henry thought. *A fucking cowboy.*

Henry calculated that it would take him eight minutes to get to the main parking lot of the campus. Class began in eleven minutes. Getting there in time wasn't completely out of the question, he told himself.

When fifteen minutes had passed and the officer hadn't yet returned, Henry contemplated getting out of the car. *Maybe if I just explain to him that I'm late for class*, he thought. Through his rearview mirror, Henry could see the officer sitting not quite thirty feet behind him in a white cruiser. He knew cops, no fewer than ten—acquaintances, neighbors, and members of his wife's family. Henry took them at their word, brave people with good intentions, minus the bad apples. But something about the air between him and this one made Henry stay put.

"The guys we know who are cops are the guys I would have never wanted to carry a gun. They were all bullies or, honestly, dumb." Andy had said this to him last year, after the murder of Oscar Grant, but some variation on this dour assessment had come up before.

"What about Jim Murphy?"

"Jim Murphy is a cop?"

"His brother Jake, too," explained Henry.

"What the fuck. That's insane. They were the nicest guys I've ever met."

"See!"

"Doesn't matter."

"'Doesn't matter'? You just said all cops were evil. And I gave you an example of two good guys."

"Even the good guys are ruined eventually. You can't have a two-tiered system of power in society. People walking around with a license to kill. That'll corrupt anyone, especially in an uneven society that uses the pretext of poverty to legitimize racism."

Henry twisted his lips and shook his head. He was sprawled out on their parents' couch in his usual special-occasion getup: a dark blue Tommy Hilfiger polo shirt adorned with a gold necklace and a crucifix charm, dark blue jeans, impeccably kept white sneakers, hair closely shorn at the sides and a strip of short curl at the top, gelled into something indestructible.

He'd just eaten too much of the pernil and the tres leches cake that Álvaro's sister had brought for Álvaro's birthday, against the wishes of Rosario, who'd prepared chicken skewers and a slew of vegan dishes from a cookbook Andy had gifted her for her birthday—green bean salad, potato salad with an egg-free mayo, even a strawberry shortcake with coconut cream—in hopes of establishing healthier traditions.

"You know what your problem is, Andy? You don't trust anyone. You have to give people the benefit of the doubt."

"Okay. Fine. I'll just keep hoping for the best and let the world continue as it is. But keep in mind that each of those police salaries, plus their cars and weapons, is probably equal to two social workers or two schoolteachers or a floor of beds in a homeless shelter."

"Dude, you just want bad guys running around loose?"

"Bad guys? Listen to yourself. This isn't *He-Man*. People with well-paying jobs and health care don't steal. People who take vacations and can send their kids to decent schools don't kill. People who don't feel trapped don't do *bad* things."

"Rich people kill."

"Yeah, but I'm talking about averages here, not outliers."

Henry's face took on a minor distortion, somewhere between discomfort and paralysis; it signaled the end of their discussion. Henry rarely shied away from a disagreement with friends or his wife, but he avoided arguments with Andy. He wanted, as an adult, to have the relationship with his brother that he hadn't had as a kid. He wanted one person in his life with whom there was no tension. Better to change the subject. Or walk away, which Henry had been doing for years.

The brother who visited nowadays wasn't the one that Henry had once known. Andy had always been a pain in the ass, but at least they'd been on the same plane. Now, Andy was like a substitute teacher. The kind who actually tries to get work done instead of giving the students time to socialize. But he wasn't all bad. Andy gave good advice about work, about school, about Ellie, about how to deal with their parents. And even when he was annoying, he had a point.

In order to reduce the risk of disagreement or discomfort, Andy and Henry stuck to the past. *Remember* became the introduction to every one of their conversations. Remember when the Ultimate Warrior beat Hulk Hogan at WrestleMania VII? No, it was at VI. Remember when mom got drunk and fell while trying to limbo at cousin Lina's wedding? Remember Sister Paula? She's a lesbian now. Remember Donny Donatelli? He's a meth head. Remember Tony's? It closed last month.

As the authoritative source on all things related to their home, their town, 1980s pop culture, major league sports, and fast food menus, Henry became the de facto gatekeeper of their past, and, in these instances, retained the mantle of big brother, an outcome that suited them both.

Next time, slow down," said the officer, after handing Henry back his license, registration, and the ticket.

"I was speeding, officer?" Henry was, by that point, furious. He'd been sitting in the car for twenty-five minutes, long enough to witness the officer smoking a cigarette and talking on his cell phone.

"Have a good day," responded the uniformed man in such an uncaring, perfunctory manner as to suggest that he meant the opposite.

Fifty-five miles per hour, read the ticket. The fine was ninety-five dollars. The speed limit on that road was fifty.

Andy would have screamed racism, Henry thought. Racial profiling, he would have said. *RDW*, he'd said many times. "R, record police encounters with your phone. *D*, do not consent to any searches. And *W*, write down car and badge numbers. Simple."

Simple? Maybe with the cops where Andy lived, but here, there was no way he could get away with any of that, Henry thought. Besides, that's not who he was. To be that person would have required him to live another way. And although Henry could recall many of these types of encounters, he chose instead to focus on the ones that had been friendly and professional. He thought of the Murphys. Really good guys. They'd all gone fishing together last year. Chartered a boat. Caught sea bass. They weren't racist. They spoke positively about Obama. A few bad guys couldn't give everyone else a bad name. Henry believed this, despite never having been pulled over by the same cop twice, and despite the guys at work all admitting that they'd been pulled over once at some point in their lives, for driving drunk or hitting ninety on the interstate, while he'd already been pulled over two times that year—and it was only February.

Henry stared at the dashboard clock until it came into focus. Then he pulled away from the shoulder and crossed the six nearly empty lanes, U-turning back toward home. He would rather miss class than walk into the room twenty minutes late. All of the eighteen-year-olds staring at an old guy with a gut and a marinara stain, neither of which could be concealed by his tie. And he was starving. He would have spent the entire class shifting in his seat, trying to prevent the grumbling. This was all a stupid idea anyway. Not even his idea. Andy and his parents had encouraged him to give school another try. They'd called Ellie and encouraged her to encourage him too. A family effort. *Never too late*, Andy had said, at least once a year for almost fifteen years. It was Andy who, after one brief conversation, had sent the list of prerequisites Henry would need to get his associate's degree and apply to a radiology technician school.

"Ellie's cousin works at a hospital. She says you can make eighty thousand a year doing radiology, up to one hundred twenty thousand with overtime. She gets good PTO, good insurance, and a pension because she's union." That's all Henry had said to trigger Andy's emails and texts.

Henry wanted to go back to school, but he used the pretext of family pressure as a cushion and an escape hatch. If it all went awry, he could easily blame someone else. *This was all your idea anyway.*

Henry had tried seven times to go to college since high school. Each time there was a reason to back out or drop out. Once, he developed pneumonia and missed too many classes to catch up. One year, midsemester, Henry decided that he needed to find a night job because of all the costs that came with the new baby. Another year, it was pneumonia again. Another time, he dropped a class too late in the semester and as a consequence he lost his financial aid. Then, the second baby. This time, Henry argued, was his last chance. "I'm too old to keep trying. Third kid on the way. I don't see myself as a guy with three kids starting college again. It's now or never."

It was never.

After this most recent false start, Henry resolved to ask Ikbir for a raise instead. He worked on commission, but there was a base salary, too—miserable, but something. Ikbir was the type of boss who didn't say no capriciously, who sent fruit baskets when children were born, who allowed for proper lunch hours—not like the miserly thirty minutes at other places—who each Christmas gave his employees a heavily discounted VCR, CD, or DVD player, or in Henry's case, PlayStations, Xboxes, and Nintendo consoles. Ikbir increased base salaries twenty-five cents every year, but Henry was determined to ask for a dollar more, knowing well that Ikbir wouldn't want to risk losing him before the holidays.

Henry had left Uncle Billy's many times over the years, to work at a bank, a supermarket, an office supply store, a coffee shop, a pet clinic, and a few fast food restaurants. From stocker to cashier to barista to receptionist to shift supervisor and eventually manager; but inevitably he'd hit a ceiling. There was either no place farther to go, or he couldn't without a college degree.

"My supervisor doesn't know shit. I had to train him," Henry complained to Ellie during his penultimate career shift as a bill collector at the corporate offices of Be Well, the hospital empire. "He's the boss's son. That's all his qualifications."

There'd always be someone who'd swoop in and take credit for Henry's accomplishments or ideas or who'd scapegoat him for their own inadequacies. Henry's quarrel wasn't with the natural order of things; he understood that there were more levels in life above him than beneath. But how to unlock them? Where was the key to exit this netherworld full of expectations and responsibilities but bereft of power or control?

The edges of Henry's heretofore good nature were well frayed by his early thirties.

"He didn't even train us on the new reporting system like he was supposed to, but he wrote us up because Corporate tore him a new one. He's an asshole. He came down on me the hardest. I know it's because I'm making more calls and follow-ups than anyone else. Motherfucker."

"Did you try telling him that?" Ellie asked.

"He's twenty-four. He doesn't listen to shit. And he doesn't want to hear it from someone under him anyway."

"But I thought he really liked you."

"He does when he's not in hot water."

"There's nothing you can do about that. Just take deep breaths, and do your best to ignore him. Remember: *stress is toxic.* It'll make your diabetes and blood pressure worse."

"Oh, okay. I'll just do some Jedi mind tricks and convince myself I'm not stressed." Henry swigged from his Dunkin' Donuts coffee. "Easy for Andy to give advice. He has no problem paying his bills."

Ellie ran out of supportive words. Instead, she pursed her lips and raised her eyebrows, like a friendly cartoon character with little dialogue. They both stepped out of the minivan. Henry knotted his tie in the window's reflection, while Ellie waddled around to meet him. The gray at her roots was creeping upward. Her hair was no longer the vibrant red-orange it'd been when they'd met. Over the years, it'd been platinum blond, dirty blond, streaked with purple, shaved around the sides and back, and recently, jet-black. *Grandma*, Henry joked whenever the gray appeared, and the next day, she'd make an appointment. But Henry hadn't mentioned it recently, and Ellie didn't seem to care either.

They kissed, a small peck on the lips, before he petted her swollen belly. "Don't worry," he said to Ellie's midsection, "your life will be easier—or maybe not."

"Hey! Don't say that to our little piglet!"

Henry laughed, but the moment of honesty lingered.

"We'll be here at five to pick you up!" Ellie called out.

Henry had, five months earlier, had a minor stroke. He'd been driving home from work when it happened.

"I heard a pop, and pressure built up behind my ear. My vision got blurry. And I felt my face get weak. I drove straight here. I'm in the waiting room now," Henry explained to Andy over the phone from the hospital.

"A minor ischemic attack," said the cardiologist on call, after a few days and a slew of tests. He prescribed a stronger dose of cholesterol medication and a change in diet. He also told Henry to reduce his stress. The advice had since become a sort of Greek chorus. Emails from Andy, Ellie's words in the morning and at night, reminders from Rosario and Álvaro whenever he dropped the kids off for a visit. Even Patty was chiming in with text messages at night: "Honey, watch comedies. The laughter will do you good. Don't stress." It seemed everyone was encouraging him to achieve the impossible.

Without meaning to, Henry did the opposite. After the stroke, he began having anxiety and panic attacks regularly, misconstruing every pain or shortness of breath for another stroke or the onset of a cardiac episode. He pored over the pamphlets the hospital had included in his discharge paperwork, which explained that strokes begat strokes. This was why he'd left Uncle Billy's for the job at the clinic. He'd assumed that a desk job would be better for him than the stress of selling large-screen television sets to indecisive customers who were incapable of emptying their car trunks before coming to buy appliances. Since the stroke, Ellie had assumed the role of chauffeur. She feared what would happen if he were to have another stroke while he was driving. Henry pretended to put up a fight, but he was relieved to have her attention and to have one less task in his day. This happened to coincide with the repossession of Ellie's old jeep, which streamlined the decision-making.

Henry called Andy often in those months after his stroke.

"You think the tightness in my chest is the beginning of something?"

"I don't—"

"Should I go to the hospital?"

"I'm not a doctor, Henry."

"I know, but you know this stuff."

"How many times have you gone to the ER in the last two months?"

"I don't know, eight, ten times."

"What do they say each time?"

"That I'm fine."

"Right. You've gone to the cardiologist, the pulmonologist, endocrinologist, neurologist, an eye doctor, and physical therapy. You're not healthy, but you're not dying. Did you have a chance to look at the list of counselors I sent you?"

"Not yet."

"How about the meditation class?"

"No."

"The Michael Moore documentary?"

"C'mon."

"Well, you're not going to overcome capitalism in the ER."

"Here we go."

"You work at the hospital during the week, Billy's on the weekend, you don't like either, plus the bills, plus your health, plus you have kids—do you even get to spend time with them?"

"Dude, when I get like this, I can barely brush my teeth. How am I going to be a dad?"

"Listen, you already know what I think: going back to school is the only way out of this. But you're not doing that. So now you just have to find a way to manage the stress so that it doesn't kill you."

"So you think it could kill me? The pain in my chest right now is different than the other times. And I also feel like a shortness of breath and a small headache that comes and goes."

"I can't guarantee that you're not having a stroke or a heart attack, but it seems very unlikely based on your past symptoms. If it makes you feel better, why don't you go sit in the parking lot of the ER. If it gets worse, you'll be close enough. And if it doesn't get worse, then you don't have to worry."

On some nights, before going to the ER, Henry would shower and put on his work clothes and sleep the remaining hours in the car.

When Henry wasn't analyzing elevations and dips or ghost palpitations, he was obsessing over his weight and searching for the new, this-is-the-one diet. He'd embarked on dozens of new regimens over the years—no meat, more meat, fish only, no carbs, all fats, small portions, one large banquet at noon, nothing before 1 P.M., nothing after 4 P.M., juices, pills, oils, teas, only green things, only red things, organic only, fasting. He'd spent entire paychecks on starter kits and professional consultations with diet doctors who promised results. Henry proved adept at losing a significant amount of weight immediately, which motivated him to return to the gym, and for months at a time, he'd be a new person, confident and optimistic, until the alarm clock rang and the bills arrived and the routine wore him down. One of the many doctors he saw after the stroke advised him to lose weight incrementally because sudden changes would increase the risk of a heart attack. Henry immediately took to eating more vegetables and smaller portions in an attempt to make his dinner plate resemble the perfectly constructed drawings in the stroke pamphlets. And for the last few months, it worked.

. . .

You don't look well," said Ikbir.

"Must be my blood sugar," Henry responded. "Didn't have time for dinner during the rush."

Henry had taken to skipping meals whenever he didn't prepare and pack them himself. He was trying to spend less, and the cheapest meal at Joe's was never less than twenty dollars. Athena's was about fifteen, even when he ordered from the all-day breakfast menu.

Ikbir, whose wife and brother were both diabetics, went in search of a snack for Henry. He found a granola bar in the staff room—a large closet with chairs, a microwave, a coffee machine, and a small refrigerator. When he returned, Henry was face down on the floor. Ikbir noted that the clock read 11:59 P.M. when he called the ambulance; he'd kept the store open late because of the holidays. Ikbir, a sturdy man with considerable upper-body strength for his age, wasn't able to turn Henry over on his own, primarily because of the narrowness of the aisle. For leverage, he pressed his feet against the top-loading washing machine on display, but the resistance from Henry's dead weight forced the machine onto its hind legs. Ikbir was eventually able to get him onto his back and employ what he remembered of a CPR class he'd taken years earlier. After he felt the crack of one of Henry's ribs, he stopped and waited for the ambulance to arrive. Ikbir pulled the phone from Henry's pocket and fruitlessly typed combinations of numbers until the screen locked. The phone number he had on file for Henry was outdated. After the ambulance took him away, Ikbir drove to Rosario and Álvaro's. In the early years, when Henry was still a kid, Ikbir had driven him home several times in the rain or snow, or when it had gotten too late.

There was no doorbell. In the second-floor window, he could see the familiar blue light of a television screen pulsating intermittently. Ikbir tired of knocking and searched the dark patio for a few pebbles. He lobbed them up in the most carefully urgent manner he could manage. After several clumsy attempts, a larger light came on. Álvaro's head slowly approached the window.

Rosario called Ellie and Andy. Álvaro stayed with the children. Rosario and Ellie drove to the hospital together.

Henry was effectively dead from the moment his body hit the stained maroon carpet of the store, but Rosario asked Ellie to keep him on the respirator.

"I want his body to be warm when his father and brother arrive."

Ellie didn't want the children to see Henry pale and feeble, with a greenish hue, tubes and cables sprouting from his face, arms, and chest. Dead.

Dead and thirty-two. Rosario's father would live for another three years; he was ninety-nine. Álvaro's mother was ninety. But Enrique was dead.

Dead.

Thirty-two, and dead.

Álvaro cried intermittently, at the hospital, in the car, in the kitchen, in bed, at work, at the funeral home. Rosario, however, cried mostly at night, in the bathroom. In the days before the funeral, she busied herself planning, shopping for a new suit for Henry, learning to bake again in order to distract her grandchildren. Five days after Ikbir had found Henry, Rosario was already four pounds lighter. On the morning of the funeral, she asked Álvaro to call family members, who were driving from the city and nearby states, and tell them that they should go home after the mass; she didn't want anyone at their house. At the funeral, Álvaro thanked all of the mourners, one by one—dozens of coworkers from the various short-term jobs Henry had held over the years, a few neighbors, and a couple of high school friends. Be Well sent flowers. Álvaro had wanted to invite everyone back to their home after the funeral, but Rosario was resolute: just immediate family and Patty, the only neighbor they'd ever cared for. A couple of aunts, a few cousins, and a few more second cousins forced their way into the late lunch at Joe's anyway. They hadn't driven all that way to turn around so soon. After the meal, Álvaro collected aluminum trays of homemade food from the trunks of his relatives' cars. He apologized to everyone when Rosario refused to say goodbye and insisted on walking home. It was okay, they said. Rosario was in shock, they whispered.

The ground was covered in a thin layer of snow that crunched before vanishing beneath each of Rosario's footsteps. Andy followed after.

"I feel as if I've lost a finger on each hand," Rosario said to him, as they waited for a lull in traffic so they could cross the street. Andy looped his arm through hers. It was the first thing she'd said since barking at the server for bringing fried instead of sautéed calamari.

"Andrés? I want to tell you something. I'm not proud of this, but I need to say it."

"Say whatever you want, Mom."

"I knew this was going to happen. I knew it. Your brother was a good person, but very lost."

"It wasn't so bad."

"Hmm . . . Andy, don't do that. We all thought it. I felt it, that he was going to die young. I had nightmares. Once—que dios me perdone—I told myself that maybe, when the moment arrived, I would feel relief. Not for me, but for him. For years, he'd been sick. Always anxious. Moody. Angry. Eating so much, spending his money on garbage. Pura basura, Andy. You know how many bill collectors called us every week? So many QVC boxes came to our house because he didn't want Ellie to see. Basura. It was like an obsession. One time, your father went down to your brother's basement to help him replace the boiler. He said there were at least fifty boxes down there. All garbage. Compulsive obsessive disease."

"Obsessive compulsive disorder?"

"Yes. Your brother had something like that. What else do you call it when someone doesn't have enough to pay their bills or take care of their family but spends like that?"

"Mom, some people take trips to Paris."

Andy, who had no problem criticizing Henry in life, was suddenly uneasy. "Trolls."

"Mom, don't be mean."

"No, mi amor. He bought troll dolls. He told your father he was saving dolls because they would be worth something someday. Can you believe that? I can't."

Rosario's eyes were moist and lined with a thin network of jagged red lines—she hadn't slept more than a few hours each of the previous nights. She set her purse atop a concrete bollard in the strip-mall parking lot they were crossing and pulled out a folded pink tissue to wipe her nose.

"Don't think like this, Mom. What's the point?"

"Listen to me, Andrés. Whatever I have done to ruin your life, por favor, find a way to fix it. I'm an old lady. I can't fix anything, but you are still young. Go to therapy. Yell at me. Hit me if you want. Just don't hold it all in. Don't repeat our mistakes. Your brother is exactly who we made him to be. And his failures are my failures. He's dead because I'm being punished for what I did wrong."

"Mom, don't—"

"No! Now, listen: I'm allowed to be wrong. And you're allowed to be better. It doesn't hurt me to be wrong. I'm not the person I used to be. With age—you'll appreciate this one day—it gets easier to see where you went wrong. I was young. I didn't know anything. Nada nada nada. I hated it in this country. I hated your father for leaving me here, in this town. I hated that I didn't know anyone. I hated the weather. I hated estos Americanos de mierda and the way they looked at me. You don't believe me. You think I'm crazy, but they looked at me. In the supermarket, at the school, at church, everywhere I went, I looked up, and they were staring at me. Never smiling. Never once. They never said hello. They never offered to help me with the groceries or to hold the door open. Eran bebés ustedes, and sometimes you were little devils, like all children, screaming and fighting, and these people just stared. 'Can't you control your children?' Strangers yelling at me. Motherfuck everyone!"

Rosario's hand chopped through the air, as if she were slaying demons. She walked briskly, a half-step ahead of Andy, her warm breath forming a cloud that replenished faster than it could dissipate, like a short steam train.

"I didn't want you or your brother to face that, so I became overprotective. It was worse for Enrique. He should have been playing outside with other children, or in a daycare, but I was afraid. I thought they would hurt him. I thought my job was to protect him from all of that. But I should have done the opposite. I should have taken him to the playgrounds. I should have been louder. And dressed how I wanted. I should have fought back more than I did. But I thought it was better to kill everyone with kindness. To smile and walk away. To make them think they had no effect on me. Instead, I made Henry a coward. No, not a coward. Afraid of life. He never wanted to leave my side. Nunca. And when I went back to work, he resented me for it. He started getting bad grades and skipping school. And to make it worse, he didn't have many friends. He wasn't like you, remember? It didn't come easy. The parents didn't call me to ask if Henry could come over and play.

That was my fault too. I should have called those parents. I should have said, 'You ignorant assholes! Fuck you! Fuck you! Motherfuck you!'"

Rosario froze, her arm raised in a clenched fist, tears streaming down her made-up face. Andy, too, remained still. Rosario cursed so infrequently, but this was the occasion for it, he thought. Now was the time for cursing.

"Mom, none of this shit is anyone's fault. This is bigger than us."

"Sí lo es. Es mi culpa. I remember one time—I will never forget this— two little boys called him that word."

"Which word?"

"The one against la gente negra. I was picking him up from school. In kindergarten. And I heard two little boys telling him he was dirty. Dirty because of his skin. 'Are you a . . . ?' You know what. That's what they asked him. And I looked up at their mothers, and they didn't do anything to correct those boys. ¡Americanos ignorantes de mierda! I never took him back there. That was why I wanted you in Catholic schools. St. Peter y St. Ignatius weren't perfect, but they saved you. I know you don't believe in anything, but as degenerate as the Catholic church is, at least God was there. And even if he doesn't protect against everything, he protects against some things. Many of those kids came from good families. Better than the ones that went to the public schools."

"Oh, Mom."

"Ya sé lo que vas a decir, 'Public schools are good.' Maybe. But it's different now. You don't know how it was before. Those schools used to be scary. Everyone was scared of sending their kids there. And we wanted you and your brother to have a chance. It doesn't matter now. It's too late. I can't have him back now. My baby." Again, Rosario stopped to blow her nose. She inhaled deeply and shook her head. "One day, Andy, you will know this. Your first baby. It's hard for you to imagine, but Henry was like my friend. I was his mother, but he was my only friend. The only person I talked to every day. The only person who listened to me. We ate together and sang together and learned English together. I had one job in this world and I failed—"

"Don't say that. Please. You're a great mother. I love you, and Henry loved you too. You know that. And you know what? It couldn't have been all bad because Henry was a good dad. And his kids are amazing."

Rosario patted Andy's hand. "You're right," she said.

"Mom, don't put this all on yourself. You made choices. Dad made choices. So did I. And most of all, Henry made choices for himself."

"Sí, ya lo sé. But what I did was the cause of the life that Henry had."

"Mom, there are so many things that contribute. You don't know for sure. I know you don't like me saying this, but don't forget that capitalism—"

"Andrés, please! I know you're trying to help, but I don't need a lecture right now."

20

MARTYRDOM

'm just going to get this out in the open. I sensed during my last visit that you're not completely okay with it"—I raise my hands, and with two fingers from each, I affect quotation marks around *it*—"but can you try and get over it for a minute, so that I can feel comfortable being honest?"

Simone slides up straight in her chair. I can't help but stare at her knees; I brought her a tub of shea butter when I was here last, and now her arms and legs are glistening.

"How dare you? I'm not a troglodyte, Andy." Simone takes on a sportive British accent.

I remember now that Simone was a fan of accents, and Jane Austen. She was a born mimic. Midway through any movie, she could intone the actor's voice: Jodie Foster's West Virginian in *Silence of the Lambs*, Alicia Silverstone's valley girl in *Clueless*, Tina Turner's Tennessee-British hybrid in *Mad Max: Beyond the Thunderdome*. She watched *Cool Runnings* in the eighth grade and sporadically pretended to be Jamaican for a year, until Sister Kay sent a letter home asking that Simone's parents talk to her about reverting to her natural voice. I always believed Simone would end up an actor or at least on *Saturday Night Live.*

"Andy, I may not agree with all the parts of your life, but I love you just the same," she says earnestly in the all-white lounge. This morning, we're tucked in a corner, behind a large pillar that hides us from the other patients.

I wonder if Simone's adult-onset homophobia is a reflection of self-hatred or a coping mechanism. Is it possible that life, in her mind, is scary enough without adding the complications of sexuality and its concomitant layer of discrimination? It has to be something like this. She was, after all, a lesbian. She can't suddenly not be. Even in the age of sexual fluidity, Simone's butchness is one of her defining characteristics. Or maybe I'm not remembering well. Maybe her queerness was implied but never confirmed. Maybe she was just being a curious human who wasn't ever and would never be a lesbian. Maybe she was simply self-assured in her sexuality, like a Canadian. Maybe I was projecting my own experience onto her.

I accept her piousness as good enough because I need someone to talk to. About Jeremy.

"Jeremy?" Simone turns her gaze up toward the ceiling, a pockmarked grid of cork panels. "Jeremy . . . wait—Jeremy Jeremy?"

"Yeah."

"You still talk to him? You kept in touch with him but not me?"

I explain everything. I tell her about the reunion, the pot, the secret high school relationship, the plan to escape, the current secret relationship, etc. Simone nods along, occasionally sliding a hand over her mouth as her eyes grow. When I finish recounting everything, she says nothing. Almost nothing. She squints as if she's just stubbed her toe or looked into the sun. I can't tell if she's distracted by her own thoughts or analyzing mine. Best guess: she's disappointed. I've probably broken a couple of major commandments and a few minor ones.

"You bastard," sluices out with a passive, perfectly neutral tone, but at a formidable volume. "How can you still be hung up on that guy? He only ever makes you an asshole."

As her words hang in the air, I lean back and catch a sliver of the wider space. I see a few people I don't recognize from previous visits. I wonder how often new patients come to this facility. I wonder who has left and where their lives take place. I prepared myself this morning for the glares and the claustrophobia, and I'm almost comfortable, even if a little embarrassed by Simone's shouting. I'm sure everyone here heard her call me a bastard and an asshole.

"Please explain," I say, although I don't really want an explanation. "How was I an asshole?"

"Nothing. Just remembering he was the reason you ditched me in high school. Now I get it."

"I didn't ditch you."

"Dude, you ghosted me before ghosting was a thing. Jeremy was suddenly your bestie, and you completely forgot about me. You didn't give a shit after my dad died."

I feel an urge to defend myself, to deny her version of the events, especially because she's wrong about her dad. He died before things got serious with Jeremy. But there's a chance she's right about everything else. I gave a shit, but probably not enough.

"I'm sorry," I say.

"S'okay," she responds. "That was a long time ago. You were a kid." Simone caps her muted absolution with a shrug. "I was too."

I don't need this shit crosses my mind. I mean, give me a freaking break. This isn't all my fault. Maybe if society hadn't been so completely demoralizing for queer youth, I might have found a way to incorporate my relationship with Jeremy into my social life. As it happened, I was effectively forced into a double life.

"It's not going to work," Simone says.

"What isn't going to work?"

"The thing with Jeremy."

"What makes you so sure?"

"What you have back home is the real thing. I can see that when you talk about Marco. Jeremy is just a flash from the past, like me. When you get back home, you'll forget all of it. Work on what you have."

Simone speaks with a certainty and clarity that's in stark contrast to the surroundings. She's like a car breaking through a low-hanging fog. Why is she still here?

"You don't think there's even a small chance that Jeremy could leave his wife, and we get to live out the lives we were meant to have?"

"Is that what you want?"

"No. I don't know. Probably not."

Simone's eyes disappear beneath her lids. She sighs, before bringing her hands together in a soft clap and wringing them. "Did you see *You've Got Mail?*" she asks.

"Yeah. But I don't remember any of it, except for the bookstore. And everyone's white. And the mom from *All in the Family* is in it."

"Dude, you continue to be the weirdest person I know. Focus. Remember, before Tom Hanks's plane crashes, he's going to marry Meg Ryan? And when he's finally rescued, he comes back to her, but she's already with someone else? And she tells him that he's the love of her life, but she's moved on."

"I think that's *Cast—*"

"That's kinda like this. You've both moved on. And if you try to come back to the past, you're going to mess up your future. Yeah, it's sad what happened between you two, but it's not worth the disruption."

"Maybe you're—"

"Besides, you said he has kids?"

"Yeah."

"Don't do that to them. They don't deserve it."

I had hoped Simone's advice would be more impulsive. I expected her to tell me to run away with Jeremy. To take a chance. I don't even know if that's what I want, but I wanted someone to advocate for it.

We talk for a while longer about her comic books, which she works on at night and keeps under her bed. "They'll steal anything here. Everything," she says.

I offer to buy a few. I say it to be helpful, but it comes across as odd because she wasn't offering.

"Yeah? That would be amazing," she says. "I can bring them next time."

I say "okay" several times, hoping to bring the conversation to a natural close, but it's not natural, and she doesn't catch on anyway. I accompany my seventh or eighth *okay* with a clear gesture: I stand up. Today's visit has to be short because my dad is only getting bloodwork done. I suspect he's already propped up against the car.

Simone and I continue chatting as we walk.

"How long do you think before you get to leave this place?"

"Honestly, I don't know. I thought I'd be out of here by now. My mom's waiting for papers to sign or something. Soon, I hope."

"You want to leave?"

Simone comes to a stop. I keep going a few feet before I realize she's making a point.

"What kinda question is that?" she asks.

"I don't know. I just meant, there must be something spa-like about this experience, no? Easier than the world."

"No, Andy. Not even a little. Have you ever been to a spa?"

"Sorry. I just meant that, sometimes, I have days when the world feels too much, and I wish I could stay home."

"Andy, who would choose this? Look around. I can't go outside. I can't cut my toenails without supervision. I can't have sushi. My shit gets stolen. This is almost like prison." Simone looks down at her own physique, raises her arms, and curls her hands into soft fists. "If I wasn't able to defend myself, who knows what might have happened to me by now. I'm not afraid of the world out there. I think it's afraid of me, but I'm not afraid of it. So, yeah, I want to leave here as soon as possible."

"I'm sorry. I should've—"

"You don't have to keep apologizing. In just a few days, you've become my best friend again. I don't care what you say, as long as you keep coming back. Okay?"

I fear I'm not who she expects or who she needs, but I don't overthink it. "Okay," I respond.

"And thank you for the Swedish Fish." Simone lifts the brown paper bag and smiles. "I'm going to have just a few a day," she explains, "so they last."

"There's also dental floss there—the little picks with string," I say. "I think they look like fancy cheese slicers."

"Monkey wrenches," Simone says.

21

THE HOLY SPIRIT

When was the last time you took Phyllis out dancing? A good husband would take his wife out."

"Why are you messing with those group boat trips when you could buy your own boat? You're a professor. Not a gas station attendant."

"Leather boots. You don't own leather boots. You should own leather boots."

At first, he found himself turning around, looking for people who weren't there. On the street, he swore he'd heard someone calling out for him: "Wesley! Over here!" Sometimes, they seemed like familiar voices. Once, he swore he heard his dead mother: "Wes, the refrigerator door. Why do you never close it?" When the voices started giving him unsolicited advice and straight up commands, he convinced himself they weren't coming from the outside world, no matter how distant they were. They were just passing thoughts, Wesley told himself. Or dreams he was reliving. But he couldn't shake the feeling that the voices were waiting for him to respond. That, however unwittingly, he was participating in a conversation.

Along with the voices, there was exhaustion. Fatigue that hadn't been there before, not since he was a kid, and only on the summer nights when he'd finish slicing and bagging the fruit that his mother would sell in the park. Next came the paranoia. Everyone was ignoring him, he thought. And the voices chimed in on that too. "You're not being invited to anything, you know that, right?" The dean claimed to have forgotten to invite him to a lunch. A month later, he wasn't invited to an "impromptu" dinner. Then someone else excluded him from an after-work birthday celebration for a colleague.

This is exactly what Wesley had expected before he'd taken the position. They were going to outdo themselves praising him when it was convenient, use him for accreditation meetings in order to fool the inspectors into believing that their faculty was keeping up with the times. Racial harmony, they'd say, and showcase him as part of affirmative action quotas on their funding applications, but they would never fully respect him.

You knew that's what they were fixing to do all along.

The problem with some mental illnesses is that they closely mirror a life oppressed. When the spate of slights came, Wesley couldn't understand why they were coming in that moment and with such frequency, but it never occurred to him that they were anything other than the assertion of whiteness. Several times, he had been a lone voice at faculty meetings. Whenever protests swept the campus, he argued for faculty involvement. When the union called for a strike, it was Wesley who suggested an auxiliary fund for adjunct faculty. At a recent meeting, he'd suggested a course on slavery and reparations. All of which had elicited courteous discomfort but not scorn. Wesley wasn't surprised by any of it. Politically speaking, he often felt that he was fifty years in the future while everyone else was fifty in the past. There were, however, other discourtesies, more institutional in nature, like Wesley's tenure review process, which began later than it did for some of his younger and newer colleagues; his office, which was the third smallest, after his two female colleagues; and his campus parking permit, although he didn't drive to work, for which he was always "next in line." In fact, white supremacy and mental illness were locked in a dead heat, egging each other on, two forces on a course for collision.

You might be as worthless as they think you are.

Wesley was a self-aware person in most respects, but he was having dif-ficulty distinguishing between what was real and what felt real. *The perceived is real insofar as its consequences* was something he was known to say. He wanted, however, the certainty to be able to draw a distinction. There were extreme things, but those were clear. Then there were the things he couldn't help but question despite knowing the answers. Everything that happened to him at work, on the expressway (did everyone get cut off and flipped off as much as he did, he wondered?), on his block (he didn't want to go to their pool parties and barbecues, but as far as he was concerned, he was being denied the right to decline their invitations), and in the supermarket (on no fewer than a dozen occasions, elderly women had reminded him that he needed to pay for the gum or magazine he'd barely just grabbed while wait-ing in line for the cashier) had always given an air of conspiracy to life, but now it was more ominous and urgent. Had he let his guard down? Those who conspired may not have been working in concert, but the ubiquity and frequency of their actions formed a delicate, detailed, and formidable web, in which he found himself trapped.

They don't want you here.

Wes, is there anything you want to talk about? Is everything alright at home?"

The dean sat behind a wide, dark wood desk, in a gray tweed suit. He was a new dean, a new hire from an even more prestigious university. He wore bow ties and smoked a pipe. He was an unambiguously eccentric person—in the afternoons, he wandered the floor, watering the plants from his can of diet soda. "It enlivens them," he would say.

"Now, Dean Wilklow."

"Call me Bob, please."

"Bob, I don't think I know what you mean. I'm fine."

"Listen, and I don't want you to take this the wrong way. You know I'm a hip guy. Aren't I?" Bob paused here for confirmation from Wesley but continued when Wesley hesitated. "And I pride myself on treating every-one equally, so you would be misguided to call my intentions into doubt. Wouldn't you agree, Wes?"

Not affirming Bob's intentions twice in one conversation might have constituted an intractable besmirching of his character. "Yes, Bob. I would have to agree with that."

"Good, good, so you'll believe me when I say that I'm only mentioning this out of concern. After all, there's nothing wrong with a drink from time to time. I, myself, am guilty of a Wednesday martini, and sometimes, a Friday one as well"—here, Bob slapped his desk with exaggerated joviality—"but I know that I have to be in control at work. You know what I mean?"

"Of course."

"We can't be slurring and nodding off, speaking in word salad. That's when we know we've gone too far. This is academia, Wes. We have an image to uphold."

"Bob, I don't think I'm following you."

"Are you drunk now, Wes?"

"Absolutely not! What? I—"

"No need to get bent out of shape. Let's keep the emotions in check and have a productive conversation."

"But I mean it, Bob. I haven't touched a single drink. Ever at work."

"Wes, several of your colleagues have seen you slumped at your desk. They say they've heard you speaking incoherently. I, myself, have walked past your office before and heard you talking to yourself."

"I might have been on the phone with a student or, or—maybe it was Phyllis."

Wesley's clumsy defenses only seemed, judging by Bob's avuncular, institutional stare, to implicate him further.

When it was all over, he suggested that Wesley take some personal time.

"I'm going to sue. I have to sue. There's no other way."

"It's incredible. I don't know what to say. Are you sure that's what he said?" asked Phyllis.

"'Several of your colleagues think you're a drunk,' he said. Several! I knew this would come eventually. They're after me. They've always been after me, but I was too stupid, stuck on this kumbaya vibe." Wesley paced the kitchen, his hands steepled over his nose and mouth, then massaging his entire face, as if he were smearing sunscreen. "Be honest, baby, have you seen me walking in drunk? Do you see any proof that I'm an alcoholic?"

"Please. Of course not." Phyllis had been slicing up apples for an evening snack, something she had been doing lately in order to avoid succumbing to her well-known cheese hankerings, but the knife was, at present, jabbed into the fruit as she gave Wesley her attention. "This is madness. There's got to be an explanation. You sure there's no other Black person in your department? They're capable of mistaking you for Harry Belafonte, Sly Stone, and Clarence Thomas all at once."

"Only other Black folks in that building are a few students and the janitors."

Phyllis slapped the counter, scattering the apple slices. "That's it! They must have seen a student or a janitor taking a nap."

"At my desk?"

"If they can't tell the difference between the who, how are they gonna keep track of the where?"

Wesley shut one eye. Then he ran a hand through his closely cut hair, accentuating in the process a clear recession, two inlets at either end of a rounded coastline. "You think?"

"Of course. This is what they do. This sort of mistaken identity is well within their norm."

Wesley slowed his pacing and tapped two fingers onto his mustache. He looked past Phyllis, toward the white cabinetry. "I'm tired, sure, but everyone's tired," he whispered. "No. No. I'm not doing this. These motherfuckers are trying to force me out any way they can. But they don't know who they're messing with."

Phyllis, who typically couldn't restrain herself from being honest with Wesley, kept quiet and nodded. This was a time for unrestrained support. But, for the first time in a long time, she felt fear. They couldn't live on her salary alone. Their savings would buy them time, but they both needed to work to sustain the life they'd settled into. She wanted to encourage Wesley to stand up for himself, but her own sister, Sam, had left one law firm for another recently because she was, as she described it, "getting it two ways: for being Black and for being a woman." She'd made it a point, however, to secure the second job before leaving the first. "It's good to have values, but it's better still to have a paycheck," she'd said.

Phyllis hadn't noticed fatigue or slurring in Wesley, but she'd also been working on a research study that had required her to travel south several times over the last year. Might she have missed something in Wesley while she was away? In fact, recently she'd told Sam that Wesley had been less engaged. "We're both working plenty, but he seems almost bored. Or lost in thought." She'd thought it was about her, that she'd become less appealing to him. Then again, Wes had always been playful, silly even. It was difficult to tell when his mood and demeanor weren't merely reflections of his personality. But even now, as he detailed the conversation with the dean, he eschewed eye contact. Is that what his colleagues had noted? Phyllis also remembered all of the times he'd called out "What?" across the room, unprompted. Then again, that tended to happen while he was watching TV. She didn't have a large enough sample to extrapolate anything. They both left early in the mornings, and he often came home on the train after hers, just in time for dinner or just after. On Saturdays, he was off fishing, sometimes with Simone. Late nights and Sundays were their only times together. One thing was for sure; Phyllis knew it wasn't alcohol. Wes couldn't handle more than a couple of beers or a glass of wine before he would begin tracing the back of her ears or her neck or her knee or any other exposed patch of skin, and then lead her to their bedroom. Certainly, that wasn't happening these days. If he'd been drinking more, she'd know about it.

The rest came quickly. More voices, hallucinations, conspiracies, highs, crashes. For someone who'd been so orderly all of his life, the loss of control only compounded the effect. During the moments of lucidity, Wesley crumbled at the sight of himself, his unkempt hair, his unbrushed teeth, his ruffled clothes.

Phyllis consulted a few psychiatrists before she found one who seemed genuinely concerned.

There were three types of pills. Then a fourth. There was weight gain and insomnia. More weight gain. Extreme lethargy. Chronic dry mouth and spasms. Wesley also developed tics, sudden forceful movements of his limbs. Once, at a friend's place for dinner, he knocked over a plate of asparagus and a glass of wine—white, luckily. "'The Holy Spirit,' my mother would have said," Wesley offered by way of an explanation.

It took nearly a year of managing the illness before Wesley began to more accurately resemble his previous self. By then, however, he'd lost his place at the university, and he was cowed by the prospect of interviewing for new positions. "I'll make a fool of myself."

"Sam's been doing some reading. And as far as the law is concerned, schizophrenia is a disability. They can't deny you employment because of it. Sam will find someone to defend you, if need be. She said she'd do it herself. You know she won't pass up an opportunity to one-up her big sister."

In the spring, Wesley arranged job interviews, but he didn't go to any of them. That didn't keep him from telling Phyllis that he was going and meeting people and was confident that something would pan out soon. In the summer, they drove south to visit Phyllis's family. Wesley seemed himself, her parents said. But he rarely left the porch, where he drank lemonade and committed to "a season of fiction." Wesley read the entire Easy Rawlins series by Walter Mosley and Stephen King's Dark Tower books. In the fall, while Simone was in school and Phyllis was at work, he spent his early mornings fishing; the party boats weren't as crowded on weekdays, just him and the old men who ashed their cigars into the bay. Afterward, he'd trade a couple of sea bass for an off-menu duck congee at a nearby restaurant. In the afternoons, he'd sit in the short stacks of the local library. By October, he'd read Octavia Butler's entire catalog. While he anxiously awaited the follow-up to *Parable of the Sower*, he put Ursula Le Guin's Hainish Cycle on hold. In fact, he was on his way to the library when the crash happened.

The passenger of the oncoming car claimed he saw Wesley's face. "No way. He knew what he was doing. He wasn't having a seizure," said the man who owned the town's pool supply store a few blocks away.

Phyllis argued to the police and to the insurance company that her husband was experiencing a side effect of the medications and must have spasmed just before swerving into the other lane. But she also entertained the notion that Wesley had intentionally swerved into the other lane. "The tics had stopped," she said to Sam. "He'd found the right regimen of pills. He was an excellent driver."

The mental illness had been nothing short of embarrassing for him. Wesley had managed the schizophrenia, but he hadn't quite acclimated to it. And although he hadn't intimated a preference for death over his new circumstances, he had become a blurrier version of himself. Slower and more distant too. "To be expected," the psychiatrist in the city had said. "Time is our best friend in these matters." Time had indeed proved useful. Wesley seemed to have regained his enjoyment of life, his curiosity about where the world was headed, his hope, his drive to pore over history for clues to the future. As dim as the previous year had been, it couldn't have shrouded a lifetime of light. The thought crossed Phyllis's mind nonetheless.

In the end, the autopsy revealed arterial blockage. Wesley had had a heart attack.

The life insurance company sent checks. With them, Phyllis paid off the house and her car, set aside enough for five years' worth of modest vacations and four years of tuition at a mid-level college, and bought Simone a new car.

She'll figure it out, Wesley said to Phyllis whenever Simone toppled over or tried to manage a fork or sound out a word or ride a bicycle. *Let her get up on her own* was the general parenting ethos in their home. Later, Phyllis would fear that she hadn't done enough to support Simone. But at the outset, she and Wesley wanted above all to equip her with the most important of human tools: confidence. If she had that, she wouldn't need much else.

Simone was a self-assured kid, unafraid to try and experiment and complain and demand. Wesley proudly described his daughter as fearless and funny. She made her parents laugh with her impressions and mimicry of just about anyone they encountered in life (the Polish postman, the Senegalese neighbors, the Italian grandmother who ran the bakery) and on TV (Pee-wee Herman, Bert, Ernie). They even got a kick out of her calling them by their first names ("Good morrow, dear Wesley. Parting is such sorrow, sweet Phyllis"). But Phyllis found room to worry, beginning in elementary school.

"Don't you see how she wears that sweater on her head? Pretends to comb it. 'Don't you love my beautiful flowing hair, momma?' she asked me the other day. She wants to be She-Ra, she told me, 'because of her beautiful skin.' And she chose George Michael over Anita Baker at the record store."

"George Michael ain't bad," said Wesley, half a smile already creeping up.

"Be serious, Wes."

"I am being serious. He's much better now that he's on his own. And you own 'Careless Whisper.'"

"Our daughter only sees white people—not just on TV, but at school and in this neighborhood—and it's going to mess up her self-image. It already has!"

Phyllis took to redecorating. Next to the posters of biomes and the correlated histories of life on Earth, she put up images of Angela Davis and Sojourner Truth. She filled Simone's shelves with her books by Toni Morrison, Audre Lorde, Nella Larsen, James Baldwin, and Zora Neale Hurston. At night, Phyllis read her *Sassafrass, Cypress & Indigo*. When she turned twelve, Wesley read to her from *The Autobiography of Malcolm X*. They played Jessye Norman and Leontyne Price records on Sunday mornings, Miles Davis and Charlie Parker in the evenings. They watched concert videos of Richard Pryor and of Nina Simone, her namesake, and they let Simone sing "Mississippi Goddam," despite discouraging cursing otherwise. They listened to Donny Hathaway, Rose Royce, Shalamar, Evelyn King, Frankie Beverly, Curtis Mayfield, Anita, Aretha, Luther, Stevie, and Prince, but didn't allow her to watch *Purple Rain*. They rented *The Wiz, Sounder, Lady Sings the Blues, Shaft, Roots, Cooley High, Daughters of the Dust, Krush Groove, Hollywood Shuffle*. They took her to see everything by Spike Lee and the works of Faith Ringgold, William Johnson, and Jacob Lawrence, and they watched reruns of *Sanford and Son, Good Times*, and *The Jeffersons*. They door-knocked as a family for Jesse Jackson's presidential campaign. And when the Pearl Jam posters appeared, Phyllis gifted Simone two tickets to the Janet Jackson and Tony! Toni! Toné! concert and plenty of pocket money for new posters and T-shirts.

When Sam came to visit, she joked that Phyllis's place was like the headquarters of the Black Panther Party. "Don't you think you're overdoing it a bit? *Sounder*? You like that movie?"

"It's a fine film, Sam. And you have no idea how strong the tide is. One day, you'll see."

Phyllis and Wesley did everything so that Simone could see herself reflected in the world because they knew no one else would make the effort. They never stopped worrying about how their daughter would be treated, but they hoped they'd given her a sufficient buffer. And, by and by, she seemed to be finding her way.

·   ·   ·

After Wesley died, Phyllis left her untenured position in the city and found a job teaching earth science at a public school in a wealthy hamlet farther east, believing it would be better to be closer to home. But by this point, crossing paths with Simone was by chance or from the bleachers. In the fall, she had volleyball. In the winter, Simone joined the basketball team, which Phyllis assumed was somehow a tribute to Wesley, who had, for years, encouraged Simone to try out. In the spring was lacrosse. Simone kept busy, and whenever Phyllis worried about the toll of Wesley's death, she told herself that he had died just when Simone needed a father least. She was young enough to adapt, but mature enough to understand and process the loss. They cried plenty—sometimes apart; sometimes together. They ate ice cream and watched *The X-Files*. They spoke his name and never felt embarrassed or awkward in the moments when they'd forgotten that he was dead.

In this way, evidence of Simone's illness was obfuscated. Wesley's death had been like a loud, all-consuming *pop*, lasting only for a moment but leaving the sound of everything muffled afterward.

Simone had been old enough to understand what was happening to her father in the year before the car accident, but she'd chosen not to. Instead, she focused only on what she'd been told: *Dad was just being silly* and *Dad isn't feeling well* and *Dad needs rest*. She never asked questions about her father's illness, and since no one volunteered answers, she deduced that it was easier, and possibly important, that she not know everything. Frankly, the truth scared Simone. Not the objective truth, but its details and implications. Better to keep quiet. Wesley's death was more shrouding for the cause.

Youth, too, concealed. The similarities between father and daughter were easy to overlook because Simone's symptoms were easily ascribable to adolescence. She was moody and withdrawn. She kept an odd sleep schedule. At times, she wavered in her commitment to friends, school, and sport. Phyllis excused it all because she saw a path forward for her. Multiple paths. Simone hadn't excelled in school, but a B average and an impeccable sports profile attracted the attention of scouts. In the spring of her senior year, Simone received several offers from Division I schools to play lacrosse, volleyball, and basketball.

The subtle shifts in Simone's personality and demeanor had eluded her friends too. Her laughter had become a raspy, intermittent giggle that surfaced when she was high, and sometimes when she wasn't. And her characteristic ebullience was by turns magnified or completely absent, which was easy to miss or to pin on a bad day, a good day, a silly mood, a low test score, caffeine, pot, exhaustion. But who would have noticed?

Andy had become an inconsistent person. He was always with Jeremy—not a bad guy, but certainly not worth all of the attention, Simone thought. Rhonda was dealing with her boyfriend's drama, sneaking away on weekends to visit him in jail. Simone couldn't understand his appeal either. Maybe, she thought, her friends were infatuated with attention. There was Eleanor, too. A nice, but excessively real, person who made truth seem less like a virtue and more like a dare. As for Mary, Simone's relationship with her had bloomed in the darkness and wilted otherwise, like the poisonous vespertines of the *Datura* genus, beautiful trumpet-shaped flowers that Phyllis had taught her to avoid. The avoidance of Mary meant also a distance from Simone's clique of athletic girls.

"She have a boyfriend?" asked Sam during one of the daily early-morning calls with Phyllis.

"No. That tall boy I told you about disappeared as soon as he arrived."

In the spring, Simone had briefly dated Mark. He played basketball and had thin legs. He came to the house twice but barely spoke a word. Simone had sex with him primarily because she wanted to see what the fuss was about. Throughout, she repressed the desire to laugh. She didn't want to hurt Mark's feelings, but she'd found the entire encounter funny—the act itself, but also the shapes of everything, including its participants, and the way all of the parts fit together. Afterward, she resisted the urge to cry because she couldn't quite pinpoint the cause of her tears.

"She's out all the time, but her only boy friend was Andy. Haven't seen hide nor hair of him in ages."

"The skinny boy with the ears that was at her little birthday party."

"That's the one. And I know he wasn't interested."

"Why?"

"You know what I mean."

"What?" asked Sam.

"I don't think Simone was his . . . type."

"Oh. Yeah, well, that's bound to happen."

"More and more these days."

"You think about Simone being that way? I mean, she likes her baggy jeans. And she's quite the athlete."

"Those are stereotypes, Samantha. You know better than that," Phyllis said playfully. "Yes, it has crossed my mind before, and you know it. It's possible, but I'll deal with that when I have no other choice."

The college was only three hours away, but they split the driving in thirds; Phyllis took the middle hour. From the moment they exited the highway, the campus sprawled into life. Simone scanned the new landscape and was filled instantly with a desperation to be set free. Phyllis alternated between saying "slow down" and "stop sign ahead." After they'd decorated Simone's room—Pearl Jam but thankfully Bob Marley, too—they ate dinner at a kitschy Mexican restaurant where the visible staff was white. Throughout the meal, Phyllis offered up errant greeting-card thoughts that she had been jotting down for the last few weeks.

"Your father loved you tremendously."

"I know, Mom."

"You're a brilliant, beautiful woman, and you'll achieve everything you want."

"I know, Mom."

Phyllis hadn't realized how much she loved hearing Simone call her *mom*, until she'd resumed doing so in the aftermath of Wesley's death.

"Do what you have to do to comply with the scholarships, but don't forget your studies. The sports will end one day; the knowledge will stay with you forever."

"You've said that to me a hundred times. Dad, too."

"And study a second language. The biggest—"

"Regret of your life was not having learned French in college. I know, I know."

"Well, it's true. Your father, too, wished he'd learned another language. But don't waste your time with French. It's completely useless, unless you plan to work at the United Nations. Even then, they can translate for you. Be strategic. Spanish or Mandarin or Urdu or Arabic. Think of something that will come in handy one day."

"I've already signed up for intro Spanish."

"Oh, right. Good. And remember—"

"Mom! You're repeating yourself. We've talked about everything already."

"No, we haven't. We could talk forever and not cover everything. But it's true, you'll learn most of it for yourself." Phyllis tapped softly at the sides of her hair, as if she were looking into a mirror. "One more thing. You have your own style, and that's fine, but please moisturize. Skin and hair. There's eczema in our family and dermatologists—"

"Don't bother to see these things on our skin. Yes, I know, Mom."

"Well, it's true. You have to protect yourself. I packed a spray bottle in your bag. A little water and a little conditioner is enough. A few spritzes in the morning before you go to class. It'll keep your hair healthy."

"Mom, c'mon. Black hair one-oh-one, really?"

"Don't sass me, young lady."

Simone and Phyllis both laughed, first a small hiss, then something with more flight, like punctured balloons zipping through the air. This moment, thought Phyllis, this is how she would remember their goodbye. Then she corralled the gaggle of hot sauce bottles into the center of the table, and reached across with both hands. Simone waited a second before extending her own hands. When she finally did, she felt the energy, the love, the loss, and the regrets that were racing through her mother. The two of them remained clasped until the server brought the check.

In the months leading up to this goodbye, Phyllis had been startled by the realization that Simone was the only other person in her life. The thought of her daughter leaving shattered the cocoon that had encased her during the previous year. It brought the sorrow out of the darkness, made it into something tangible with unambiguous boundaries, with a roof, doors, and windows. Phyllis quickly stepped outside of it for fear that Simone's departure would leave her trapped, alone. In a short period of time, Phyllis attempted to compensate for everything she felt she hadn't done right or better. They flew west to visit cousins, drove south to visit grandparents and north to go camping. Phyllis made an effort to be kinder and more attentive. She sat on her judgments, suppressed the nitpicking. She wanted her daughter's memories to be fond ones, unshadowed by the previous year's traumas.

Phyllis wasn't afraid to stay behind. She'd grown used to the town and its people, and while neither elicited her affections, they were the devils she knew. Even the parents of those evil children (all the Michaels and Josephs) had come by with food and condolences after Wesley's death. Those who hadn't nodded or smiled in the days that followed. No, Phyllis didn't worry for her own future; she feared for her daughter. Simone's life was commencing, and it would move speedily. She'd be a woman with her own life and new reference points and experiences the next time they'd meet. Phyllis had worked at the campus bookstore every summer during her college years, only going home for holidays and brief visits. She was prepared for her daughter to do the same.

"I just want her to be happy," she'd often said to Wesley. "Please let her be happy."

"She will be," Wesley responded breezily, in a reassuring even if unconvincing manner. Phyllis allowed herself to believe it anyway. But now she wondered what Wesley had been truly thinking. *Was he there with me, or was he already lost inside the maze of his mind?*

All they could do was love her: on that they agreed. Love her until they couldn't love any more. They were certainly firm, but always in the service of her safety. In retrospect, Phyllis wished she hadn't made Simone carry an adult's dignity at such a young age. She'd done her best to let her be, but there were moments when she'd flash Simone a stern look that said, *You're better than that*. Too often Phyllis had let other people dictate how they'd lived. Periodically she'd reminded herself that a life spent proving people wrong wasn't a life at all.

"I don't want her to be angry."

"Can't help that. A bit of bitter comes with the territory. It can make you nimble and powerful too."

This was the sort of sermonizing that could drive Phyllis up a wall, even when Wesley was right.

"Fine then. I want her to be more powerful and less angry than me. As long as it moves in that direction, I'll be content."

Every day was a leap, filled with anxious hope, sometimes with their eyes closed. It seemed to be working. Even when they feared that Simone was too adventurous: they'd found the tobacco pipes and rolling papers; Wesley had smelled the cigarettes on her; Phyllis had heard her tiptoe in at two and three in the morning, sometimes with friends, but more often alone, the chorus of stumbling, knocking into furniture, the refrigerator door being flung open and into the wall, glasses coming down carelessly onto the counter.

Phyllis worried about what complete sovereignty would spell for Simone.

As they sat across from each other at the Mexican restaurant that night, only a bite of flan between them, before Phyllis went back to her hotel room and Simone disappeared onto campus and back to her dorm room, Phyllis recognized something in her daughter's face. Something that she'd seen in Wesley's. A look. Or really, the absence of a look. A vacancy in her eyes. Simone wasn't but two feet away, but it might as well have been miles. As if she'd left well before they'd parted.

Simone would spend most of the next twenty years claiming that she had two years of college under her belt, but that wasn't accurate. After the first semester, a letter went home saying that she was in danger of being kicked out because of poor grades and unsatisfactory attendance. To complicate matters, near the end of her first year, she broke her arm after drunkenly falling off of her bed. She wasn't able to train in the summer; by the time the new year rolled around, she'd lost her scholarship. Phyllis paid for the second year and for a tutor, but Simone showed no signs of improvement.

It was in this second year that the late-night calls began. Simone was either drunk or high. Phyllis couldn't distinguish between the two, but she was frightened.

"Your father and I didn't work hard to raise an addict!" she'd yell, after several failed attempts at compassion. "I won't pay another dime for that school if you don't get your act together."

During one call, Simone grew exasperated and hung up. They didn't talk for weeks after that. On another occasion, Simone told her mother not to worry about her; her inner voices were guiding her. Phyllis at first assumed Simone was speaking figuratively, but during subsequent calls, Simone again referenced the voices. At some point, she switched to first-person plural.

"Don't worry, Phyllis. We're on the right track. We'll find our way."

The regrets soon became an obsession for Phyllis. She should have worked less; stayed home more. She should have addressed this earlier. She and Wesley should have discussed his health with Simone. They shouldn't have hidden anything. But Phyllis had believed there was time. Besides, she was barely keeping afloat trying to manage Wesley's illness. Then she was coping with his death. Then she was preparing Simone for college. Then she was adjusting to life alone, which had been much more difficult than she'd envisioned. Re-entering the world. Meeting people. Going on a date. Two. One thing followed by another. Life had gotten in the way of truth.

Send her to Mom and Dad's," Sam suggested.

"Remember how well they got along last time?"

After Wesley's death, Phyllis's parents had come up and stayed with her for two weeks, most of which they spent criticizing Simone's hair, clothes, piercings (nose, ear ridges, belly button), manners, vocabulary. What little relationship Simone had had with her grandparents before had been soured by that visit.

"Well, you have to find someone. You need help. You don't have people in that little town."

Later, she was more prescriptive: "If you don't get her into a psychiatric hospital soon, she's going to end up like Wes."

When Phyllis, at the behest of the school's medical clinic, came to get Simone, her daughter was unrecognizable. Her blank stare, intermittent laughter, the modulation of her voice from whisper to cackle, all of it contained a kernel of Simone's playfulness, but she was somehow magnified and discombobulated all at once.

Phyllis wanted to fix her stare onto someone and scream. She wanted someone to blame. Who? Not her. No. She had done too much of it right. She'd navigated this miserable life, one giant Indonesia-sized archipelago of indignities. She'd refrained from running over all of the horrid children and their parents. She'd never raised her voice at the harpies who'd pulled their children away from Simone in the playground. She hadn't taken a pen from her purse and stabbed any of the people who'd passed their hands freely through her daughter's hair. She hadn't burned down the university when it overlooked her for tenure. She hadn't driven south to buy a gun in order to shoot all of the people who'd taken liberties with her. The *Hey, girl* people and the *Smile more* fools and the *No need to be defensive, emotional, to get worked up, to have such an attitude, to make this about race* know-nothings. She hadn't clawed out the eyes of all the police officers—the mustached one with the potbelly who told her and Wesley that there was nothing to be done about the vandalism on their house, or the freckled one with transparent eyebrows who pulled her over for speeding one mile above the limit when everyone else was driving ten to twenty over, or the platypus-looking one at the hospital who asked her several times if she was sure her husband hadn't been on drugs. She'd maintained her composure, chosen her moments carefully, hoping that if she absorbed enough, her daughter wouldn't have to. But she'd also run away more often than she should have. Retreating coastlines and wetlands and science had felt simpler than this street and this town and this life. But somewhere along the way it all fell apart, and now she was without Wesley to pick up the pieces. At its worst, life had felt like an enormous jigsaw puzzle scattered on the floor. Now it was a mirror that had broken into an infinite and irredeemable number of shards, and Phyllis stood over it alone.

22
SAINT JOSEPH

This is my longest stay here in twenty years. Even when Henry died, I went back to the city a couple of days after the funeral. I've noticed that the longer I'm here, the more trapped, unmoored, and implicated I feel. Time bends back so far that I can't be certain of when everything is taking place. I also feel incapable of communicating effectively with my surroundings. Although everyone speaks a version of English and listens to Drake, we operate from distinct realities. Worse yet, I'm outnumbered, and I cannot see clearly the delineation between my side and theirs.

"Not yet. Maybe someday," my mom said, when I asked her about coming to live near me.

It's always been clear, from the shift of her eyes (away from me) and the way she busies herself wiping down an already-spotless counter or running water into an empty sink, that she isn't seriously entertaining the possibility. They've lived in this place nearly thrice as long as anywhere else. The city frightens them. And despite its modernization, its drop in crime, and the rise in incomes, its density alone would constitute a regression for them.

I don't hate this town. I'm uneasy in it.

It's not only the memories of my brother or the frailty of my parents. It's not the demographic either, the somehow more racially and economically integrated town that skews oddly more conservative than I remember it—everyone, it seems, has become more live-and-let-live around race, ethnicity, and sexual orientation, but they litter their lawns with conservative signs, as if social oppression is completely divorced from politics, the economy, and history. Neither is it the law-and-order mentality that keeps me from returning—although it bears repeating that there's a surfeit of police vehicles in this town, but almost no public transit infrastructure; everyone would rather employ a local paramilitary to uphold the illusion of safety than sit next to one another on a bus. Nor is my unease the result of the endless stream of racing, swerving, and honking SUVs, each one a reminder of man's weakness and his propensity to overcompensate, as well as a portent of his gas-guzzling demise. It's the sum of it all. Together they constitute a devolution.

Everyone here has a past and ancestors, just as I do, who escaped barbarity, misery, oppression, or a bad time, just as mine did, and came here in search of a dignity that wasn't exactly waiting with open arms—ditto. The American immigrant experience has been a mash-up of *The Godfather* and *Toy Story* set in a factory full of crisscrossing conveyor belts, where the only possible endpoints are a gilded throne or an incinerator.

One could weep forever thinking of the trajectories that had once pointed upward and are now perennially sloped toward hell. Ambitions that were at one point honorable have become, as a result of their inaccessibility, targets of ridicule and disdain. Intelligence, progress, proficiency, freedom of expression, separation of church and state, and solidarity are no longer valued or aspirational.

Unlike earlier waves of immigrants, today's masses are here because this country, their final destination, is responsible for their miseries back home. If not for all of the coups, dethronings, assassinations, covert missions, all-out assaults, drug wars, disinformation campaigns, faux-unity NGOs, pipelines, bilateral treaties, trilateral contracts, regional trade groups, Coke commercials, moonwalks, Peace Corps, missionaries, scholarships, brain drains, kidnappings, bribery, fraud, Academy Awards, and Avengers movies, they wouldn't have come here. They, including my parents, left countries and families and friends and restaurants and movie theaters and bookstores and crushes they'd hoped to marry and favorite guitars and inimitable ice-cream flavors and an irreplaceable variety of fruits and vegetables, to be here, in the place that made their place uninhabitable, only to be reminded regularly that they were unwelcome, that there would always be a target on their backs, until they soon became like the first batch of pilgrims: corrupt, ignorant, spiteful, sedentary, intolerant, uncouth, fearful, and unkind boot-licking tools of fascism. In a word, American. Most of us, anyway.

It's possible that I'm unhappy here because I feel utterly useless. There's a finite amount of superficial socializing one can do in a space where one is politically outnumbered. At some point, I'm going to have to have a difficult conversation. But is this where I want my energy to go? Shouldn't I be building power and communion with other like-minded people so that we can spin the wheel with force? Anything shy of that guarantees that the process of convincing and explaining and tapping into empathy will consume energy, and we won't live to see the trajectory tip upward.

I'm not proud of myself. I know my outlook is off-putting and possibly wrong. Or maybe, incomplete. My high school class, after all, was comprised of more than two hundred students, and about half came to the reunion. What became of the rest? Who are they? Where are they? What do they believe? How do they live? Are they college professors? Social workers? Anti-racism activists? Communists? Working drag queens? Polyamorous? Dinner theater actors? Writers? Jazz musicians? Club Med instructors? Pastry chefs? Massage therapists? Software engineers? Incarcerated? Dead?

Eighty-nine degrees today. The humidity of a greenhouse. If there were any foliage in this invented, concrete town, it would be wilting. I regret not taking a car. I insisted on walking because I'm trying to make a point to my parents that I no longer need to keep making. It seems that I'm a martyr without a religion and with only two congregants.

Five long blocks and three parking lots to traverse with four bags of groceries. Already there's a lather of sweat over me, despite the shower I took before I left home and despite the supermarket tundra of only two minutes ago. Wiping my brow without assaulting myself is proving difficult because of the edges of corrugated plastic poking through the thin plastic bags—I forgot the reusable ones. It's making me hate this experience even more.

To get onto the right path, I have to first walk through a parking lot. I make an effort to walk down the center of the lane, keeping an equal distance from the rows of parked cars on either side of me. Every year, people die in parking lots.

A car behind me honks. I don't turn. I'm nearly out of harm's way; there's no need to honk.

The honking continues anyway, no longer quick, strident stabs, now a sustained blaring. I resist turning around, hoping to manage the anger that the insistent bleating has now triggered, but the longer it continues, the angrier I become. Turning around risks creating a situation that I would like to avoid. I read recently that violent crimes increase in the summer because the heat and humidity make people less patient. There are, it seems, a few ways to die in a parking lot.

"Hey!" the driver shouts.

I pretend it's for someone else and cross the main artery that connects all of the lots and storefronts. I'm no longer in the way of anyone or anything.

"Hey!" the voice continues.

The beads of sweat clinging to my forehead, upper lip, armpits, chest, and groin each descend as if on cue. The sensation irritates me further.

"What the fuck!" I shout to myself, before turning around to face my antagonist.

"Andy! Andy, it's me, Paul!"

Paul pulls up to the curb and opens his door. I don't have time to assess where this encounter is going. I'm certain he hasn't forgotten that I passive-aggressively accused him of murder in his lord's storefront church, but I don't see anger in his wide, jubilant eyes or in his Easter-yellow guayabera. Maybe he has a meth addiction.

"Andy, can I give you a ride?"

"No. I'm good. Just a few—"

"You're going to your folks'? They still over there?" Paul points in the general direction of my parents' house.

(The people in this town have such an amazing recall for location.)

I nod as vaguely as I possibly can.

"I'm okay to walk. It's a nice day—"

"It's, like, a hundred degrees."

Paul mimes wiping his brow. His inflated cheeks exhale forcefully.

"I guess global warming is real," I say, but he doesn't acknowledge it.

"Summer only started last week, right? These next few months are going to be brutal." Paul opens the back door and reaches for my bags. "Get in."

"I'm okay. I like the exercise."

"C'mon man, it's on the way for me."

Paul stares at me without malice. His arms are akimbo; his feet, too, are spread apart. There's a vulnerability to him that makes me acquiesce. "Okay, but just to the entrance of the complex. You can leave me at the security gate." Paul strikes me as someone who would regularly visit my parents, given the opportunity. Kindness as a recruitment strategy. "I don't have one of the clickers to get in," I explain, in case he doubts me, "and I don't know the new manual code. It changes every year."

"No problem."

I hop into his Mazda. It's a hatchback, the shape of a station wagon. A practical car. The car Jesus would drive.

From the rearview mirror hang at least three pieces of religious paraphernalia: a small wooden cross, a white string of rosary beads, and a laminated prayer card of the kind that are given out at funerals. These accessories were typical in the cars around town when I was growing up, but in the city, I only ever see them in taxis. I've always associated them with Catholicism, but now I wonder if they're universally Christian.

"St. Joseph," Paul says. He's caught me eyeing his decor. "That's my mom's prayer card. I've had it all my life."

I recall now that he never knew his mother. I recall, too, that St. Joseph is Jesus's earthly father, his stepfather in a way. I can't think of a more thankless role than being the stepfather of Jesus Christ. Years ago, I watched a PBS documentary that noted the multi-decade age discrepancy between Mary and Joseph. I wonder how much of a choice Mary had in marrying him. I've wondered, too, about how different these arranged marriages in the Bible are from the ones that are wedged into the humanitarian pretexts our government employs to garner sympathy for its illegal wars in the Middle

East. The Judeo-Christian tradition is full of the extremist practices that we condemn elsewhere today. Why, I've wondered, don't Democrats draw parallels between the Taliban and the pro-life crowd? ISIS and the Mormons? A savvy campaign could weave in some 9/11 first-responder imagery. *Never Forget . . . A Woman's Right to Choose.*

Paul flips down his turn signal and pulls away from the curb. He checks his mirrors and drives tentatively through the parking lot, slowing down to a crawl as we go over the speed bumps, and braking completely when the stop signs appear. He drives like a cautious person who isn't late and hasn't yet secured his place in the afterlife.

"First full week of summer for the kids," he says unprompted.

"Oh, right. My brother's kids are coming down for a visit next week."

The rhythm of our conversation stalls, and I sense what's coming next.

"I'm sorry, Andy. About your brother."

"Andrés," I say. "I prefer Andrés."

"Oh, alright. No problem."

"And thanks. About Henry."

"How's Ellie doing?"

Paul catches me off guard. I didn't know that he knew Ellie.

"She's good. You know her?"

"Know her? Ellie's cousin Billy is married to my sister's husband's cousin. She grew up like five blocks away from me."

Ellie was four years younger than my brother, and she went to public school. We ran in different circles, but I'm not surprised that those circles have points of connection. That was quite common back then.

"She came with her cousin Billy to the church once to say hi when she was in town. Beautiful kids."

I wish I didn't know this. Ellie's Catholic. She's not particularly devout, and I'm sure she has no interest in converting to whatever Paul practices, but the contact between the families makes me uneasy.

This was typical of Ellie and my brother. Indiscriminate to a fault. On the surface, a commendable trait, but in practice, it left my brother prey to the world's evils: religion, time-shares, expensive diets, binge drinking, QVC, Ponzi schemes, and counterintuitive home remedies, like fruit juices to treat diabetes. One exception was life insurance. Henry bought three policies because the salesman who came to his house used to work with him at Uncle Billy's. The payout for each policy was small because Henry was already diabetic when he bought them, but cumulatively, they were enough for Ellie to pay off their credit cards and back taxes, buy a car, and move upstate—a move that my parents and I disdained but for which I am suddenly and incredibly grateful.

Paul inches down the small ramp and turns onto a two-lane road with considerable traffic. At the light, he takes another right onto a four-lane road—he should have taken a left.

"That was it back there. But you can U-turn up here, before the gas station."

"I know. I just want to show you something. Real quick. I promise."

I'm going to die. He's going to kill me and discard my body exactly where he left the other body twenty years ago. He's much more skillful and disciplined than I anticipated. The thought of getting run over by a Ford Escalade in the supermarket parking lot has a certain appeal all of sudden.

"I have frozen peas," I say. It's the only lie I can muster. All of my energy is in my hands, one of which is gripping the armrest while the other is white-knuckled at my side. *Fuck, I could have said ice cream.* I actually bought ice cream. It's right behind us, in one of the bags. Ice cream is significantly more urgent than frozen peas.

"It'll only take a minute," he says. "I'll turn up the AC so nothing melts."

It'll still melt. Just slower, I guess.

Paul continues, at forty-eight miles per hour. We drive past Uncle Billy's, Joe's, the paintball gallery, four strip malls, each with its own bagel shop and Chinese restaurant, two sets of railroad tracks, the strip of garages where all of the town's cars get repaired, the horse-betting place, and the large field where families once gathered after school and on weekend mornings to watch their children play baseball, now, soccer. Not a single red light for almost two miles; it seems the Lord is on his side.

We drive through a rare stretch of forested land. Trees guard the road for a couple of miles. On our left, I spot new development through the thinned layer of trunks, branches, and leaves. Uniform houses, bigger than the average stock, built into faux cul-de-sac neighborhoods. This is the sort of gated community that has proliferated as income gaps have widened, social cohesion has declined, and violence and crime have increased—in that order. On my right, trees only. Along the ample, dusty shoulder, people park their cars and unload their fishing rods and tackle boxes on the weekends. Hot dog and pretzel vendors, too, set up their trucks there, near the entrance to a little-known pond. I'm surprised the fish are comestible. I'm further surprised these people don't just drive to the bay or the ocean.

Just when it seems we're out of the wooded corridor, another opening appears, a paved road, one that leads to a long-ago-shuttered psychiatric hospital hidden entirely by the forest, indicated only by a large road sign that has since been made unrecognizable with graffiti. I seem to recall that it was named after a saint, but I don't remember which one.

I see where Paul is taking us. We are officially one town north of our town. The houses are slightly bigger and better kept here. Up ahead is the interstate. Just before the on-ramp is the parking lot where conscientious commuters leave their cars during business hours and ride-share with fellow commuters or board a bus. I'd like to know who these wayfarers are because, culturally speaking, we aren't in the kind of place where someone would voluntarily give up their car, much less get into a car with someone else. We have some bus riders, but there has never been a crowded bus in this part of the world. Never. These people must be traveling from quite a way. From a more enlightened place. I also presume that these ride-share commuters are unaware that their innocent rest stop transforms into an after-hours cruising ground for gay men. But who knows?

Steer Queer.

I started coming here in the weeks before I left for college, after my relationship with Jeremy ended. Mostly out of spite, but there was genuine curiosity, too. As well as overwhelming trepidation. I drove past the lot several times before I found the nerve to drive in that first time. In those waning days of summer, the reunions and goodbyes were plentiful and debaucherous. I was often the designated driver for friends who drank, smoked, and snorted to excess; whereas I limited my consumption to three beers or two lines of coke or a few pulls from a bowl or hits from a bong. After I'd gotten all of my passengers home safely, I'd drive here.

The median age of the men was typically nearer to fifty-five than eighteen. Occasionally, I crossed paths with someone who appeared to be in their twenties. Because I was inebriated every single time I went cruising, I wasn't too concerned with the age or even the looks of the men I encountered. I searched their eyes instead. At the time, I held the suspicion that many, if not all, gay men were duplicitous HIV-positive, serial-killing pedophiles. I had been, over my brief lifetime, casually conditioned to believe this, and I didn't have any definitive proof that it wasn't true. That I wasn't these things, I believed, was merely a consequence of time and willpower.

It wasn't clear to me how Jeremy fit into all of this. It seemed our relationship had temporarily obfuscated reality. We were neither gay nor straight. We'd been too busy being in love to compartmentalize ourselves. After him, however, everything changed. All of my defenses vanished, leaving me perpetually crouched, ready to run or hide.

I was aware again that straight was normal. Straight was healthy. Straight was godly. Straight was natural. Straight was right. Straight was a line. Straight was safe. Straight was human. Straight was my brother. Straight was James Bond. Straight was Knight Rider. The Dukes of Hazzard were straight— and racist. Superheroes and cowboys were straight. My parents were straight. All parents were straight. Straight was the only way forward.

My midnight suitors and I usually drove off to nearby empty lots, where one of us hopped into the car of the other. Once, me and a guy with long blond hair who looked like a slim Fabio walked into the woods together. Without prompting, he tried to enter me with a bit of spit. The pain was so intense and unexpected that I screamed, pulled up my pants, and walked straight to my car while he heckled me. When I got home, I noticed spots of blood on the toilet paper. I spent a week panicking that my prophecy had been realized. I didn't have the faintest idea of where to get an HIV test, so I pretended it never happened. Another time, I followed a fifty-something Dan Conner–type to a motel. He climbed atop me and forced his tongue into my mouth, but his weight on my chest sent me into a panic, so I punched him in the arm as hard as I could. He immediately rolled over and apologized profusely. Then he ate me out until I came and didn't ask anything else of me.

During all of my encounters with these older, sometimes married men— rings and tan lines—I kept one eye on them and one on our surroundings, in particular the locks on their car doors. Somehow, I found a way to be perfectly and unwaveringly aroused, as well as frightened. The irony of course was that the older men, who left me most uneasy and on guard, were the most tender, passionate, and respectful, not only expert cartographers of the body, but almost reverential with their tongues, lips, and fingers—grateful, I realize now, to have a young man to devour, to have a young man's attention.

The younger men, those who were within ten years of my age, tended to be more aggressive, disrespectful even. I'd been spoiled with Jeremy, whose passion was somehow always gentle. These men, however, were likely to try to fuck without lube or protection, and never wanted to be topped. I learned to be prepared, to sense when they were transitioning from excited to aggressive. One guy pressed my face and body against a tree in the wooded area on the other side of the interstate. When I felt his tumescence slide between my legs, I thrust my head and back against him with considerable force. He lost his footing and stumbled, which he somehow mistook as playfulness. He responded by pressing his forearm against the back of my neck, scraping my face against the bark in the process. Again, his rock-hard flesh appeared against my back. It was then that I shoved him more forcefully and pulled up my pants. He lay on the ground dazed, while I ran back to my car, trying to listen for footsteps.

"What happened to your face?" my mother later asked.

"I walked into a tree."

"A tree? What tree?"

After each encounter, I drove away quickly, making sure to complicate my route home, for fear that I was being followed.

Gay, after all, was dangerous. Gay was violent. Gay was unclean. Gay was abnormal. Gay was sick. Gay was an illness. Gay was a phase. Gay was a secret. Gay was effeminate. Gay was crossdressing. Gay was transvestite. Gay was one earring. Gay was the one character on *Melrose Place*. Gay was a late-night miniseries on Bravo. Gay was a death sentence. Gay was a target. Gay was a target. Gay was a target.

One time, I was arrested. It was the Saturday of Thanksgiving break during my freshman year, my first time home since I'd left for college. I'd gone out with Greg, Sal, and Alex to an all-ages club tucked between a Subway and a nail salon. We met up with a dozen other friends, several of whom were also home from school. It was a techno-themed night, and we all took ecstasy, danced, and sweated profusely. At some point, when everyone seemed to have paired up, I slipped away and drove toward Steer Queer. It had snowed that day, and I remember well that everything was coated in frost— roads, utility poles, cars. I overcompensated for the slickness by driving below the speed limit. The cop who pulled me over claimed it was for driving suspiciously. I spent the night in the drunk tank, high as a kite—exhausted, wide awake, and afraid to close my eyes. By the time Greg picked me up from the county jail and drove me home, I'd missed my ride back to school—a student in my dorm who lived twenty miles east of my town, in a coastal hamlet I'd never heard of. I told my parents I'd overslept at Greg's. My mother didn't say anything, but her face narrowed—brow and eyes. Henry drove me to the bus depot and bought me a cup of coffee, a bag of Doritos, and eye drops.

After the arrest, I used my loan money to hire a lawyer, I borrowed my roommate's car to drive home for three court appearances, and I completed twenty hours of community service hacking brush at a farm a few miles from campus. A classmate whom I told about the arrest said that having a record would make it difficult to apply to law school or medical school. I panicked after that. In college, I wasn't only surrounded by resources and wealth I had never before imagined, I was privy to them. The possibilities of life were suddenly concrete, and my hometown felt like a rejection of all that. Going back wasn't only a rewinding of the clock, it was a devolution.

That memorable Thanksgiving break was the last time I ever saw a friend from high school, until the reunion last week.

W hat are we doing here, Paul?"

"I want to tell you what happened," he says. "The night I came here."

"Listen, man, that was a long time ago, and I don't want to know anything more about it."

"You're the one who brought it up."

"But I'm not going to say anything. What's done is done."

I'm afraid, but I'm also angry. Angry at myself for getting into this killer's car. And angry at myself for betraying the gay man who died all those years ago. This is typical of my temperament: bluster, piss, vinegar, bark, and hot coils ensconced in a proclivity for avoiding confrontation and pleasing others. Whether this is genetic, epigenetic, or Pavlovian is hard to say.

Paul pulls into the lot and finds space by the desolate bus stop. He tussles with the gearshift until it's firmly in park. I pull my phone from my pocket and compose a message for Marco: "in car with killer paul from h.s." But it dawns on me that I've never told Marco this story. Only Jeremy knows it.

"I want to explain what happened," Paul begins. "It's—"

"You really don't need to. In fact, Paul, I'd like to go home."

"Just let me show you—"

I open the door, knowing well that I may be sacrificing my groceries.

"Please," he says. His mouth is dry and I can see foam on his tongue and spit on either end of his lips. This man is perpetually dehydrated. "Please give me a few minutes. And then I'll drive you home."

I keep one foot on the pavement, but I face him with an open mind and a decisive stare.

"I came here with Fred that night. Remember Fred?"

Fred was a tall, lanky boy with thick black eyebrows and an outsized jaw, who could have been a member of the Addams Family. I don't know exactly where he lived or went to school, but there was a period in high school when Paul brought him everywhere.

"Yeah," I say.

"Well, it was his car we drove that night. We were coming home from the gym on McDowell, the one in the industrial area behind the train station. We used to go there after school—it was just a small warehouse with free weights and a few machines. Anyway, that night we went to the movies after the gym. And you have to drive right by this place when you're heading home, you know? I don't remember if it was me or Fred, but we noticed the car lights in here, and one of us joked about how funny it would be if we went in. We just meant to take a look—you know how kids are," he says.

I resist the urge to say *Not all kids.* In fact, not most kids.

"Everything's a dare," he continues. "And so we agreed, and we started driving around in here. There weren't that many cars, but they kept circling us. One guy pulled up and asked if we had a cigarette. Fred gave me one to give to him because the guy pulled up on my side. Then the guy got out of his car and walked over, and when I gave him the cigarette, he made sure to rub his fingers on my hand, and I just kinda freaked out. It was stupid. I was stupid. I can't explain why I let it get to me, you know?"

Paul, who has been looking at me intently this whole time, puts his head down, rubbing the bridge of his nose with his thumb and index finger. His change in demeanor makes me wonder how often he's thought about this, and whether he understands more about his own motivations than he's willing to admit.

"I wanted to get out of the car and beat the shit out of him, but Fred told me to relax. He had an idea. 'Follow my lead,' he said. Then he told the guy to follow us. And then we left the lot. We drove around to the other side of the expressway, to the deserted area between the movies and the highway. You know how empty that is at night. Completely dead. When we get there, the guy gets out of his car and points to a dumpster by a fence. The guy was super calm, like everything was cool. We followed him, and I remember Fred kept poking me in the back. We didn't really have a plan—I wasn't even angry anymore, I swear—but we'd already started walking, and we just went with it. Anyway, the guy must have been unbuttoning his shirt the whole time because when he stopped walking and turned around, his shirt was open and his pants were unzipped, and he just dropped to his knees and started pulling at my pants, and I just kinda snapped. Like that." Paul snaps his fingers. "Man, I just started swinging and didn't stop. And honestly, I didn't even make contact with most of my swings. But I definitely hit him. I remember that for sure. I remember that feeling, you know, when your knuckles smash against something. I felt his head and teeth. And when he fell on the ground, I started kicking him and that's when Fred joined in.

"It didn't last that long. But I can see it clear, like it was yesterday. It was warm out, and there were puddles everywhere on the ground, from the rain, and I kept stepping in them."

These last words emerge slowly, accompanied by a whoosh of emotion in the back of Paul's throat. He goes quiet.

Just then, a bald man in a short-sleeve button-down appears a few parking spots over from us. Seems he's actually a commuter. Or maybe someone who went out drinking last night and left his car overnight. Paul and I don't move, as if our stillness makes us invisible. The man searches his pockets with tremendous frustration. "Fuck this shit," he says, and slaps the roof of his charcoal-gray Ford Fiesta. He rifles through his bag until he pulls out keys. He closes his eyes and exhales deeply before opening the door, starting the engine, and driving away.

"What did he say?" I ask Paul.

"Who?"

"The guy on the ground."

"He didn't. He didn't say much. He moaned a lot."

"He didn't say anything?"

"I don't know. At first, he cursed at us. *Fuck you* or *You fucking assholes.* Then he yelled *stop* a few times."

"Jesus, Paul."

"I swear he was alive when we left him. I swear."

"Well, he fucking died, so it doesn't really matter how you left him."

Paul bites down on his lips. He tries to speak, but only a few guttural sounds make their way out. His hand searches the console between us, but he doesn't find whatever he's looking for. Then he leans forward, his face practically on the wheel. His arms hang long and loose at his feet. He pulls a creased napkin from beneath his seat and brings it to his nose.

"There was one more thing."

"I don't care."

"You don't have to do this," Paul says.

"Do what?" I ask.

"No. That's what the guy said: 'You don't have to do this.'"

Paul's face is aquiver, and tears fall from his eyes. "When I think of it now, all I see are two wild beasts, and I hear this voice of reason. And we ignored him."

If it were anyone else, or if Paul were admitting to anything else, I would make an effort to console him, even superficially, but I don't feel sympathy for him. Just pity. A malicious sort of pity. Dear Lord, smite this piece of shit.

Paul wipes his face and blows into the disintegrating napkin.

"Can you please drive me home?"

Paul leans back. His chin points toward the sky, leaving his short neck exposed—vulnerable and within arm's reach. There'd be a symmetry to my slashing his throat. Here. In this place. Why is this thought even crossing my mind?

"I hoped we could go to the place where we left him," Paul says.

"What? Why? No. Paul, take me back or I'm calling a cab."

Paul places both hands at the top of the steering wheel, side by side. Then he pulls them apart slowly, along the vinyl circle, until his hands meet again at the bottom.

"Haven't you ever done something stupid? Something you regret?" he asks.

Stupidity and regret are two different things. "Of course," I respond.

Paul remains silent, as if in prayer. He rests his head on the wheel. I open the door wider and look around. In this very lot, I've done any number of stupid things—driving drunk, driving high, mixing drugs, unprotected sex. But regret is another thing. A unique emotion.

I think back to Henry.

He came up to visit me at college a few times. During his visit my freshman year, I developed the most severe strep throat of my life. My tonsils were swollen to a point where I couldn't swallow my own saliva. Henry nursed me back to health with a mixture of ibuprofen and a ginger-lemon-honey-anise tea, whose ingredients he had to walk off-campus to find.

The following year, he visited again. My mother had encouraged him, hoping that being on a college campus might inspirit him—after the previous visit, he'd gone as far as requesting applications from various colleges.

Henry and I got along quite well whenever he visited. In fact, after I left home, we stopped fighting with each other altogether.

While I was in class, Henry would shop for groceries or use my school ID to work out in the gym. At the time, he was going through a body-conscious phase. Since Thanksgiving and Christmas, he'd shed nearly forty pounds.

It was during that visit my sophomore year that I told him I was gay. It happened in the basement of a tavern that had been around since the Coolidge administration and whose claim to fame was a visit from FDR, an event that was memorialized in a framed black-and-white photograph affixed above the spirits. The dark wood walls and floors were splitting and replete with ghostly water stains, giving the impression that the establishment hadn't been renovated since the New Deal.

"How do you know?"

"I just do."

"Okay," he said, before chugging the contents of his mug.

Between us sat a large plastic pitcher of PBR and a plate with the cold, congealed cheese left over from the nachos we'd just devoured.

"Are you going to be okay?" he asked.

"What do you mean?"

Henry's face became an assemblage of folds and curved lines: pity and worry. I wondered if he, too, equated being gay with AIDS and pedophilia and Dahmer.

I nodded.

"But what about Erin?" he asked, while scraping the hardened orange-yellow from the plate.

Erin was a girl I'd dated briefly freshman year.

"She moved back to Arizona. She didn't like the East Coast. Too busy, she said."

"Busy?" Henry looked at me cockeyed. "This is the smallest town I've ever been in."

He made a valid point.

"You gonna tell mom and dad?" he asked.

"Someday. Probably."

"What do you mean probably? You gonna keep this a secret? Don't be such a fag—a chickenshit. Want me to tell them?"

"No, don't. I'll deal with this."

"I could tell them it's me. That I'm the one. The gay. After they're done losing their shit, we can tell them it's you."

I did my best to talk Henry out of his plan, and I assumed that I had.

There was a lot of silence after that, during which I feared he was growing uncomfortable around me.

And then suddenly, he announced that he had diabetes.

"What?"

"Yeah, doctor told me last summer."

"Shit. You're only twenty-two."

"I know." Henry put his head down. "That's why I'm keeping in shape."

"Fuck, Henry. How did you let this happen?"

"I know. I know."

"Do mom and dad know?"

"You kidding? They're gonna kill me."

Just then, the bartender came around and asked us to finish up. The pitcher was three-quarters full. We swallowed what was already in our glass mugs and refilled them. We drank those in an instant too.

"You know, I've been thinking," he said, as we made our way back to my apartment.

"That's an improvement."

"Shut up, dickweed. I was thinking that community college is probably community college anywhere, right?" Henry asked.

"Probably."

"I could go to school here, no?"

"Don't see why not."

"Cool. We could even get a place together."

"Really?"

"Sure, like old times. I'll bring the Nintendo 64. It's really cool," he said, "3-D."

I nodded without much conviction. My bladder was about to burst, and I couldn't focus on a future farther than my bathroom.

I would have liked for Henry to live nearby, but not necessarily with me. I didn't think I could be fully myself with him around. Luckily, I wouldn't have to choose. Henry's plan would never take shape without my help. I would have had to remind him of what he'd proposed, I'd have had to track down the nearby community colleges, and I would have had to help him fill out his applications and financial aid forms. Then I would have spent the subsequent years reminding him to go to class and to study for his exams. None of which came to pass.

And yet, of all the lofty ideas and unformed plans that Henry ever had, this strikes me as the one that might have paid dividends. This is maybe something that I regret.

▌ am sorry with all of my heart and soul," Paul says, without looking at me. "Pray with me, Andy."

I turn back toward him. "What?"

Paul puts his arms out, palms up. He doesn't wait for me to say no.

Lord, I am a sinner.

I ask humbly for you to make me whole again,

So that I may continue my life's work,

To fulfill your promises.

I have learned from my mistakes.

I ask you to forgive me.

Protect me.

Guide me so that I never again run astray of your path.

I thank you, Holy Father, for bringing your son Andrés into my life again.

For helping me to see that I have caused pain.

For helping me to see that there is a difference between sin and sinner.

Lord, I am on this earth to serve you.

Do to me what you will.

Do to me what I deserve.

He lost me at sinner.

23
MARGARITAS

I don't care that much about God," my mother says, before pouring a splash of oat milk into her coffee.

"What? Since when?"

"Since a long time," she says. "I believe there is something there watching over us, but I don't care like I used to."

She gets up to put the milk away, but stops the refrigerator door before it swings shut. "¿Quieres?"

"No, thanks. Black is fine."

My mom and I are drunk. Our first time together.

We're alone. My dad wasn't feeling well after dinner and went to bed early. She and I sneaked out to the Mexican restaurant nearby. It's a family-owned place that appeared in the years after I left home. It's beautifully gaudy and upbeat, and the food is terrible. My mom and I shared two orders of chips and guacamole while we drank two-for-one margaritas. Six margaritas in all. No salt. High blood pressure.

I avoided drinking with my parents until I was in my early thirties, well after I'd come out to them. Prior to that, I feared the honesty that might ensue.

Even now, I don't allow for more than three drinks. There are still things they don't know. Things that are private and stories that would bring them shame. I've never told them about the DUI. I don't want them to know about the sex clubs or the orgies or Marco's infidelity and now mine. I imagine myself intoxicated and these stories pouring out of my mouth, like grains of rice through a small tear in a bag.

"You don't have to worry about us. You've been here more than you had to. Tu papá y yo estamos muy agradecidos." My mother hiccups between the reassurances and gratitude. "But we're also stronger than we look."

"I know," I say instinctively, but I don't know it. My mother wants more than anything to feel protected after a lifetime of insecurity, but she doesn't want me to feel obliged to protect her. She wants it to come naturally. It does come naturally.

"I mean it. When my mother got older, I felt a lot of guilt. I couldn't be there to help her. I never want you to feel that."

"Different life, mom. She was far away, and—"

"I know where she was. I'm not sad now. This is how life is. We get old. We die. And I'm allowed to feel sad, but guilt takes up energy. You're young, and you have your husband, and, maybe, one day"—she looks down and swirls the coffee with a small spoon—"children."

"Mom. You know Marco and—"

"That Marco and you don't know if you're ready. Ya sé. Ya sé. But you'll never be ready. Trust me when I say that no one is ever ready. And you're already more prepared than we were. You have your degrees, your home, your savings. You're sophisticated people who can do whatever you want. Any child would be lucky to have you as parents. I mean that, Andy."

"Thanks, Momma."

"Okay, but really, promise me that you won't wait any more. Don't be so thoughtful about everything. Be human. You're old, mi'jo. Forty is already too old to start a family."

"I'm still thirty-seven, Mom. How dare you!" I say, before laughing.

My mother rests one elbow on the table and buries her face in her hand. She snorts laughter before slowly composing herself.

"It's true," she says.

"What?"

"At any moment, your opportunities will disappear."

"Okay."

"And you can't have just one child. Everyone needs a brother or a sister."

"Geez, mom. Let's get the first one, and then we'll see."

"Don't get upset."

"I'm not."

We sip our coffees and set them down. And for a long while, nothing interrupts the silence between and around us, least of all a desire to interrupt the silence.

Marco and my mother agree. If it were up to him, we would have already adopted five children. He mentioned it casually as we lay in his bed, about a month into our courtship. He wanted to finish up his surgical residency and work at a hospital somewhere warm, he wanted to learn to play the guitar, he wanted to take me to Santo Domingo, and he wanted a big family. It was early days, and everything was whimsical future talk. I mentioned Dominican food, and he said he'd take me to a place uptown with the best mofongo. I said I knew where we could find the best pupusas in the city, and he couldn't wait to go.

"I came from a big family, and frankly, it's dope. You'll see. Matter of fact, you should meet them. Maybe next weekend, if you want."

"They're cool . . . with it?" I asked.

"It? You mean me? Or us?"

"With being gay?" I explained.

"Yeah, of course."

"Really? Cool."

"We're a big, tight family. They don't always say the right things, but they're solid. Your family isn't?"

"No, they are. I mean, it took them a bit to adapt, but we're just the four of us. And anyway, family comes first."

Marco smiled and curled the arm he'd wrapped around my shoulder, drawing me toward him.

"In my case, it helps that my parents aren't super religious. They go to church on Sundays, but they're pretty secular."

"Same," he said. "But my parents are even worse; they only go to church on Easter and Christmas, and for baptisms, weddings, and funerals."

"That's great that your family is so cool. I thought maybe being Dominican might make it harder."

"Wow." Marco retracted his arm from around me and sat up. He produced a twisted smile that was more of a grimace. Even before the last word had escaped my mouth, I knew I'd offended him.

"Forget it. I don't know."

"I mean, something like that needs room to breathe," he said. "My family isn't grand marshaling pride parades, but they're down."

"Of course. I'm sorry. I just kinda always believed Dominicans were more machista and closed-minded when it comes to this stuff."

"This stuff? You mean, life?"

"No. I—"

"Listen, not sure where this is all coming from, but my folks aren't whatever you think they are."

Typically, I'm adept at staying quiet and thinking through my ignorance. This was one of those stupid observations or unformed theories that runs through one's mind too quickly to be tackled. Truth was, the ignorance was even more convoluted than I'd let on. Not only had I ascribed a heightened degree of homophobia to Dominicans, I'd also factored in the homophobia I'd believed was common among Black people. It wasn't as if I felt that there was something inherently closed-minded about being Black or Dominican or Black Dominican, but I was thinking of socioeconomic rungs based on historical oppression. I was thinking of white supremacy as a massive anvil, and of how hard it is to grow beneath that kind of weight. But my thinking somehow transformed into assumptions, of the kind that only add more weight.

Marco was kind enough not to recriminate more, but he looked at me the way someone looks at an old dog with three legs.

The odd thing was that by the time I'd met Marco, I considered myself relatively well versed in the histories of colonialism and oppression in this world. I'd already rejected, in theory if not yet fully in practice, the white supremacist rubrics for language, culture, style, and self-worth that had defined my understanding of what it meant to be oneself in this world, but apparently, I hadn't scrubbed myself clean.

After that day, Marco stopped calling and messaging with the same élan. He wasn't rude, but he wasn't interested anymore. He was kind enough to wait for me to get the hint, instead of dumping me outright.

That encounter stayed with me for a long time. I couldn't understand why I had held onto such archaic notions. Why had I allowed a few superficial markers to determine how I would interact with others? I'd dated white men before Marco. I'd contended with their assumptions and discomforts. And yet, somehow I had cast myself in the role of the white guy.

In brief, I had fallen prey to the Latinx hierarchy. A lens, really. A racist lens, with tiers and a color gradient. At the top, unsurprisingly, sit European Latinxs ("whitinos"), irrespective of nationality or ethnicity; this layer includes most of Buenos Aires and most of the upper castes of all Latin American countries. Diego Maradona is the sole occupant of the next tier. Next are the mestizaje that lean more European than Indigenous, excluding anyone with visible African diaspora ancestry. Below them are the mestizaje that lean more Indigenous than European, still excluding Black Latinxs of all kinds. Each of these tiers is then stratified by nationality, beginning with white Argentines who don't live in the capital, Chileans who disdain Argentines, followed by non-coastal Colombians—despite how large el costeño Gabriel García Márquez looms globally—the Mexican actor Cantinflas, and other South Americans. Peruvians of Japanese descent follow. The subsequent tier is occupied by Central Americans, again stratified by genotype, but still not inclusive of Black people. Below them is the trifecta—Puerto Ricans, the Mexicans who haven't won Oscars, and Dominicans—all of whom, not coincidentally, have some of the longest, most oppressive histories with the United States. The penultimate tier includes Indigenous people without African ancestry, who were labeled "Indios," as per the ignorance of fifteenth-century imperialists. Last are all the permutations of the African diaspora: Black Indigenous, Black Latinx, and Afro-descendientes; Morenos and Pretos; Creoles and Maroons; Miskitos, Raizales, and Garifunas; countries with plurality or majority Black populations, like Belize, Panama, Guyana, Suriname, French Guiana, Haiti, Trinidad and Tobago, Jamaica, and all heretofore unmentioned Caribbean nations. This tier, too, is subject to discrimination, based on hue and shade.

Cubans are their own category and merit a secondary analysis. After all, their revolution continues. They somehow stood up to the Empire and have thus far survived, giving them an almost magical status.

In any case, no amount of post-breakup social mapping reunited Marco and me.

And then Henry had his stroke.

I set aside my ego and messaged Marco right away. I wanted to be sure that the doctors were giving Henry the best treatment. I wanted him to receive the care that rich white people receive.

Marco responded immediately. He called my brother and helped him find a cardiologist and an endocrinologist. But that did nothing to reignite our relationship. We'd been reduced to text-messaging acquaintances.

A few weeks after Henry died, Marco reached out to see how Henry was doing. I waited a day before responding, unsure about how to communicate something like this over text.

"Mi'jo, I'm so sorry," he responded. "Is there anything I can do?"

"I'm okay. But I appreciate the offer."

That week, he sent me an order of pig trotters and a bowl of spicy fish cake soup from the Korean restaurant where we'd gone on our third date. He remembered that I'd enjoyed the meal.

In the days that followed, Marco checked up on me regularly. After a week, he invited me to see *Avatar*. He bought the tickets. He bought jumbo popcorn, sour gummy bears, chocolate-covered almonds, and a large ginger ale. After the movie, which he loved—I, however, couldn't help but think of how many better movies could have been made with the CGI budget alone—he offered to walk me home. We didn't get far before we gave up and flagged down a taxi. He refused to let me pay the fare, just as he'd refused to let me pay him for the movie tickets. The entire night had been about taking care of me—door holding and handholding and, later, a masterclass in eating me out. The degree of chivalry was outside of the usual boundaries of comfort for me, but I gave myself to the moment and to him.

A few months later, Marco introduced me to his family, on the occasion of his cousin Ricky's daughter's christening. After the church ceremony, fifty of us (family, friends, neighbors) crammed into the three-bedroom railroad-style apartment, where Marco had lived with his parents, three siblings, and Ricky. From the front door through to the fire escape, there were people laughing, drinking, and eating from small plates, and children running around in flower-print dresses and bowties, all of whom took turns interrupting whatever they were doing to introduce themselves, to offer me wine, beer, blessings, shrimp, stewed beef, pastries, cake, rum, a place to sit, a handheld fan, their spot in line for the bathroom. The camaraderie—in Spanish, in English, in heavily accented English, in Spanglish—moved through the tight quarters like the pleasant scent of a familiar perfume. I was reminded of the handful of post-sacrament family gatherings I'd attended in my youth, in similarly crowded apartments. There was a thread between my upbringing and Marco's, one I hadn't been missing or didn't know I'd been missing, and it drew me deeper into our relationship.

Since meeting Marco's family, I've thought a fair bit about the community that surrounded Marco when he was growing up. I wondered how it had affected his confidence and temperament. His poise and self-assuredness have stood in stark contrast to my doubts and anxieties, which I'd previously attributed to the financial insecurity and consequent stress of my formative years. But Marco's mother was an informal beautician for the neighborhood, and his father was a non-union plumber, and they'd had more mouths to feed. The obvious difference was that Marco had been raised in a large and proud family within an even larger community where he saw himself reflected every day, in the people, in the food, in the stores, in the billboards, in the music he heard from passing cars.

Which isn't to say that Marco's life isn't full of indignities. At least once a week, he encounters a white person who thinks it's exotic that a Black person can speak Spanish and a non-Black Latinx person who congratulates him for speaking the language so well. Not only does Marco have to be Black in the world at large, he has to navigate being Black among Latinx people, as well as being Afro-Latinx around African Americans. He also has his tía Selma who wants all his cousins to marry white people: "Mejor. Pelo bueno."

No, Marco's life isn't easier, but he weathers everything better than I do, which comes as no surprise. Research has shown that minorities who live in areas with more people like themselves are healthier than those who live outside of their communities. Being outnumbered, it seems, takes a physical and psychological toll.

My mother finishes her coffee and folds the white cloth napkin into a large triangle. She continues folding and unfolding until she's made something resembling a ship's hull. "You know, I don't wish I had more children. Not even after your brother died."

I nod slowly but remain quiet. It's only nine, but it's later on our faces. I haven't had a drink since the reunion, nearly ten days ago. I feel hungover instead of euphoric. I don't have it in me to rehash the past. "I should probably get to bed," I say. "I have to be up early tomorrow."

"Andy, can I tell you something?" The napkin is now a pocket square. "I don't have to tell you this, and maybe you don't want to know. But I want you to know."

Before she begins, I put my hand up and walk over to the stove. I turn on its dim light and turn off the blinding bulbs overhead. All of my childhood memories are framed in a soft orange light, like a photograph that hasn't been stored properly, but when I come home now, the lighting is hospital grade.

"I think you're mature enough to know more about your mother." She lands her warm, smooth hand atop mine with a small tap. "I had trouble getting pregnant—"

"I know this already—"

"Esssssscucha, Andy." My mother is drunkenly sibilant, but she is otherwise a straight, composed line of a person: head erect, neck long, shoulders back, arms flat on the table. "I had trouble staying pregnant. But after you, my body changed. And I was able to stay pregnant. Twice."

Her eyes disappear momentarily, but her face doesn't contort with embarrassment. Modesty takes her gaze downward. Cultural norms then drag her fingers through her hair before they trace a few wild strands behind her ears. "Pero no quería más."

"I thought you always wanted a big family."

"When I was young, yes. And even after I met your father, I wanted to have lots of children. That's how I grew up. Someone was always around.

There was always another person to be with. I thought families had to have lots of kids—sisters, brothers, cousins, neighbors. I wanted that. That's what I thought life was. But *I* became different. Your father and I were always working. Always running. Always worried. Always in trouble. Siempre estrés. It made me sick. The doctors never believed me, but I knew something was affecting me. My body was telling me not to bring another child into this life. So we stopped, tu papá y yo. And then, I went to work at the bank, and boom!" My mother brings her hands together with a loud slap. "I got pregnant, but I didn't feel different. What was I supposed to do?"

My mom stays quiet just long enough for me to wonder if I should attempt a reply.

"I couldn't keep it," she says. "I didn't."

Until this moment, my mother was one of the very few women in my life who had not had an abortion, as far as I knew. I can't explain why, but the revelation makes her more realistic. Or more righteous. I'm curious about who accompanied her. My father probably wouldn't have been able to take the time off work. Wait. Does my father know?

"It's okay," I say. "What's done is done. You didn't do anything wrong."

"I know. I have never regretted, not for one moment, my abortions. I regret many things, but not that."

My abortions.

"I knew stress before I came to this country, but it was a different stress here."

My mom left El Salvador before the official start of the civil war, but even then, the country had been ramping up toward conflict as well as recovering from previous struggles. Teresa, my mom's older sister, was the revolutionary of the family. An actual gun-running, farmer-training Maoist who left school to live in the mountains.

A few summers ago, Teresa visited. It was her first time in the United States, which she'd boycotted for most of my life—she blamed it for all of the world's ills, not least of all for her country's travails. For over forty years, she'd refused invitations. Civil war, work, and my grandparents' frailty were her excuses for not traveling. When Henry died she reversed course, but there hadn't been enough time to secure a travel visa. When my grandfather died, so did the last of her alibis.

"The arrogance. The sheer arrogance of this neoliberal regime. I begged your mother not to leave. I tried to get her to go to meetings. Did she tell you that?"

On a scorching afternoon, Teresa and I sat on the patio of my parents' house because she preferred the furtiveness of wasps to the slow death of air-conditioning. We drank expensive rosé and ate shrimp cocktails—my mother had wanted everything to be luxurious during Teresa's visit because "she never does anything for herself. She's never traveled anywhere by plane before. She already hates this country. I want her to like something while she's here."

Teresa was forthcoming about her revolutionary days and about the hatred (now, a distaste) she once held for this country, the place where my mother had made her life. She spoke with the authority and vocabulary of a professor, someone who could defend herself in a crowded room. It filled me with pride to hear her informed and fearless criticism of my country, and I was left wondering who my mother might have been had she never come here.

"Your mother was never inclined toward fighting injustice. It wasn't her road in this life." My aunt was dispassionate in her assessments, without the slightest suggestion of judgement or denigration. "Some people do, and some people simply don't."

With time, Teresa had grown staid about revolution and hewed closer to religion, but she didn't regret her participation, even if she felt there wasn't a verifiable difference to show for it.

"The goal was to maintain our sovereignty in the shadow of this. El gran imperio yanqui." Teresa set her glass of wine down on the plastic patio table in order to extend her arms wide. "But we failed. We are now one large warehouse for your malls and cafés. What we have is a false independence. But you should visit. If you like shrimp, you'll have delicious, enormous ones. Not this," she said while grimacing toward the perimeter of pink, anemic apostrophes hanging from her plate.

Teresa was fierce, but her countenance was dull, bereft of emotion, not only in that moment, but throughout her visit. She was neither upset, nor angry, nor unattractive, nor unappealing. But there was less verve in her than in the average human. In fact, making her smile required an effort I was never able to muster. Only one time, while she and my mother reminisced about something that one of their aunts had once said to a nun or a police officer or a magistrate, did she accede to a moment of levity, and it was quite the uproar. Otherwise, Teresa's face remained taut and her eyes indifferent, and yet, she appeared younger than her younger sister—my mother. My aunt moved with the confidence and elegance of her advanced age, in a body that wasn't under threat—she was a human who was ablating at an appropriate rate.

A very different stress here," my mother continues. "I think you know what I mean. You lived it too. You know." My mother purses her lips and dips her head a few degrees, performing apology. I'm already envisioning the heartburn tonight and the hangover tomorrow from the margaritas.

"It wasn't so bad," I say, but I don't think either of us believes me.

"I thought it was the life of an immigrant, and because we chose it, we couldn't complain."

I nod, unsure of what's expected of me.

"Do you have anything to say? A reaction?"

"Oh. Well. I'm not going to lie, you've surprised me."

"Does my honesty upset you?"

"No. Not at all. You know my politics, Mom. I would have driven you to the clinic if you needed it. I'll take you right now if you want to have another one."

My mother looks at me with googly eyes and emits a fireball of cackling. I laugh too. It takes a moment for her to catch her breath. When she does, she dabs the napkin to her eyes and exhales, whistle-like sighs. "Oh, Andy, thank you for that." She caresses her crossed forearms and smiles.

"When Enrique died, I thought about those two abortions," she says. "I always wondered if they were girls. That would have been nice to have two and two, no?"

I just wish the one sibling I had had gotten his shit together.

"There were some months when we almost gave up," she says. "Sold the house and moved to El Salvador or Colombia."

"It got that bad? I don't remember that."

My mother's heavy head bobbles in various directions. "Good. I'm glad you don't remember."

"Everything happens for a reason," I say.

"¿Quién sabe? Sometimes there's no reason."

My mom has always consoled us with this very platitude: *Everything happens for a reason*. I don't subscribe to her theory, but I'm disappointed that her own words don't comfort her when she most needs them. And now, she might erroneously believe that I've converted to this way of thinking.

"Some things come naturally, but most don't. My instinct was to protect. But when I look back on those early years, I don't know if I was trying to protect you kids or me."

"Wow, Mom."

"¿Qué?"

"Now I know where all of my overthinking and processing comes from."

She smiles and slides her hand across the top of mine.

"I should have let him join the military."

"Don't say that."

"Maybe it would have straightened him out. Controlled his diabetes."

"He wouldn't have had fewer problems, just different problems," I say dismissively, disappointed that my mother's negative view of the military— her most progressive touchstone—has changed so drastically.

"But at least he'd be alive."

"We can't be sure of that. Look at the last fifteen years in Iraq, Afghanistan, Syria, Libya. And those are just the wars we know about. He might have come home thin, but, like you always said, maybe without his legs and traumatized."

"Oof, no," my mother says. "I don't want to think that." As the words leave her mouth, a yawn takes over. "Maybe you're right," she whispers, before changing the subject. "I'm going to have heartburn. Those margaritas are going to wake me up in the middle of the night."

"Have some yogurt," I say. "Or I can make you some lemon water."

Her lower lip juts out, and she shakes her head. "I have a pill upstairs."

I convince her to have a few spoonfuls of the yogurt I bought for my own acid reflux. I explain about the lactobacillus and the probiotic effect. It either brings up the pH balance or it breaks down carbohydrate molecules that bloat the stomach and allow for acids to travel up the esophagus. I'm not entirely certain, but it works for me.

"Okay," she says.

. . .

While I'm brushing my teeth, my mother taps lightly on the door, which I've left ajar. "Sorry, honey, but I need to get my medicine."

Before leaving the bathroom, she hugs me tightly, in a way that constricts my movement; my toothbrush hangs from my mouth. "You don't have to come back," she says.

"Wuh?"

"You don't have to come back all the time. I mean, to take care of us. Ellie is coming down with the kids next week. And as soon as your father is healthy, we're going to visit them more often."

"That's great, but I don't mind taking care of you," I say.

My mom rips two squares of toilet paper from the roll anchored onto the wall and wipes the toothpaste dripping from my chin.

"We appreciate that. But promise me that you won't live worried about us."

We're not made this way. Maybe in some families children don't worry about their parents and parents don't assume that every call is a distress signal. But not in ours.

There are places in this world where people worry less intensely and with less frequency. Places where the hierarchy isn't stretched tall and people aren't perched high above their loved ones. Egalitarian places, where families don't have to be self-contained battalions constantly defending against their neighbors and other strangers. But not here.

"I promise," I say, so that she will leave in peace.

I rinse out my mouth and floss hastily. I try to think of something besides the ignominious march toward death. Only Jeremy and Marco come to mind.

Marco is crossing over the Sahara at this very moment. Jeremy is across town. He would come meet me if I asked him to. He'd make up some excuse to his wife and be here in fifteen minutes.

I split the difference. I remain faithful by masturbating in my childhood bedroom while thinking of my high school boyfriend. Later, I send my husband a see-you-soon text.

24

GETAWAY

To ride a bicycle along the wide boulevards, commercial corridors, and immense, frenetic intersections of the suburbs is to take your life into your own hands. The number, size, and speed of the cars (beside, in front, behind, across) makes me feel like the smallest kid in the playground. And probably not the smallest because the smallest child is used to being the smallest one and has therefore developed unique coping mechanisms. That child can do an astounding number of pull-ups or dive headlong and supine down a steep slide or make his way across the monkey bars in record time. Or maybe they're resolutely awkward, delicate, and unfit but witty beyond their years, capable of ridiculing the other children in debilitating ways that make everyone laugh, including the child who is in fact the humor's target, because the smallest child cannot risk a mutiny; he remains, after all, the smallest. No, I'm not that child. I must be the fifth- or sixth-smallest because I don't know what it feels like to be extremely isolated or denigrated. My coping skills, consequently, aren't as deft. And they don't need to be because I am not first in line for pain or glory. I'm also not as consumed by the anticipation of pain or glory. I have just enough confidence not to care enough. But not enough to be undaunted. This was me then, and it's me now, except for the better-constructed ten-speed bicycle, the one I bought for my father a few years ago, in the hopes that it would help him stave off diabetes and lower his cholesterol.

A few months ago, my father died. A complication from the surgery required another surgery, which then led to sepsis. It all happened quickly.

We're approaching winter, but the summer's warmth lingers in an almost portentous way. It's only two miles to Simone's house, but I chose to cut the travel time by biking instead of walking, so that I would have enough time with her before meeting Alex, the decorated bus driver and one of the few Latinx friends I had in high school, for a drink. I'm on a roll with reunions. Two weeks ago, I succumbed to Marie's onslaught of text messages, which continued through the end of summer, and the fall. By scanning her social media accounts, I learned that she voted for Trump. I also deduced that her husband is Guatemalan and a chef at a nearby Italian restaurant, the only one that passes for "fine dining" within a three-town radius. Their children are all a mixed-race, wide-faced white. I also saw an innocuous and wilty post about racial harmony, which included an image of multicolored hands grasping one another; it was meant as a lamentation for the murders of Armando García-Muro and Philando Castile, who were gunned down by the police, on whom she didn't waste a single word of criticism. She did, however, take time to praise "peaceful protestors" and lambast "looters."

Sure, it's all about peace until her favorite hockey team wins the Stanley Cup, then it's about the patriotism of overturned cars and garbage fires.

At first, I ignored her messages, primarily because she's a "special needs counselor" who supports Trump, exhibiting one of the more severe cases of dramatic irony I'd ever witnessed. But she kept texting.

We met up at Ruby Tuesday, which wasn't altogether terrible. We spent most of our time reminiscing about dead nuns and vague parties. I couldn't shake her politics though, which she must have sensed because, at one point, she went out of her way to defend her support for Trump.

"I just wanted something different. Ya know? I was done with the Clintons, and Obama—it's not a race thing—was bad for the country. I wanted to shake things up," she said, as if she were writing a soap opera's storyline. "It felt like everything was speeding out of control."

I remained silent, resisting the urge to ask how her decision had worked out for the country, instead sipping the shot of peppermint-infused liqueur that she'd ordered surreptitiously, as a way to celebrate our reunion.

"He says what he means. That's refreshing," Marie said, when I kept quiet.

I did my best to channel Marco, who works at a hospital where a couple of his poorest patients, as well as the hospital's CEO, are Trump supporters— the demonically rich, the earnestly inane, and white supremacists—but he still treats them with kindness. In fact, I managed to keep an open mind through the next round of drinks, the nachos, and the final round of lagers. We talked about high school friends—turns out Mikey C. is a high school teacher in the Bay Area—her family trip to Disney World, which was, according to her, amazing because Steve—Esteban, her husband—has a cousin who works there, and as a result, they were able to skip all the lines, a luxury I wholeheartedly endorsed as the best way to visit an amusement park. We also talked about Gianni's, the restaurant where Steve works, which I recalled as the prom night and Valentine's Day spot. Marie drunkenly confided in me that the owner has a cocaine addiction and he makes the bartenders fill their top-shelf bottles with well liquor. ("And can you believe the cosmos are fourteen dollars?")

Our time together, no doubt aided by the alcohol and fried food, had autocorrected after the Trump deviation, but then the third round of appetizers arrived. Something about the restaurant runner—his brown skin or his Mesoamerican facial features—triggered a conversation about immigration and an offhand remark about "the people who take our jobs." After that burst of unambiguous xenophobia surfaced, I checked out mentally. I suppressed the urge to remind Marie that she was sitting across from the child of "the people who take our jobs" and that she was married to "the people who take our jobs." I thought instead about the 40 percent of Latinx folks who voted for Reagan and Bush Jr., and the nearly 30 percent who voted for Trump, including many of the very "people who take our jobs." Her husband was undoubtedly one of these self-hating scoundrels, the kind who never forgets to close the door behind him.

Since that night, I've successfully ignored four of Marie's emoji-bloated texts.

Later today, Alex and I—his wife Charisse might join, if they can find a sitter—are going to Paddy's, one of the many Irish pub-cum-dance clubs in the area, which I know very little about because by the time I was of age, I'd already left. Many times, Henry had suggested we go for a drink at Paddy's, McClain's, McDougal's, O'Reilly's, Flanny's, Daly's, the Rusty Leprechaun, the Gold Pot, or Lucky Irene's, but I'd been uneasy about it. About being out in this world, around these people.

It won't, however, be my first time going to Paddy's. The first time was a few weeks ago, with Greg, the real estate agent who's been married three times, and Sal, the Costco manager who doesn't believe a woman can run the country. Alex was driving a night shift and couldn't make it, which is why we made plans for today.

I reconnected with these guys through Greg, after I reached out to him, in the wake of my father's death. For the last few weeks, Greg's been showing my mother apartments in a few of the coastal towns—elevator and walking distance from a supermarket required.

"Too much of your father is everywhere. I thought the memories would be comforting. They're not."

Marco and I invited my mother to live with us, but she declined. "I'm not that old," she explained. "But when the baby comes, I'll be there all the time."

My father is buried in the same expensive cemetery as my brother, but they're far apart. A quarter of a mile's worth of gray stones separates their resting places.

It surprised me that my father didn't want to be cremated. In life, he was a humble person uninterested in attention and disdainful of frills, apart from a later-in-life affection for mani-pedis. I recall vividly at his sister's funeral him saying that all the ceremonial fuss was a waste of money. "¿Qué van a saber los muertos?"

My father had always been like this. Whenever we'd ask him what he wanted for his birthday or Christmas, he'd respond more or less the same thing. In my youth, it was *Be good to your mother, wash the dishes, and don't fight.* After I left for college, it was *Be the best student.* At some point, he started asking me to *Be good* and for warm wool socks—he had terrible circulation. One year—I might have imagined this—he responded, *Be good to yourself.* Typically, we'd ignore his wishes and buy him white shirts, tuxedo pants, or orthopedic clogs, the mainstays of his work uniform. With this spartan history in mind, I thought my father wouldn't care what became of him in death or, at the very least, would insist on taking up as little space as possible. My mother says that when the sepsis spread, he needed to be heavily medicated, and he slipped in and out of consciousness, often conflating the past, the present, his dreams, and his hallucinations, at times believing my mother was his mother, or asking why Henry wasn't coming to see him. Through it all, he was certain that he wasn't going to survive and that my mother should do whatever she needed to do to be happy after he was gone. He also made her promise that she wouldn't spend much on the funeral because he was worried that the life insurance would not be enough for her. But during a near-final moment of clarity, he said, "Quiero estar a la par de Henry."

My mother has plenty of money. As confident as my father was of himself, he didn't trust life. He took it for granted that it wouldn't go to plan in this country, so he and my mother bought nearly half a million dollars in life insurance in the early eighties. With all of the lottery tickets my father bought in his lifetime, it's bittersweet that he cannot benefit from this one.

My mother and I are going to the cemetery tomorrow. We've been doing this every Sunday since the funeral.

"Just for a year," she said to me after our fifth visit. "You don't have to come with me, if you don't want to."

My mother and I typically bring lunch and sit on the grass, somewhere between my brother and my father.

The cemetery itself is part luxurious golf course and part cluttered farmland, except that in the place of holes and crops are small US flags and white wooden crosses. There are several acres dotted with thousands of granite and bronze squares, rectangles, semicircles, plaques. In some areas, hundreds upon hundreds of identical white stone tablets sprout from the earth in neat rows, like horse teeth or a carefully curated domino rally. I supposed those were designated for veterans or very wealthy people.

I hadn't expected to feel catharsis from sitting in a burial ground. I thought it might feel like a chore or an insincere gesture, but in fact, it's a gentle acclimation to life without a father or a brother. And for my mother, who insists on time alone at my father's grave, it's a long goodbye.

For most of the ride to Simone's, I've managed to stay in the bike lane. It was painted a few months ago. I can't imagine who this lane was painted for since I have never seen a single cyclist apart from the scatterplot fellowships of roving adolescents, who will no doubt continue to occupy any part of the road they desire. I'm content nonetheless.

I just passed an Islamic center. I don't know if it's new or if I hadn't previously bothered to notice. It's as big and boxy and beige as everything else in this town and therefore easy to miss. Is there such a sizable Muslim population here? Are they peppered throughout the town or do they occupy a few square blocks? Or is this now the hub for all the Muslims in the area? I can't imagine this sitting well with the other residents. Have there been protests or vandalism?

I could have driven my dad's Prius, which my mother doesn't want to sell yet, but I made a covenant with myself a few months ago: if I continued returning, I wouldn't shrink away from who I am. I would walk places. Take the bus. Ride a bicycle. I wouldn't use plastic bags. I would make eye contact. I would go out to the local bars for a drink. I would talk honestly about my life and not obfuscate my political views. I would engage, in earnest, with my environment.

I've managed to stick to my self-imposed self-pact. Sometimes, it's easy— my mother has a surfeit of reusable market bags. Sometimes, it's not—it's getting cold, and I can't always walk or bike places. I'm treating the town like a getaway, as if I were a stranger who stumbled upon it. I'm swallowing my fears and doing the things that need to be done when one parent dies and the other needs help. I'm also socializing somewhat regularly. I'm going out at night, mostly alone because my mother doesn't want to do anything that might be construed as marginally celebratory.

Of note: in the last few weeks, I've outed myself to a number of garrulous bartenders and soft-faced diners. The conversations typically called for it, but I nevertheless had to swallow the sort of throat-seizing trepidation that I rarely experience anymore in the city. My circumspection doesn't stem only from the individuals and the bumper stickers; it's the voting records of the town and a limp horror-movie aura that accompanies everything.

There have been plenty of awkward fumbles in response to my outing and a few long silences, but I've never felt unsafe.

Dealing with sexual orientation is easy relative to other identities. My phenotype still requires me to submit to a battery of poorly crafted anthropological questions—too pedestrian to list. My political persuasion, too, is another slat on the rickety bridge affixed to the edges of this town.

In all potentially prickly encounters, I take a multilayered approach. I begin obliquely and play ignorant by asking a series of questions on the topic at hand. For example, the murders of Black people by police have come up on occasion. As far as I'm concerned, anything short of a sweeping condemnation constitutes an irredeemable lack of character, but that sort of posture, however righteous, is untenable here because there is always someone who is related to a cop, and sometimes, it's the entire wainscoted dining room, and I am, in this case, an unarmed party of one. I wade cautiously. I try common sense: *Guns to a group of people with little education and training?* I try education: *You ever heard of the Stanford Prison Experiment?* I revert to common sense: *You know the crime rate ebbs and flows with unemployment.* I steer clear of full-on justice; I don't, for example, bring up the wealth gap or mention reparations. I use real-life examples: *Lots of Black and brown men in my life, in three-piece suits or polo shirts or hoodies, have been stopped by the police for doing absolutely nothing wrong.* I never overshare; I haven't yet told them about the cop in college who singled me out of a group of drunken white people for being too loud and threatened to arrest me, or about the cops who detained me in a small New England town, in the days after 9/11, for being Arab-looking, or about all of the cops who have been generally nasty when I've asked them for directions or inquired about a nearby incident. Whether my abstentions are self-preservation or self-consciousness—or both—I'm not sure. Sometimes, however, I employ supposition, which runs a close second to personal experience: *I consider myself a law-abiding person, but I'm not sure how I would react if someone ran up to me with a gun and didn't identify themselves. And even if they did identify* themselves as a cop, I might instinctively fight back if they were accosting or choking me. I, for one, have a tendency toward claustrophobia, and I can't imagine remaining calm in that sort of situation. Usually, the other person gives some ground. I suspect it taps into the libertarian streak of conservative folk and of Americans in general. Once, a guy with a crooked nose and a button-down shirt tucked well into his khakis, who was digging through a heaping plate of marinara-drenched fried calamari, shook his head at me and turned away from our conversation. His dad, he explained, was a retired police officer, and there were good guys in the world and there were bad guys, and there was no way I was going to convince him of anything. We kept mostly to ourselves after that interaction. Later, when it came time for him to settle his bill, he plopped his wallet and keys onto the bar. One of his many keychains read: *Global Warming? It's Called Summer, Stupid.* Another read: *Don't Like Abortions? Don't Have One.*

Sounded about right.

Over the last few months, I've come to an important realization: I'm from nowhere. I'm no longer from here. I'm not from there.

I didn't grow up around "my people." I spent most of my life surrounded by white people who didn't take me seriously one way or another. I went to college and continued surrounding myself with white people—whether that was intentional or not is for future psychologists to decipher. Then I moved to a neighborhood in the city that I could afford. It was mostly working-class, mostly Black and Latinx. I was part of the gentrification wave that forced many of them out.

At some point, maybe fifteen years ago, when I realized that I had been a negative agent for change, I contemplated banishing myself from where I lived and going back to where I'd come from. This town. I calculated that my money would go significantly farther here. I'd have more space, and I could still commute into the city. After a couple of years, I would run for the town board. Then county council. *Poor kid done well comes back to give back.* In the city, I have a small voice, but here I could sway the conversation: *More buses! More schoolteachers! More social workers!* In fact, it was around then that the incidence of gang-related crime increased, mostly in the surrounding towns, but the resulting fear had made everyone more conservative. As a pillar of this community, I could have served as a counterexample—the gangs are mostly made up of Central Americans—and contributed to more productive solutions to crime.

I couldn't go through with it, however. In part, I didn't want to, but I also doubted how effective I could be.

I can't quite go through with it now either. Marco offered to move back here after my father died. "Whatever you want, Orejas. I can commute or work at a hospital nearby."

Marco has come out a few times since the funeral. This weekend, he's at his mom's place: cousin Ricky's fiftieth birthday party. Two hundred people are going to fill the basement of the community center where he used to play basketball as a kid, and where all the quinceañeras and wedding receptions took place. As much as I love his family, that's a level of joy I'm not ready for yet.

My crusade to re-insert myself back into this town doesn't consist only of going to Irish pubs and chain restaurants. I also go to Jalisco, Hal's Catfish Emporium, Veena's, Patties by Indira, Pedro's, Queen of Sheba, Pupusas Hechas Por Gloria, Samayah's, Empanadas a la Orden, Four Seasons of Hanoi, and Mashiko. None of which existed when I lived here. I also learned that Paddy's, the Irish bar-club, is co-owned by a Puerto Rican couple.

Wherever I end up, I sit at the bar, so that at the very least I have one person I can talk to. Not everyone who works in these places lives in the town, but most do; no one travels particularly far. I'm rarely more than two degrees removed from anyone I meet. And if we don't have someone in common directly, we're familiar with the same places: the diner, the other diner, the various playgrounds, the church, the elementary school, the roller-skating rink, Dunkin' Donuts. When in doubt, *What's your favorite pizza place?* can lead to a robust conversation—something the town has in common with the city.

By Sunday evening, I'm ready to leave. I hop on the commuter train the way someone with a wig and a fake passport rushes onto the last plane while guards and henchmen swarm the runway. But it's not all terrible. There are also fleeting moments within hopeful conversations, when it occurs to me that the very fact of being human is potential enough. On those occasions, I feel a deep desire to get to know this place better. Desire and effort are essential. It won't happen accidentally, the way it does in the city, where the density throws our differences into stark relief, forcing us to decode and demystify our incompatibilities—city-dwellers aren't open-minded as much as we are inured to one another.

During these visits, I've also noticed that the bulwarks have been breached; there's at least one non-white family on each block, beginning the life that my family did more than forty years ago. Sometimes, when I come across one of the newer immigrants, I want to beg them to go back to the city. *Don't trade in proximity to your communities or to humanity for more space! You'll die younger because of it!* But maybe this is the way. They are, after all, the successful immigrants who traveled, not in a wave, but in a slow-moving brook, unaware of what had roared before. Their children will achieve enough to open doors for the rest.

I guess it's possible. But is it truly worth it?

Through it all, the Black part of town remains mostly undisturbed. That section is as segregated today as it was when I was a child. I'm told there's more crime now. *You don't want to be out there at night.* But that's the sort of slander I've been hearing all my life about the city.

The town also has an interesting, diffuse community of mixed-raced and mixed-culture families. For starters, my brother and his wife, Jeremy and Tonya, Alex and Charisse, and Paul and Graciela. There is more than a smattering of light-brown and racially ambiguous children. And maybe this is how the town will eventually integrate, which would be typical of this country's history: you can only truly participate by first giving up part of yourself.

I know nothing of what's become of the Indigenous families, who haven't in my lifetime had much representation here. They're nearby still; there are also two reservations farther east. I know this because my brother used to go to powwows and fairs. I never fully understood why. It seemed like gawking to me, but for Henry it was nearly spiritual. "They really care about everything. Where it comes from and where it's going."

Henry decorated his rearview mirror with dream catchers, and he collected hand-crafted teepees. I feared his affinity bordered on cultural appropriation, and I hated the idea of my brother contributing to a dehumanizing type of mythologizing, but he told me it was a sign of respect. He said it so earnestly that I chose to believe him.

"Besides, Ellie is one-sixteenth Cherokee princess."

"Seriously? What does that even mean?"

"I don't know. Probably her ancestors were next in line for the Cherokee crown or whatever."

"Did the Cherokee people have princesses?"

Henry's face shrugged. "That's what Ellie thinks. No big deal. She's proud of it."

"If you're both really proud, why not push the government to return the land to the local tribes? Or to compensate them for what's been stolen? Or how about we dynamite anything with Columbus's name on it?"

"Sign me up! I'm all fucking for it!"

This was as heated an encounter as Henry and I ever had as adults. There were never any hard feelings, but these sorts of conversations conditioned us to have fewer conversations. This one in particular took place in his car, while we waited for my train to arrive, after I'd visited for Thanksgiving.

"I don't understand why you have to be like that. Such an ass sheriff about everything. If I support the land stuff, does it matter if I mess up and say the wrong thing?"

It was an interesting point.

Does it matter? I think so. If we're not actively fighting oppression then we probably shouldn't be contributing to it in any way, big or small. But how does one explain that one private comment doesn't make a difference, that it's the agglomeration of comments and beliefs that creates a culture that permits ridiculing American Indians and using them as logos and mascots, which then trivializes their injustices and makes political gains less likely? How could I have made my brother see that? And was that really the best use of our time together?

"Alright, alright. Put a cork in it. The train's coming. Do you already have your ticket?"

"Yeah."

"See you in a month?"

"Yes. Send me a list of gift ideas for the kids. I don't want to buy them shit they won't like."

"Okay. I'll tell Ellie to message you."

Then we hugged, and I got out of the car. A few weeks later, he had the heart attack at work.

Simone's house was painted blue this week. During last week's visit, her mother was fretting about the impending work.

"I don't trust them. And I have jury duty, so I can't be here to make sure they don't mess it up. Last time we had the house painted was about twenty years ago, and they left everything azure. Everything. The gutters, the window shutters, the garage, all the trim. Even the mailbox! I mean, really, who would do that? Why would you paint absolutely everything? Seems odd to me. I don't see other houses that look like that." Phyllis raised an incriminating eyebrow.

The uncertainty of mistakes. Are they really mistakes? There's no way to ever know, but it only means she has to worry twice about everything. Micromanage every last detail.

"There were no contrasts. The house looked hideous. Suddenly, we were one-dimensional," Phyllis explained.

Her voice now crackles, static-like. It's deeper and has more vibrato than I remember. It's the voice of a lifelong smoker, but I have never seen her smoke. She looks almost exactly the same as she did when I was a kid. She's gray on her crown and has a bit more sag and wrinkle to her skin, but she's still tall and lithe, with hair close-cropped at the sides and larger on top in a natural style. She was the first person I ever heard say, "no fuss, no muss."

Today, Phyllis is standing outside when I arrive. She has a cup of coffee in her hands, and she's wearing a long, pink bathrobe; it's thin and embroidered, like lingerie, but not risqué. Simone told me recently that her mother has a boyfriend, a guy she met online. "They go fishing and line dancing a lot."

"Cerulean!" Phyllis shouts, when I bike into the driveway. She extends her free hand outward, as if she were singing the final number of a musical. "Do you like it?" She's referring to the house.

"Looks great! And three-dimensional!"

Phyllis laughs and walks with me toward the garage, where we store my bicycle.

"Lazybones is still sleeping. Can I get you a cup of joe?"

"Please."

We make our way inside, into her kitchen, where Phyllis gives a brief update on her research. She and her team of graduate students are tracking local efforts to restore the beaches through a strategy of natural defenses. "Oyster reefs, replanting grasses, rocks, dredging up sand," she explained last week. Part of the study includes studying the Shinnecock, on whose land much of the preservation is taking place. "The first will be the last. The irony," she said. "But it's still not enough. Half the world's beaches will be gone by the end of this century."

"Wow," I responded, realizing that I know next to nothing about coastlines, and that as afraid as I am of global warming, there is always room for more fear.

"Aren't we humans lovely?" she added. "The dinosaurs would be proud."

Phyllis and I sit at the kitchen counter for nearly an hour before she tells me to go down and wake Simone up.

"Those meds are a lifesaver, but they sap her energy. But my baby is doing okay. No longer under the devil's spell." Phyllis tenderly squeezes my shoulder, like a well-meaning coach.

She doesn't mean Lucifer himself. She means Trump. Last week, she told me that she'd known Simone was taking a turn for the worse earlier this year, before the hospitalization, because she hadn't been sleeping well. "And I was certain we were in for a ride when she started talking about making this country great again. I said, 'Can you be more specific: during slavery, Jim Crow, or ever since?' This illness isn't for the faint of heart, Andrés. My baby has gotten religious and more conservative, and I think it's the schizophrenia. I can't prove that, of course, but I'm curious about whether there's a correlation."

I make sure to step loud and heavy on each step as I make my way to the basement. When I arrive, Simone is rousing herself. She's tangled in her comforter. On the floor beside her is an N. K. Jemisin book, an acoustic guitar, a sketch pad, and a plate with a couple of mildly oxidized apple slices, a breaded chicken nugget, and a smear of ketchup.

"Andy!" she says while rubbing her eyes. "You just get here?"

"I was up with your mom for a bit."

"Hold on a minute," she says and rolls out of bed. "I have to pee and brush my teeth."

When Simone returns, she folds up the pull-out couch, and we sit. She tells me about her week, including her choices for classes next semester. Simone wants to study psychology: "If they count life experience, I've got all the prerequisites."

We sit for forty minutes or so before making our way back upstairs. She scrambles eggs and toasts bread. Her mother is either outside or in her room.

Simone seems to be doing well, but she laments her night-owl sleep schedule. Although she's composed and focused, there's also a grogginess to her.

"You ready?" I ask after she's done eating.

"Let's go."

I read online that routines are healthy for people managing their mental illness, which I found amusing because routines are essential for my survival. Simone and I have taken to walking around the block during our weekend visits. Sometimes it's her only outing of the day.

The block is a long rectangle. And we take it slowly. We make it last nearly twenty minutes. Sometimes we circle it twice. At the point farthest from her house, she raises her hand to signal east, across the street and toward a row of trees that rise above the triangle tops of the houses. "That's where Jeremy lives, right?"

"Yup."

"You going to visit him after this?"

"Nope."

"You talked to him again?"

"Not since the last time."

"Good," she says.

Jeremy and I got together one more time on the day before I went back home, the day that Marco got back from his trip to Namibia. We didn't have sex, but it was a charged goodbye. I told him that I didn't want to see him anymore. It was too fraught, and I couldn't make my peace with his cheating.

"What about your cheating?" he asked.

"I told my husband everything."

That was a lie, but since I was going to tell Marco everything, it felt more like a divination.

"Does he care?"

"He cares, but he's not upset. He's not like that. But I don't want to keep doing this."

"You sure?" he asked.

I nodded, and he became quietly angry. His breathing sped up and his nostrils flared slightly. Something about his immaturity convinced me that I was making the right decision.

I hadn't expected that Jeremy would come to my father's funeral, primarily because of Marco, but he showed up. He came alone and wore a black suit and a thin black tie. He was right out of an adolescent dream. When he hugged me, I began to cry. The accumulation of varying emotions came to a head in that moment. I didn't know what to do because I didn't want Marco to think that my crying meant anything extraordinary. Neither did I want Jeremy to get the wrong idea. Luckily, Marco was still inside of the church with my mother.

Marco had to get back to work a few days after the funeral, but I stayed with my mom for a week longer. Ellie took a few days off work before driving back upstate. She and the kids stayed with Ellie's cousin, who still lives nearby. It was Ellie who told me that Paul had closed up the church and left town. "They went to stay with his wife's family down south." That news filled me with tremendous relief, as if the eye of Sauron had turned forever in another direction.

During those days after the funeral, Jeremy messaged me a few times. I tried at first to ignore him. Then I explained that I couldn't see him because I wanted to spend time with my nieces and nephew, whom I see only a few times a year. But he continued texting, and I eventually gave in.

We met at the basketball courts behind the middle school. Like teenagers, we sat on the hoods of our cars. At one point, he rolled a blunt and shot-gunned smoke into my mouth. Then he pulled the blunt away and kissed me. We ended up on the dark grass, our backs wet from the previous day's rain. We were both otherworldly high, a mixture of thrilled and detached. Suddenly, he was giving me head, and while I was enjoying it, it felt as if I were watching a homemade porn that wasn't all that good. I shouted at him to stop, knowing full well that if I wasn't forceful in my objections, he would continue.

"What? Why?"

"We can't do this. I'm not cut out for this."

"What, sex?"

"Having an affair. I'm not being holier than thou; I just can't handle the stress of it."

Jeremy rolled off of me and seemed to be pouting, but it was difficult to tell in the dark.

"Hey, don't be this way. I've had two loves in my life: you and Marco. And I know without a doubt that Marco is it. And I don't want to do anything to jeopardize it."

I'd attempted a gentle honesty, but my words landed heavily. Jeremy's face and shoulders sank, like a boy who'd been picked last for the team—a feeling I could relate to, not least of all because we were near the very courts where I had been picked last many times. I felt particularly bad because I had felt him light up only seconds before when I'd named him one of the loves of my life.

After that, he didn't message me again for a few days. "Need weed?" was all he texted.

I declined.

I've thought about him over the last few months, fleetingly, the way one conjures up portions of a vivid, ponderous dream the morning after. Going home makes it impossible to forget the past, but it also ushers the past into the present, reconstructing it, making it easier to face. From time to time, I've gotten a little lonely or drunk and almost messaged Jeremy, but I've held strong. I promised Marco.

"After what I did, I'm in no position to call you out for anything," he said, when I told him about everything that had happened with Jeremy while he'd been away. I kept the retelling vague, and Marco didn't press for details. He laced his arms around me, looked into my eyes, and said, "I'd prefer you didn't have contact with him." I was relieved that he wasn't upset, but I would have liked a bit more of a reaction.

. . .

think you made the right move," Simone says, now that we're back in her kitchen, each of us perched on a stool. "More coffee?"

"No. I'm good. I could bike back to the city with the caffeine I have inside of me. Truth is, I should get going. I want to get home, spend some time with my mom."

"How is she?"

"Okay, I guess. She's obsessed with wanting to clean out the house. She wants me to help her pack up my dad's clothes."

"Ouch."

"She seems to be okay, but I'm expecting a big emotional crash at some point."

"Maybe it already happened." Simone tips back her head to take in the remains of her coffee. The mug reads *Jesse Jackson '88* over a faded rainbow. "When you weren't around."

"It's possible."

"You know the difference between your dad dying and mine is twenty-one years? That's old enough to drink. A full adult. You ever think like that," she asks, "about the age of time?"

"Sorta. Maybe not exactly like that."

Simone grabs the baby-blue terrycloth robe from the couch where she'd left it earlier. She drapes herself in it and cinches up the belt, in the process covering up the faded, tattered Janet Jackson T-shirt she'd been wearing, the one she bought at a concert nearly twenty-five years ago. It was my first concert. We arrived late and missed the opening act, Tony! Toni! Toné!

She leads me to the garage and takes out my bike. Before I mount it, Simone puts her hand on my back. I feel the love in her touch. I see it, too. Her stare comes through a thin layer of tears. Every time I say goodbye to her this happens.

"Next week?" she asks.

"Yes, but it might have to be on Sunday because my brother's wife and the kids are coming for a visit on Saturday. That okay?"

"I'll be here either way."

"See you then."

"You know, Andy, I am going to visit *you* one day. None of this one-way traffic."

"Perfect. We have an overpriced pull-out couch that never gets used."

few Sundays later, the morning begins with a light, unexpected snow. My mother and I are quiet during breakfast, which has become a routine for us. It's not a silence that discomfits. It's a tribute, in a way, to my father, who would have filled the quiet with a joke or a summary of a newspaper article or a plea for me to watch one of a number of videos sent to him via Facebook by a relative in Colombia. Sometimes I wonder if my mother fears that engaging in conversation will mean that my father isn't missed or, worse, wasn't necessary.

My mother suggests we go to the cemetery early. "Va a bajar la temperatura. Mucho frío hoy," she says. "We can pick up Marco from the train station on the way to the restaurant."

It's almost Christmas, and my mother suggests we go out to lunch instead of eating at the cemetery in the cold.

"A Marco le gusta sushi, no?"

"Mom, we've eaten sushi with him dozens of times. He loves it."

"That's right. Must have slipped my mind."

My mom has been more forgetful than usual. I hope it's a natural decay and not the beginnings of something serious.

When I was younger, I wished that my parents would both die at the same time; I couldn't bear to imagine one trying to survive without the other. But I find myself grateful that my father went first. He would have been lost on his own. He'd be unshaven and hungover and unmedicated. My mother still keeps a clean house and paints an impeccable, subtle face on herself. I am grateful that she is still here.

"Their California rolls are heaven. All of the ingredients are very healthy and fresh. The man and woman who run the place are the owners. Lo hacen todo. Cocinan, limpian, sirven. There are only a few tables, but they're always full. You know, your father always wanted to open his own restaurant. He would have been great. He was such a people person."

"But you never wanted that, no?"

"Of course not. That's something you have to do when you're young and have the energy."

When we get to the cemetery, my mother tells me to go with Henry. "I want to spend time with your father first. Ve con tu hermano." She says this every week.

My mother loves that I'm here with her, doing this. She worried often that Henry and I weren't close enough.

I worried about that too. After Henry's death, I spent a few years blaming myself for not having been more available to him. I wondered if he'd just needed more people in his life. Someone to complain to. Someone to reassure him. I could have helped lessen the cortisol coursing through him. He had me, and I could have reminded him of that. While he was alive, I chose to believe that whatever we had between us was mutual, but I wonder now if he was waiting for me.

Henry's bronze plaque is dusted with snow. I squat beside it and lightly wipe the surface with my glove. It's cold, but not intolerably so; the cloudless sky gives the sun free reign.

I tell Henry about the adoption plans, about how we've passed the initial round of state requirements: "All that's left to do is a few classes and to get chosen."

I tell him about how Ellie and the kids are doing. I tell him that they're healthy and growing, and that I set aside money for them every month for an emergency fund. Ellie is fine financially, but in the last year of his life, at the end of every anxiety-ridden phone call, I promised Henry that I'd take care of his family if something ever happened to him.

Henry and I talk more now than we ever did when he was alive.

A few visits ago, I told him about the high school reunion at Joe's. I also told him about Paul and what happened all those years ago at Steer Queer. I didn't have to wonder what Henry would have said. I know it: *Mind your business. You weren't there. This is old news. Don't start trouble.*

It's the same advice I'd been giving myself for a long time. In fact, if my advice were a person, it'd be almost twenty-one years old. But just for the hell of it, I spent some time recently searching online, in the local papers mostly, trying to reconcile Paul's account of that night with my memories:

gay bashing, steer queer, 1997, 1996. Nothing. Then: *dead man found near park & ride 1996, 1997.* Again, nothing.

Actually, I'm not certain of what Henry's advice would be. He might have empathized with the dead man's parents. He might have wanted to give them closure. Maybe.

At another visit, when I'd run out of things to say, I said the obvious: "Henry, Dad died." Then I waited for the news to sink in. "I'm sure Mom already told you, but I wasn't sure. Anyway, Mom's doing alright. I've been coming home more. I think she might sell the house and find something smaller. I'm trying to get her to come to the city, but she's scared. Ellie also asked her to go live upstate with them. Mom said no to her too. She won't admit it, but I think she's afraid of leaving this place. It's understandable."

I stayed quiet for another moment, wondering how the dead felt about being interrupted, knowing full well that they don't care.

The wind is whistling, and it nips at my face and wrists. I see my mom making her way through the maze of stones. She looks small and weak. She's neither. But something about the way she shelters her face from the wind while taking deliberately small steps projects fragility. I guess she is fragile after a point.

"Henry, Mom's on her way over. But I want to say something. Two things, actually. One, I'm sorry I wasn't a better brother. I don't have time to elaborate on that now, but just accept that as a blanket apology.

"Second, I want to thank you. I know about what happened all those years ago with Jeremy. Before I left for college. You somehow convinced him to let me go. Honestly, if I had found this out ten or fifteen years sooner, I might have been pissed, but these past months have been eye-opening. You made the right decision for me, and I'm grateful.

"Anyway, that's all. Mom's like ten feet away. I love you, Henry. And don't worry about Ellie and the boys. If they need me, I'm here. Oh! I almost forgot! I think Venus Williams is going to retire. Did I tell you that she made it all the way to the semifinals of the US Open, after making the finals at Wimbledon, the fourth round at the French, and the final at the Australian, where she lost to . . . guess who?

"Yup, baby sister. It's a shame about that, but it was still one of Venus's best years, even if she didn't win a damn thing."

ACKNOWLEDGMENTS

Baby L. and Baby C., for holding up a mirror and for making this all the more interesting.

Ernesto, Maria, and Nathalia, for going through it too. Cindy, Mickey, and Keith, for joining the party.

Margie, for taking care of us all.

Robert Guinsler, for persisting.

Danny Vazquez, for taking me with you.

The folks at Astra House—Rachael, Alisa, Tiffany, Sarah, Jordan, Olivia, Rola, Alessandra, and Ben—for making this all happen. And Julie McCarroll, for the fine-tooth comb.

Lisa Chen and Hugh Ryan, for making a solitary career enjoyable.

Apogee Journal, in particular Frankie Ochoa, for inviting me in.

The readers: Ana Melo, Anika Gzifa, Catie Napjus, David Johnson, Gene Laughorne, Jael Humphrey, Josh Glaser, Katie Kendall, Kimberly Kelly, Michele Hoos, Radhika Singh, Robin Moore, Sofia Santana, Stacy Delong, Traci Arnold, and Veena Chintam.

The educators and researchers: Amy Hagopian, Cindy Watts, Clarence Spigner, David Williams, Dietmar Schirmer, Jonathan Jackson, Karen Hartfield, Karina Walters, Kate Pickett, Luisa Borrell, Mrs. Keeler, Nancy Amidei, Richard Wilkinson, Roxanne Dunbar-Ortiz, Sharyne Shiu-Thornton, and Stephen Bezruchka.

The incubators: Jerome Foundation, Lower Manhattan Cultural Council, New York Foundation for the Arts, and New York State Council on the Arts.

Chayo and Jimmy, for defying the expectations that I had of us.

Ms. Elena, Claudia Patricia, Martín, Poli, Saran, and Lucas, just because.

LL, OBCC, Regeneración, and OWS folks, for arriving at the right times.

Everyone involved in the making of *The Great Leveller* (Paul Sen, 1996), including the macaques at Wake Forest, the baboons in the Serengeti, the civil servants of Whitehall, and the residents of Roseto, PA, for shedding light on the solutions.

Rumaan Alam, for your generosity.

All of the people who held the door open.

Everyone who struggles because they have no other choice, because it's right, because they see a way out.

Especially those who don't use time as an excuse for avoidance.

And anyone who fights for reparation, repatriation, transformation, truth, and reconciliation.

ABOUT THE AUTHOR

PHOTO BY MATIAS PELENUR

Alejandro Varela (he/him) is a writer based in New York. His graduate studies were in public health and his writing has appeared in *The Point Magazine, Boston Review, Harper's Magazine, The Rumpus, Joyland Magazine, The Brooklyn Rail, The Offing, Blunderbuss Magazine, Pariahs* (an anthology, SFA Press, 2016), *the Southampton Review,* and *The New Republic.* He was a 2019 Jerome Fellow in Literature, a resident in the Lower Manhattan Cultural Council's 2017–2018 Workspace program, and a 2017 NYSCA/NYFA Artist Fellow in Nonfiction.